A HANGING

MATTER

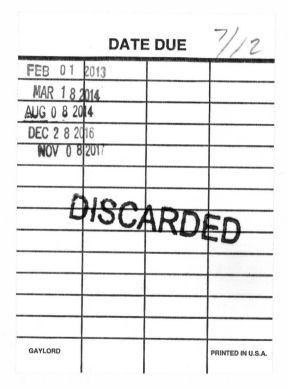

DATE DUE			7/12
FEB 01 2013			
MAR 18 2014			
AUG 0 8 2014			
DEC 2 8 2016			
NOV 0 8 2017			
	DISCARDED		
GAYLORD			PRINTED IN U.S.A.

Historical Fiction Published by McBooks Press

BY ALEXANDER KENT
Midshipman Bolitho
Stand into Danger
In Gallant Company
Sloop of War
To Glory We Steer
Command a King's Ship
Passage to Mutiny
With All Despatch
Form Line of Battle!
Enemy in Sight!
The Flag Captain
Signal–Close Action!
The Inshore Squadron
A Tradition of Victory
Success to the Brave
Colours Aloft!
Honour this Day
The Only Victor
Beyond the Reef
The Darkening Sea
For My Country's Freedom
Cross of St George
Sword of Honour
Second to None
Relentless Pursuit

BY DUDLEY POPE
Ramage
Ramage & The Drumbeat
Ramage & The Freebooters
Governor Ramage R.N.
Ramage's Prize
Ramage & The Guillotine
Ramage's Diamond
Ramage's Mutiny
Ramage & The Rebels
The Ramage Touch
Ramage's Signal
Ramage & The Renegades
Ramage's Devil
Ramage's Trial
Ramage's Challenge

BY DAVID DONACHIE
The Devil's Own Luck
The Dying Trade
A Hanging Matter
An Element of Chance

BY DEWEY LAMBDIN
The French Admiral

BY CAPTAIN FREDERICK MARRYAT
Frank Mildmay OR
  The Naval Officer
The King's Own
Mr Midshipman Easy
Newton Forster OR
  The Merchant Service
Snarleyyow OR
  The Dog Fiend
The Privateersman
The Phantom Ship

BY JAN NEEDLE
A Fine Boy for Killing
The Wicked Trade

BY IRV C. ROGERS
Motoo Eetee

BY NICHOLAS NICASTRO
The Eighteenth Captain

BY C. NORTHCOTE PARKINSON
The Guernseyman
Devil to Pay
The Fireship

BY W. CLARK RUSSELL
Wreck of the Grosvenor
Yarn of Old Harbour Town

BY RAFAEL SABATINI
Captain Blood

BY MICHAEL SCOTT
Tom Cringle's Log

BY A.D. HOWDEN SMITH
Porto Bello Gold

BY DOUGLAS REEMAN
Badge of Glory
First to Land

BY R.F. DELDERFIELD
Too Few for Drums
Seven Men of Gascony

BY V.A. STUART
Victors and Lords
The Sepoy Mutiny
Massacre at Cawnpore

A Hanging Matter

DAVID DONACHIE

THE PRIVATEERSMAN MYSTERIES, NO 3

MCBOOKS PRESS
ITHACA, NEW YORK

Published by McBooks Press 2002
Copyright © David Donachie 1991
First published in the United Kingdom in 1991
by Macmillan London, Limited

Cover painting by Geoff Hunt

Library of Congress Cataloging-in-Publication Data

Donachie, David, (1944–
A hanging matter / by David Donachie.
    p.   cm. — (The privateersman mysteries ; no 3)
    ISBN 1-59013-016-2 (alk. paper)
    1. Ludlow, Harry (fictitious character)—Fiction 2. Great Britain—
History, Naval—Fiction. 3. Privateering—Fiction. 4. Smuggling—
Fiction. I. Title
PR6053.O483 H36 2002
823'.914—dc21   2002000135

Distributed to the book trade by
LPC Group, 22 Broad St., Suite 34, Milford, CT 06460
800-729-6078.

Additional copies of this book may be ordered from any
bookstore or directly from McBooks Press, 120 West State Street,
Ithaca, NY 14850. Please include $3.50 postage and handling with
mail orders. New York State residents must add sales tax. All
McBooks Press publications can also be ordered by calling toll-free
1-888-BOOKS11 (1-888-266-5711).
Please call to request a free catalog.

Visit the McBooks Press website at www.mcbooks.com.
Printed in the United States of America

9 8 7 6 5 4 3 2 1

To Pamela and Michael

Deal is a most villainous place. It is full of filthy looking people. Great desolation of abomination has been going on here; tremendous barracks, partly pulled down and partly tumbling down, and partly occupied by soldiers. Every thing seems upon the perish. I was glad to hurry along through it, and leave its inns and public-houses to be occupied by the tarred, and trowsered, and blue and buff crew, whose very vinicage I always destest.

WILLIAM COBBETT.
Rural Rides 1823

THE WORDS OPPOSITE were written some thirty years after the action that takes place in this book, when the town was suffering from the recession caused by the end of the Napoleonic Wars. Cobbett did not stay long enough to witness the new war that had broken out between the excise and the smugglers, a conflict that, once the state had provided the resources in ships and men, could only end one way. Slowly, due to a combination of official harassment and increasing free trade, the industry was smothered.

But during the war the activities of the contrabandiers were vital to the area, just as they were vital to the enemy. To term smuggling as a way of life on the East Kent coast was almost understatement. Napoleon could not have fought his campaigns without the gold that these men smuggled into France. So important were they to the French economy that the government allotted them a portion of Dunkirk harbour for their own use. Unfortunately, they were so rowdy that the burghers of Dunkirk complained and the Emperor had them moved to Gravelines. An early case of the English hooligan abroad?

Today Deal stands as the last Georgian seaside town in England, a model example of that remarkable and elegant age. The anchorage is comparatively empty, unless there is a great storm in the Channel. Yet the history is not far from the surface. *A Hanging Matter* is a work of fiction, yet some of the characters did exist. The landscape still does!

The Goodwin Sands remain as a formidable barrier guarding the coast, as do two of the three Tudor castles. Boats, fewer in number, are still hauled high upon the beach, though the town behind has become more respectable. The Hope and Anchor is fictitious, though there is a public house on the site. The Paragon has disappeared. Portobello Court is now a charming cul-de-sac of white cottages. The Ship Inn stands where it did in the 1790s and the Griffin's Head at Chillenden still provides good food and drink for travellers. And if you look closely, you will see that the owner of the Griffin, at the time this book is set, was a widow called Naomi Smith.

DAVID DONACHIE
DEAL, 1993

PROLOGUE

THEY WERE getting noisier, the more they drank, and their voices echoed off the low rafters of the Griffin's Head. They'd already turned a few disapproving heads with their boisterous behaviour. Three men, young, dissolute, but well dressed: these bucks were no doubt wealthy. They had money to spend, plus an air of easy assurance about them. Outside stood a coachload of contraband, with armed servants left to guard it. Such creatures were not an uncommon sight at the Griffin's Head, for it lay on the route between Deal and Canterbury. Many a well-heeled individual made his way to the coast to buy his untaxed goods direct from the smugglers that infested the Kentish shore, returning by this route and avoiding the Dover to London road with its ever-present nosy excisemen.

Tite, sipping his ale, took a step backwards and peered myopically through the doorway, his attention attracted by a sharp, feminine squeal. With his poor eyesight, and at this distance, the faces were something of a blur, but the picture was plain enough. The men were laughing as the serving girl Polly Pratchitt in some distress struggled to get free. Two tenant farmers at the bar of the small tap-room who could see through the hatch into the main parlour removed their pipes from their mouths and shook their heads. What they murmured to each other made him move through the doorway that led into the main parlour in the hope of a proper view.

Unfortunately Polly was just a blur, running back towards the kitchens, attempting to cover her naked breasts with the tattered remnants of the blouse one of the bucks had torn away. He smiled. It was little wonder that they'd chosen to jest with her; she was a nubile creature, with an ample bosom that needed no support, one designed by nature to catch the roving eye. Hoots of derision followed her fleeing form as those who'd combined to assault her yelled noisily for more claret, as well as a sight of more bare flesh. He grinned: he was as partial as the next man to the sight of a naked breast. He put his tankard on the nearest empty table and made for the kitchen, jerking himself into the gait of a man with an urgent need to relieve himself.

He was in luck. Polly, feeling safe in the kitchen, had removed the torn blouse so that she and her friends could assess the damage and engrossed in the task they failed to register the hunched figure in the doorway. Tite, a mere three feet away, got a heart-warming eyeful of Polly's exposed flesh from waist to neck. The shout that followed his grunt of pleasure was accompanied by a flurry of activity, as Polly and her friends panicked in their attempts to render her decent.

"Get away, you dirty, slimy old bugger!"

"Can't a man have a piss?" growled Tite, determined to trot out his excuse.

"Filthy old sod," hissed Amy Igglesden, the oldest of the girls. "It wouldn't surprise me if you piss in the kitchen!"

But she addressed this remark to an empty doorway, for he had exited through the back of the inn. He turned and faced the outside wall, close to the partially open window, and unfastened his breeches. He was half angry, half amused at the stream of abuse directed at him, his age, and his probable abilities which wafted out through the open kitchen window.

"Never you heed my age, girls," he chuckled softly to himself. "Old Tite can still manage enough of a gallop to pleasure any of you lot."

As the thin trickle of water began to play on the wattled walls, his mind wandered off to the past and to his days at sea. He'd served the late admiral when the man was a mere lieutenant and kept the post as his master rose in rank. It had been a good life. As a personal servant, Tite wasn't subject to the harsh discipline of the other hands. They were denied shore-leave, for they could-n't be trusted not to desert. He, given the task of stocking his master's private larder, got ashore often. As a man who knew how to turn a coin from such a lucrative post, Tite always had the means to visit the local bawdy-houses. There had been more per-manent attachments, of course, some that lasted months if his master was lacking a ship. But in the main he'd gratified his lusts on whores, of all shapes, sizes, ages, and colour.

"I say that they're going to get worse. An' tearing at Polly's blouse is not to be borne. We should rouse out Mrs Smith to sort them out."

That remark, from Amy Igglesden, dragged Tite's mind back from his fond, wistful memories. He'd assumed that Naomi Smith, the young widow who owned the Griffin's Head, was absent; it was her habit to visit her late husband's grave each morning, to change the flowers. What was she doing upstairs with all this tur-moil below? She was strict about the way her customers behaved. She harboured a particular dislike for those who preyed on the poverty of the people who lived on the coast, seeing poor men, with wives and children to feed, forced into smuggling to feed the vanity of others. There was little choice, since there were few alter-native methods of turning an honest coin in these parts, even if the war with France had broken out again.

To lay a hand on one of Naomi's girls was an outrage that called for a drubbing in the horse trough. Had she been in the tap-room or the parlour those boisterous bucks would have been shown the door before they'd got halfway down their first bottle. Tite had seen it happen before, when customers got out of hand. And if things took a turn for the worse, Naomi had the loyalty of her regular customers to back her up.

Polly answered Amy. "She said that she and the gentleman were not to be disturbed. Not at any price."

Now Tite's ears were positively twitching. For a man who'd been reminiscing about past fancies, such words as these struck an immediate chord. When a lady with the good looks of Naomi

Smith entertained a gentleman, and said she was not to be disturbed, it could mean only one thing. He knew she was no widowed wallflower, despite her daily visit to the cemetery. The late admiral's son, who just happened to own the land on which the Griffin's Head stood, had a relationship with Naomi Smith that he suspected went beyond mere politeness.

Tite, assuming an innocent air, walked away from the building towards the stables. That, he knew from experience, gave the best view. As he passed the wood-shed he saw Naomi's small cart safe in the stable, its empty shafts pointing towards the red-tiled roof. But it was the horse in the next stall, a dappled grey mare, that took his attention. He recognized it at once. It came from the stables at Cheyne Court. He'd seen it that very morning leaving the house, bearing his master's brother-in-law, a man he loathed. Tite spun round to look back at Naomi's window. There was someone, wearing a wig and a black coat, standing with his back to the window. Then he moved away.

Tite hurried back the way he'd come, slipping past the kitchen without being seen then turning right and making for the bottom of the stairs. The rowdy trio in the parlour were now singing a loud and vulgar version of "Tom Bowling," which made it hard to hear the conversation that was taking place on the landing, but he recognized the voices. The unmistakable Scottish burr of Lord Drumdryan, and the deep, slightly rasping voice of Naomi Smith.

Here with his arse bare lies lucky Tom Bowling,
The darling of our crew . . .

"I'm flattered, of course," said Lord Drumdryan. "But I do have a dinner arranged for that . . ."

Tite missed the rest, which was lost in the next censored verse of the song.

His form was of the manliest beauty,
His heart was kind and soft.

Naomi's voice was clear enough, but Tite missed her opening

words. ". . . afterwards. I have told the girls what I plan, and they are very taken with the notion."

Faithful below he did his duty
And now he's gone aloft,
Still with his breeches doffed.

Singing gave way to unrestrained laughter. They banged their tankards on the table, demanding more claret.

"I fear your guests are getting out of hand, madam."

"I must attend to them," said Naomi. "But I'd be obliged if you'd tell me how you view my invitation."

The polite tone in Drumdryan's voice seemed oily to someone as ill disposed as Tite. "It would seem churlish to refuse, madam. I can do nothing but accept."

Naomi grew a touch louder. "Then I can go ahead with the arrangements?"

"By all means."

The sound of the lady's feet on the stairs had Tite dashing away. Reclaiming his ale, he took station by a window that looked out over the front of the inn, his eye on the road that led back to Knowlton Court, muttering under his breath and wondering what value such knowledge might have. His train of thought was broken by Naomi's voice. It was low, quiet, but firm, and right behind him.

"My hospitality does not extend to an allowance of filthy songs. You will have nothing more, sirs. You will pay for what you've consumed, and leave."

"My dear Barrington," said the one with his back to the wall, "I fear we are under threat. And from such a handsome creature."

"Why, madam," said Barrington, the nearest of the trio, responding to his friend's sally, "I have yet to eat or drink my fill. It would break my heart to depart prematurely. Especially from such a pretty morsel as you."

He was flushed with wine, and his wig was a touch askew. His exaggerated air of gallantry did nothing to dent Naomi Smith's resolve. Her face was set hard, and she stood, hands behind her back, eyeing her three "customers" by turns.

"You may well have a broken head if you stay, sir."

The young man called Barrington turned to sneer at his companions, for he couldn't see the cudgel she carried, which was hidden in the folds of her dress.

"Break my head indeed! I have more in mind to break some wench's hymen."

The idea obviously appealed to the third one, who'd spent the last minute in a careful examination of Naomi's figure.

"Too late for that, Barrington. But she's a spirited mare, an' no mistake. Mind, I'd rather engage myself to the one with the large udders."

"My good friend Stanly, here, wishes to bed the serving wench. Her name is Polly, I gather. He may even consent to buy her a new blouse. Do you have a tariff for the creature?"

The voice didn't change. "You have a bill to pay, sir, for food and drink, which are the only things on offer in the Griffin's Head. You may leave it on the table. Be so good as to settle now, before matters take a nasty turn."

Barrington looked past her, as if searching the room for some other form of compulsion. He noted the men who'd filled the doorway to the small tap-room, observed Tite standing by the window, and cast a jaundiced eye at the ragtag collection of customers in the half-filled parlour. In a strange place he couldn't know how many were local, how they'd react if he attempted to bait the owner, so his response carried an element of bluff, rather than any threat.

"Am I to be so addressed by a mere woman?"

"This mere woman happens to own the premises, sir," said Naomi.

Barrington leant forward, his face stiffening as he looked up at her. "Then you will cease your insolence, madam. If you do not, my friends and I will reduce the furniture to matchwood."

It was Blake who added the words that mattered. He couldn't

see Barrington's face, couldn't observe the bluff. He took his friend's bellicose statement at value, and decided to overlay it with a threat of his own.

"And perhaps, madam, we will take from you, and that milch cow who served us, something you seem unwilling to offer, even for a decent price. Indeed you may wish to remove your blouse, and afford us a view, to save it from the same fate as the other trollop's."

There was no word of warning. No cry of anger. Naomi's cudgel took Barrington right on the forehead. He was catapulted out of his chair by the force of the blow and ended up in a crumpled heap on the wooden floor. The other two scrambled to their feet, but the upraised club, in the hands of a woman clearly determined to use it, made them pause.

Naomi wasn't calm now. Her bosom heaved with anger or effort and her voice was like ice. "Pay, gentlemen, or I'll ask my regulars to douse you in the trough." This statement was greeted with a collective growl from all the men in the room. Polly Pratchitt stood by the kitchen door with a meat cleaver in her hand. The only other sound was that of coins rolling on the tabletop. "Now take this vermin and load him into your coach."

The place was silent as the two others, suddenly sober, sought to comply. They lifted Barrington between them and staggered towards the door. But Naomi wasn't finished.

"Should you be tempted to seek revenge, sirs, I would count the cost of your contraband cargo. Then ask yourself if you're willing to lose both that and your liberty when you're brought before the local magistrate and gaoled for transporting unexcised goods."

The thought of the contraband made Tite turn back to the window. But he didn't look at the heavily laden coach. Instead his eye caught the rear end of the dappled mare heading up the hill towards Cheyne Court. He swore under his breath. Lord Drumdryan, who must have known that there was trouble in the parlour, had ridden off, leaving Naomi Smith to deal with

matters herself. What could she see in a man like that? No one
with an eye to see or an ear to listen could doubt that he was
enjoying a dalliance with the lady. What would his master say
when he found out that his brother-in-law had moved into a bed
that had welcomed him? There would be the devil to pay and no
pitch hot.

"Come back soon, Captain," murmured Tite. For he knew that
Harry Ludlow wouldn't have behaved so badly. He'd have behaved
like a man and turfed those noisy buggers out single-handed.

He'd had a lot to drink by the time he started on the journey
home and staggering as he was, he was nearly run down by the
man on the horse. He had time to curse at the disappearing hind-
quarters of the animal and through his bleary gaze he saw the
flash of a red military coat.

"Damn bullocks!" he cried, waving a drunken fist.

But the rider, if he heard him, didn't bother to respond.

CHAPTER ONE

JAMES LUDLOW'S face creased with pain as the coach bounced over another frozen rut. The driver had little choice, attempting to increase their speed by weaving his way through the mass of fleeing refugees. In this milling crowd of exhausted humanity, men, women, and children each bore a bundle containing their meagre possessions. It was a mob which only maintained any forward motion because it was heading in one direction: away from the cannon which could be heard booming to the south. The faces of those they passed who retained sufficient energy to raise their heads said more about the horror of war than James's expression, or his words, which seemed exaggerated in proximity to such evident hardship.

"Damn it, Harry. If I ever complain about the discomfort of life aboard ship, you have my full permission to staple me to the deck."

Harry Ludlow was suffering as much of a buffeting as his brother, constantly moving his musket to ensure it didn't accidentally go off. But having spent most of his life at sea, often in conditions that made this crowded Flemish road seem like the pathway to paradise, he was less prone to grousing. James, a more domestic creature by far, tended to be loud about his comfort, aboard ship as much as anywhere else. Pender, their servant, perched atop their sea-chests at the rear of the coach, aimed a grim smile at the back of James's head. For him, being spared the need to walk, like the flotsam of humanity around them, served as a source of deep pleasure.

"I should have a care, brother, lest I remember that," said Harry, his breath forming clouds of vapour in the freezing air. "I've known you to complain of cramped quarters and fetid odours before we ever won our anchor."

James was in a foul mood, and the landscape, under the grey and threatening sky, seemed to match his temper. There was nothing in the gloomy countryside to alleviate the depressed spirit. It was flat and featureless, windswept and treeless. The roadway showed more evidence of defeat than these fleeing refugees. They'd passed several carts laden with the wounded and anyone who cared to look closely would see that many of the tattered uniforms were British. Their driver, sitting on the elevated box, used his whip again, forcing the horses to drag the coach out of yet another frozen trough. It lurched dangerously to one side, causing several people to jump clear.

James ignored their cries of protest. He gave the coachman's ample buttocks a sour look as he continued, shifting himself again in a vain attempt to ease his discomfort. "The privations that you sailors tolerate never cease to amaze me, brother. Even the most elevated soul aboard the ship is denied true comfort. A captain's cabin is no drawing-room, regardless of the wiles you employ to disguise it. I've seen enough ships' interiors to last me a lifetime."

"Then you'll be glad to get home."

The element of mischief in that remark was evident by the way James frowned. But he directed the resulting ire at the coachman, not his elder brother. "All this about the French being hard on our heels is so much stuff. A canard designed to increase this villian's fee."

The guns boomed out once more, as if to give the lie to James's words. Harry, again shifting his musket slightly, looked to the south, towards the front lines. True, those cannon were a good way off, and they would represent the epicentre of any battle. But the French would have cavalry patrols out. The mob on the road were afraid of the danger, even if James was not. They'd been told the French border was teeming with an army of Jacobins, afire with revolutionary fervour, and determined to "free" their fellow sufferers to the north, the poor benighted peasants who lived in Flanders. Given the news from France, it was hardly surprising if quite a few of the locals felt the need to decline the offer.

Having disposed of their own royal house the French were now bent on exporting the benefits of *Liberté, Égalité, Fraternité* to all those who shared their borders. But those high-minded sentiments included the Terror, which travelled with the guillotine as its bloody mistress. The revolutionary despots had set the whole of Europe alight. The Ludlow brothers' route home from Genoa had been determined by that one fact, as they'd skirted a host of potential battlefields, making the trip very much longer. They were now faced with the prospect of undertaking a Channel crossing at the end of October, a notorious period in a stretch of water not renowned for gentility even in the height of summer.

"You may very well be correct, James. The guns are miles away. But I for one shall follow the evidence of my own eyes. And what I observe looks remarkably like an army in retreat."

James could see as well as his brother. He too had noticed that the Allied troops they'd encountered were mainly heading north. But he was not to be deflected by that, or such reasoning. If anything the idea made him even angrier.

"This fellow we've hired to drive us should be on the boards. I've never known such an actor."

As if to underscore James's words, the driver, who'd already performed the same manoeuvre several times, turned on his box and gave James Ludlow a most fearful look. If he didn't comprehend the meaning of the words, he could not fail to quail at the look in his irascible passenger's eye.

"I reckoned when he'd dunned us out of our money for this trip, a fee which I still consider exorbitant, he would dispense with the need for such melodrama. Yet here he is, still favouring me every two minutes with a terrified roll of the eyes."

Harry Ludlow had also been made curious by the coachman's actions. But it was only on this occasion, by careful scrutiny, that he discovered the true reason for the man's anxiety. Being a sailor to his fingertips, and a rougher man by far than the elegant James, he rarely managed the languid tone of voice, the air of bored indifference that his younger brother, in better mood, found so effortless. But he did so now, even going so far as to feign a yawn.

"I would hazard that, at this moment, you frighten the poor fellow somewhat more than the French."

James was surprised. "In God's name, why?"

Harry affected another elaborate yawn, then flicked a gloved hand towards his brother's lap. "Have you observed the direction in which your musket is pointing?"

James looked down at the long gun on his lap. Then his eyes lifted as he followed the line of the barrel, till he found himself once more looking at the ample posterior of their coachman, straining at the leather breeches he wore.

"I dare say," Harry continued, "on this treacherous, uneven surface, and having to weave his way through this mob, he fears you may inadvertantly discharge your weapon."

Pender laughed, his teeth flashing in the grim daylight, his voice heavy with false foreboding. "You might leave him with more holes in that part of his body than he truly requires, your honour."

James quickly moved his musket then spun round to look at their servant, trying to maintain his angry look. But his twinkling eyes betrayed him. He was clearly amused. "A tempting thought, Pender, such a tempting thought."

They could no longer hear the distant cannonfire, but that did nothing to lessen the hint of panic in the air. Flushing was bulging at the seams. The little fishing port had to deal with an army landing supplies in one direction, east, while the wealthier citizens of Flanders fled west, seeking the security of the English shore. Added to this mix were the casualties, as well as a good number of soldiers who'd become separated from their units. Every hostelry, which in this sleepy backwater didn't amount to much, was full to bursting, and the narrow streets teemed with coaches and carts, none of which could be brought to consider giving way to their fellow *émigrés*. The Ludlow brothers had been sat in the same spot for twenty minutes, listening to the shouts and catcalls, which were tinged with desperation, while those intent on flight tried to sort out some bottleneck further ahead. Pender had gone to investigate, returning with a glum expression on his normally cheerful face.

"We'd be better off walking from here, your honour. An overloaded Berlin coach has cast its wheel. Can't see them jackin' it up with what they has aboard, so they'll be at that repair for an age."

"Right then, Pender. Light along into the town and see if there's somewhere we can get some dinner, and fetch a couple of porters to lug our sea-chests."

Pender nodded, then turned and pushed his way back through the crowds that hemmed in the coach. Harry turned to James, who had been silent for some time. "I doubt that a room will be easy to come by, with the place so crowded. And if the rumours are to be believed the French could arrive at any moment. It might be better, right off, to seek out a berth aboard a ship, rather than try and spend any time here."

James didn't even raise his eyes. "Do as you think fit, Harry."

It was all there in his demeanour. Normally James was a keen observer of all that went on around him, his painter's eye obsessed with detail. The emotions, especially the fear in the faces of their fellow travellers, should have been a source of deep curiosity; Harry, who even without a particular destination or a pursuing army was always in a hurry, had remonstrated with him often about his dilatory ways. Not now. All the things that he had put to the back of his mind while they'd travelled from Italy had clearly returned to haunt him, and Harry shared some of the evident disappointment. He'd been given good grounds to feel that the matter had resolved itself, given the lapse of time and the distractions they'd encountered. Now, on the last leg, as they were about to take ship for England, all the reasons why James had left were crowding in on him.

Harry spoke gently. "We can't stay here, James. But we could go north to Amsterdam."

James finally raised his eyes, looking at Harry directly. Then he smiled. "No, brother. You have the right of it." He slapped his thigh, in a most uncharacteristically hearty gesture. "Forgive me for being poor company, Harry. The prospect of getting home seems to have dried in me."

"Perhaps things will have resolved themselves to your advantage."

James replied gamely, smiling, but his eyes still told of his reluctance. "Perhaps. But first we must eat, I'm close to starving." His eyes lit on the coachman's back, and the man's stoic acceptance of all that was happening ahead annoyed him, for his face clouded again. "Nearly as much as I am bored of staring at this fool's arse."

"I'm glad that joining me at sea has done something for your language. I imagine your rich friends and clients will remark on how salty it seems."

James leant forward and touched Harry's knee. "I have gained a great deal from being with you, brother, both on land and at sea. If I seem a little down, it's not your doing."

Pender's return, with two grubby porters, saved them both embarrassment, for though they were friends they had the good manners to avoid too much intimacy, each well aware that certain areas of their lives were not open for discussion. The driver turned as the porters took their chests off the back of the coach, his eyes holding that universal gleam of a man hoping for a reward. It would have been hard to tell what James was thinking when the fellow caught his eye, but the look was more than enough to kill any hope of extra remuneration.

If anything, the crowds had increased. The dirt on the road had long since thawed and the pounding feet had turned it into mud. Harry and James slithered and slid in the sucking morass as they followed Pender and the porters, elbowing their way through the mass of bodies. It was with some relief that they ducked into the straw-covered courtyard of the tavern. A small urchin dashed forward with his bucket and brush, eager to clean the gentlemen's boots for the sake of a coin. Not having the heart to dismiss him, they both stood while he sloshed around their feet, talking non-stop in a barrage of conversation that neither of them could comprehend.

"This young fellow seems to have transferred most of the mud from my boots to the hem of my coat!" said James; yet he was grinning, and Harry was glad to observe that the pleasure was in his eyes as well as his smile. This was more like the James of old. His own coat was in a similar condition, but that did nothing to dent his generosity. The coin he gave the boy was a good deal bigger than his services, or his expertise, deserved.

They had to duck low to enter the tavern, both coughing immediately as the warm air, laden with pipe-smoke, filled their lungs. Pender was sitting against the wall by the blazing fire, guarding their sea-chests, his coat open and his face red with the heat. He addressed them directly, without rising to his feet, his soft Hampshire burr seeming to add a feeling of welcome to their surroundings.

"I bespoke the owner, your honours, who has enough of English to be understood, and he says that he couldn't even find us a place in the stable." The eyes twinkled in his red face. "We are, as you might say, worse off than Joseph and Mary."

An observer might have wondered at a servant addressing his master so, finding it odd that he dared to sit, let alone exercise his wit, in their presence. Yet neither of the Ludlow brothers seemed affected. For them Pender was more than a servant, if something less than an equal.

"I'm more interested in food than a bed," said James, opening his coat gratefully to welcome the heat of the fire.

"That he can provide, though I reckon, being so busy, he'll charge for it."

"Damn the expense," said Harry, who was as sharp-set as his brother. "Get us a table, Pender, and tell the landlord to dig out some decent wine. And while you're about it, tax him to see if he knows of any berths on a ship heading for Kent."

◆ ◆ ◆

They were sitting in a high-backed booth talking quietly. James hacked off another piece of the tough fowl and waved it in his brother's direction. "This bird is a Methuselan creature, judging by its texture. The cook has sought and failed to make it palatable with this rich sauce."

Harry stopped with the food halfway to his mouth. "I'm rather enjoying it."

"The cold air must have dulled your tastes, brother."

Harry barely heard him. He'd turned as soon as he observed the stranger approach. He knew him for a sailor right away. It was in his rolling gait, as well as the weather-beaten face. He had salt and pepper hair, worn long and loose, with two tufts high on each cheek. His clothes, though of a decent quality, were streaked with salt, and the brass buttons that lined each facing were dull and green rather than shiny bright. Harry, looking at the singular tufts of hair, had the vague impression that he had seen him somewhere before, but he couldn't place him.

"Mr Ludlow?" he said, looking from one to the other, his heavy eyebrows creased in confusion.

"We are both of that name, sir," said Harry.

The man gave a small bow, then sniffed loudly. "Tobias Bertles, gentlemen, Captain of the *Planet*. She's a snow, sir, which is a broad and comfortable class of vessel. I have had words with your man, an' he says you are in urgent need of a crossing."

"That we are, Captain Bertles," said James, quickly. He knew he'd cut Harry off, just as he knew that it would have been wise to question the word "urgent." Moving over on his seat to give room, he pointed to the huge platter in the middle of the table. "Would you care to join us? For we have here a dish that seems to please sailors."

Bertles missed the sarcasm, just as he missed the fact that the remark was aimed at the brother, not him. He slid easily into the booth and gave Harry, on the other side of the table, a happy jerk of the head.

"Why, I wouldn't say no to a feed, sir, if there be some spare."

"Dig in, sir," said James, pushing his plate towards their guest. "Though I would advise you to have a care for your teeth."

Bertles looked at him, perplexed, the tufts of greying hair on his ruddy cheeks twitching slightly. As he ducked his head to take a mouthful of food, he swung his brown eyes towards Harry, with a look that begged to know if he was being practised on, only to find himself under examination. His name meant nothing to Harry. But he hated the idea that he could forget a face.

"My brother has refined tastes, Captain. He finds the bird is not to his liking. As to pleasing sailors, he refers to me."

Bertles nodded sharply, as if that information was obvious.

"Without a ship, of course," replied Harry.

"I sail on the ebb, sir."

"Nothing could suit us better," said James. "That is, if you have an available berth."

"I can offer you only my wardroom, sir, which you needs must share with me, my officers, and another passenger, for my own cabin has been given over to a married couple."

"Your destination in England, Captain?" asked Harry.

Bertles looked at him directly as he replied, as if he was challenging Harry to place him. "I hail from Deal, sir. It is to there I shall return, weather permitting."

That smacked of remarkable good fortune, for Deal was the anchorage closest to the Ludlow house at Chillenden.

"Then it only remains for you to name a price," said James.

"So you are bound for Deal!" said Bertles, smacking the table, as though he'd solved a puzzle. He sat forward slightly, evidence of some eagerness. James, who was about to reply in the affirmative, felt the gentle pressure of Harry's foot on his own.

"The Kent coast suits, Captain Bertles, though landing in the Downs will still leave us a journey."

The other man's eyes narrowed, bringing his heavy eyebrows close to the tufts of hair on his cheeks. But the accompanying smile was knowing. Bertles was used to bargaining. "Makes no odds,

Mr Ludlow, do it, for if you seek another berth you could be stranded here. If I hear things aright, Flushing ain't going too healthy for an Englishman. An' I dare say you've seen as many wounded as I."

"Are you transporting any of them?" asked Harry.

"No, sir, I am not. Tobias Bertles operates for cash on the barrel, not for some slip of paper that the Horse Guards will pay out on, rock bottom, at their convenience. An' I'm not short on passengers. There's many a well-heeled local trying to get away from the Jacobins. Such a flood has pushed prices pretty high. Not that I'd favour a foreigner over a fellow Englishman, you understand. But I cannot be required to ask less than the going rate."

"Which is?" said Harry, still pressing down on James's foot. His eyes were fixed on those of Bertles.

"Twenty-five guineas a nob."

"Ten," said Harry immediately, holding up his hand to stop Bertles's reply. "And before you protest, Captain, that you will be made penniless, be aware that I've sailed these waters many times, both in peace and war."

Bertles held Harry's gaze, though his eyes moved fractionally, as if seeking a chink in his adversary's resolve. Finally he spoke.

"I dare say you have, at that. But anything less than fifteen would be robbery."

"Done," said James. Harry started to glare at him, which he responded to with a smile. "My foot was going numb."

Bertles took another mouthful of food, ignoring the sauce which ran down his chin, and looked from one to the other, wondering what these two "passengers" were about. But the price pleased him and he clapped James on the shoulder. "Well, sir. For fifteen guineas I shall include a capital dinner."

James looked at the plate, so recently his own. "Tell me, Captain, what did you think of the fowl?"

"Why, it's tasty, sir. Very tasty." He ducked to eat again, and so missed the look of despair in James Ludlow's eyes.

◆ ◆ ◆

They'd barely finished their cheese when the hullaballoo commenced. The news that was spreading like wildfire in the streets soon penetrated to their inn, rippling through the packed room like a tidal wave. Voices were raised in evident alarm and the crowd seemed to disperse as soon as they comprehended the information. Suddenly the room was empty, except for Pender, who'd pushed his way forward, against the flow of the crowd, his face creased with anxiety.

"The French are at the gates, your honour," he said to Harry. "Cavalry in the main. Whoever's in charge here has thrown up a defensive line with some of the troops that were bringing in the stores."

"That won't hold," Bertles observed calmly. "There's scarce five hundred soldiers in the whole port."

"It would seem prudent to get under way, Captain," said James.

"It may be prudent to board ship, sir. But I'll not be shifted by a ravaging pack of Jacobins. I will sail on the ebb as I originally intended."

"Far be it from me to question your decisions, sir—"

Harry interrupted James, lest he offend Bertles. If Flushing had been invested, even by a cavalry screen, they needed him now, more than ever. "Don't be alarmed, brother. The French will attempt nothing till they've fetched up some artillery—"

Bertles now cut in. "By which time our lads will have torched their stores and be ready to either take ship or offer surrender."

"So you apprehend no real danger?" asked James.

The tufts of hair on Bertles's cheeks twitched as he replied. "Unless the Jacobins have learnt to walk on water, Mr Ludlow, unlikely you'll grant me, then the answer must be no."

He picked up the bottle on the table, which was still half full. "I'd say we've got time to finish this, sir, and toast damnation to the French."

James knew he'd been the butt of Bertles's condescension, so his reply was a trifle sharp. "Forgive me if I decline, Captain. I cannot abide the damning of an entire race."

CHAPTER TWO

TOBIAS BERTLES'S "capital dinner" came as a pleasant surprise, for though it was plain, the food was of the very best quality. Fresh fish to start, herrings and turbot, followed by a fine bowl of brawn, with a proper English roast as the main course. No part of the beast was to be wasted and this was accompanied by a remove of sweetbreads and faggots.

The captain had reclaimed his tiny cabin to entertain his passengers and since the *Planet* was riding gently at anchor, it was more like a shore-based affair than a nautical one, with only the occasional exploding warehouse, with the dull boom and accompanying flash, to remind them of their situation. Bertles, who'd appeared a trifle shifty on first acquaintance, blossomed in the role of host, introducing his guests to each other in a grand voice and pressing upon them a glass of sillery to "whet their whistle." But with barely enough room to accommodate the five extra diners and a red-hot stove contributing to the warmth, it was an intimate dinner, and every time the door opened to admit another dish the blast of freezing air made all present shiver.

The married couple were military, a middle-aged major of engineers, Franks, and his young wife Polly, decidedly pretty, with a cornflour complexion and blonde curls. But the lady was unsuited to mixed company, since she could not let a word pass her lips that didn't have more than one interpretation. That she was innocent and completely unaware of this fault entertained the Ludlows and infuriated her husband as she delivered every sally with her blue eyes wide and excited and her blonde hair escaping, one curl at a time, from under a very fetching cap. Franks felt the need to explain his presence at the table when his fellow soldiers were engaged in a desperate attempt to throw up some kind of fortifications to protect the town: he had offered his services and been politely declined. The colonel in charge of the operation had informed him that the earthworks he was digging were a sham: he had no intention of trying to protect Flushing. Their first purpose was to give the French pause, their second to reduce the danger of panic in the town itself, which would seriously hamper his attempts to destroy what he could before withdrawing his men to their transports, something he fully intended to do before the day was out.

The other passenger was a young man from Warwickshire named Wentworth, whose family traded into the Low Countries, selling the new manufactures and startling innovations that spewed out of the factories springing up in such towns as Birmingham. He was tall and thin, with fair hair and a serious demeanour made more apparent by a pair of half spectacles which continually slipped to the end of his nose. His conversation, which was plentiful, for he was a garrulous soul, consisted entirely of profit and opportunity, even extending to those avenues, like the sale of armaments, which had been opened up by this latest war. Yet it was mixed with a string of complaints about everything he'd encountered: Flemish food and manners, the roads, the inns, and the attitude of the locals to the glittering opportunities he represented to them. The fact that their country was suffering invasion was held a poor excuse for such behaviour. Harry and James, who would rather have listened to Polly Franks any day, were bored rigid by the time they were called to eat. The dinner, however, once they sat down, was very convivial.

Having embarked these few passengers, the *Planet* had none of the desperate air of the other ships in the harbour. The anchorage was full of small boats, busy loading casualties, portable stores, and refugees by torchlight. None of that panic penetrated this cabin. The crossing, Bertles assured them, would be brief, for the wind was steady in the east, its prevailing quarter. So they regaled each other with background and anecdotes, in the shallow fashion that people in transit do.

"I have travelled extensively in these parts, sir," said Wentworth, who had, to Harry's relief, turned his attention to Major Franks, "and it is not just the fortifications that are in need of an overhaul."

"Pray, sir, not fortifications," cried Polly. "I have suffered enough in that area for a lifetime. There is nothing in life more tedious than to be surrounded by men, all ardent . . ." She paused at that point and took a mouthful of turbot, leaving her fellow diners in anticipation. ". . . in the matter of castles and the like. If they are not intent in sticking things up, they want to take them down. And guns, poking this way and that. Poking things out and blasting away! I wonder if it's all men ever consider."

"Gentlemen," said Franks hurriedly, "I have been attempting to persuade the Dutch to renovate their fortress line, especially in the light of what is happening not two miles from where we sit." Franks had originally been sent across from Shorncliffe to look at the Flemish forts that lined the border with France. Many had long since fallen into disrepair, and those capable of offering some resistance had suffered from the incursions, earlier in the year, of the French army under Doumouriez. He had of course deserted to the Royalist cause and the invasion had collapsed. But the threat resurfaced, with new armies, under generals like Pichegru and Lazare Hoche, more committed to the Revolution. A hasty programme of rebuilding was essential. But they had not heeded the advice and all the Allied armies had paid the penalty. Franks had tried the same persuasive tactics on the Dutch further north. But despite the evidence of their own eyes, it would not prevail.

"Do you think the burghers of the Rhine towns will heed your advice?" asked Harry.

"Certainly they will rebuild, but only if we subsidize them with British gold, Mr Ludlow. They are no more willing to fend for themselves than any other nation in Europe."

James interjected at this point. As a man who had initially

welcomed the Revolution in '89, he felt that despite the recent excesses there was a case to be made for the French. "Our Gallic foes do not seem to seek our subsidies. Nor do they seem to require your advice. They are sustained by the strength of their ideas."

"What are these brown balls, Captain Bertles?" demanded Polly, poking at a dish on the table. Her husband, who'd been about to bristle at James, had to divert his energies immediately. "They are faggots, my dear."

"Are they, husband. I don't think I've ever seen one so big." She turned a dazzling smile on their host. "I dare say they are not meant to be taken whole. Why, I'm sure I would choke if I were to swallow a ball that size."

"Major Franks, allow me to apologize," said James, trying not to grin at Polly's latest gaffe. He realized the lack of tact involved in defending the Revolution to a serving officer who had just witnessed his army in full retreat. "I spoke hastily and too freely." It didn't emerge well, but the good major took it in the proper spirit: "Being an Englishmen, sir, I am conscious of the benefits of liberty."

The conversation flowed, as did the food and ale, with James and the major deeply embedded in his concerns over Dutch fortifications. "For the French are not idle, Mr Ludlow."

Polly, who'd been busy hearing of Mr Wentworth's Birmingham buttons, a penny a pair by the newest process, rose to the unoffered bait once more. "They'll come again, Mr Ludlow, even if they are repulsed. And I should know, sir. I hear it morning, noon, and night from my husband. The French are forever coming. But I hope they never arrive, for they are frightful, sir, given to all manner of rapine . . ."

It is impossible to put two sailors within ten feet of each other, particularly those who captain their own ships, without the talk turning to the sea and its hazards and the nature of ships and fellow sailors good, bad, and downright criminal.

Harry was very tempted to ask if they'd met before, for the feeling that they had was as strong as ever. But Bertles gave no indication that this might be the case, nor left a gap in the conversation for him to enquire. And his questions regarding Harry's recent movements were merely polite, with scant attention paid to the answers. Not that Harry volunteered much. Bertles was left unaware that he was dining in the presence of a very successful privateer; nor did Harry divulge any of the strange events of the last eighteen months since he and his brother had set sail from England. He confined the conversation to the ports they'd visited and the sights they'd seen.

Below decks, Pender, close-mouthed by nature and given to withholding information as a lifetime habit, showed equal restraint. But his companions probed nevertheless, curious about all the passengers, and sailors being a gossipy lot, the name Ludlow quickly rang a bell, forcing Pender to confirm certain facts. The wealth and potency of the Ludlow brothers was readily conceded, as was their parentage. After all, who but a wealthy man could carry a personal servant halfway round the Continent? But for all the answers he gave, he avoided more. His response to an endless stream of lower-deck questions, with pots of ale provided to wash down his supper, seemed to leave his companions somewhat dissatisfied.

"It must be a fine thing to have your pa as an admiral," said one of the men at the mess table, who'd tired at last of asking questions about the brothers.

"There's admirals and admirals," said another. "Some ain't got a pot to piss in. But, like I said already, I heard o' the name Ludlow, and I seem to remember that he'd done all right."

Pender looked at the man over the rim of his tankard. Admiral Ludlow had done more than all right. He'd made a mint from the West Indies command. But that fact was also none of their concern, so he left them to wait in vain as he sipped his ale. Seeing, finally, that they were getting nowhere, they changed the subject.

"Now what's the military cove doing with a wife half his age?"

"If'n you don't know the answer to that, then you're as thick as a plank. It won't only be the swell that's rockin' the barky this night."

Things were no less amusing in the main cabin. Bertles, like most of his guests, perspiring freely, was clearly pleased at the air of conviviality. As soon as the cloth was removed he set forth the port and a large bowl of nuts. Major Franks's face froze as he saw it; he knew what was coming.

"Nuts!" cried Polly gaily, her face now flushed with the addition of port wine. "I long to crush a pair beween my hands. My father could manage it, but the art of crushing nuts has ever eluded me." Her husband looked at the deck-beams above his head, as if seeking deliverance. But he could not be unaware that the other men envied him, none more so than young Mr Wentworth, who'd made every endeavour to monopolize Polly Franks this last hour. James was enchanted, thinking her a creature from another age, positively Jacobean in her wit. He was game to paint her for free and said as much. She trilled dismissively. James was too well mannered to add how sought after he was in fashionable London circles. Harry, who would have spoken up for his brother's talent, missed this exchange, registering instead the different motion of the ship. But he soon turned back to join in the conversation. To him Polly spoke of home and comfort, of England and domesticity. Like all sailors he longed for it at sea, and chafed to be away again once he'd tasted it.

Yet she had made him hanker after more than that. Even if her speech caused mirth, she had an independence that reminded him forcibly of the one person he was looking forward to seeing again more than any other. He was a healthy bachelor, prey to the same desires as any man, and since nature had favoured him with looks and birth with money he'd enjoyed the favours of a good number of the fairer sex. As a sailor, these things were transitory, of course; but there was one relationship which could be said to be more than that, without ever threatening to place a curb on him, something he would resent.

When it came to Naomi Smith, jealous souls mouthed *droit de seigneur,* which only demonstrated how little they knew her. Their relationship had nothing to do with pleasuring her landlord. Naomi, widowed young and now sole owner of the Griffin's Head, seemed as determined to remain as unentangled as Harry himself. Decidedly pretty and obviously secure, she'd been exposed to innumerable offers of marriage; most had been subjected to a good-humoured refusal. Not that she was all jollity.

She was as prone as Polly to speak as she found, though less likely to make a gaffe: she paid little heed to the nature of the gender of her company, cast her own opinions instead of borrowing them from others, and disdained to seek defence from mere males. She could, in short, stand up for herself. Some men found such behaviour unbecoming. Harry Ludlow esteemed it.

His mind was dragged back to the present by his host's topping up his glass. Bertles, continuing round the table, was evidently pleased. He poured port liberally into Polly's glass, well aware that he owed some of the success of his dinner to her. All complimented her husband and extolled his good fortune in having a wife like Polly. He remained silent in the face of this. But if he had been challenged on his own attitude, Major Franks would have opined that they didn't have to live with her.

"My lady and gentlemen," said Bertles, rising to his feet, "forgive me, I feel the ebb tide under our counter. I must see to the unmooring of the ship."

He reached behind him, to a desk which had been pushed out of the way to accommodate the diners, and fetched an inkstand, plus a leather-bound folder, with the name of the ship picked out in gold tooling.

"One request, since I may not have time to join you again, this being such a busy anchorage. You must enter your names on the manifest. I also like to have the comments of my passengers noted, be they favourable or not. If you would be so good as to list your names and addresses, with your occupations and opinions, on the ship's manifest, here in this ledger, you would be doing me a service."

"Will a favourable comment gain a reduction in the crossing fee?" asked Wentworth. He tried to make it sound like a jest, but he failed, for it was plain he meant it.

"After such a fine dinner, sir?" said James nailing him.

Bertles, who seemed less full of ale, wine, and port than his guests, beamed at him, his little tufts of hair twitching on his puffed-up cheeks. He watched as Harry filled in his details in the folder. Such examination was unwelcome. Not that his name and address presented any problem. The difficulty arose with his occupation. He had no desire to put down privateer. But ship's captain hardly seemed sufficient for someone who nowadays never sailed in a vessel he hadn't bought. Harry scribbled ship owner and put the quill back in the stand.

"I trust I will not be in the way if I join you on deck," he said, pushing the folder across the table as he began to rise to his feet. He stopped when he saw the flicker in Bertles's eyes, as though he was about to refuse, which left him half in and half out of the chair.

"Of course not," said Bertles, with a sudden smile.

James was on his feet in a flash, though bent double to avoid the low overhead beams. "I am in no way the sailor that my brother is, Captain. But if I promise to stay out of harm's way, I too would welcome the air."

The pause was too long by a second, as if Bertles was seeking another motive for the request. But he nodded eventually, bowing slightly as he replied, "By all means."

Mr Wentworth looked at the soldier, as if hoping he too would go on deck. But Franks was not about to leave a young bachelor alone with his wife, even if the sweat was visibly running down his face. He wanted to keep an eye on this overly solicitous young fellow. The look the major gave Wentworth, and what it portended,

tended, was so obvious as to kill all other conversation. In the awkward silence that followed, Bertles's request that they list their names was forgotten.

The chill air made Harry shiver as he came on deck. It was a clear night, with the moon near full in a sky ablaze of stars. Torches flared across the whole anchorage as boats plied to and fro carrying the last of the wounded. Blazing buildings were dotted around the town, with an obvious arc of fire inland where the colonel was destroying houses to provide a clear field of fire. What would the locals say, having sacrificed their homes, when they saw the troops marching for the jetty, and the safety of their transports?

The wind was still in the east, slightly north, faint but steady. The hands had been called and were already bringing the *Planet* over her bower. As they plucked it from the mud, the bows started to swing on the ebb tide, slowly coming round till they pointed towards the open sea. The bower was catted, the dripping cable stowed. Then they bent the stern anchor to the capstan and the ship was pulled back till that was free. Men ran to set the sails at Bertles's command, rushing up the shrouds and along the ratlines to let loose the reefed topsails.

James was watching his brother during these manoeuvres. It was easy to observe the pleasure it gave him to be back at sea. His head was back, his nostrils seeming to twitch at every odour.

"They seem an efficient crew, brother," he said.

"They are. Bertles would be wise to take care, lest the navy press the lot of them."

Bertles conned the ship out of the bay himself, neatly avoiding the bloated traffic. The swell increased as they left the shelter of the land, and with the sea running south there was little leeway to impede their progress. They stood, both quiet, each alone with his own thoughts, as more sails were set. The *Planet* heeled slightly and her bows now dipped steadily into the black water of the North Sea.

James yawned throughout the entire manoeuvre. "Sea air, Harry. I'd forgotten how it brings on sleep."

"True," said his brother, but whatever it was bringing on for Harry Ludlow, sleep was the least of it.

Harry was awake long before the *Planet* dropped anchor. The movement of feet on the deck throughout the night had filtered into his consciousness, though not enough to bring him fully round. But the ship's changing course, with the consequent alteration in the motion, went deeper, and he opened an eye. He knew instinctively that either the wind had shifted or they'd come round on a quite different heading. By the time the hands slipped the stern anchor over the side, he was wide awake and somewhat curious.

He lay in the darkness, noting the creaking of the capstan and the sound of ropes running through blocks as a ship's boat was hauled up and over the side. Bertles had said, quite firmly, they were making straight for the Downs, with his course set to bring them into the Gull Stream, north of the Goodwin Sands off Ramsgate. Not with all the wind in the world could they have made a landfall already, unless it was on the coast they'd just left.

Harry couldn't contain his curiosity. James snored gently on the other side of the tiny cabin, and it was with some difficulty that he raised himself and shrugged on his greatcoat without waking him. The wardroom stove was open, giving out enough light from the coals to see his way out on to the main-deck. He stood in the waist, looking up at the star-filled sky, listening to the sounds of whispered conversations.

He knew instinctively that whatever Bertles and his crew were up to, it wasn't legal: sailors went about their duties as the task dictated, and if that disturbed their passengers' slumber, so be it. Which left him wondering whether his curiosity was wise. Whatever they were doing was none of his business. He'd wondered already, when he'd first seen the *Planet* riding high at anchor, at the apparent lack of a cargo. He'd surmised that Bertles was content, on a return journey to England, with his quota of fare-paying passengers. Bertles's reluctance to accept soldiers was nothing to remark on. A captain so employed could wait years for his bill to be paid. Then he realized that he'd not enquired as to what the *Planet* carried on the outer voyage, nor looked at the manifest when he'd added his name and occupation. And there was none of the air of a recently unloaded ship about her when they'd come aboard.

He smiled to himself, thinking that Bertles was no fool. It was most likely to be smuggling, since Deal was the most porous place in the whole of the south of England, with a shingle beach ten miles long for the smuggler to land his cargo. Preventative officers were few and far between; getting unlicensed goods ashore was a business with relatively little risk. The mere act of carrying passengers gave a reason for Bertles to be at sea, just as the tariff they paid gave him an income. The excise might be thin on the ground, but they'd soon smoke an owner with money to spend, who maintained and sailed a merchant ship which bore no cargo. He turned below, more amused than angry, when the first shot rang out.

CHAPTER THREE

HARRY WAS ON DECK in a flash, registering the fusillade that followed the first shot. All attempts at silence on deck had been abandoned as men shouted in alarm. The ship's lantern had been extinguished. Bertles, a mere silhouette, was standing on the poop, calling out orders to cut the cable and make sail, as well as shouting at something over the stern. Harry saw the axes flash and the line on the stern anchor cut. He leant over the side, peering towards the barely visible shore. He could just see the outline of the topmasts of at least three more vessels and noted that they also went without a light before his attention was drawn to the flashing oars of two ship's boats, racing across the water towards the *Planet*.

"Captain Bertles!" he shouted. "What's amiss?"

He couldn't see the man's face as he spun round, but the voice left him in no doubt of the master's anger. "How dare you, sir. Get off my deck this instant."

Harry ignored him as he made his way aft, and Bertles had turned away from him to yell encouragement to his boat crews. Everyone on board was preoccupied, too busy to impede his progress. He climbed the ladder to the poop before Bertles, turning back, realized that the passenger had not obeyed his injunction. The pistol was out of his belt and aimed at his passenger's head before he could open his mouth to speak.

"Damn you, sir!" cried Bertles. "Do I have to down you with a ball to be obeyed?"

"I demand to know what's going on!"

The gun waved menacingly, but Bertles had turned to look over the stern. "I have no time for your demands, sir." His shout rent the air: "Move your arses, you lazy buggers!"

He turned and pushed past Harry, leaning on the taffrail to shout at the men on deck. "Get a line ready to lash on to the boats." There would be no time to get either aboard, so Bertles would need to tow them.

"Captain Bertles—" demanded Harry.

He ducked as the pistol swung at his head, feeling it whistle by his ear. His reaction was a reflex and his fist came up with his body catching Bertles in the stomach. The captain fell forward, the gun dropping from his hand. Set at half-cock, it discharged itself with a loud bang, the ball thudding into the rail. Bertles was bent over, gasping for breath. Harry hauled him upright, waiting while he sucked enough air into his winded lungs to talk.

"Now, Captain, explain."

"We are in mortal danger, sir," panted Bertles. "I must get my ship under way."

Harry shook him roughly. "I demand an explanation."

"In time, Mr Ludlow. But for Heaven's sake let me get to sea."

Harry let him go. Bertles immediately shot down the ladder to the quarterdeck, taking the wheel himself, and, despite Harry's punch, shouting out a string of orders to set all sail. The *Planet* was already moving, for the forecourse and main staysail were down, with hands hauling on the inner and outer jibs like demons. Still afire with curiosity, he turned to look at the ship's boats, now close enough to take a line from the *Planet*, as Bertles called for topsails.

The other ships were still distant silhouettes, but the one nearest was setting her sails as quickly as the *Planet*. He strained to make out her shape, to see what manner of vessel she was, but the lack of light defeated him. It was only as she swung round, with her anchors inboard, that he realized she was a square-rigger, with three masts. Difficult to be sure, but some kind of trading barque? He turned and looked up at the *Planet's* top hamper. A merchant snow, broad of beam and poorly rigged, she'd need something special to outrun any three-masted ship, and nothing he could see aloft gave him any confidence that she would do so.

Three crewmen bundled on to the poop. One took an end on the line they carried and lashed it to a cleat, while another jumped up and balanced precariously on the rail. He swung the line round his head and then cast it out. Harry saw the flash of phosphorescence as it hit the water between the leading boat and the ship, heard the cry that told all of them that the throw had been accurate. The jolly-boat, behind the cutter, had lashed itself to the larger boat's stern.

The rope creaked as the cutter took the tow. One of the sailors released the line on the cleat as the other took the strain. Using the cleat as a stop, they hauled on the line to bring the two boats closer to the ship. Feeling useless, Harry took an end of the line and heaved along with the hands.

Both boats had been hauled alongside, with the oarsmen jumping nimbly aboard, despite the fact that the *Planet* was now making some three knots. He'd been joined on the poop by James and Major Franks. Pender arrived last, well wrapped up against the cold, and bearing the brothers' greatcoats.

"Smuggling, I think," he said, when James first asked him what was happening. "Bertles put the ship about once we were asleep. I imagine that he touched on the coast of France."

"Then who was shooting at us?" asked Franks, with a fine grasp of the essentials.

Harry lifted a hand slightly to indicate Bertles, still busy trimming his sails. "I shall ask the captain as soon as he has a moment. There were other ships anchored off the coast."

"Do we need weapons, your honour?" asked Pender.

Harry looked at the pistol that still lay at his feet. "We might, Pender. Bertles has already tried to crown me once."

He looked over his shoulder at the black sea, shot across with glinting shafts of moonlight. There was nothing visible, but he didn't doubt for a second that the other ship had been setting sail for a pursuit. "Apart from the risk from Bertles, I'd be very surprised if we are not being chased."

His servant was gone before he finished the sentence. But what he said alarmed Franks. "Is my wife in any danger, sir?"

"That I cannot say, Major. But I think wisdom dictates that she be up and dressed."

Franks went down the ladder as Pender returned to the deck. His hands were empty. "The captain has posted a couple of guards to mind our dunnage. I can't get near it."

"Damn the man," snapped James, making ready to go and investigate.

Harry grabbed his arm to restrain him. "These men were armed, I take it?" Pender nodded. "I thought they must be," said Harry, with a smile.

Pender smiled too, his teeth white in the moonlight. "If they hadn't been, I wouldn't have come back empty-handed."

"Captain Bertles," shouted Harry. "You are taking unwarranted liberties in keeping us from our possessions. I think you most certainly owe us an apology and some degree of enlightenment."

Bertles kept his hands on the wheel, but he turned to reply. "You'd best mind your tongue, sir, for you've laid hands on me this night. That is not something Tobias Bertles is likely to let pass."

"Who is chasing us?" asked Harry.

"There ain't no one chasing us, Mr Ludlow. Those that had a mind to do so were too slow off the mark."

Harry turned and walked aft to the taffrail, peering out into the darkness. The light of the moon flickering off something fixed his attention. He stared hard and the faint, dark outline of a ship under sail formed before his eyes. He didn't just turn to tell Bertles. He had a voice that could carry to the tops in a full gale.

"I hate to disappoint you, sir, but if you care to look astern you will observe that someone has been more nimble than you supposed."

The *Planet* jibbed slightly as Bertles let go of the wheel. Harry heard him curse as he told another to take the con. He kept his eyes fixed on the other ship as Bertles thudded up the ladder behind him. The man was breathing heavily as he joined Harry and the others at the rail.

"Where away?"

Harry raised his hand slowly, pointing to a spot two points to larboard off the stern. "He's a better sailer than we are, Captain. And faster. If he holds his course he'll take your wind when he catches us."

Bertles swore under his breath and Harry thought he heard something remarkably like a whimper.

"Now, sir. I really think an explanation is necessary."

Bertles ignored him. His head was back, searching the clear sky.

"One cloud," he said to himself. "Oh, Lord, just one decent cloud."

"Will you answer my brother, sir. It's intolerable to be so used."

Bertles turned and gave James a cold look. "Get below, all of you."

"Not until you answer," said James.

Even in the moonlight you could tell that he was angry. All his earlier bonhomie had quite gone. "You can do so willing, or you can do so with a pike up your arse. But go below you will!"

By stretching a point, Harry led them into the small cabin instead of going below decks. Major Franks had raised his wife and she was fully dressed, wearing the same cream dress which had so flattered her youthful figure at dinner.

"Who's chasing us, Harry, a revenue cutter?" asked James.

His brother was already at the sternlights, moving the damask curtains aside a fraction to peer through the thick glass. James soon joined him and Harry spoke quietly, not wishing to alarm the others.

"I don't know much more than you, James, but it's neither a cutter nor a revenue man. That is unless he's French."

"French!" said James out loud. Mrs Franks put her hand to her mouth in alarm. The major moved to comfort her, and also to admonish her, for she seemed set to speak. "Not one word, my dear, is that clear?" She nodded meekly.

The door to the cabin flew open and young Mr Wentworth, his eyes still full of sleep, was pushed in to join them. The door was slammed shut again.

"What the devil is going on?" said Wentworth.

"You were asleep?" asked Harry, shaking his head in wonder that anyone could have slept through such a commotion, forgetting how Bertles had plied them with drink.

Wentworth, somewhat bleary-eyed and pasty, looked as though he'd taken extra advantage of Bertles's generosity. He was watching Pender, as he searched the cabin for weapons. "I was until I was dragged from my cot. The sailor said we were in some danger!"

"Did he say who from?" asked James.

"No, sir, he did not. I shall ask Captain Bertles."

"I don't think that will be possible. He has confined us all here in the most direct way. And I believe if you open that door you will find an armed man outside."

"Armed man! What are you talking about, Mr Ludlow?" He spun and pulled at the door. As it flew open the barrel of a musket poked through. The grim face of the man holding it left the young man in no doubt of his intentions.

"Back inside," snapped the sailor with the gun, before he reached out with his free hand and slammed the door shut again.

"Any luck, Pender?" asked Harry.

"Nothing," replied his servant. "He must keep his armoury someplace else."

"I should think his entire range of weapons is in the hands of his men."

"I've got my knife, your honour, but that's all."

"Will someone explain to me what is happening!" cried Wentworth, petulantly.

"I too am confused, Mr Ludlow," said Franks.

Harry nodded, but he did not explain right away. "Pender, the light." As soon as the cabin was in darkness, he pulled back the curtains, explaining what had happened as he did so, all the time struggling with the catches to try and open a window. But this was a North Sea vessel. If the windows were opened it was a rare event, for the catches were rusty and stiff.

"They are involved in smuggling, Major Franks. There seemed to be a squadron of ships anchored in the same bay and I believe it was they who fired on us. Why, I don't know. And you are as aware as anyone of Captain Bertles's failure to answer my enquiries."

"Why lock us in here?" said James angrily. "Does he think we care if he's smuggling?"

"The kindest interpretation is that he expects a fight and he wishes to protect us."

"I don't believe that and neither do you."

"Pender, can you get this damned window open."

Major Franks coughed slightly, forcing Harry to apologize for his language. Pender went to the window, pulling a knife from his boot. He ignored the catches and stuck his knife into the side with the hinge.

"Take hold of the frame, Captain Ludlow, otherwise Mr Bertles's window is going to end up in the drink."

"Let it," said James. "And may our host shortly follow."

Harry did as he was bidden, though like James he cared nothing for the casement. But what he was about needed to be kept secret from those above his head. Pender was digging away. He turned to Harry, who was holding the catch, and the enquiring look on his master's face produced a wide grin. "Always go through the hinges, your honour. They're usually a sight easier than the lock."

There was a slow wrenching sound as the frame came away from the surround. A blast of cold air greeted them as they spun the casement and lifted the window inboard.

"The wind is still in the north-east," said Harry.

"Is that a good thing?" asked Major Franks, who'd left his

wife's side in an attempt to discover what Harry was looking at. But he was thwarted, both for an answer and a view, by the other man's body, hanging half out of the casement, searching the moonlit sea for the other vessel. He saw her, a ghostly presence in the blue light, just abaft the beam. He'd altered course, sailing large with full advantage of the wind, and he was still overhauling the *Planet*.

The cloud that suddenly covered the moon had the effect of a light going out, plunging the cabin into complete darkness. Harry watched as the other ship hauled round, no doubt aware that the clouds beginning to cover the sky would make the *Planet* near invisible. Harry watched as the darkness raced across the sea between the ships, felt the *Planet* heel as Bertles put his helm down. He could hear the creak of the maincourse yard as it was hauled round to change the ship's heading. The sails on the other ship turned from ghostly white to a black and threatening silhouette, with an ever decreasing strip of pale blue light behind it.

It was a perfect situation for Bertles to evade his pursuer. For though they could still see him, it was doubtful if their pursuer could see the *Planet*. Harry pulled himself back through the frame, vigorously rubbing his bare hands together, trying to get them warm, before addressing the blackness of the interior.

"I cannot say if it's a good thing for us, but Bertles has at least won some time. We may, at last, find out what he intends."

"Would it be an idea to put that winder back, your honour?" said Pender. "No sense in letting them know what we've been about."

"Make it so, Pender."

"Let me help," said James, stepping forward.

"God help anyone who leans on this, Mr James," said Pender. "They'll be pitched into the wake and drown for sure."

Slightly breathless from his exertions, James's reply had none of the usual languid sarcasm. "If the swine who owns the window goes near it, push him hard."

Most of that long winter night was spent in a series of elaborate manoeuvres. Harry lost track of the number of times that Bertles altered course in his attempt to evade his pursuers. Despite endless speculation, with Wentworth barely pausing for breath as he complained loudly at being ill used, no one could advance a convincing reason as to why they were in such a situation.

Harry felt the way come off the ship and knew they were heaving to. The scrape of the cutter was clearly audible as it was pulled alongside and he heard the creak of loaded ropes running through blocks as it was hauled aboard. He peered out of the salt-streaked sternlights. The sky was now only half obscured by cloud, with the silver linings giving off a small amount of light. He turned to look at his fellow passengers. They sat silent, rocking on the swell, wondering what would happen next.

CHAPTER FOUR

AS THE DOOR swung open, the shaded lantern faintly illuminating the cabin gave enough light to show Bertles's long pepper and salt hair and the two tufts on his cheekbones, making him look like a ghost. The pistol that came up in his hand brooked no argument. "Out of here, the lot of you."

They filed out of the cabin on to the deck. Harry could see their sea-chests were piled by the gangway. Men were lifting barrels aboard, obviously from the jolly-boat which they'd been towing since the pursuit began. As he stood there trying to make sense of what was happening two sailors came out behind him carrying the possessions of Major and Mrs Franks.

"I should wrap up warm, ma'am," said Bertles, taking Polly Franks's cloak and draping it round her. "For it's a chill night and likely to get even colder."

"What are you about, Bertles?" snapped Harry.

"Why, it's time for us to part company, Ludlow."

"Part company, man? We're in the middle of the North Sea," said James angrily.

"Then ain't it handy your brother bein' a privateer."

Harry stared hard at him, wondering how he knew that, as James made to move forward. But two seamen grabbed his arms to restrain him. Bertles stuck the pistol into his stomach. Then his eyes turned to Harry. "I owe you for that clout you gave me earlier, Ludlow."

Harry's heart was in his mouth. Then felt Pender push his knife, blade forward, into his hand. He kept his voice as steady as he could. "Then take it out on me, sir, not my brother."

"How can I, Ludlow? I intend to put you lot over the side in that there boat. Without you to navigate, this little party will die. I wouldn't want to have that on my conscience, now would I? But this here brother of yours is only a painter, an' has been very vocal as to how he's useless at sea."

James's voice was even and phlegmatic, almost bored. "If you're going to pull the trigger, Bertles, do so. But spare us your observations, and most of all the idea that you possess a conscience."

The captain's knee came up and took him hard in the groin. He doubled up in agony and Bertles whipped his head with the pistol. Not hard, but enough to knock over a man already bent double. He stood over his writhing victim, breathing heavily, though his exertions had been slight. Harry watched the gun closely, ready to lunge at him with Pender's knife.

"Pull the trigger, indeed. What does he take me for, a murderer?"

He lifted his eyes to meet Harry's again, but the gun stayed where it was, hanging by his side.

"I'd say we're all square, Ludlow."

Pender's mouth was close to his ear, the whisper quiet but urgent. "It's all show, your honour. He's doin' it to impress his crew."

Being at the front of the group Harry couldn't reply, nor could he agree, much as he trusted his servant's instincts. Polly Franks had gasped when Bertles hit James. Now she was sobbing quietly on her husband's shoulder. Bertles lifted the pistol again and tucked it under her chin, forcing it up. Her husband moved to intervene but the gun was on him in a second. When Bertles spoke, it was to Polly Franks, and her alone.

"It could be worse. Maybe you'd like to stay aboard the *Planet* with me." She looked away in disgust, burying her head in the major's shoulder again. "You'd get pleasure from it, Polly Franks, that I do assure you. Happen you'd get to chew on one of them balls you was on about earlier."

Bertles laughed and turned to include his silent crew. None of them seemed to share his merriment. Having observed this, the captain looked down at James, who lay still on the ground, his hands held between his legs.

"I should say his'll be a fair size in the morning, mind. Happen you should go along after all."

That did produce the odd smile from the crew. Harry stepped forward, the knife tucked out of sight up his arm. Bertles stepped back, but he wasn't in any way alarmed.

"He's all yours, Mr Ludlow. Or should I say *Captain* Ludlow, since you're about to take command of a boat again?"

Harry helped James to his feet and led him over to the side of the ship so that he could lean on the bulwarks.

"Stuff's all aboard," said one of the men.

"Right, get their chests into the jolly-boat." His men didn't rush to obey as he turned his attention back to his passengers. Everything they did was undertaken with a palpable air of reluctance.

"I've provisioned her with water and biscuit for two days. That should be more'n enough to get you to a landfall."

"What's our position?" asked Harry.

"Don't rightly know, with all that twistin' and turning," said Bertles. He was smiling again, about to crack another joke. "But it won't be hard, will it, Ludlow? You just wait for daylight. If you want to go to France you head into it. If you want to go to England, sail the other way. There's a mast in the boat, and canvas. Failing the wind, you can use the oars."

"I think, on balance, we'd all rather stay aboard."

"That's not an available choice. I've got to go blue water for a bit, and I don't want a load of snivelling passengers along."

The murmur from the crew was faint, but it was there.

"Who are you running from, Bertles?" asked Harry.

"Who says I'm running?" he growled.

"All that twisting and turning, not to mention the way you cut your cable . . ."

With his men now shifting from foot to foot, Bertles looked at the cloudy sky, broken in the distance. "Never you mind, Ludlow.

Just you get yourself into the jolly-boat. 'Cause if you don't I'll throw the lot of you over the side. I can't expect these clouds to hide me forever."

"I'm not going anywhere," said Wentworth, who'd not uttered a word since they'd come on deck. Now he'd pulled himself erect, hat in hand, his fair hair lifting slightly in the breeze and the light from Bertles's shaded lantern flashing off his spectacles.

"Well, ain't you now?" said Bertles, amused.

"I've paid for my passage, sir," said the young man, squaring his shoulders even more. "And I demand you take us to our destination."

Bertles looked round the assembled faces in wonder. "Lord in heaven, the next thing you know he'll be demanding his money back." He turned to a pair of the sailors guarding them. "Throw that cheeky young bastard into the boat."

"Captain Bertles!" cried Wentworth.

That angered him. His head shook as he shouted at the young man. "Stow your gab, or by God I'll order 'em to throw you and miss."

For the first time Harry knew that Pender was right. The man's actions were all for show. But Bertles would kill one of them if he had to. He needed his crew more than he needed his passengers. Harry moved between them, took the young man's arm, and led him over to the rail to stand beside his brother, still bent double from Bertles's blow.

"Come, Mr Wentworth. If this wind holds, in a sound boat with a decent sail, we'll beat Captain Bertles to the Downs."

Bertles was clearly relieved by Harry's intervention, so much so that he made another heavy-handed attempt at humour. "There you are, Mr Wentworth. Happen I should charge you Post rates."

"Are you all right, James?" said Harry softly, turning away from a very dissatisfied Wentworth. His brother nodded slowly. "Pender, help my brother into the boat. Major Franks, please ensure that both you and your wife are well wrapped up. You too, Mr Wentworth."

The sailors had stowed their chests. Harry stood at the gangway and helped the others down into the boat, which rocked gently on the swell. Less than ten feet from stem to stern, there was barely enough room for them all and the combined weight of passengers and baggage would take the gunwales perilously close to the waterline. He was just about to get down himself when Bertles took his arm, pulling him close.

"No doubt you think I'm a treacherous bastard, Ludlow." Harry just looked at him without replying, so Bertles continued. "What's in your mind don't bother me none. But I'll tell you this. I'm doin' you a favour. You've seen that ship that was after us. Well, let me tell you our destination ain't no great secret. If she shows her topsails above your horizon, then forget the Downs. You put your helm down and get as far away as you can. You'll be safer in France than on that deck."

With that Bertles turned away and gave the order to make sail.

As soon as they were away from the side of the ship, Harry set about altering the balance of the jolly-boat, moving chests and people to bring her down by the stern so that his rudder would bite. Mrs Franks and the major occupied the thwarts near the bow, with James and Wentworth amidships. Harry and Pender, with most of the baggage, sat in the stern, which allowed them to swing the boom of the small triangular sail without asking anyone to shift.

The *Planet* had disappeared in minutes, swallowed up by the night. It was impossible for Harry to see in the dark, but experience helped as he lashed the top of the triangular sail to the top of the mast. Then he stepped it, pushing it through the grommets on the boom, with Pender helping him to get it upright. As he worked, looping the line on to the wood through the eyelets in the sail, the others sat in complete silence, still like statues, as though numb. That was probably true in the case of the Franks and Wentworth, but he knew James was just waiting for him to finish his task. Nothing would stop his brother from asking about their situation. James waited till he had set the sail and hauled it taut, careful about the setting for he wished to keep their speed to a minimum.

"Are we done, Harry?"

"We're not badly off, James. The boat seems sound enough, the weather is clement, and the wind is in our favour."

"Was what you said to Mr Wentworth aboard the *Planet* the truth?"

"We would be better off with a stronger wind," said Harry, looking at the sky. "And I don't doubt in these waters we'll get one before long. If it stays in the east, then we'll be in England in time for dinner."

Harry could almost feel James's disbelief. His brother was always complaining about his sanguine nature. But at sea he would be at a loss to disagree. That, and the need not to alarm the others, kept him silent. And Harry didn't feel like further explanation. Their situation held no terrors for him at all, provided the weather held. He'd been afloat most of his life, since his father entered him on the books of his man-o'-war as a ship's boy. His years in the King's Navy had included many an occasion when he found himself in a small boat, well out of sight of land.

"I do not wish to sail her too hard till daylight, since I don't know our position, though I'll be able to have a guess at a suitable heading if the sky clears."

"The stars?" asked Major Franks.

"The conjunction of Arcturus and Vega will suffice, Major!"

The edge of the cloud covering the moon grew steadily more luminous, which made the cloud itself, as the sea around them, look ever more black and threatening. The moon suddenly lit up the southern horizon with a silver glow and Harry saw the tips of the three masts right away. He could not be sure it was the same ship, but what Bertles had said had stayed with him. The captain of the *Planet* knew the ship, and he knew who commanded her. He was so afraid of whoever that was he was even avoiding his home port.

Harry was very confident of his ability to get the jolly-boat and its passengers to a safe landfall. But after the events of the night, still a mystery, he wasn't sure what fate would await them if they went aboard the ship chasing the *Planet,* a ship that had been anchored off the shore without lights. Bertles had seemed decent enough until things turned against him. It was all a question of what credence you gave his parting words. Harry ran them over in his mind, and as he recalled the urgency and fear in Bertles's voice he made his decision. They were safer where they were, where all the factors were known. He hauled on the boom, put the tiller down, and did his very best to stay out of the approaching ring of bright moonlight.

"Harry . . . ?"

James had also seen the ship. "Quiet, James. And that goes for all of you. Pender, stand by to get the mast down double quick."

His servant was no doubt as mystified as James, but he didn't question Harry Ludlow's orders. If Major Franks harboured any doubts, he held them in check, prepared to bow to another professional, clearly at home in his own field. But Wentworth, as talkative as ever, was not to be silenced. "I don't recall us electing you to lead us, Mr Ludlow."

"Was there time?" snapped Harry.

"That is neither here nor there, sir. We have a ship close by, which will surely prove a safer haven than this small boat."

"I think it's the ship that was chasing Bertles."

Wentworth's voice grew louder and even more querulous. "Then all the more reason to hail them, surely."

"Captain Bertles said we'd do better to avoid them."

"And you believed him, sir!"

Harry's voice was hard, for he could see the illogicality of his action with the same degree of clarity that affected Wentworth. And he needed to still his own doubts as well as those of the younger man.

"I have no time for explanations, Mr Wentworth. But as the only person capable of getting us safely to shore, I will exercise the right to steer the boat anywhere I want. Now you shall oblige me by remaining silent, for sound carries a long way at sea."

"I will—"

Harry cut off his protest at once. "Otherwise I will be forced to gag you."

"This is an outrage."

"Do be quiet, Mr Wentworth," said James, "or I fear I shall be the one given the task."

"I shall abide by whatever decision you make," said Franks.

"Thank you, Major," said Harry.

That show of support effectively silenced Wentworth. The jolly-boat heeled as they sailed into the wind. Harry took several turns on the rope to tighten the sail, then sat on the counter, using his weight to steady the boat. They were moving faster now, as Harry sought both darkness and distance. They might spot him, but even if they did, he hoped he'd be far enough distant to avoid investigation. It all depended on how keen the captain of that barque was on finding Bertles.

The light from the moon, behind that shifting cloud, was coming their way. Harry called to Pender, unlashed the boom so that the sail flapped uselessly, and pushed the tiller to bring her round, bows on to the swell. Then he stood to help take the mast down.

"Down in the boat, everyone," he called softly, "and no talking."

The moon appeared from behind the cloud, suddenly bathing the whole sea around them in a bright light. The silhouette of the barque was a good mile off now. If she saw the jolly-boat at all, it didn't interest her enough to change course. The ship ploughed on, then disappeared as the next cloud obscured the moon.

"Are we allowed an explanation now, Harry?" whispered James.

Harry couldn't resist baiting him a little now, since the matter had been resolved. He couldn't catch that ship now, even if he wanted to.

"Is one necessary?"

"It most certainly is!" snapped Wentworth.

"The ship that was after the *Planet* was engaged in the same trade, I think. In other words, another smuggler. Bertles had cause to be frightened of whoever sails her. I shall show the same caution and avoid contact."

"This is nonsense, Mr Ludlow," said Wentworth. "How can you tell anything in the dark? It could well be a British warship. And I repeat, surely we'd be safer aboard that than stuck here in this coracle."

"If it is a smuggler, it could be another Bertles, Mr Wentworth. Or maybe something even worse. I feel safer where we are."

The young man was not mollified. "I do feel that we should be consulted as to any future course of action, Ludlow. I, for one, will not meekly submit myself to your instructions."

"Shall I heave him over the side, Captain?" growled Pender, careful to make sure only Harry heard.

"I am at a loss to know whose instructions we should be under, Mr Wentworth," said James sharply. "I will have you know that, at sea, I repose nothing but faith in my brother. If I enquired as to the situation, it was for the purpose of information, not to foment dissent."

"I am not to be ordered about, sir," snapped the young man. "Nor moved about the ocean at another's whim."

Surprisingly, it was Polly Franks who spoke, her voice small and subdued, but all the more effective for being so. "Do be quiet, Mr Wentworth. Or if you must speak, direct your breath on to the sail."

"Let's have the mast up again, Pender. Then break out some of that water and biscuit so we can fortify ourselves against the cold."

"There's brandy in my chest," said Franks. "That may serve us better than ship's water."

"Splendid," said Harry. "Let's have a tot to raise our spirits."

Both James and Wentworth grunted, but for entirely different reasons.

CHAPTER FIVE

WITH THE STARS to guide him, Harry was certain of his course, knowing that as the clouds came over again he only needed a steady hand on the tiller to maintain his heading. But the sky cleared again, with the moon dipping towards the earth, he couldn't credit the evidence of his own eyes.

He'd spent enough time at sea looking for other ships to know that even with a rendezvous it was a very chancy business. Yet he was in the presence of both the ships he wished to avoid. The *Planet* was doing its best, with all sails set, but whoever was chasing Bertles was overhauling him easily.

The two ships were very close together, with the three-master edging down to take the *Planet*'s wind. Worse than that, they were heading straight for him. Harry cursed loudly, then apologized to Mrs Franks, as he put the boat about, sailing into the wind, well off their course.

He heard the sound of musket fire across the water, but nothing larger. In the main, smugglers relied on speed, superior skill, or guile to outwit any pursuer, rather than heavy armament: Bertles, supposedly a merchantman, had a couple of four-pounders on his deck, but they were so badly cared for that to fire them might endanger his own crew more than his enemy. The crack of the muskets grew louder, and with the space between shots Harry had the impression that it was only one gun replying. He recalled the faces of Bertles's crew. Not sullen, but not well pleased at the way things had turned out. Perhaps they'd refused to fire off the guns, leaving their captain to do his best with a solitary musket.

The three-master took the wind right out of the *Planet*'s sails leaving them flapping uselessly, and put his helm down hard. Harry heard the crunch as the two ships collided, then the yells of the boarding party as they leapt aboard. He waited for the sound of battle joined, of metal on metal as sword and pike clashed, of the screams of men excited and wounded. Nothing came across the water except an eerie silence. With a quick glance at the sky, Harry trimmed the sail to bring the jolly-boat round. He put them on a heading that would take him past the stern of both vessels.

"They are between us and our landfall," he said quickly. "Please maintain silence as we go round them."

"For God's sake, why, sir?" said Wentworth. "Surely Captain Bertles's enemies must be our friends?"

A single scream came across the water, of a man in great pain. The kind of pain that precedes a slow death. The agonized voice rose and fell. Mrs Franks put her hands to her ears to shut out the horrifying sound. All eyes, bar hers, were on the two ships. The huge stern lanterns were now lit, creating a pool of light which clearly showed them lashed together. Harry edged away a fraction more, to stay out of the arc of those bright lights. "I don't know who our friends are, Mr Wentworth," said Harry. "You will forgive me if I treat them all as potential enemies until I'm sure."

If Wentworth had words to say, they were checked by the final scream, a sound more terrifying than those that had gone before, followed by a cheer. Harry saw the blood-stained body rise from the deck, saw the legs kick wildly as the man was hauled up to hang by his neck from the maincourse yard.

Curiosity made Harry edge closer. He had the safety of those stern lanterns, which would illuminate anyone standing by the rail and make it near impossible for anyone aboard the ships to see beyond the circle of golden light into the darkness beyond. No one in the boat said a word. The voices from the deck, faint at first, grew suddenly clear across the calm water. Bertles was speaking desperately, though his words belied the tone.

"I'll not beg, if'n that's what you're after."

The voice that answered was high, almost girlish, with a singing quality and a rolling accent. But it carried, too, for it was full of amused disbelief. "Who says that begging will do for you? You're way beyond that, Tobias Bertles. There's only one fate for a thievin' git like you."

"So string me up, like you did to him, an' get it over with."

"You could have saved him some pain, Bertles. All I asked was what you did with the other sod I'm after. It was a bad notion sending him off with the passengers. It won't save the bastard, either. If you'd told me instead, happen I'd have let him that's hangin' die quick."

There was a pause, filled with a low moaning sound which seemed to come from more than one throat. The sound of men sobbing and begging came across the water.

"You see, Bertles, I can be merciful." That was followed by a a girlish giggle. Then the high voice rose, screaming out as if the man was giving orders in a gale of wind. "Haul away, lads, handsomely now."

Harry could hear the ropes running through the blocks. The choking sound of hemp closing on a dozen throats was unforgettable. Each line was now tense, straining on its load. Suddenly the victims rose above the sides of the ship, each one arched, struggling to get his feet back on the deck. Bodies jerked as the man on their line gave another heave. Up and up they went, until the rigging was full of writhing sailors, legs flailing as the life was choked out of them, the whole scene overlain with the sound of laughter and cheering from those who strung them up.

"My God!" said James, his voice soft with horrified wonder. "They're hanging everyone aboard."

The voice sang out again. "See, Bertles. Now that be mercy, for I could have done it one by one, with each man awaiting, with the last man dying a dozen deaths." Silence fell as the men aloft expired, their kicking feet eventually stilled, till they swung like decorations on a grisly tree. Then that high voice came again, soft at first, but rising higher as he pronounced the last man's fate.

"And now for you, Bertles. I sees you as a traitor as well as a thief. Now in the olden days, when someone did the dirty, they wasn't as soft as they are now. It was more'n just a hanging they got. Lord, no. They was hung, drawn, and quartered. You know what that means, don't you? And they weren't hung by the neck so that the drawin' and quarterin' caused no pain. No, Bertles, they was suspended in a frame, and as their vitals was pulled out of their gut they could see it all. I've often wondered if they were gone by the time they was chopped. Now I've a mind to afford you something special, but I don't have the frame. So we'll put aside the hanging part, and just concentrate on the rest."

The voice changed, going even higher, like a choirboy straining for a top note, as the prospect of what was to come raised the degree of his excitement. Harry was so engrossed in the words that he'd drifted close, into the edge of the light thrown by the stern lanterns. Pender, white faced, touched his arm and Harry pressed on the tiller as he took the strain on the boom. As they drifted away the voice faded, but not before they heard the last words.

"But I'll not have you spoiling my fun, Bertles. So I'm going to strip your hide off before anything else. Every inch of skin off your useless body. Strip the bastard down."

"Do you still wish to go aboard, Mr Wentworth?" asked James, sombrely.

The young man didn't reply. But he shook his head as the first of Bertles's screams, each one accompanied by a loud cheer, came at them across the intervening sea. They seemed to follow them for an age as they put some distance between their boat and the two ships. Bertles died slowly, his terrible cries echoing across the water, but no man's heart could endure what he suffered and eventually they ceased.

Harry saw the first flames lick the rigging, which showed him that the barque had fended off the *Planet*. The fire grew brighter still, and the inert figures swung in the rigging like the victims of a pagan feast. The ship went up like a torch, much faster than it should. Harry cursed and shouted at Pender. They hauled on the mast to get it down, lest the white canvas should be illuminated by the sudden flaring of the fire. The whole sea was lit up for half a mile as the upper sails caught fire. Harry could see the light reflected on the faces in the boat as he struggled with the mast.

"Look away!" he shouted. The flaring sails died, which decreased the illuminated area, though the blazing ship, with the barque close by, was still plain to the eye. Harry watched anxiously as the other ship's bowsprit swung round. He had no way of knowing if they'd been observed, for they were too far away to hear any shout. But his heart sank as the ship, silhouetted against the burning *Planet,* ceased to swing. Sails were going up rapidly and the bows were pointed straight at them.

"Get the sail back up, quick," he shouted to Pender. "James. Get our pistols out of their cases and load them. Major Franks, if you have any weapons in your chest, I suggest we get them out as well."

"They're after us?" asked James, ducking under the boom to get at their sea-chests.

"I think so," said Harry, hauling on the sail to get it taut. "I can't be sure."

"Can we outsail them?"

Harry, as he sat on the rim of the boat and leant back, strove to put as much confidence in his answer as he could. "Possibly. It's too early to tell. Pender, over here alongside me. Let's get her heeled over. It'll increase her speed if I can trim the sail round a bit more."

If James knew he was lying, he kept the information to himself. Harry had little hope that what he said was true. A three-masted vessel, even badly handled and with a bottom covered in weed, would catch a jolly-boat in this wind, for the pressure was much greater on her higher, larger sails. With a fore-and-aft rig he might have a chance if the wind swung right round into the west, but he couldn't reverse his course to make it so. A square-rigged ship would just put down his helm and head him off. And what if she carried cannon? Even if he could somehow evade her, they'd be too close to those guns to survive.

He looked at the sky, which was beginning to lighten in the east, then back towards the rim of fire on the surface, all that remained of the *Planet*. Imperceptibly the ship pursuing them took shape. It was impossible to say yet if it was gaining, but he had to work on that assumption. Harry was making a host of calculations, quite naturally, and would have been at a loss to explain himself if called upon to do so. The sight of geese, flying in a line high above his head, made him ease the boom out further; at this time of year, they were heading west, migrating via the marshes of southern England. This lifted him and Pender out of the water and he teased the sail in and out as he sought the proper balance between the force of the wind on the canvas and the effect of that on a boat lacking any kind of keel.

"James, Mr Wentworth, come to this side of the boat," he shouted.

"Should we throw the luggage overboard?" asked James.

Harry shook his head. Without a keel the weight of their luggage, right in the bottom of the boat, was likely to help rather than hinder them. His mind was clear and unencumbered as he eased their small boat round so it was right before the wind. That would force his pursuer to do the same, nullifying the advantage of most of his sails, since the wind, right aft, could only play upon the rearmost canvas. He'd sailed these waters many times before and by his reckoning, which was as much guesswork as anything scientific, they were on course for the Downs. He had no doubt they were headed west, for the sun popped red-edged above the horizon behind them.

He thought back to the times he sailed off the Goodwins, that great bar of treacherous sand, the graveyard of many a ship, that provided such a large, safe anchorage. The wind in these parts tended to be a prevailing easterly, though there was a chance it would swing round to a land breeze, or drop away altogether at first light.

The gentle swell lifted them at the same moment it raised their pursuer. The bows were full of men, all looking right ahead. If he'd had the slightest doubt they were after the jolly-boat that was laid to rest. His eyes took in the sails. That captain with the singular voice had his main-topgallants aloft, in an attempt to compensate for his lack of foresails. And he was gaining. Not much, but enough. It was a race to see if Harry could make a landfall before they came up on them. As to why they were being pursued, he didn't know and he didn't care. Nor was he likely to find out. Whoever was conning that ship had a choice. With cannon he could blow them out of the water. Or he could heave to and take them aboard. There was another choice; to run his bows over them and pitch them into the sea to drown.

The sun disappeared behind the rim of cloud which covered the Channel. That cloud would be over the French coast. But knowing that gave him little idea of his own proximity to the Downs. The thought that really troubled him was if he was further north, heading into the Thames estuary, that great bight of open water would give his pursuer more room to chase him. If that was the case all he could hope for was the sight of another ship, to make their pursuer shear off.

"Harry!"

James's voice brought him out of his private thoughts. He looked into his brother's eyes. James kept his voice as low as he could, but in the confined space it was impossible to avoid it being overheard.

"I think it would be better to let us know the truth of our situation."

All eyes were on him, waiting expectantly. He was tempted to lie again, but he realized they must have registered the size of the ship, compared to how it had seemed at first light.

"If you're inclined to prayer, any of you, this would be a good time to seek Divine intercession."

"I know I'm no sailor, Harry," said James. "But would a change of course help?"

James was asking because he couldn't stay silent. It was against his nature. "We're making good speed. With our single sail we're getting the very best out of the wind that we can, while denying him the use of most of his canvas. A change of course would slow us down and allow him to increase his speed, that is, unless we have a complete change of wind."

"We have no sure knowledge that this fellow means us ill," said Wentworth. "Perhaps if we stopped running away and threw ourselves on his charity."

The thought was not his alone. Major and Mrs Franks looked as though they might agree. After what he'd heard, that fact astounded him. Harry was tired, from being up all night and from sailing the boat, so perhaps he could have been more gentle. He looked at the pistols in the major's hands. "I should discharge but one of those, Major. You will need the other ball for your wife."

"You bastard!"

Harry swung round to look at Pender. Then he realized his servant's words were directed at their pursuer. Even in the short time that they'd had their conversation he could observe how much they'd gained. He could also see that they were coming round, adjusting their yards and setting sails on the fore- and mizen-masts, trying to gain even more speed, which seemed odd given that they were winning on their quarry already.

Harry saw the first of the huge flock of migrating birds. Thrushes, they were flying as hard as they could towards a shore he couldn't see. Seagulls flew above them, their gimlet eyes on the weaker birds as they sank towards the surface of the ocean. Many wouldn't make it, some finally drowning from exhaustion a few feet from the beach. But if they were so low above the water, they had to have covered most of the distance. He eased the boom a trifle and stood up, placing his feet on the rim of the boat to gain height.

"Masts ahead!" he yelled.

James stood too, forcing Harry to jump back down, as his brother's action had an alarming effect on the balance of the jolly-boat.

"Are they ships? A fleet?"

"No, James," Harry snapped. "And you will see them just as clearly in a moment if you sit down."

James did as he was bid, sheepishly aware that in his enthusiasm he'd behaved in a very lubberly way. All eyes were now on the western horizon as the first tip of what looked like thin black sticks rose to pierce the grey sky.

"Look at the tilt on them, James," shouted Harry eagerly. "They are wrecks. Dozens of them. That is the Goodwin Sands."

James knew Deal, though not as well as Harry, who'd been stationed there while serving in the Navy. But he'd been partially raised not six miles away in the estate their father had purchased after retiring from the West Indies command, Cheyne Court in the parish of Chillenden. He'd seen that sight many a time from the shore, the innumerable wrecks littering the treacherous hazard slowly sucked under by the constantly shifting sand.

Those sails behind him would be visible from the shore, so that Deal pilots, who kept a sharp lookout for any potential fees, would be wondering about them. But their boats, set to intercept ships coming into the anchorage, would be out to the north and south, covering the Gull Stream which led to the Pool of London, or the southern approaches close to the demarcation line with Dover. But they would be unlikely to see him, because the jolly-boat was too low in the water.

Harry looked back, cursing as he saw that the barque had made a substantial gain. Then, as he ran over in his mind a chart of what lay ahead, his heart lifted. They had one chance, and only one, which depended on their distance from the sands and the state of the tide. He was on his toes now, leaning back with the rope attached to the boom grasped in his hand, trying to see if there was a line of breakers close ahead. The first flash of white made him yell with excitement. He now knew why his pursuer had altered course to put on more sail, for from his higher elevation he'd seen those waves breaking on the Goodwins long before.

"James, get ready to chuck the baggage over the side. We may need to lighten the boat."

Time now seemed to stand still. They watched as the bowsprit got closer and closer, with their pursuer edging first slightly to the north, then to the south so that the master could keep all his sails in play. The faces that lined the forepeak grew from mere white blobs to people with features. There was nothing of excitement of the chase in their looks, mere cold-blooded murder.

"Major Franks, if you fancy a shot with your pistols, I am bored with being stared at."

The heads disappeared as soon as the soldier raised them, though he had little chance of hitting anything at this distance, especially on such a mobile platform. As he fired they all heard the high-pitched girlish voice order his targets to mind their duties. Only one head re-appeared, a fellow with a beard so thick it entirely obscured his features, leaving only small, close-set eyes visible under his hat. There was a musket in his hands, but he wasn't looking at the jolly-boat, he had his eyes on the line of white breakers cascading over the approaching sandbar. Yet they were not breaking evenly, in a continuous line. There was a wide gap, off to his starboard side, where the water was calm. Harry prayed it was the Kellet Gut, a deep-water channel that led into the safety of the anchorage. If the man trying to kill them was local he'd know it, and he might use it to cut Harry off from safety.

There was only one way to stop him, though it entailed a degree of extra risk. Harry hauled on the boom and the tiller, steering for the southern tip of the channel. The barque followed, seeming to leap forward as the wind, now coming in over her quarter, acted on her sails. Everyone in the boat, bar Pender, was staring at him, wondering what he was about. He had neither the time, the breath, nor the inclination to explain. With this wind, if he could force his pursuer south of the neck, there would be no way the man could come about to pursue him. The barque edged up slightly, with the bowsprit now aimed to cut off his wind as a prelude to running him down.

The ship rose and fell as the swell increased in the rapidly shoaling sea. White water creamed from the bow, with screeching gulls, suddenly numerous and oblivious to the drama being played out, diving across them. The man with the beard had called six of his men forward and they now leant on the rail, each bearing a musket. The tip of the bowsprit seemed, at times, as it swung on the upward roll, to be above Harry's head, yet when it dipped it missed the stern of the jolly-boat by a good ten yards. But it was inching closer, with that bearded, piggy-eyed face ever present. He was using his arms to command the helmsman, and ignoring Major Franks's attempt, futile in the heaving sea, to hit him with a pistol ball.

The muskets were aiming now. It was no easy task, for the two vessels were moving in different directions; but the ship was coming so close that they would be bound to hit something. The noise, like a huge, sighing gust of wind, surprised Harry as much as anyone else. The air was suddenly full of small migrating birds, thrashing around looking for a place to land and rest. The bows of the ship were covered in them, and Harry could see the men with the muskets thrashing around to try and clear the way for a clean shot. One of the men discharged his weapon, which only added to the confusion, as the escaping thrushes collided with those still trying to land.

The first sight of white broken water under their counter lifted Harry's spirits. The seabed was shelving fast. As he eased the boom to adjust to the loss of weight, James threw the baggage overboard. With no keel, he had a very shallow draught. But that ship could not draw less than twenty feet, and if he could sail over the sands, drawing his pursuer after him, there was every chance that he would turn the tables and draw his opponent into mortal danger. If he struck the Goodwins at speed, he'd certainly lose his masts, and with luck, he'd damage his ship irreparably.

They were now abreast of the southern neck of the Kellet Gut. It was going to be a close-run thing, with no certainty that Harry himself wouldn't get stuck in the sands as he changed course. No man in his right mind would go straight for shoal water, even in a small boat, unless he was certain of the tide. Harry trimmed his course to keep the wind, bringing their pursuer even closer. Shouting his orders, Harry, followed by Pender, let fly the sail and ducked under the boom. He hauled hard and used his foot to kick round on the tiller, completely changing course as he headed for the foam breaking round the northern spit of the Gut.

His pursuer followed him round, attempting to beat the leeway of the falling tide and swing his ship. His speed helped and the bows were now a matter of feet from their starboard side. A wave came under the ship, lifting it high and aiming it towards them. It started to drop as the same water lifted the jolly-boat. For a moment it looked as though the little vessel was going to be smashed into the sea. The water around them was a mass of spurts as the men finally fired off their muskets. Harry, concentrating on the task ahead, had no time to look and see if anyone had sustained a wound. Suddenly the barque seemed to shudder, as the way came off her and the bows, forced round by the leeway, swung rapidly round till they were heading south.

Harry knew why. They were over the sands. He prayed he would not get stuck so close to his adversary. Those muskets would be reloaded soon. But, regardless of that risk, he had no choice but to loosen his grip and slow his speed, for the last thing he could afford was to ground the boat. If necessary, they'd all have to get out and push, hoping that the sands beneath their feet were solid enough to support their weight. Once in the deep waters of the Kellet Gut they would have to row like the devil. He fully expected that a boat would be over the side of that barque, intent on continuing the pursuit.

"Oars, Pender," he called as the jolly-boat slowed and drifted sideways. They lay along the side and Pender had his looped over the protruding thole before Harry even got his into position. As the two oars bit the water they heard the voice again, screaming at them in a frightful tone that sounded like a hurricane ripping through the rigging. They only saw the top of the head, hidden under a tricorn hat. The man's arm was back and as he screamed out his words he threw something at them with all his might.

"Here, you sods. You live another day, but not many more. Take this ashore with you. And make it plain to all that the same fate attended this bugger awaits anyone else who seeks to poach my trade."

The object spun through the air so swiftly that it was impossible to identify the blur. But they knew soon enough when it landed in Polly Franks's lap, staining her cream dress with dark blood. He'd used the pepper and salt hair to throw it, and given its length that afforded him a lot of purchase. The tufts were still there on the cheeks. But there was no life in the wide staring eyes. Polly Franks screamed, lifted Tobias Bertles's head out of her lap with both hands, and threw it into the deepening water of the Kellet Gut . . .

They heard the laugh, high pitched, giggling, and deranged. It nearly drowned out her screams.

CHAPTER SIX

POLLY was still sobbing as they approached the shore. Mr Wentworth had been sick over the side and had kept his head there ever since. In such a busy anchorage, with an entire fleet of men-o'-war, and with hundreds of ships waiting to take on stores and hands, many a head gazing over the bulwarks of ships they passed must have wondered what was afoot. But their shouted questions were ignored. Harry, deliberately avoiding the public quays, headed for the beach, and as he heard the soft crunch of the bows run into the shingle he felt his tension ease. He collapsed over the tiller, exhausted, more from the thought of what might have happened than the effort. They sat there for a while, rocking on the gentle waves that hissed over the stones.

Pender, equally spent, recovered first, and jumping over the side called to a couple of longshoremen to help haul them out of the water. Major Franks was out next, to aid his distraught, sobbing wife on to dry land. The boatmen lifted Wentworth out and James helped Harry to stand upright. "Thank you, Harry," he said gently.

"Who was he?" asked Harry, shivering, for he was, like the others, soaked to the skin.

"He must be known, brother. But let us keep our counsel for the present. We shall have to report what happened to a magistrate. Perhaps they will have some knowledge of him."

Harry looked up and down the strand, which seemed to stretch endlessly in either direction, covered in boats, wherries, hoys, smacks, and the odd twelve-oared Deal cutter, which along with the cabinned luggers was the favoured boat of the local smugglers.

This was where Tobias Bertles hailed from, or so he said. And that was fitting for a man who laid claim to be an "Honest Thief," for despite others' claims to the title, they had landed in the contraband capital of southern England.

They made their way slowly up the steep shingle, through the great blocks of chalk hurled ashore by some storm, and into the alley that separated the Three Kings from the next door property. The smell of fish was overpowering as they passed the nets hanging out to dry in the wooden sheds, and it seemed to bear down on them as the high buildings shut out the light. They emerged on to the busy street that fronted the lower part of the town. Beach Street was full of carts and horses, laden with all manner of supplies for the ships that victualled here in what had become in the last hundred years one of the busiest seaports in England, despite the lack of a proper harbour.

Harry led them into the warm interior of the Three Kings, its darkly gleaming oak panelling reflecting the glow from the blazing logs in the open grate, and Pender took station by the hallway fire, in possession of the men's coats. It was crowded, with many a naval officer and ship's captain ashore to take breakfast. While Harry searched for the landlord, James went straight in to the parlour, and spoke urgently to an army captain taking his ease by the fire. The redcoat was out of his seat in a second, only too willing to offer it to a fellow officer's wife who was patently in some distress.

Polly Franks was still white as a sheet and mute from her ordeal. Her husband got her into the chair and ordered hot wine spiced with brandy for the entire party, then found a spare chair and brought it over for Wentworth. The young man, still racked with sickness, sank into it gratefully, his head in his hands. Franks then crouched down beside Polly, holding his wife's hand as the warmth penetrated her soaking cloak, making her shiver.

"I think her cloak is hindering her recovery," said James. They helped her to take it off, exposing her cream dress and the great streaks of blood and sea water that stained the front. The officer who'd given up his seat stood awkwardly on the other side of the wide inglenook.

"If I can be of any service, sir," he said, bowing slightly. "Captain Latham of the Westmorland Militia."

Harry came in just as Franks was standing up to introduce himself. Latham pulled himself a little straighter when the major gave his rank.

"Not a room to be had, I'm afraid. The place is full," said Harry glumly. "I'm told the Royal Exchange is even worse."

James took his arm. "Then let's at the very least see about some food."

"You appear to be in some distress, sir," said Latham. They were all wet and bedraggled, with drawn faces, and the wretched Wentworth was vocal in his suffering, moaning slightly as he rocked back and forth, so close to the fire that his wet breeches were beginning to steam.

"You would not credit what we've been through, sir," said Franks, looking up. "Not if it was told to you in a month of Sundays. Cast adrift in the middle of the Channel by one black-hearted villain then pursued to near damnation by one even worse, and obliged to cast every stitch we own into the sea to effect an escape."

"I have a room here, sir. You would do me an honour if you'd allow me to place it at your disposal."

"Why, that's a most handsome offer, Captain Latham," said Franks, standing upright. "And one, on behalf of my wife, I most heartily accept."

The young soldier turned to Harry and James. "I'm afraid it is but one room, gentlemen."

"It must go to Mrs Franks," said James. "But allow me to thank you for your concern."

"But this will never do, sir. I must find Hogbin and insist he provides you with a place to dry your clothes." He saw the enquiring look in the eyes. "Why, he owns the Three Kings, sir."

"I am aware of that," said Harry, who'd come across Hogbin on more than one occasion. "I've met the gentleman, and from my recollection he's not a man to insist with."

Latham smiled. "But I shall ask his daughter, sir, who I do assure you is a much more amenable creature. Major Franks, sir, allow me to show you to my room."

"I'd forgotten Hogbin's name," said James wearily as Latham led the couple towards the stairs. "But I do recall him as an extremely irascible soul."

Harry smiled wearily, taking one boot away from the flames and replacing it with another. "He has too many admirals, rich merchants, and Indiamen captains occupying his chambers to be polite to anyone without a title. The fellow on the desk took great pleasure in alluding to a recent visit by the Duke of York."

"I take it you were suitably humbled, brother."

"I told him to warm the damn Duke's bed," snapped Harry. "For judging by his army's performance he'll be on his way back to the Horse Guards within the month."

James turned to find a man behind him, bearing a tray full of steaming tankards.

"Gentleman ordered this. Hot wine and brandy."

Harry took one for himself and one for Wentworth. James took a third and the servant looked askance at the two left on his tray, then at James. This was accompanied by a loud, insolent sniff.

"Take those to our man. He's in the hallway by the fire," said Harry.

"Both of them?" asked the servant.

"Yes," growled Harry, taking a gentle sip of the scorching brew.

"This fellow's your servant, you say?"

"He is," replied James.

The man was plainly displeased with the idea of waiting on him. Another loud sniff. "How will I know who he is?"

"Simple," said Harry, with a glare that made the man tremble. "He'll have steam rising off him in great clouds."

Latham obviously had a way with Hogbin's daughter, for she appeared before their tankards were empty, favouring them with a curt introduction. Broad of beam, with a jolly round face, she was nevertheless formidable. The drink had revived Wentworth somewhat, and that, added to the heat of the fire, had brought a bit of colour into his cheeks. But his attempts at gallantry with Cath Hogbin fell flat, broken on both her natural resolve and his patent exhaustion. If anything his words angered her and the three men were hustled unceremoniously down the stairs, shown into a private parlour at the back of the basement, and ordered to strip. Harry made sure that Pender would be taken care of.

"I'll have your man taken down to the kitchens. Now, every stitch, gentlemen, if you please, for I can see that you're drenched to your smallclothes." She banked up the fire. "While you're about that, I'll fetch you some towels."

"Would it be possible to fetch the towels first?" asked Wentworth modestly.

She laughed without turning. "Lord, gentlemen, if you've been in that there sea, bone-marrow freezing as I know, I don't suppose you'll have much showing to embarrass a grown woman."

James was already getting out of his breeches. Harry had his shirt off. Only Wentworth, his eyes riveted to Cath Hogbin's ample buttocks, was still in his wet coat.

"Nevertheless, Miss Hogbin. Decency demands."

She turned one hand up at the side of her head to mask her eyes as she made her way to the door. "If you insist, sir."

"And writing materials, if that is possible," said Harry. He turned to James. "We cannot just turn up at Cheyne Court, quite possibly with guests, without letting Anne know we're coming."

Cath Hogbin did everything required of her with bustling efficiency. Drying, brushing, and pressing wet clothes was plainly something the staff at the Three Kings were used to, for it wasn't long before all three men were dressed once more. They were informed that Captain Latham had a table in the dining-room and earnestly hoped they would join him for a late breakfast. Harry sought out Cath Hogbin first, to post his letter and to pay for some food for Pender.

"Why, Captain Latham has seen to that already, Mr Ludlow. Your fellow Pender has got his feet under the kitchen table like an old friend, and no mistake." Her grin was replaced by a mock frown. "Mind, if he interferes much more with the maids doing their work, I'll sling him out in the street."

This threat was followed by another smile. It was plain that Pender had made an impression on her. But that was as nothing to the delight she took in using Latham's name. Her eyes glowed at the mere mention of him, and he was heaped with no end of praise for being "a true gent." He was undeniably handsome, with a slim figure encased in a tight red uniform, a ready, heartwarming smile, unmarked olive skin, and large, soft brown eyes. The slightly hooked nose hinted at mixed blood, as well as providing a hint of steel in an otherwise gentle face. If Harry had harboured any doubts as to a lowly captain's ability to maintain a room at the Three Kings, they were laid to rest. As long as Cath Hogbin had a say, and she was obviously cut from a similar mould to her father, no elevated person, not even a prince of the blood royal, would dislodge her "true gent."

That was not an appellation that Harry was inclined to argue with. Latham had been the soul of kindness. Sitting down to a substantial breakfast, he informed them that Mrs Franks was asleep in his bed, with the good major beside her. A physician had been called, had bled her, then pronounced confidently that she needed no more than a decent rest. Her dress, alas, was beyond redemption, but Latham had sent for something she could travel in.

Harry and James, with the odd bitter aside from Wentworth, outlined what had happened in the last 24 hours, a tale which produced no shock in Latham's face. Yet the words that followed contained a degree of genuine feeling.

"Why, they're all villains in these parts, Captain Ludlow! There's hardly a man on the coast of Kent who isn't smuggling. I had one of my own men shot dead in Beach Street, not a month ago, while guarding a load of seized contraband."

He paused, as if embarrassed to express so much emotion, then smiled, showing a good set of white teeth. "Not that I'm a puritan in such matters, you understand. I like untaxed brandy as much as the next man. But the degree of lawlessness that attends their activities, not to mention their rivalries and disputes, is alarming. There's no end of murder and rioting in the streets. The Preventative Officers go in constant fear of their lives. And they don't confine themselves to stealing from the revenue, either."

"Am I to understand you too have suffered, Captain Latham?" asked James, who knew only too well the reputation of the Deal smugglers. He been at Cheyne Court in the early '80s, when they'd beaten back the army, sent to curb their activities, and burned down the Customs House to underline the strength of their feeling.

The younger man brushed a crumb off the sleeve of his red tunic. "I have, sir, though I hasten to add the loss is not personal. If you take a walk in the direction of Walmer Castle you will observe a new set of buildings being erected. They are barracks, sir, which will in time house enough troops to police this entire coast."

"Then they must be substantial," said Harry, "and costly. Does the loss to the revenue justify the expense?"

"That is not their true purpose, Captain Ludlow, at least in wartime. You, being from these parts, and a sailor, must know how much Deal has expanded. We find we are embarking an increasing number of troops from here to destinations all over the globe. We require proper barracks to house them. The locals resent being forced to billet them. Yet if they are accommodated in tents they have all the diseases rampant before they ever get aboard ship. As I say, that is in wartime."

It was hard for such an open, honest fellow as Latham to look cruel and heartless. But he managed it, as he went on to outline what would happen in peacetime.

"Billy Pitt, as you may be aware, has the Cinque Ports sinecure. He dines at this very inn when he visits. I've had it from his own lips that the barracks will be fully occupied, peace or war, with the troops put to protective duties so that the revenue officers can do their work."

"They have tried troops before," said Harry, dismissively. "The locals fought them to a standstill. Pitt even tried burning all the boats on the beach in '84. All he managed was a bonanza for the boatbuilders."

Wentworth, who'd been eating steadily, finally raised his head from his dish and spoke. "One wonders whether the entire country would not benefit from the creation of a body of men charged and paid to do proper policing."

"My God, sir," said Latham, his brown eyes popping slightly. "A *gendarmerie!* What a perfectly tyrannical notion."

"The use of the army, generally scum from the gaols, can hardly be said to be better," added Wentworth tactlessly.

James could see that Latham was struggling to stay polite and he cut in. "You alluded to loss, sir, but did not go on to explain."

"Ah yes," said the young captain, brought back to the root of his subject. "Bricks and mortar, sir."

They all looked confused at this, exchanging curious glances.

"You can't construct a barracks without bricks and mortar. Just as you can't stop them being stolen, no matter how well you set your pickets. If you wander around Deal, sir, you will observe a great deal of building taking place, mostly of private houses. It is my honest contention that most of the materials are stolen from the barracks site."

Latham leant forward, lowering his voice. "I could understand if the locals didn't take to the barracks, as it's likely to interfere with their nefarious trade. But it ain't that. It's just plain villainy. Most of them, under the guise of being honest traders, have joined the local Fencibles to defend the coast against the French. You can see them on a Sunday, all puffed up in their uniforms. They parade about, fire off a useless fusillade, then retire to the Hamburgh Ensign to toast their bravery. Yet the same fellows finance the trade, or at the very least turn a blind eye. There is not a man

amongst them who isn't building something, and as to my bricks
. . . I lose little when the sea is calm and the 'Honest Thieves' are
busy, but let there be a storm, with those smuggling coves tied up
to the shore, and my bricks and mortar disappear by the ton.
They're not 'Honest Thieves' then. They are true miscreants, sir,
for if they will not steal one thing, they'll purloin another. The
naval yard is another favoured target."

"Then you will have frequent dealing with a magistrate," said
James.

Latham frowned. "Frequent is barely the word, sir. I call upon
the mayor daily if the wind is foul. And it is quite useless."

"Why so?"

"Mr Temple is in the process of building a new house himself.
I have heard him complain loudly that the excise tax on bricks is
ruining him. But that is all so much stuff to blind me. Since no
one who ever steals from the barracks is brought to book, I cannot help but feel that the materials he himself is using are suspect.
Surely, even in the dark of night, it cannot be hard to apprehend
a man with a cartload of bricks and lime, especially running along
these newly paved roads they're so proud of. Surely not even the
well-practised folk of this town can turn their famous blind eye
to that. Yet they do. I have come to believe, in my six months
here, that the whole parish is implicated in this villainy."

There was no innate kindness in Latham's look now, rather a
glint that would gladly see a man broken at the wheel. And his
voice had a harsh tone, so unlike his normal kindly manner. "I
tell you, gentlemen, you may search the town of Deal for an honest man till your face turns blue, for you will do so in vain."

CHAPTER SEVEN

ON THEIR WAY to Temple's chambers they observed the building taking place. New houses were springing up everywhere along Beach Street, crammed into the tight spaces that had previously served as boatyards. There was also some evidence of a burgeoning civic pride, with the streets new-paved with Yorkshire stone. They passed the Customs House, gutted by the riotous mob and still a shell after all these years. The gaping windows and forlorn look caused James to speculate on the seeming absence in Deal of any Preventative Officers. Normally they had at least one member of the excise set as a tidewatcher on the public quays to intercept and examine incoming ships.

"They were shifted to Sandown Castle, I believe," said Harry. "Which tells you all you need to know about how they are perceived."

"It's certainly a damp piece of accommodation, unless they've rebuilt the moat."

The castle, one of three built by Henry VIII to protect the coast, had succumbed to erosion. The sea now beat against the stone walls, undermining them; in time the whole edifice would slip into the sea.

"I think not. It has the virtue of being the furthest from the public quays. It makes for a long walk and a lonely vigil, which is hardly an inducement to zeal."

James frowned. "They must mount a telescope on the battlements, Harry. Could they have observed our predicament?"

"Having a telescope is one thing, brother, manning it quite another. We'd stand more chance with the Deal pilots. They're

always on the lookout for a fee. But being to seaward of the Goodwins would make us hard to spot from the shore."

James, seemingly restored to his dilatory ways, stopped to look
at a corner house in the middle stages of construction; the builder
was adding false window spaces to the side elevation, arched fol-
lies which were already bricked up, to give it the appearance of
an older dwelling which had been subject to (and sought to avoid)
payment of the window tax. "See, Harry, there is no honesty anywhere. Even the simplest affair, regardless of the source of
materials, is corrupt. The good captain was right, though I will
admit that Latham, when lambasting Kent as a place awash with
villainy, only alluded to the coastal strip. I'm glad he didn't refer
to Cheyne, or Chillenden parish. If he had I would have found
myself called upon to defend them."

Harry had walked on and now turned impatiently to hurry
James along. His mind, not much taken with builders and their
wiles, had turned to the man who'd tried to murder them, trying,
through the words he'd heard, to discern a clue that would help
the magistrate apprehend the fellow. Then there was the late Tobias
Bertles and his nefarious activities, plus the nagging feeling of a
previous encounter that had been with him since they'd first met.
James's reference to the soldier broke his train of thought. He took
his arm to hurry him along.

"Captain Latham, as you've no doubt observed, James, has
impeccable manners. He knows as well as us how deep smuggling
goes in these parts, just as he's aware that Chillenden is a mere
six miles from the nearest stretch of beach. The name Ludlow
would be recognized, certainly by Cath Hogbin, so he would not
insult us by even remotely suggesting that we are . . ." Harry
waved his hand, searching for the word he wanted to complete
the sentence. James obliged with one of his own, though certainly
not the one that his brother was seeking. "Involved?"

"Don't be silly, James. How could we possibly be involved?"
snapped Harry.

"Why not, brother?" James replied. "As you've just observed, Chillenden is close to the shore . . ."

"I've always preferred to avoid such entanglements myself."

Whatever thoughts those words induced made James reclaim his arm. He stopped again and his eyes took on a sad look. "It must be a fine thing to be so free, Harry. But are you truly detached? I wonder how such things are perceived by others. Hardly in the best light, I fancy. You know how it ails me to agree with Arthur . . ."

"What are you driving at?" said Harry suspiciously. James detested their brother-in-law, Lord Drumdryan. Introduced into the household after the death of their mother, he had assumed a hand in James's education, much to the chagrin of the younger man, who could barely tolerate the idea that his sister had married anyone. Harry, absent at sea during most of James's formative years, often felt that he had benefited more than he should from the invidious comparisons drawn by his younger brother between the upright, housebound Arthur and his rather raffish absentee self. "This day has been singular enough, brother," he continued. "If I find you agreeing with Arthur I'll demand to be pinched into wakefulness."

James stopped to lean on one of the numerous capstans which lined the seaward side of Beach Street, adopting a rather wistful air. "Not that I've ever discussed Naomi Smith with Arthur, but I don't doubt that he thoroughly disapproves, in just the same way that he censors me for what happened with Caroline Farrar."

"Naomi?"

"Has our absence made the name unfamiliar?"

Harry shook his head. "What brought this on?"

"The word entanglements, Harry. I'm not privy to the details of your relationship with the lady—"

"Nor will you be, brother."

James ignored the slightly sharp tone. "I wondered if you intended to take up where you left off."

Harry didn't reply right away, sifting what James had said to seek his true aim. There was, given James's nature, just a possibility that he was being baited. Yet his brother knew that his relationship with Naomi Smith was not a subject for family jokes, any more than James's own "entanglements" lent themselves to drolleries. Possibly James was turning the conversation towards his potential concerns as a way of avoiding contemplation of his own.

He'd come to sea with Harry after a very public affair with another man's wife. It had ended messily, leaving him a physical and emotional wreck. No doubt he was wondering how he would be received on his return, for they'd not even exchanged a letter these last months. Nor, for that matter, had Harry. But then his case was different. There was a lack of true intimacy that excluded letter-writing. In the rare moments when he contemplated his relationship with Naomi Smith, he'd realized that deep and friendly as it was, their liaison was certainly no more than a convenience. Nothing like the grand passion that James had both enjoyed and suffered.

Naomi was a widow, and happy to remain so. The idea of marrying her had never entered Harry's head. For all that they enjoyed each other's company, talking a great deal and laughing at the same things, there existed a gulf between them that both wished to preserve.

"I doubt the question should be addressed to me, brother. If you knew anything about Naomi, you'd realize that she is as likely to decide as I. Not, by the by, that it's any of your business. And if we are going to discuss Arthur's capacity for disapproval, then we shall be at it all day."

James finally grinned. "Upon my soul, brother. An acid remark about Arthur! For a moment, you sounded just like me."

Harry swung his fist at James's head. But it had no force, just as his smiling face held no malice.

They were sitting in the quiet anteroom to Mr Temple's chambers before James became serious once more. These rooms were attached to the side of his house, and given the scale of lawlessness described by Latham it was remarkable they were so empty. Pender had been left at the Three Kings, delighted to keep his feet under the kitchen table.

"Can I make one observation, Harry, regarding the events of the last 24 hours?" He waved his hand around the deserted room. "I am happy we are here, preparing to hand these matters over to the proper authorities. I half feared, given your nature, that once ashore you would go charging about Deal yourself, asking questions."

Harry yawned and stretched out his feet. "You malign me, brother."

The single raised eyebrow took enough issue with that statement. The words James used were unnecessary. "Do I, indeed?"

That eyebrow engendered little more than mild pique. Harry Ludlow was aware of some of his habits, if less certain of the depth that took them perilously close to becoming faults.

"Come along, James. You cannot see the difference between being in England, with the law close at hand, and being at the mercy of some other quite arbitrary power. Certainly I'm curious about that fellow who chased us. I am determined to know his name. Equally, I would love to meet him at sea in a ship of my own. Should I do so, well out of sight of any other authority than the fates, I will most certainly exact revenge. But here, ashore, or even within reach of the shore, I am as subject to the law as he is. And since there is such a thing available, I'm content to let others do the work of bringing him to justice."

It was clear his brother didn't believe him. With good reason. To James's mind, Harry had a bad temper, few scruples, and an abiding curiosity, coupled to a need to delve into things that didn't concern him that had nearly proved fatal on more than one occasion.

"Would you say you have learned your lesson, then?"

Harry was shocked at that. "Lesson? That is an exceedingly

curious way to put things, brother. I admit the need to see things in the whole, just as I will own to being dissatisfied with matters left incomplete. But even you must acknowledge this: I've only ever enquired into subjects that directly affected us."

James opened his mouth to disagree. He had ample ammunition with which to nail Harry. But he was saved from a contrary observation by the door on the other side of the room, which opened abruptly to admit a squat, black-coated individual, quite clearly in hurry, judging by his fussy manner and the scowl of impatience on his square, red face. He was in the act of cramming a round black hat on to the full wig that identified his profession. The eyes, bright blue, shot up at the sight of Harry and James occupying his anteroom, as though that was in itself an offence.

"Mr Temple?" asked James as they both stood up.

"I am, sir," replied Temple, sidling towards the outer door.

"We have come to report a grave felony."

The face, under the powdered wig and round black hat, screwed up in distaste, giving him the appearance of a badly executed beer jug.

"Why, that is most inconvenient, sir."

"Inconvenient!" snapped Harry. "You are Mr Temple, the magistrate?"

"I believe I have already said so. But you will observe I am in somewhat of a hurry. I have other matters to attend to at this moment."

It was James's turn to be sharp, but he kept his voice low, for he feared to scare the man. "Matters more important than murder, Mr Temple?"

The older man looked flustered and confused, edging still closer to the street door.

"Why, yes. I must go to the site of my new house, which is at this very moment at a critical stage in its construction. Believe me, sir, if you knew what blackguards builders are you would put nothing before a constant check on their labours. And I am, gentlemen, already late for the installation of my carved oak staircase."

"Your staircase be damned, sir," said James, again without raising his voice.

The eyebrows shot up and the wig slipped a touch as Temple jerked his head, plainly accustomed to a greater degree of respect.

"Does the name Tobias Bertles mean anything to you?" asked Harry.

The look of impatience was back. "Of course it does."

"A ship's captain who sailed from here, if I'm not mistaken?"

That got a sharp nod, but his hand again reached out to open the door. It stopped midway as Harry barked at him.

"Then we are here to report his murder, Mr Temple. Not only that, but the unnatural death of his entire crew, who I take it also came from Deal."

"And his ship, the *Planet,* burnt to the waterline," added James.

Temple's scowl deepened. "Bertles, murdered?"

"Yes," replied Harry, relieved that at last he was getting through. "In the most shocking, cruel manner. Skinned alive, with his crew hung from the yards above his head."

The magistrate's eyes narrowed. "They were aboard ship?"

"Naturally, sir."

"And where did all this take place?"

"At sea, sir; I cannot be certain of the exact location, but let us assume it was midway between here and the coast of France."

The door was open in a flash, a look of relief coursing across his face. "Bless my soul, that's nought to do with me, sirs. Now I really must attend to my staircase."

"Then who is it to do with?" yelled Harry to Temple's retreating back.

The magistrate stopped and spun round, his square face even redder with anger. "Try the Admiralty, sir, I only attend to felonious behaviour in the St George's parish of Deal."

James had been warned by Harry that the navy would very likely do nothing without specific orders, but his brother insisted that it was an avenue that needed to be explored, if only to make matters clear. But Harry balked at any attempt to involve Admiral Duncan, who had command of the fleet stationed in the Downs. Duncan had known their father well, and both senior officers, vying for lucrative commands, had cordially disliked each other. Thomas Ludlow's sons would get no welcome and precious little help from that quarter. Instead he directed James to the shore installation, a more permanent local feature than a fleet, which could up anchor and be off at the bang of a signal gun.

The Port Admiral, McBride, was up in London for the parliamentary session, leaving a Captain Billings in command of the naval yard. He was certainly more amenable, if no more helpful, than Temple. He listened carefully, without interrupting. He offered them a glass of Madeira and some tipsy cake his wife had made, and as he did so he put the case firmly back in the bailiwick of Mr Magistrate Temple.

"Mutiny and piracy are our purview, gentlemen," he said, talking awkwardly, for his wife's cake was crumbly. "But with plain murder, I cannot see that the navy is involved."

"Is the taking and burning of ships not piracy?" asked James, allowing himself a nibble of cake for the sake of politeness.

"Why certainly, if you shift cargo out of them before you set your torch. But I believe as you described it, sir, this was not the case. Besides, it is plain from your tale that both sets of rogues were intent on smuggling, which puts them outside the law in any case."

"You seem to forget, Captain, that the very same man tried to drown us, and we are entirely innocent."

Billings looked away at that, as though the idea of entire innocence was uncomfortable. "That is most certainly the magistrate's responsibility."

"He maintains that it is not, since it happened at sea."

Billings sighed. "It is exceedingly burdensome, the way others seek to load the navy with their tasks. As if fighting the French were not enough."

"So how would you suggest we proceed, sir?" asked Harry, well aware that James was getting nowhere.

The captain sat for a moment, thinking, though whether he was concerned with their problem or confounding the French wasn't clear. Then his eyes lit up. "A body would turn the trick, sir, especially if he was a local man, positively identified. I recall your saying that Bertles was such. Temple would have to act in that event. Even the detached head would suffice. What a pity the lady threw it overboard. It would have served your case admirably."

"Failing that?" asked Harry, impatiently.

"You could approach the Preventative Officers, since the whole thing clearly involves smuggling. They are based at Sandown Castle. But I cannot see that they will undertake an investigation into an act of murder. They suffer too much from that themselves. They can't even hang on to the goods they seize. The villains shot a soldier not a month back."

"Captain Latham told us of that," said James.

"But did he tell you contraband disappeared, never to be found? The Preventatives' task is near impossible. Why, some years back, one young fellow was buried alive in a cellar not half a mile from this very room. I even recall his name, it was so shockin'. Charlie Taverner. To this day they have yet to apprehend his murderers. If you recount details of a smuggler's demise, in however horrible a fashion, the Preventatives are more likely to cry 'good riddance' than take any action to find the culprit."

James slammed down his plate, sending bits of cake all over the polished surface of Billings's desk. "There must be some authority that can act."

The captain frowned at seeing his wife's culinary efforts so ill used. "Even if it did take place at sea, I'd say it's a matter for the Lord Chancellor."

"Not personally, surely," replied James with deliberate sarcasm. "I happen to know that he hates water."

The remark plainly missed its mark, for Billings didn't respond, either to the name or the gibe alluding to Thurlow's love of the bottle. The idea had taken root, and his voice became quite excited as he pursued the idea. "The Lord Chancellor could then order the requisite investigation. Force Temple to act, don't you see. You will of course require affidavits sworn before a notary by all the passengers, stating what they saw and heard."

Billings picked up the plate from the centre of the desk, took another mouthful of cake, spitting crumbs in all directions as he concluded. It was hard to decide if the cake, not being properly set, added to his sudden loss of verve.

"But even then I fear Mr Temple will insist on a corpse. He is, as you may have already noted, a trifle tardy in the execution of his duties. Even the might of the Lord Chancellor might fail to stir him. More cake?"

CHAPTER EIGHT

BILLINGS PROVED CORRECT. The magistrate having been run to earth again, all his misgivings about the lack of a body were borne out. Though Temple was much more courteous: as he informed them with evident delight his staircase had been fitted with extraordinary ease.

"Sound carpentry and good oak, sir. That is the secret. Plus a wary eye on the owner's part."

"Well, sir," said James, "now that the nation can safely ascend your stairs, perhaps you will be so kind as to advise us of what to do?"

Temple was still gazing wistfully toward a future full of set bricks and dried mortar, of social gatherings in his glittering upstairs drawing-room, so his reply was a touch absentminded.

"Advise you, sir? What about?"

Harry snapped at that, convinced the man was being deliberately obtuse. "The trifling matter of a dozen murders, plus the attempt on our lives."

Temple looked at him, as if struggling to concentrate. "Oh, yes, I recall it now. You said Bertles had been done in."

"Along with his crew. And you would blench if I told you how in proper detail."

"So Bertles has finally met his maker," said Temple, shaking his head and smiling. "A rum cove, to my mind, who would do mischief for its own sake. Not that he couldn't make you laugh, sir. No, he was good at that. I dare say the Devil will chuckle at Bertles, even as he singes him."

Temple's look changed then and the smile evaporated, lest he be involved in an association. He carried on hurriedly. "Not that I knew him well, you understand. Our relationship was not personal."

"Does he have next of kin?" asked Harry.

Temple rubbed his chin thoughtfully. "There was a wife, but I seem to remember she died of consumption."

"What about the families of the crew?"

"Since I don't know who they are, it would be mere speculation to say."

Even James's well-honed air of indifference found such a lack of curiosity unbearable. "They should be sought out, sir, just as surely as they should be told."

Temple shrugged, unaware of any rebuke. "Oh, I dare say they already know; news gets around the town amazing quick."

"Then perhaps they, or the dead men's friends, might have some knowledge of who committed this foul deed."

Temple's indifference was insufferable, for his response to James's suggestion was another shrug of the shoulders. Nor did his words ring with any urgency.

"They may well. And if they care to bring me proof of a crime committed outside my area, I would most certainly pass it on to the proper authority."

"And who might that be?"

"I told you, sir, the navy."

"We have already approached Captain Billings at the navy yard. He was quite firm that it was none of his concern."

Temple shook his head sadly. "Is it any wonder the country is in its present condition? No one seems willing to stir themselves, even to undertake their proper duties."

They'd fought hard to keep their tempers, both brothers knowing that tact was necessary with such a person as Temple. But they could not contain themselves in the face of such patent hypocrisy. Both protested at once, but Harry's voice, louder through practice, overbore James. The small panes of glass in the leaded windows shook at the sound.

"One would scarce need to look further than this room, sir. I have heard Deal described as a place without the benefit of law. Exposure to your company leaves me no doubt where the cause of that lies."

Temple half rose out of the chair to protest. James finally got to say his piece. "You will prosper in your new home, sir, for I have it on excellent authority that every brick has a layer of criminality to hold it in place."

That knocked the magistrate back into his chair. "What do you mean, sir?"

"I allude, sir, to the source of your materials. Free bricks must please you. Never mind if the military barracks are never completed. It is plain that you consort with thieves for your own personal gain, instead of apprehending them."

Temple recovered somewhat, even though the blood rushed into his cheeks. He pointed a square-tipped finger at James Ludlow.

"That is a calumny, sir, for which, if you repeat it, I shall see you beggared. For there is, thank God, a law of slander. And how dare you come in here and harangue me."

James, having got the floor from Harry, would not yield it. "You deserve it, sir. You are content to let murderers escape rather than bestir yourself."

"I have already told you that the case lies outside my jurisdiction. My duties end at the shoreline. This is not London, sir, with your fancy Bow Street johnnies nabbing a villain in time for a piece in the next day's *Register*. This is the real world, where a man enforces the law as those who pay see fit, which in Deal parish does not run to much. I have two watchmen on my book, a sergeant-at-mace and his deputy, whose sole concern is to avoid paying for their nightly drink. They are served in such endeavours by a blind eye, not zeal."

"There are widows and orphans out there, sir. Will the parish support them?" asked Harry.

Temple half stood again, fists on the desk, his square face suffused with anger.

"How dare you, sir! This parish is second to none in its care of mariners' dependants. It is only out of the same well of goodness that I've tolerated your presence so far, Mr Ludlow. You are a stranger in this town. But Tobias Bertles was not, nor was his trade. All that carrying of passengers, which he brayed to the rafters, was so much eyewash. He and his men knew what risks they ran."

"From the Preventatives and excisemen, Mr Temple, whom I'm sure do not stoop to murder and the burning of ships."

"Don't mention Preventatives and excisemen to me, sir. They are a confounded nuisance. Why, they disturb the peace more than those they're set to apprehend. There's murder in the streets when they seize goods and a near riot every time they nab someone. And they're more like to be the victim than the felon, which leads to no end of work and complication. Had Bertles faced his end ashore, or even if you'd fetched his body back, I might have taken an interest. But you have not. In truth, I don't even know whether the story you have recounted is mere fancy!"

James grabbed Harry's arm, pulling him away from the desk. His brother was coming mighty close to fetching the older man a buffet around the ears. The action seemed to calm him. He turned away from the magistrate. "We will do no good here, James, for Mr Temple is a mere placeman."

Temple exploded. "How dare you, sir!"

Harry's voice was like ice as he turned slowly to face the older man. "A placeman, sir, whose sole concern is for a heavy pocket. And rest assured, Mr Temple, that I shall repeat that on the street. Sue me if you wish, for I look forward to hearing you list your contrary achievements before a higher court. Good day to you."

It took a good deal of claret, liberally poured by an amused Latham, to calm the Ludlow brothers.

"I cannot say that it amuses me," said James.

"Perhaps I am become accustomed, Mr Ludlow, for I cannot pretend even to mild surprise."

Mr Wentworth was as confused as the Ludlows. For once his carping seemed well placed. "Surely there must be some authority responsible for piracy and the like. What about Trinity House?"

Harry patiently explained that the Downs, its wardens and pilots, had liberties guaranteed by Act of Parliament. The writ of Trinity House had no effect in these parts.

"It is the navy," he continued, "for only they have the means to catch criminals on the high seas. The Revenue have but one cutter, and that is moored at Dover. But how do we get them to respond, that's the rub. Short of a complaint directly to the Admiralty, I cannot see that we will achieve much. They would need to be directed to act. If the magistrate bestirred himself and issued a general warrant, Duncan would have to do something, for fear of repercussions. But if Temple sits on his hands, so will they. Their attitude will be the same. Felons have killed each other, and good riddance. We are all still alive, so where is the harm."

Wentworth made a rather grand gesture, his hand sweeping the anchorage outside the window, full of men-o'-war. "But we have ships in abundance here. Surely their task is to make the seas safe?"

"Against the enemy, Mr Wentworth, against the French fleet. They will chase after a smuggler on the way to France, for he's likely to be carrying gold. The officers and crew receive their share of that from the Exchequer, in the same manner as if they'd taken a prize. But the chasing of contrabandiers, beyond that, is not their concern. For instance, they will not seek to apprehend one on the way home, regardless of how much brandy he has aboard."

Pender came into the parlour and walked towards the window seat. Harry had sent him to to search out the Preventative Officers, but he had to report they were not at their stations, with no one at Sandown Castle prepared to cast an opinion as to where they'd gone, and he sent him back to the warmth of the kitchen.

"You cannot tell me their only care is for money," said Wentworth, resuming the conversation. The shock he exhibited was overdone, especially from a man who was clearly, on the evidence of even such a short acquaintance, both parsimonious and greedy.

"That is, I'm afraid, the truth," said Latham. "There was a blazing row in here few weeks ago. Some of the local merchant captains were upbraiding a group of naval officers at their dinner."

Latham leant forward and emptied the bottle into their glasses, before signalling for another.

"A French privateer took a ship just inside the sands. It was a clear day and the gunfire was plainly audible. Indeed one officer sent for a telescope so that he could observe the action, which was then described to his fellow diners."

"Of which you were one, I take it?" said James.

"I was indeed, though at a separate table. A *chasse-marée,* I think they termed the Frenchman, was in a running fight with an English merchantman. The French boarded and took her, carrying her off towards Boulogne."

"Did the navy not pursue them?" asked Wentworth, his face holding his customary heightened sense of outrage.

"No, Mr Wentworth. The navy did not. Not a man-o'-war so much as shivered a sail, though they must have had a better view from their rigging than the men ashore. And as for those officers in the dining-room, they, sir, once the matter was concluded, went back to their victuals. Hence the party of irate merchant captains who sought to upbraid them. They felt the navy was neglecting its duty."

"Neglect of naval duty is not uncommon," said James, looking into the deep red wine in his glass.

Harry gave him a sharp look. Having been a King's officer himself he knew more than the others about the nature of the problem. He was generally willing to put their case, even though he himself had been forced to resign his commission in questionable circumstances.

"It is easy to carp, Mr Wentworth. But you cannot comprehend the restraints that the Navy Board places on serving officers. An admiral is responsible for his fleet, a captain for his ship. Should either set off in pursuit of a privateer, which you will find are generally nimble sailers, risking spars and sails and firing off their cannon, then they would enrage their superiors, for they would consider that the officer had endangered his ship to no purpose. And anything they lost, or used in the way of powder and shot, would have to be replaced out of their own pockets."

"Is that not the task of a ship-of-war, Harry? Or are they to be merely polished and displayed like brasswork on a door?"

"And is it not the duty of the navy to protect our shipping, sir? After all, our nation lives by trade. Damn the French privateers, but could they not at least recover the prize?" Wentworth addressed this question to Latham, who smiled in reply.

"I am *au fait* with the arguments, Mr Wentworth. And as a military man, subject to the same constraints in the execution of my duties, I can sympathize with the difficulties attendant upon the officers of the navy. But I also heard the opposite view, most forcefully and loudly expressed by the merchant captains."

He looked at Harry as if he represented the source of enlightenment. "I must say that it does appear a trifle odd that Admiral Duncan forbids his frigates to chase enemy privateers, and lets them carry off cargoes from right under his nose."

"The key is in the word *prize,* Captain Latham. A ship is not a lawful prize until it has been in possession of the enemy for 24 hours. If it is recovered inside that limit, then it is merely handed back to the owners. Clearly, with the enemy shore so close, any ships which are taken are safely anchored under French cannon. The navy will not pursue a ship, at their own expense, for no financial gain."

James was about to speak, about to bait him further. But Harry held his hand up to stop him.

"And before you all castigate that as an ignoble attitude, you should enquire as to why it is so. It is those very same commercial captains, or rather the ships' owners, who order it so. Laws are made in Parliament, gentlemen, where the commercial lobby far outstrips the service in power. They would rather lose a ship than see the navy rewarded, too soon, for recapturing it. So be it. Such people only have themselves to blame."

Wentworth's nose was up, his face bearing a look of high dudgeon. "Well, I'm sure what you say is true, Captain Ludlow. But it is nevertheless a scandal. No less a scandal than the fact that a villain can threaten our lives and nearly take them, yet no one seems to care. I shall not let it rest, I do assure you."

Latham made a swift gesture to silence him, for he'd observed that Major and Mrs Franks had come downstairs to join them. "A change of subject is in order, I think, Mr Wentworth. We would not wish Mrs Franks to recall her terrors."

Wentworth's hard, angry look softened as he turned, and a thin, salacious smile appeared as he gazed on Polly Franks. He adjusted his stock and his spectacles, which had slipped in his anger to the very end of his nose, then brushed his grey coat, like a preening bird. Polly was wearing her new dress of dark burgundy silk, and her hair had been restored to some of its former glory. They were all on their feet as she approached, pleased to observe that she seemed quite her old self. And if they doubted her recovery, the words she said, in a voice loud enough to turn every head in the room, was sufficient to convince them that she was, in all respects, back to normal.

"Why, Captain Latham," she trilled. "How can I ever thank you for letting me share your bed?"

CHAPTER NINE

"THERE MUST be a way out of it," said Harry, unhappily.

They were walking back to the Three Kings, having seen Major and Mrs Franks off in the coach to Dover, where they could change for another to take them to Hythe. Addresses had been exchanged and the promise of letters made, with an invitation to visit Cheyne Court should they find themselves in the vicinity. It was the way that Wentworth had picked up on this that had caused Harry's gloom, for he'd virtually forced an invitation for himself out of James.

Added to that, his behaviour towards Polly Franks had bordered on the licentious, for once Major Franks had left to arrange their travel he'd treated her like a girl to be courted rather than as a married woman whose husband was hard by. Perhaps the most embarrassing thing for the others present had been his assurance to her that he, and he alone, would bring to justice the men who'd tried to murder them. No mention was made of the fact that the Ludlow brothers had tried to do that very thing. Indeed, the way Mr Wentworth related it, though without actually saying so, everyone else had been too busy drinking and eating to take any action at all.

James gave Harry's words due consideration before replying, for he was no more happy about the prospect before them. "I can't see how. Perhaps there is a naval expression that would suffice."

"There are several, but given our recent adventures I cannot bring myself to use them."

"Then it seems we must suffer his company a little longer,

Harry." His normally passive face closed up angrily. "Perhaps he and Arthur can bore each other to an early grave."

James would dearly have loved to go straight to London, avoiding the family home altogether. But much as he disliked his brother-in-law he could not ignore his sister, Anne. She would be badly hurt if she heard he'd been so close and travelled by. As they approached the Three Kings they saw Pender standing with the horses they'd ordered.

"Perhaps we could just leave without him," said Harry, indicating the waiting animals.

"That wouldn't deter Wentworth. He knows where we live, and he does insist that since he intends to take coach from Canterbury it's on his way to Birmingham."

"Excuse me, sir."

The voice was weedy and as Harry turned, responding to the tug on his sleeve, he saw the abject look in the woman's eyes. She was thin and wasted, with her bones sticking out of her gaunt face. The children beside her were as filthy as she, and equally undernourished.

"Word has it that Tobias Bertles is dead, an' his whole crew with him?"

"I regret to tell you that is true," Harry replied, automatically reaching for a coin, for it was plain by the look of supplication that her man had been on the *Planet*. Thieves they might be, but their charges depended on them to eat.

The other voice wasn't weak. It was loud and harsh. "What are you about, Bridie Pruitt?"

The woman's head spun round, but not before Harry saw the fear in her eyes. Passers-by, at first made curious by the loud voice, hurriedly looked away, or found good reason to go about their business when they recognized the source. The terrified children had clutched at their mother, grabbing the rags that passed for a skirt. The man approaching them was well fed, tall, and stocky, wearing a dun-coloured coat, good breeches and boots, and a shiny leather meat-porter's hat. He had a huge white scar down one side of his ruddy face, and the way he swung the club in his hand told you that it was there to be used.

"The lady posed a question to me," said Harry. He saw, out of the corner of his eyes, that Pender had moved away from the hitching post and was coming round behind the interloper.

The man didn't look at Harry. He kept his eyes on the woman. "Then she's changed her mind, ain't you, Bridie."

Bridie nodded her thin head quickly and slipped round him, leaving the man staring at Harry. "We takes care of our own, mate, so you can put your conscience money back in yer purse."

The voice was deep and rasping, the sound of a man who liked his gin as well as his pipe. The black eyes regarded Harry steadily.

"Was her man serving with Bertles?"

"Same goes for her troubles, friend. They're our concern, not yours."

"Did you know Bertles?" asked James.

The head of the club twitched slightly. For the first time Harry noticed that it was a mass of intricate carving, but he couldn't make out the detail. The man's voice brought his attention back to the ruddy, scarred face.

"You ought to be careful with questions. They can lead to unwelcome bother."

Harry moved closer. He wanted to be inside the arc of that club, rather than on the end of it, if the man decided to use it. "The same man who killed Bertles tried to kill us. I have some interest in his identity."

"You're alive, friend. I'd settle at that if I was you." The eyes flicked to the side, but he didn't look behind him as he raised the carved club a touch higher. Harry saw serpents and dragons in the woodwork. "An' I'd tell that cove, who I take to be a servant of yours, to stay away from my back, else I'll need to give him a taste of this."

"Easier said than done, mate," replied Pender, evenly.

The man finally turned, but kept the club pointed downwards. He walked past Pender, stopping to look him in the eye as well.

"If I ever meet you when I have a mind for a brawl, then I'll be happy to put you to the test. You and your lords and masters. Meanwhile, if'n I was you, I'd get aboard them horses and put Deal an' what happened last night behind you."

It was only when he'd gone that Harry realized how still the street had become. No one had dared look in their direction. He'd rarely seen the "blind eye" so prevalent. All those by an alleyway had used it. People too close to melt away had found many other things to occupy their attention. Movement restarted as soon as he was gone, and in seconds it was the same as before, full of bustle and noise, as though nothing untoward had taken place.

"Now who was that fellow?" asked James.

Pender grinned. "Shouldn't be too hard to find out, your honour. There wasn't a man or woman in the street didn't recognize him. Ain't surprising, mind. An ugly bugger like that tends to be known to all."

"Did you notice the club?" said Harry.

"I did," replied Pender. "Wouldn't be much doubt who hit you if'n he used that."

"Cephas Quested," said Pender. "He's a batman for a mob called the Aldington gang, an' a right terror by all accounts."

"The Aldington gang?" said James, raising his eyebrows. But he neither expected nor received an answer, for a gang in these parts engaged in only one occupation.

"And the girl?" asked Harry. She'd been no more than that, for all that she had two children.

Pender grinned. "I was told to mind my nose. One question answered was sufficient. But I doubt that they knew."

Neither Harry nor James enquired as to whom he'd asked. That was Pender's business. And here in the street, where they could be overheard, their servant would refuse to tell them anyway.

Pender looked at the crowded roadway, full of people and

traffic. "They're a close-mouthed lot round here, an' no error. Makes me hanker after home."

He looked at Harry in an odd way, and it was only then that the realization dawned on his captain that Pender's family, whom he not seen since he went to sea eighteen months before, would if all had gone well be at Cheyne Court. Harry had sent instructions for them to be fetched from Portsmouth. Pender, normally a still, self-contained person, was fidgety, impatient to leave. But patience he had to have. There was no sign of Wentworth, which left Harry mulling things over again. He suddenly remembered a nagging doubt.

"Pender, did you tell the crew of the *Planet* that I was a privateer?" His servant took that badly, for he was proud of his discretion. Harry tried the same question on James as a way of avoiding his eye. "I didn't talk to the crew," replied James.

"Don't be obtuse, brother."

James shook his head slowly. "I don't think the subject of your occupation ever came up."

"Then how did Bertles know? I made a point of not telling him. Yet I distinctly remember him using the word, saying that it was handy, me being a privateer. That was when he was about to put us in the boat."

Harry hesitated, for he knew he was on tenuous ground. "You remember when he came to our table in Flushing . . ."

"Nothing will ever erase his enjoyment of that bird."

"I smoked he was a sailor, right away. But I also had the feeling that I'd seen him before somewhere."

"You've been a lot of places, your honour," said Pender. "Could've been anywhere."

Harry shook his head, suddenly certain of one thing. "No. It was in England. Perhaps even here in Deal."

James made the observation Harry most feared. "One sailor looks much like another, Harry."

"True." Harry slapped his horse on the flank. "Where is that damned fellow, James."

The cry that hallowed across the road dashed any hopes, briefly considered, of leaving Wentworth behind. He made his way with some difficulty through the rutted mixture of mud and dung to join them.

"I trust I have not kept you waiting, gentlemen."

"We are impatient to be off," replied Harry stiffly, hoisting his foot into his horse's stirrup. "I have a mind to be home before dark."

But Wentworth's social armour was easy defence against the rebuke. He just grinned at the brothers, already mounted, and took the reins of Pender's horse out of his hands.

"I have put the time to good use, I do assure you. Thomas Wentworth is not a man to be trifled with, sir, by land or sea. Polly Franks can rest easy in her bed. That fellow who tried to kill us needs to be brought to heel and I shall do it."

"And how will that be?" asked James.

Wentworth pushed his half-spectacles up his nose, fixing James with an expression which testified to a superior ability. "Let us just say, sir, that you will be amazed at my ingenuity."

He was up on the animal before anyone could protest. Pender shook his head at his audacity. Harry, more taken with the way he'd usurped the horse than the words he'd said, looked to the sky to contain himself. It was left to James to do the necessary.

"Pender, go to Mr Hogbin and bespeak another horse."

"Aye aye, sir," said Pender, moving away, favouring Wentworth with a baleful look as he did so. Not being a rider, he'd picked a quiet mare for himself, an animal he'd been assured by the farrier was as steady as the man's own armchair.

"Have you extended another invitation?" asked Wentworth, looking around him.

"I'm sorry?" said James, perplexed.

"The other horse. I wondered if you had engaged yourself to another guest."

"It is for Pender," said Harry, through clenched teeth.

Wentworth's eyebrows shot up, an action which pushed his half spectacles down again, perilously close to the end of his nose.

"Your servant, mounted on a horse? What a quaint fancy. I doubt even the ogre Robespierre ran to such a levelling notion."

They rode away from the tang of the sea, up the gentle slope towards home, passing through the old town of Deal with its quiet red-brick houses aglow in the dying rays of the sun and on into open country. The sky was clear, blue and cold, with a heavy frost promised. Every spire and naked tree stood stark against the sky-line. Wentworth talked incessantly, unaware that his fellow travellers were occupied with their own thoughts.

Harry, quite deliberately now, pushed the events of the last 24 hours to the back of his mind. He had no intention of leaving things as they stood: he was not a man to forget attempted murder. But given that there was so little he could accomplish without information, the matter was better left, for the present at least. Perhaps Arthur, who dealt with things political as well as matters financial on his behalf, and who knew the local oligarchy much better than he, could propose a solution.

He was happy to be heading for home. But he wondered how quickly he'd be embroiled in running Cheyne Court and the estate. Providence had given him a brother-in-law who lacked a fortune and was thus willing to look after the Ludlows' considerable possessions and take the regard that came with such responsibility. Having control of the Ludlows' two parliamentary seats guaranteed him the ear of those in power. It was a world which had little attraction for Harry; Arthur Drumdryan found it extremely congenial. The heir to Cheyne Court was grateful for this mutually beneficial arrangement, for it left him free to go away to sea when he chose, which was often, since it was the only place he was truly happy. Of course, Arthur rarely missed an opportunity to inform him that such behaviour was immature.

James harboured the same thoughts, but for different reasons. He liked Cheyne only on those occasions when Arthur was absent. There was a degree of mutual antipathy which no amount of sisterly pleading could overcome. He had grown up in the house, motherless, with an elder sister who'd expended most of her regard on him. The arrival of an impecunious Scotsman, brother to one of his father's officers, had, regardless of his title, thrown young James's world into disarray. Especially since Lord Drumdryan, who prided himself on his manners, had seen it as his duty to take a hand in the young man's education.

But it wasn't just Arthur's presence which would make him chafe to be off. He also had a number of pressing matters to attend to in London, not least the need to reintroduce himself into society. It would be interesting to see if people were still as anxious to have him paint their portrait. The cause of his absence from London had become common knowledge. His very public affair with another man's wife had caused a scandal, though the effect on him had been hidden by his absence. Was he truly his old self again? Only exposure to the root of that problem would tell him if such a thing was possible.

Pender was too preoccupied trying to stay on his horse, a very skittish Arab, to think of anything else. Yet he, too, had much to ponder when the ride was over. He had been a thief and a good one. But the law, such as it was, closed in on the best of them, especially when their success excited the envy of less-talented practitioners. He'd left Portsmouth one step ahead of the sheriff's grasp, taking the best route that he could out of a wartime seaport by joining the King's Navy. The last he'd seen of his wife and family was their fearful faces as he climbed out of the back window, leaving them to face the tipstaff hammering on the front door. The feelings engendered at the prospect of seeing his wife again were mixed, though he was curious to see how his bairns were faring. If anyone had mentioned domestic bliss to him he would have looked at them strangely, not knowing of what they spoke. His life to date precluded it. In Pender's world a man wed just ahead of a birth and a father's wrath, then struggled to keep a roof over the family's heads and food in its mouths. He'd succeeded better than most, though never enough to satisfy the girl he married, whose partiality to gin had been a constant source of friction. The last words she'd spoken to him, as he'd dived out the window, would not come under the heading of conjugal endearments. Yet he'd sent her the king's bounty when he signed on, and made what arrangements he could to give her the docket that would allow her to draw his pay.

He lifted his head from the horse's neck for a fraction, to look around. Harry and James were doing the same, taking in the familiar sights. Few were at work in the fields at this time of day, especially in October, though the orchards were still busy. The starlings bustled in the hedgerows, occasionally wheeling aloft in their hundreds, filling the air with whistling. The sky was now a frozen blue, beginning to fade to grey in the east. The smell was winter, with the cold sharp air mingling with a hint of smoke. Every chimney, from the merest hovel to the tall pipes above nearby Betshanger House, had slow black plumes rising. They heard the sound of guns going off, as someone hunted in the woods over towards Eastry Court, once a king's palace, as the owners were forever reminding them. The land continued to rise and fall as they traversed the shallow valleys, slightly higher each time as the chalk downland rose gently from the shoreline. Soon Harry and James rode on to their own land, and though husbandry was not Harry's long suit he cast a curious eye over the fields, keen to observe any improvements, to demonstrate to his brother-in-law that he still took an interest.

The great windmill, larger than the others that dotted the landscape, stood stark against the top of the hill, the first sight of something close to home. They skirted the woods to come on the house from the front, which faced the dying sun, their first sight the six red-brick chimneys of Cheyne Court above the surrounding trees. As the light began to fade they rode up the grassy avenue towards the huge iron gates.

They'd already been identified. Anne would have had someone keeping a sharp eye out at the top of the house. The grass turned to gravel as they rode through the entrance, skirting the round section of lawn with its familiar statue. The sunset turned the beautifully proportioned red-brick house a blood colour, while the glass in the huge sash windows reflected the sunset behind them. The servants stood all in a line on the steps between the two gleaming brass cannon, ready to welcome their master home. Even Wentworth ceased his relentless jabbering, and had the good grace to drop his horse to the rear, so that the owner of the house could be the first to dismount.

Harry searched for his sister, but she wasn't there. He smiled as he remembered. Being a stickler for good manners, Arthur would have restrained her. Anne was a naturally ebullient creature who constantly fell below his high expectations. Harry had heard the argument many times, for Anne, in years gone by, would go to welcome anyone who called, even the lowliest new curate from another parish. Arthur, who'd visited Versailles as a young man, and took his etiquette from the rigidly polite French court, would remind her that ladies did not wait outside to greet anyone, even brothers. That was an honour that might only be granted to the likes of a royal duke. Ladies waited, properly seated, in the drawing-room to receive new arrivals.

They dismounted, Harry and James reeling off the servants' names, returning the greetings of those who had been in their service for years, while acknowledging the few unfamiliar faces. There was a diffidence with Harry which was lacking with James, for he'd grown up here while Harry had been away at sea and to most of the servants James was still the mischievous boy who'd driven them to distraction. Most present had scolded him at one time. Not one of them could envisage anyone ever scolding Harry Ludlow. He represented a different kettle of fish altogether, though he was popular for his kindly manner and obvious consideration. Tite, his toothless gums quite obvious, stepped forward.

"This is Pender," Harry said. "Please see he's taken care of."

"It's grand to have you back, sir," said Tite. "The place isn't the same without there be a sailor in the house."

"Well, there are three sailors now, Tite," said James. "For Pender is one too."

James knew the old man well, even better than Harry. Tite had a strong sense of hierarchy, a hang-over from his navy days, plus a sharp tongue and a bad temper, which sometimes made for difficulties below stairs. Tagging Pender as a fellow sailor was the best way he could choose of easing the new arrival into that society where neither he nor his brother, regardless of how acrimonious a dispute became, dared set foot. Tite looked at Wentworth, still mounted, his face curious.

James waved an elegant hand, placing his fingers on the chest of his buttoned-up greatcoat. "You seek the third sailor, Tite. Look no further, for Harry has turned me, too, into a proper tar."

The old man showed his bare gums again in a broad smile. "That wouldn't be, even if the good God willed it, Master James."

James leant forward and spoke softly, his mouth close to the old man's hairy ear. "Allow me the delusion, Tite, for I intend to treat my brother-in-law to some salty language."

Tite pulled a face. He suspected, quite rightly, that absent any other authority, like the proper master of the house, Lady Drumdryan's husband was always trying to replace him. That Arthur had good grounds for his desire never occurred to the old man.

"Well, if you's stuck for a word, your honour, you come and see me. My memory can still rake up the odd blaspheme."

"Tite, please attend to our guest as well: Mr Wentworth," said Harry, interrupting this intimacy. Right then all knew how much their master cared for this "guest," for he'd seen to Pender, clearly a servant, well before him.

Tite fixed him with an unfriendly eye. "Your baggage will be along presently, I take it."

"You see me as I stand," said Wentworth, slightly surprised to be addressed so on the doorstep. "Just like your master, I lost all my possessions at sea."

Tite's old and rheumy eyes swung round on to Harry enquiringly, but he just indicated Pender. "You can have it from this source, Tite. I must wait upon my sister."

"You need some hot grog, mate, on a raw night like this."

Harry smiled, for in reverting to that way of talking Tite had demonstrated that Pender was in good hands. And no wonder. He thought him another sailor, and one with a tale to relate. James knew better, but said nothing. The old man shooed away most of the servants, then turned to point to the two brass cannon, with their neat piles of black shot, which sat one on either side of the entrance. They were Tite's pride and joy, a relic from the admiral's last command. He polished them with loving care, and fired them on the king's birthday.

"I wanted to fire the guns, your honour, to welcome you home, like. Her Ladyship was game enough, but he would have none of it."

"Save them for royalty, Tite," said Harry. "I don't merit a salute."

The old man bent down and rubbed the crest on one of the barrels, but his watery eyes stayed on his master. "They don't get enough use. They need to fire a ball from time to time, else how will we know they're true?"

"If you plan to fire a ball, Tite," said James wickedly, "I should spin them round and aim them into the hallway."

Cheyne's familiar smell filled Harry's nostrils. Old polished wood gleamed on the walls and floors. The welcoming fire blazed in the great open grate in the hallway. The last of the light was going and by the lanterns illuminating either side of the door he looked up at his father's dominating portrait. The admiral was in full dress, resplendent in a mass of gold lace and sparkling decorations, with the red sash of the Order of the Bath across his snow-white waistcoat. James had painted it while still quite young. Harry could never look at it without wondering what his father had said when it was unveiled, for James had put a hundred-gun ship, under full sail, with a vice-admiral's pennant atop the mainmast. That flag, the insignia of his father's command, and the other flags, streamed backwards from the masts. The admiral would have spotted that error as quickly as Harry, for they should, of course, have been streaming towards the bows. Had he said anything?

Harry never had. It seemed churlish, for James had caught his father well. His brother was a devotee of Allan Ramsey, who seemed to escape his general condemnation of things Scottish. He agreed with Ramsey that a portrait painter had a duty to see beyond the mere face, a duty to look for an expression that would give some clue to the soul of his sitter. Admiral Ludlow, in James's picture, had a stern eye, with a hint of eager avarice. Yet there was warmth there, plus a feeling of pride easily dented. It was very much the man his eldest son remembered. The flag hurt, for Harry knew that he would never follow in his father's footsteps, never hoist his own pennant above a king's ship.

Tite, with that liberality that only an old retainer can muster, fussed round them, brushing cloth and adjusting coats, until finally, with a sharp and approving nod, he pronounced them fit to be seen in decent company. As he took Pender below stairs, the brothers, tailed by Wentworth, made their way into the drawing-room.

The scene before them seemed staged, with Arthur, bewigged, his pallid, fine-boned complexion rigidly composed, dressed in an outfit of pale cream silk. He stood, in an elegant pose, by the flickering fire, one hand resting on the mantel. Their sister sat on a chaise-longue, her dress carefully arranged to billow around her feet. But the picture dissolved immediately. Harry barely had time to register that Anne had gained some weight before she was out of her chair in a flash, hugging them both and dancing round in delight, unconcerned by her husband's stern look of disapproval.

"Arthur," said Harry, finally detaching himself.

Lord Drumdryan took his hand off the mantel, and placing it gently on his chest gave a small bow, leg forward in the prescribed Versailles manner. His linen handkerchief swung elegantly over the front of his coat. For a moment Harry was left staring at the powdered wig on the top of his head. Then he raised himself again, to reveal the very slightest of smiles, which smacked of good manners rather than pleasure. A touch of red peeped through the powder on his face. Harry didn't doubt he was pleased to see him, for within the bounds of Arthur's reserve they esteemed each other. But displays of emotion were, in Lord Drumdryan's French-trained mind, bad manners. Yet, for all that, there was hint in his look of a rigidity that was greater than normal.

"It is truly good to have you safely home, Harry."

The smile disappeared to be replaced by a frown, for James had swung Anne into the air, sending her skirts flying. She caught his eye in her travels and quickly stopped her brother, comporting herself properly with a blush. The frown stayed on his face as he bowed again, and the single word "James" had little warmth.

"I am glad to see you looking so hearty, Arthur," said James languidly. "Quite your old self. Or is that colour in your cheeks brought about by proximity to the fire?"

"Allow me to name Mr Wentworth," said Harry quickly, not wanting James and Arthur to bait one another quite so quickly. "He was a passenger with us, and suffered the same distress."

"Ah," said Arthur, addressing Wentworth, who rated no more than a polite nod. "My brother-in-law alluded to the circumstances of your ordeal in his note. I will not press for further details, sir, it is too early to do so. But we are much of a size. If I can be of any assistance in the article of clothing, I am at your service."

He looked around the room, his green eyes, under pale ginger lashes, taking them all in. Tall bespectacled Wentworth, young and gauche, slightly awed by the surroundings and his courtly, old-world demeanour. Harry, who in his mud-spattered breeches looked more out of place than usual in a drawing-room. James, equally stained, but somehow without effect on his natural grace. Then Anne, plump, happy, and rosy cheeked, her arm clutched round the waist of her brother in the most unsuitable way.

"I had expected you sooner, Harry," said Arthur, "thank God your note arrived in time for me to cancel a previous engagement."

He turned to pull the bell. "You are late for dinner, of course, but we held it."

Harry, who had every right to order dinner in his own house whenever he chose, had to stop himself from apologizing. James, at whom this propriatorial display had been aimed, bit his tongue as Anne's fingers dug into his waist. The door opened and one of the footmen entered carrying a tray with glasses and two bottles of iced champagne. Harry turned to look at his brother-in-law, for this seemed excessive just to celebrate his homecoming.

"You will oblige me, James, if you allow my wife's feet to remain firmly on the floor."

"That is not a matter on which I will accept instruction," replied James coldly.

Arthur's green eyes danced slightly. He smiled at him wolfishly, as though James had stumbled into some trap. "Odd, James. For all your skill with the brush, you cannot observe the very obvious fact that Lady Drumdryan is with child. I think that calls for a glass of champagne, don't you?"

CHAPTER TEN

THE ANNOUNCEMENT had failed to lift the occasion, the euphoria and congratulations that had greeted Arthur's news evaporating by the time they'd finished their soup, and the feeling made Harry uncomfortable. A lack of true gaiety was not unusual with Arthur at the head of the table; he had the French habit of discussing each culinary course set before him in reverential detail. Yet Harry had the impression that he was overdoing even that on this occasion. Left in sole charge of Cheyne, Arthur had undertaken the task of training the cook in the art of French cuisine and the success of his regime was put before them, course after course. Yet his observations lacked that leavening of wit that generally rendered them entertaining instead of tedious. And it wasn't the presence of an unexpected guest that made Arthur seem a little sour. If anything, Wentworth at the dinner table was a godsend, for his incessant chatter partially restrained James and Arthur, and Arthur's rigid manners would not let him show, even by the flick of an eyebrow, that he was bored. He listened, with a bland expression on his face, to all the details of the latest processes for the cheap manufacture of any number of goods; the prospects of startling inventions emanating from the Soho works of Boulton and Watt; plus a lengthy paean to the benefits of turnpike roads and navigation canals, while Harry, Anne, and James exchanged family reminiscences at the other end of the table.

But Wentworth and his technical peregrinations could not quite keep the combatants apart. Harry had a fleeting feeling of *déjà vu* as James and Arthur fell to discussing events current and historical. Arthur, the third son of an impecunious Scottish nobleman, saw himself as something of a *grand seigneur,* and his political beliefs matched this conception. James was a radical, imbued with the notions of the class of people with whom he had habitually moved, a point of view which he termed "the spirit of the age."

"I cannot pretend a lack of amazement," said Arthur, his voice betraying the slight burr of his Scottish origins. "That I should come to agree with Edmund Burke on any matter is startling. But all his predictions about the course of the French turmoil have most regrettably been borne out."

"Perhaps one day you'll even agree with Fox," said James.

"Never," snapped Arthur, who hated the leader of the opposition with a passion. "The man does nothing but lick the Prince of Wales's boots. Mr Fox has been mighty silent, skulking in St Ann's House, since those murdering villians chopped off the queen's head."

James paused. Any right-thinking man could not consider that act as anything other than outright barbarism. "I would not disagree that things in France have taken a turn for the worse—"

Arthur interrupted, his thin ginger eyebrows knotted together. "That is a fine way to put it, James. They murder their princes and you name it a turn for the worse!"

James allowed himself a smile. "I don't think that we in England are fit to lecture anyone on the removal of kings. And I believe the Scottish habit is to send them south so that others may sully their hands at the block. That is, if they don't knife them first. Good will come of the Revolution in time, just as it did when our forebears took the head of the first Charles. You should be well content, Arthur, unless you still hanker after Stuart absolutism. I, for one, welcome a constitutional settlement in which the king is subject to the will of the people."

Harry felt as if he'd never been away. It was Tory Arthur versus Whiggish James. His sister saw the way things were headed and tried to lighten the atmosphere with an anecdote. "I believe Mr Burke, on receiving the news of the poor queen's murder, took a knife into the chamber of the House of Commons, and in a dramatic flourish, in the middle of his speech about the Jacobin terror, threw it into the floor by the point."

She paused, her face assuming that look which presaged a witticism. "Mr Sheridan quite ruined the effect by enquiring if he'd fetched along a fork."

"I dare say he was drunk, as he usually is," said Arthur, sourly, deliberately spoiling his wife's efforts.

James Ludlow cut in quickly, leaning forward to make his point. "I should have a care as regards to such accusations, Arthur. Pitt is no stranger to the bottle. And he is not aided by placing so much faith in a Scottish sot like Dundas."

Harry's attempt to say something to avert a clash was too slow. James knew that Arthur was much attached to his fellow Scot, Henry Dundas. Billy Pitt's right-hand man had all the reins of government in his hand and was master of a great deal of profitable patronage. Arthur added expediency to his natural desire to support a fellow-countryman. Indeed the two rotten-borough seats the Ludlow estate controlled, managed by Arthur, had been pledged to support Dundas in the House of Commons. The Ludlows' support of the Ministry meant they expected any request they tendered to receive a positive response. This had borne fruit already. Harry had put to sea eighteen months before, sailing as a privateer in a fast schooner called the *Medusa;* Dundas had expedited the granting of his letters of marque, as well as providing his crew with exemptions so that they could not be pressed into the navy.

But Arthur was too long in the tooth to allow James's gibes to pierce his skin. He replied smoothly. "I have had occasion to observe, James, that some men can drink and still keep a clear head for business, while others, normally quite abstemious, cannot handle their own affairs competently, let alone those of the nation."

Arthur took good care to emphasize the word "affair." He might just have well called Lady Farrar by name. Her spendthrift husband had objected vehemently to being publicly cuckolded and reminded his wife where her duty lay. James had no option but to withdraw, a loss which had nearly ruined him. His silence in response to Arthur's barbed comment was evidence that even an oblique mention of Caroline still had the capacity to wound. Arthur signalled to the footman standing behind Harry's chair and addressed his next remark to a rather confused Wentworth.

"You will forgive me, sir, if Captain Ludlow and I retire, for we have many matters to discuss."

"Tonight?" said Harry, slightly surprised.

Arthur gave him a look that brooked no refusal, though he went through the formalities. "I trust you will oblige me, Harry, for there is much to report. That is unless you are too fatigued."

Harry looked at his sister, sure that she would rescue him from the need to undertake such labours so soon. No one knew better than Anne how much he disliked looking over domestic accounts. But she turned away from his look of supplication, which only served to reinforce Harry's impression that things were far from right.

"Come, Mr Wentworth," said Anne. "You may return to the drawing-room with James and me, to play cards."

"I should go, Harry," said James, with a wicked gleam in his eye. "Arthur obviously feels the burden of playing host to a man in his own house. He longs to relinquish the load."

Arthur's voice was as smooth as the silk of his coat. "How right you are, James. I am not as comfortable with dependancy as you. But I reassure myself in that I, at least, make a contribution."

There was, quite simply, no one who could get under James's skin like Arthur. The younger Ludlow was a man who could turn an insult on its head with ease, in any company bar this. When he replied, he lacked his normal sang-froid.

"Then I hope you've kept account of your domestic consumption, Arthur."

Arthur permitted himself another slight smile. "I keep account of everything, James, including the 'burdens' placed on me by wayward relations."

"James," said Anne pleadingly, as her brother opened his mouth to speak.

"My dear," said Arthur. "Pray let him speak. You know as well as I how we have missed his well-honed wit. After all, locked away in the country as we are, we depend on James to keep us abreast of what people of fashion consider amusing."

Harry cut in quickly. "I think you said something about business, Arthur." He stood up abruptly, forcing everyone else to follow suit. But Arthur wasn't finished, requesting James to stay behind for a second while Wentworth and his wife headed for the drawing-room. Arthur delivered his blow as soon as the door closed behind them.

"While you have been away, James, Lord Farrar has issued a writ against you for criminal conversation with his wife. I have, at some expense, managed to delay matters. But I was obliged, since I knew you were in the country, to write to our attorneys as soon as I received Harry's note from Deal. Thus the case will be heard shortly."

"Is he seeking damages?" asked James coldly.

Arthur nodded. "Fifteen thousand guineas."

"Is he aware what such a case will do to his wife's reputation?" asked Harry.

Arthur smiled at James, but it was a cold, heartless look. "Given the very public nature of their affair, I doubt her reputation will suffer."

"Damn you," said James, as Harry held up his hand.

"From what James tells me, the man's sole interest is in money." He turned to his brother, who was quite pale. "Buy him off, James. And if your own means don't run to the cost, you may call upon me."

Arthur had angered Harry and he knew it. But he had paid James back for his earlier gibes, and he looked like a man who considered it well worthwhile.

"Him being a Scotchman don't help." Tite hit the table with the flat of his gnarled hand. "You can't trust a Scotchman. Look what they got up to in '45. And he might say it was never so, but his papa was behind Pretender Charlie all the way."

Pender nodded without understanding. The events of the Jacobite rebellion were lost in the mists of time. He hadn't even been born. And as for Scotchmen, the few he'd met were neither better nor worse than any other, so he was indifferent to the tag. All this talk was just another indication of Tite's loyalties. He would discuss Lord Drumdryan, unflatteringly, till breakfast. But he was less willing to open up about the Ludlows. Pender was just as close-mouthed about how he come into the family service. If Harry Ludlow wanted to tell Tite about that he would do so. Besides, Pender's mind was on other things, for it was clear from what Tite said that his family had not yet come to Cheyne Court and that worried him.

"What are you like with a musket?"

The question surprised him. "I knows how to handle one."

"Good," said Tite.

"An' why would that be?"

The old man's blue, rheumy eyes narrowed just a touch. The voice, which hitherto had been reasonably friendly, took on harsher note.

"I don't know what way you attended of Captain Ludlow at sea, or on land for that matter. But whatever you did won't be necessary here at Cheyne, 'cause he'll be well cared for by others. But you can't just sit here, soaking up his food, without doin' summat. His lordship has enclosed most of the Cheyne land, so all those he hasn't employed are idle. They don't think to labour so as to fill their pot, which means there's work to do at night. You might as well take out a musket against poachers, as sit on your arse doing nowt."

"I've no mind to blaze off at a hungry man, Mr Tite."

"Even if he's robbin' your master?" demanded the old man, staring at him hard.

Pender's voice was even, and his eyes were every bit as steady as old Tite's. "That's somethin' I shall put to Captain Ludlow, should he ask me."

They sat silently, eyes locked, as Tite tried to stare him down. The old man cherished his authority, that was plain, and he didn't want anyone in the house outside it. But Pender was not one to buckle, even to the likes of Harry Ludlow. He didn't have a servile bone in his body and his attachment to Harry and James had been forged by necessity, before turning into one engendered by respect. But the respect was mutual. Pender was not above telling them, in his way, that they were over-stepping the mark. So he was not about to be put upon by this old man, and if that meant he had to appear like a proper hardcase, so be it.

"I don't think you quite understand your station, Pender," said Tite.

Pender leant forward, elbows on the kitchen table, and smiled.

"I do, old man. Just as much as I smoke your game. Now I know that the captain has itchy feet, so I don't reckon that he an' I will be here all that long. You leave me be an' I'll cause you no trouble. But don't order me about, mate, or the place won't be the same, ever again, even after we are long gone."

Tite wasn't easily cowed. He'd dealt with this problem all his life. It was always the same. You had to set out who was bossman. And in Cheyne Court, he considered that to be his prerogative.

"I see I'll have to have words about you."

Pender leant back in the chair with a smile, and softened his tone. "Do that, mate. But in the meantime, if you want something done, you just ask. Seein' as how I'm an obligin' sort, you might just get a result." Tite smiled too, showing his gums, sure that he'd won. The threat of him having words with Harry Ludlow had put this bugger in his place. But for all Pender was smiling, his next words had ample force to change that. "Mind, just you be sure you say please. For if you don't I'll shove my fist so far up your withered arse folks'll think you've got a new set of shiny white teeth."

The old servant padded up the hall, stopping at the entrance to the drawing-room. The voices inside were muffled by the doors, but he could hear enough to comprehend that they were playing cards. He shuffled from foot to foot, not quite sure what to do. It was always the same with a bit of dirt. You could never tell the value till you'd spilled the beans. Tite desperately wanted to talk to James Ludlow. He could tell him if his brother was still sweet on Naomi Smith. He certainly had been the last time he was home, but Tite, having shifted his own connubial allegiances all his life, wanted to be sure. If things still stood as they had, then maybe he could settle Drumdryan's hash once and for all.

Not that you could ever tell with Harry Ludlow. He was too like his father. Tite recalled many a time when he slipped a secret to the admiral only to find he was the one getting a verbal keel-hauling, instead of the person he'd split on. There was no way of telling in advance. He made his way down to the door of the library and listened to the faint voices of Harry and Drumdryan, wondering whether he should say anything at all.

"No need to make my mind up, right off. But once I know how the land lies . . ."

Tite stopped suddenly, for he realized that he was talking to himself. And talking loud enough to be overheard.

"I'm getting old," he said, as he headed back to his room. There was rum there, and peace to think out loud if he wanted to. "A few measures of grog, an' then I'll go out and get after them bloody poachers."

CHAPTER ELEVEN

"I FIRED OFF a complaint to Thurlow as soon as I received your note," said Arthur. "Just as well, it seems. I don't know Deal well, but the lack of zeal in country magistrates is a national scandal."

Harry was surprised, first that his brother-in-law had been so quick off the mark, and secondly that he'd taken the matter to such an elevated authority as the Lord Chancellor himself. Then he recalled the earlier conversation with the naval captain, Billings. That had been the correct suggestion as far as he was concerned, so perhaps Arthur had acted wisely. Yet for some reason he looked piqued at the need to explain, another manifestation of Arthur's discomfort since his return.

"I'm surprised you didn't wait to hear about things in more detail."

He tried hard not to make that sound like a rebuke. But the sour look on Arthur's face told him he'd failed.

"The wheels of justice grind slowly, Harry. I felt it best to get something off immediately. I cannot believe someone as impatient as you could disagree."

Arthur's green eyes held Harry's in a steady gaze, as if waiting for another challenge.

The wheels of justice move too slowly for me, thought Harry, who had half resolved to ignore James's strictures and ask around himself. For that reason he said nothing, knowing Arthur's reaction.

"What about Pender's family?" he asked, changing the subject.

Arthur dropped the stare, and looked at the papers in his lap. "We've had no luck there, I'm afraid."

Harry scowled. "I am committed to this."

"Your letters left me in no doubt how important it was. I sent a man all the way to Portsmouth, Harry, but he failed to locate them."

Harry smiled. "I should think, if they are related to Pender, they're well versed in the arts of avoidance."

"That makes him sound like a very unsavoury character."

Harry had no intention of letting Arthur know Pender's true profession. That was something that was behind him now. "He's just the opposite, Arthur, and another effort must be made to find them. As I said, I gave Pender my word."

Arthur nodded, but his eyes held a quizzical expression. Harry knew he would agree with the keeping of his word. It was the reasons why such an undertaking had been given that engaged his curiosity.

"Your letter only hinted . . ."

Harry was reminded how much he left out in his communications with Arthur. He stayed with the bare facts regarding the sinking of his ship, the *Medusa,* and although he'd alluded to subsequent difficulties, he hadn't stated how serious matters had become. And saying now that James had faced death by hanging would do nothing to aid relations between them. It would just be another stick Arthur would use to beat his brother. He knew even less about the sordid events that had taken place in Genoa.

"He saved my life, Arthur, and he helped me to save James as well."

The mention of James made Arthur purse his lips slightly. But he could see the gleam of determination in Harry's eye, just as he could discern his desire that the conversation should move on.

"Then he deserves such gratitude. Do you intend to retain him as a servant?"

Harry smiled. "I intend to ask him to remain with me. The choice will be his."

Arthur decided not to pursue the remark, instead pointing towards the desk. The great pile of ledgers, which contained the details of every act that Arthur had undertaken, lay unopened, save the one relating his privateering activities in the *Medusa*. Harry had no intention of opening any of the others tonight. After all, being here alone with Arthur provided a splendid opportunity to find out if anything was indeed amiss. He'd always felt that the situation at Cheyne was one he and Arthur found mutually beneficial. Yet something had changed, and it surely wasn't just the imminent arrival of a child. He set himself to find out why.

Yet, in Arthur, he was dealing with a person well versed in the art of avoiding definitive statements. His brother-in-law dissembled expertly. He wished Harry to know that he was not entirely happy, without ever giving the impression that he was in any way complaining. Finally tiring of verbal fencing, Harry decided to try a more direct approach.

"I realize that I have shamefully abused you, Arthur."

The other man's gaze didn't flicker by so much as an eyelash. "Abused me, Harry? What an odd thing to say. You give me the run of your house, food and drink, as well as something to do. I am, in your absence, seen as the *seigneur* of Cheyne. When I write to the ministry on your behalf, I carry the weight of a man of parts. The government is well aware that I appoint the parliamentary representation. As a consequence they show me a great deal of respect. I hardly call that abuse."

"For all you say, you're not content."

Arthur raised a quizzical eyebrow. "Few humans are content, in my experience."

"Perhaps if you were to outline to me what it is that you want . . ."

"I don't want anything," said Arthur coldly.

Harry could interpret that quite easily. Arthur wanted something, but he was not prepared to ask for it. He put the matter aside for further consideration and turned back to business. The ledgers relating to the income from Cheyne would wait till the morrow, for he knew that Arthur was scrupulous in that regard.

But there were other matters that required clarification. There

were the figures relating to the profits that he'd made from privateering at the outbreak of the war with France. He'd got to
sea in double quick time, before most of the incoming French
merchant ships knew that the conflict had started. Two of the
prizes he'd taken had been deep-laden ships from India. Arthur
showed him the results of his cruise, with a net profit of £90,000,
which did not include a sum of gold that he'd traded in at the
port of Genoa.

For a moment his mind turned to the ship he lost and the events
that had forced him home from the Mediterranean. He'd also had
a ship, sunk in the Bay of Biscay by the King's Navy, which had
curtailed a successful cruise as a privateer. How went his compensation claim?

"I insured the ship, Harry, at the Lloyd's Coffee House. If there
is a case for compensation, I'm sure that they will be able to pursue it far better than we. You will find the sum for that has been
entered."

Harry nodded happily, and continued his interrogation. What
of the crew who'd been pressed into the navy?

Arthur's fingers were still ranging across the ledger. "I was just
coming to that. All the shares which were owed to the crew are
invested in government stock, earning interest while they serve
King George. Some of those who sailed with you have deserted.
I must say they add up to a surprising number. All have come here
and been paid their proportion of the profits."

"Then what?" asked Harry eagerly. These men could form the
nucleus of a new crew once he had another ship.

"Since their impressment was illegal, I have given them protection. They are already provided with funds, but I added that
they would be paid a retainer until I knew what you required. I
had hoped you would say in your letters, but these were exceedingly vague about your intentions."

Arthur's jaundiced look lent effect to his next statement. "I told
them to return to their homes and await you, not anticipating the
time you would take."

Harry flushed slightly. The length of time they'd taken on their trip from Genoa couldn't merely be explained away by the threat of French incursions. James belonged to that community of artists, writers, painters, and sculptors which was truly international. Every stop on their way home had been to visit someone whose reputation James esteemed. They'd been royally entertained, and given the nature of the work their hosts performed, their kindness, and the society they moved in, the Ludlow brothers' dalliance had included more than visits to studios and the like. He deflected an explanation by asking another string of questions. Was the letter of marque that permitted him to sail as a privateer still valid? What method had Arthur employed to alert the men who'd deserted to his return? Did his exemptions, which forbade the navy to press men out of his ship at sea, still hold good for a different crew? As was usual in such discussions, Arthur pounced on the last question first.

"Am I to understand, by that enquiry regarding a crew, that you plan to return to sea?" It was clear he disliked the idea. His fine-boned face, the natural pallor heightened by powder, was screwed up in displeasure. But then he always had disapproved, since he saw Harry squandering the opportunities his patrimony had given him. For Lord Drumdryan all this charging around the oceans of the world was nonsense. A man as wealthy as Harry Ludlow, if he wished to increase his fortune, as well as his position in the world, should go to London, not to sea.

Harry nodded. "You know I cannot abide a long sojourn ashore, Arthur, especially with the opportunities that war brings."

"I shall advance my usual arguments against such a course, Harry, but add two points. You are older, and should by now be wiser, and the war has made my previous observations even more potent. Given the fortunate position that you hold, together with the improvements that have been made to the estates, an increase in your wealth is near unavoidable. Add the tenuous nature of the ministry's hold on a majority in the house, and you could, if you wish, secure some telling and profitable sinecures for your continued support."

Harry indicated the figures on the open ledger before him relating to his previous cruise. "As for profit, Arthur, there is a great deal of that at sea."

Arthur flicked a hand towards the unopened ledgers, a more substantial pile.

"Let us leave aside the increased yields from land. I have placed the books relating to your investments near the top. You will observe, when you finally consent to look, that every stock has shown a considerable increase."

Harry smiled. "Would that be the case if I had charge of my own affairs? Who knows, I might lose the lot."

Unusually, his smile was not returned. Generally, when upbraiding him for his love of the sea, Arthur had behaved like an indulgent parent, despite their being the same age. Now the deep disapproval was plain in his look, even if good manners sought to disguise it, and when he spoke his well-modulated voice, with that slight Scottish brogue, carried a hint of asperity.

"This is plainly nonsense, for I refer to Bank of England and East India stock, and five per cent Consols. All as safe as this house. But there have been any number of less regular investments you could have undertaken, nearly all of which have prospered, if you'd been on hand to take advantage of them."

"Why didn't you take them if they were offered?" asked Harry.

"I did, on my own behalf. But my stewardship of your affairs does not extend to commercial speculation, Harry."

"I don't recall ever saying that was the case."

"I don't suppose you ever did," replied Arthur stiffly. "It would not be necessary to do so."

Harry was getting nowhere, either with Arthur or the pile of ledgers. But he knew that only the books would open up to reveal anything. With his brother-in-law he needed more subtlety and that in turn required time. Much against his earlier wishes, he pulled a ledger from the top of the pile and opened it.

"Your guest," said Arthur, who'd clearly not expected Harry to actually peruse the accounts tonight.

"You take care of him, Arthur," said Harry, glumly, "and if you can find a way to shift him off to Birmingham, please do so."

Arthur stood up. "Perhaps the spirits of the night will oblige, it being Halloween."

"Is it Halloween?" asked Harry.

Arthur nodded impatiently, though without cause, for the particular festival was a Scottish affair that he had introduced to the household some years back. James, along with most of the local clerics, termed it Celtic barbarism. But Harry, on the rare occasions he'd been around, had entered into the spirit of things, revelling unashamedly in what was without doubt a pagan ritual.

"I do have a dinner arranged for tomorrow, but I can shift it if you wish."

"Not on my account, Arthur," said Harry quickly.

That produced the first real expression of pleasure that Arthur allowed himself. "The heir of Goodnestone has wed since you last saw him. A charming girl called Miss Austen. She is, however, the possessor of a large family. A number of her relations have descended on the place and I have invited the entire party over to dine."

"I would not have you suspend it for the world, Arthur."

"Good. Then I wonder if you would be so kind as to inform Tite that we are having guests."

Harry opened his mouth to ask why, for Arthur could just as easily issue instructions to Tite, but the icy look in his brother-in-law's eyes killed the words in his mouth.

"He hates him, that's what."

This statement was accompanied by a telling thump as Mrs Cray threw the dough into the pile of flour on the huge wooden table. "Old sod don't think he's got any right to be here. It's got steadily worse this last year, while her ladyship's brothers have both been at sea. Not that it wasn't plain aforehand. An' it's sad to have to relate that Master James encourages the old goat. He always has."

"Old's the word, Mrs Cray," said Pender, waving a hand to keep the dust down. "Strikes me Tite ought to have been put out to grass years ago."

Her fingers squeezed the dough angrily. "The knacker's yard is where he belongs. He's got no teeth, no hair, and precious few manners. You can't make a silk purse out of a sow's ear, an' it was ever so. Tite's ways might have served aboard ship, but they're no use in a country house."

The cook kept talking as she continued to take out her anger on the dough, listing the slights she'd received from Tite, especially in the article of cooking. "His lordship has gone to no end of trouble to teach me sauces an' the like. But all Tite can say is that he likes things plain." She slammed the dough on to the bare wooden board with increased venom. "I'll give him plain, all right, one of these days. I'll fetch him round the ear with a leg of mutton an' ask him if that's plain enough."

Pender hadn't started the conversation and he suspected that Mrs Cray was hoping he'd pass on her remarks to Harry Ludlow. He'd only been in Cheyne for a few hours, yet he'd been left in no doubt that Tite was heartily disliked below stairs, much given to interfering in all manner of things, especially the preparation of meals. "Fancy French shit," as he was wont to term it, he did everything he could to ruin it. Given that Lord Drumdryan was fussy about his food, it served as Tite's way of telling him he was unwelcome. And since Lord Drumdryan wasn't master in the house, he could not replace him, even if someone told him what Tite was about.

"Be an idea to strap the old bugger to one of them cannons he's so fussy about, then set it off."

The old cook stopped her litany of complaints and looked at Pender hopefully. He smiled, the white teeth flashing in his dark-complexioned face. Pender, who hadn't taken to Tite himself, was not the type to split on anyone. But he was not daft enough, in this house, to get on the wrong side of the cook by saying so.

"I don't know that Captain Ludlow would take to that. I know he reposes great faith in her ladyship's husband."

Mrs Cray thumped the dough on the table again, sending up a great cloud of fine flour. But this time it was done with pleasure.

CHAPTER TWELVE

"I'M SORRY, PENDER."

"Ain't your fault, Captain," Pender replied, pointing at the papers in Harry's hand. "If'n people started asking about me, then my woman would take a sharp hint and drop out of view."

James cut in. He'd come to the study as soon as his brother-in-law had returned to the drawing-room. "If I may make a suggestion, it would be better if you went to look for your family on your own. You stand a better chance of finding them than any agent we could employ."

"If the man had enough money to buy information," said Harry quickly.

Pender dropped his head slightly. It was clear that his captain didn't want him to go. They both knew the risks, for there were bound to be warrants out on Pender's head. Here, at Cheyne, Harry felt he could protect him. But James would brook no argument, for the logic of what he said was inescapable.

"We could spend money to no purpose, brother. Much simpler to send Pender himself."

"It could be dangerous."

"Not for Pender," replied James. "He knows that world better than you or I."

Pender grinned, more to ease Harry's fears than anything else, for he had a few of his own to add to those already hinted at. "That's true, worst luck."

Harry was silent for a moment, still searching for another way. But he had to concede, eventually, that they were right. He patted his servant on the shoulder.

"You'll need some funds for the journey."

"He can travel to London with me, Harry," said James, quickly. "I can see him on to the Portsmouth coach personally."

"You're not staying, then?"

James shook his head, and spoke with a contrived eagerness that nailed his reason as an excuse.

"I have all the items we bought in Italy and Germany waiting for me in London. They have to be sorted out." He paused, dropping both his head and his voice slightly. "As well as other matters."

"Anne won't be pleased," said Harry.

"She'll be a damn sight less pleased, listening to Arthur and me trade insults. Besides, I'll come back for the christening."

Harry looked from one to the other. "It seems that I'm to be left here on my own."

"You are welcome to come with me," said James.

Harry thought for a moment. It was a tempting offer. But it wouldn't do. He could not entirely shirk his responsibilities, going off the very next day after an eighteen-month absence. The future looked no less gloomy. Things had changed at Cheyne. Getting away to sea, or even to London, was going to be more difficult than it had been previously. He shook his head and patted Pender again.

"For God's sake don't get taken up by the press."

"What, me, your honour," said Pender, genuinely shocked.

"The port will be swarming with them."

His servant smiled again, and this time it was genuine. The action never failed to light up his face. "They ain't managed it all the years I was living there, even in the hot press when the war started. I doubt they'll succeed now."

"Better safe than sorry, Pender," Harry replied, looking at Pender's clothing, before turning to James. "Kit him out in London, brother. Make sure he loses the appearance of a sailor."

Pender cast a worried look over James's elegant clothes, for he too, in his sartorial distress, had been forced to borrow from his old-fashioned brother-in-law.

"You leave me to choose my own garb, Captain. If Mr James dresses me up to look like him, I'll be clubbed for my purse afore I get ten feet from the coach."

"I should leave Arthur to deal with the Lord Chancellor," said Harry. Pender, aware that they were set on discussing family business, had left the room discreetly, retiring to the room near the kitchen that Mrs Cray had allotted to him.

"It will do no harm for me to talk to the Admiralty. After all, they have the ships. If anyone can lay that black-hearted villain by the heels, it's the navy. You said as much yourself. I can get to see Lord Spencer with ease. He was after a portrait before we sailed."

"Ask him if he's got any ships for sale."

"I can't ask him that," cried James, palpably shocked at the suggestion. "He's the First Lord of the Admiralty, not a ship broker."

"Then send round the prize agents for a list of their stocks."

"Why not come to London yourself? You know that I have ample space to accommodate you."

Harry grinned. "Arthur is always at me to go me to London."

"I had in mind that you come for pleasure, Harry. His aim is that you should suck up to Pitt and Dundas so as to secure a title, with his garnering a peerage by hanging on to your coat-tails."

"Has Anne said anything to you?"

"About what?"

"About being unhappy."

The angry look, which had accompanied his opinion of Arthur, disappeared, to be replaced by a benign, almost paternal expression. "I've rarely known her more content. She positively aches for motherhood."

"I get the feeling Arthur is somewhat less pleased. I wonder if he's beginning to find life at Cheyne a little tedious."

"Damn it, Harry, he should be grateful. He has everything he wants without effort."

"Not everything, I think."

James snorted derisively, frowning again as his voice rose in anger. "If he wants more let him go back into the army. I believe he still has his commission."

"An ensign's commission. He'll never get anywhere at that rank, as you know perfectly well."

"For God's sake don't advance him the money to purchase a colonelcy. Judging by what we saw in the Low Countries the army is in enough of a mire without his adding to their woes." Inasmuch as a man so refined as James could snort, he did so. "Imagine Arthur commanding a regiment."

"Father always said his elder brother was a good officer."

James positively barked his reply, as though he wanted Arthur, still in the drawing-room with Wentworth, to hear him.

"I curse the day he was allowed aboard Father's ship. And just because his brother showed promise doesn't mean that Arthur shares his talent. Mind, all these Highland Scotchmen think they are God's gift to soldiering. We take the scum of the earth and kit them out with a red coat, but the man beneath is the same. I quote you Defoe, Harry, when I say that they are some of the worst, most barbarous men alive, cruel in victory, apt to quarrel, mischievous, and even murderers in their passion."

Harry had read Defoe's *Tour* himself, many times, and he knew that his brother was being somewhat selective in his quotation.

"I think you missed out the bit about being desperate in fight, which is, after all, the very stuff of war. And I believe, James, that Defoe, in that passage, was referring to the Campbells, a tribe even the native Scots regard as treacherous."

"It's all one, brother."

It was an old argument and one which no amount of common sense would resolve. James, normally a most forgiving soul, was determined to engage in that fashionable English pastime, damning the Scots, merely because he hated his brother-in-law.

"I will not contend with you, James, otherwise I will be exposed to the bilious words of Johnson on the same subject."

James looked slightly confused for a moment, clear evidence that he had been on the brink of quoting Johnson, or at least the words that his biographer, Boswell (another Celtic parasite in James's book) saw fit to place in the great doctor's mouth.

"Have you decided to leave tomorrow?"

James shook his head, pulled at the heavy drapes, and looked out of the window at the clear, starlit sky. "The next day, I think. I promised Anne that I would stay for her guests, the party from Goodnestone. Still, I suppose we should be thankful we avoided the usual celebration of Arthur's barbarian Halloween ritual."

James traced a figure where his breath had misted the glass, then turned back to Harry, with a grimace on his handsome face. "We are in for a dull day, brother. It will be all crops and rotation from soup to pudding, with gravy boats full of rural piety. And you wonder that I want to be off?"

Harry returned the bleak look in full measure, though in truth the prospect alarmed him less than it did James. But his next thought matched his expression.

"Wentworth?"

"Is also staying to dinner tomorrow. But I have persuaded him to go with me as far as Canterbury, by the simple expedient of telling him it's free."

Harry's boots made scrunching sounds on the crust of frozen earth that covered the path. There was an eagerness in his step, added to a lack of concentration, that sometimes caused him to slip, for his thoughts were full of Naomi. He had known her husband, Tolly Smith, before he died, a man much older than she who had taken the rural taphouse and turned it into a proper coaching inn by hard work and application. Smith had been a tough individual, barrel-chested and ugly, with a touch of the smuggler in his past. But that didn't matter to his landlord, Harry's father, who was happy to peg his rent to help him prosper. He bought Naomi as a gamine young virgin from her father ostensibly to work in his kitchens. Not that anyone was fooled by that excuse.

No one in their right mind paid good money for a scullery maid. Nor would anyone search out one so pretty. A hard man, Tolly showed a surprising softness for the girl thirty years his junior. Soon she was more than a concubine, if not quite a wife. Smith then surprised everyone, not just by marrying her two years later, but by doing so in a church, with all the expense which that entailed. Their joy was brief, their marriage childless. Tolly Smith's health began to fail, till finally he'd died, in his bed, some five years previously.

Harry had been home at the time and he could well remember the grey-faced, red-eyed young widow, almost destroyed by her loss. There must have been a firm bond of lasting affection there, for whatever the season Naomi never let a day pass without visiting her late husband's grave. Harry felt a slight twinge of guilt there, for he'd paid a contribution for the headstone, a massive Portland stone affair, covered in angels, which he personally found offensively ostentatious. Then he'd promptly set about replacing the deceased in Naomi's bed.

Three times he'd gone to sea, and three times he'd returned to find her happy to welcome him. She was like some safe, untroubled haven, never shrewish as long as Harry treated her as an equal. Naomi understood that an invitation to Cheyne Court, barring the Harvest Festival, was unlikely, and never pressed for one. Nor did she ask to accompany him to Canterbury or Deal for balls and visits to the theatre. The couple shared the odd outing, to eat or allow Naomi to pick the wild flowers she was so fond of. But other than that their relationship was kept within the walls of the Griffin's Head, a liaison discreet without being secret. This was a state that suited all parties, including their neighbours, admirably.

The thin strip of moon was hidden, and the light from the stars was less apparent now, down the valley, with the tall trees that surrounded the hamlet of Chillenden creating a dark tunnel. But there was light and sound at the end of it, with the lanterns in the windows of the Griffin throwing out a welcoming glow. A black plume of smoke poured out of the tall chimney into the night sky. The thatched roof and the dun-coloured Elizabethan walls, criss-crossed with oak beams, picked up the light from the crescent moon, and the heavy frost caused every branch to sparkle, creating a magical island in the midst of the freezing landscape.

He could hear the sounds of singing, faint on the night air, which made him wonder. It was late to still be carousing. But the raised voices also caused him to hurry his step, eagerly seeking the warmth of the old coaching inn. Harry noticed the odd shapes as he came close to the building, grotesque faces, cut out and hung over lanterns, some swinging from the trees, others stuck on poles jammed in the hard earth. There were more in the windows. His mind, concentrating on other things, barely registered the fact that he'd last seen those figures when Arthur had celebrated his Halloween festival, some five years before, at Cheyne Court.

CHAPTER THIRTEEN

THE NOISE diminished a little as Harry opened the door and entered, coughing slightly as he left the cold evening air, sharp and fresh, and inhaled the near impenetrable smoke of the busy tap-room. Once inside the doorway he stopped, looking with amazement at the way the place was decorated. Oak leaves and branches covered the walls and ceiling. But the made-up faces and the costumes, worn by customers and staff alike, were even more surprising.

The girls serving the tables wore tall hats and black cloaks. They'd used soot to blacken part of their faces and grey ash on the rest, giving them the appearance of the living dead. Most of the male customers had entered into the spirit of the occasion. They too wore costumes, with devils' horns and goats' heads the most numerous embellishments.

Naomi was in the middle of the room, standing by a water butt in which some of her customers were ducking for apples. Dressed as a witch, she was wearing the largest-pointed hat in the room, no doubt to compensate for her own lack of height. She turned as he entered, partly because of the blast of cold air, but more because the singing had broken off at the arrival of this new face.

Harry could see that underneath the cloak, which swung open, as she turned, her figure was as firm as ever, that the grace of her movements was the same. And for all the soot and ash on her face, Harry observed her expression very clearly. It was quite a mixture, starting with delight, then turning to consternation, then welcoming, though the smile that accompanied that look was marred because she'd blacked out some of her teeth.

But she didn't move, and neither did Harry Ludlow. They stood, merely staring at each other, as the noise died away. Harry's confused thoughts covered the last five years in as many seconds, accompanied by an odd feeling in the pit of his stomach. Naomi, with her direct gaze and warm nature, attracted innumerable offers. Many a buck, having stopped to slake his thirst and fill his belly, had calculated the turnover of the Griffin's Head and convinced himself that someone like Naomi needed masculine protection. They were soon disabused. She was apt to fly off the handle at any travelling man who took the least liberty with her.

Men in drink often find the word "no" a hard answer to accept from a woman they desire. But accept they did, with ill grace or humour. Stories abounded of Naomi's skill in deterrence, both verbal and physical. There was a tale, oft repeated in the tap-room, of one stranger who'd disappeared, never to be heard of again.

Harry knew it was false. But the story served its purpose. Her regular customers delighted in relating this tale to any passer-by who enquired about her. Her kindness took care of the rest, for she was not one to turn a hungry soul away from her door or deny a strapped customer a tankard of ale. The small tap-room was always full of men who'd do anything for her. Those same people knew that Harry Ludlow, when he was home, enjoyed liberties denied to other men. It wasn't seen as mysterious. There was his wealth, plus his status as her landlord. Most concluded that Naomi was being practical. She, like her husband before her, paid little in the way of rent. No doubt, out of earshot, it was a cause for ribald humour, but the subject was never broached, either in her presence or his. Given Harry's position locally, not even the coarsest, dim-witted labourer would dare to joke with him about his luck.

Harry broke away from her gaze and his eyes roamed around the room, taking in, yet again, the decorations and the costumes. The look that Naomi had given him was plain. She'd been anticipating someone else, had been disappointed as her expectations were dashed, then tried to cover her confusion with a smile. But for all the display of stained teeth, there was no welcome in her eyes. Harry looked at her again, seeing now the sadness in her expression. It did not take any kind of deep penetrating thought to guess who she was expecting. Obviously practicality was her abiding trait. Nor was it possible that such a thing could remain a secret. In fact the Halloween decorations, such a rarity south of the Tweed, acted like a public statement of Arthur's usurpation. This, no doubt, was the engagement he'd been forced to cancel.

He had no hold, no rights, which justified a rebuke, either to his brother-in-law or Naomi. No wonder Arthur had been on edge, for he could not be sure how Harry would react. Suddenly those cold expressions in the library, which he'd interpreted as reluctance to speak, seemed like sneers, the same kind of looks that the customers were giving him. It was that, the knowledge that all present knew who'd displaced him, which made Harry turn angrily on his heel and barge out of the door.

He stopped by one of the masks on a pole, looking at the features that had been cut out to make a face. The tallow flickered through the holes, dancing about in the faint draught as much as his own thoughts. Harry was not humbug enough to miss the irony of the situation. If, in his absences, there had been others, they had been strangers to him, or at the very least unknown. The fact that it was his brother-in-law wounded him, and not for his sister's sake, either. Arthur, though discreet with Anne, barely sought to hide the fact from Harry, or even James, that he made regular visit to a bawdy house in Canterbury. He'd left Arthur to manage his affairs at Cheyne, and his brother-in-law had taken matters a stage further than diligence required. No wonder he'd been reserved, for Harry had spoiled his Halloween celebration, as well as what was to follow.

Like most men who cared how they were perceived, Harry Ludlow scoffed publicly at the very thought of standing on his dignity. If anyone had been around to allude to his being wounded he would have laughed in their face. But he was aware that he'd made a fool of himself, especially in the abrupt manner of his exit, and that made him livid. It was imperative for him, for his own self-esteem, that he somehow redress matters. His hand shot out. He grabbed the pole and wrenched it out of the frozen ground, raising the whole above his head like some pagan talisman.

He could say nothing to his sister's husband, either directly or by allusion, for to do so would only make his own position worse. No gentleman worth his salt would debase himself in such a way. But he had to find a method to tell Arthur that he knew, that he cared, without demeaning himself. This mask-covered lantern would do just that. He might have to renew the tallow. But when Lord Drumdryan woke in the morning, and found this totem outside the door of his bedchamber, he would know where it had come from and who had put it there.

The moon was high now, as he made his way in silence along the rock-hard paths that would bring him back to the house. The pole was across his shoulder and he could feel the slight heat from the lantern on the back of his neck. On another occasion he would have needed one to see, but not on a night like this. Lost in thought, the sound of a musket discharge made him jump, and at the crack of a passing ball he adopted a swift crouch. He pushed the lantern down, whipping off his hat to block out the glim. The voice, slurring and shouting, came clearly through the cold night air.

"Take that, you thievin' bastards!"

Tite, said Harry to himself. Still chasing poachers, at his age? He heard the thud and the strangled cry just as clearly as he'd heard the passing ball. Then a voice, high and girlish, just on the other side of the thick hedgerow, which made him crouch down much lower than before.

"Belay. There's no need to belt him again!"

"A tap like that won't kill 'im," said another voice, gruff but deferential.

The laugh was even higher than the voice, more like a childish giggle. "But the cold will. He'll freeze to death on this night, that is, unless he's too close to the house."

Several men laughed, but not out loud. But there was one of the party who was too preoccupied for humour.

"What about dogs or geese?"

The voice which replied was just as cold as it had been on Tobias Bertles's deck, for all its feminine quality. "Never known an animal yet that could face fire. We'll light our torches before we go in. Remember, straight through the windows with the turpentine, then the lamps to follow. Skewer whoever comes out, man, woman, and child. I don't want this lesson to go unheeded."

Harry should not have been shocked that no one questioned this command. He'd seen what this crew was capable of in the middle of the Channel. They were between him and the house, obviously numerous and armed, and definitely determined. He racked his brain for a way to distract them. If he could get past them and rouse out the servants, then he and Arthur could organize some form of defence.

The smell from the lantern, the odour of tallow choking on its own wax, gave him the idea. He raised it slowly as he stood himself, keeping his hat in front of the mask to cut out the light. He tried to remember exactly where he was, so that he could make for the next break in the dense undergrowth. But he'd been woolgathering. It was going to be pot luck whichever way he went, so he turned left.

It was only the fact that they were organizing themselves that allowed him to get ahead of them. And he wasn't in front by much when he saw the break in the hedgerow, signalled by the thinning silhouette of the branches against the starry sky. His opponents were stumbling along on the slippery path, making only a limited effort at silence. Harry took a deep breath and muttered a quick prayer that these men were sailors, a breed notorious for their superstition, and that they did not number any Scotchmen.

His screams rent the air and he jabbed the uncovered lantern up into the thin hedgerow. Then as he started to mix loud, semi-Celtic curses his screams were completely overborne by those of the attacking party. They saw a huge monster, ten feet tall and just as wide, towering above them, with every feature, eyes, nose, and mouth, a fiery horror. They heard the voice, now screaming, now cursing, telling them that their fate was sealed. If they were rooted to the spot with terror, it was only for a split second.

Harry knew he couldn't have scared all of them. But his vision of hellish demons had acted on enough of the party to initiate a general rout. Half the curses coming to his ears were from men being bundled over as their terrified mates panicked. The high-pitched voice of their leader, well to the rear by the sound of it, was calling out for them to stand. But his commands were issued in vain. The thud of feet on hard earth faded as the attackers fled.

There was no time to waste in self-congratulation. Harry jammed the pole into the hedgerow so that the totem stood like some kind of ethereal guardian and ran uphill. He was through the kitchen garden in seconds, heartened by the sound of his own feet as they pounded across the gravel, setting the dogs off in a frenzy of barking, which made his shouts of alarm superfluous. The whole house would be roused. But would it serve? People suddenly stirred from slumber rarely acted swiftly. And that was what was needed now, as the men, recovered, came on. They'd discover, very quickly, that the fearful terror was nothing more than a ritual mask. If they'd been a deadly crew before, they'd be made doubly so by the way he'd humiliated them.

The moon flashed on Tite's brass cannon, standing on each side of the doorway like silent sentinels. Harry cursed the latchkey as he fumbled with it. Then, throwing open the door, he saw the brass-bound chest in the hallway that the old servant used to store powder and shot. He used his best yell to call for Pender, since he knew of no one else in the house who could handle the guns, all the while wishing that he had the time to go and fetch him.

Harry threw off his greatcoat, relieved to see that the chest wasn't locked. He flung it open. Tite had several charges made up, sewn in cloth. He grabbed two bags, the powderhorn, and a couple of wads, fetched the rammer from behind the front door, and ran back out on to the front step. Loading a gun was second nature to Harry. He'd been doing it all his life. But he nevertheless cautioned himself, determined to take things at the right pace, for if he made a mistake by being hasty he might not get the time to correct it.

"Captain," said Pender, who reached the doorway just ahead of Arthur.

"Find some slowmatch," snapped Harry, barely looking up. "Get it lit and send someone for water."

"Harry," said Arthur, holding up a candelabra.

"Water," yelled Harry, who had no time for explanations. "Load every gun in the house and search that chest for grapeshot."

"Grapeshot?"

Pender pushed past Lord Drumdryan, who had recollected himself enough to issue orders that weapons and water be fetched. He rooted round in the chest till he found the impregnated thread, pulled it out, and lit it from one of Arthur's candles. It fizzed slowly, filling the doorway with smoke. James was present, and Harry barked at him to move out of the way, which his brother ignored, adding to the confusion in the confined space. Harry had removed the tampions and had the charge rammed down the gun. He stood back and looked expectantly at his servant.

"Nothing, your honour," said Pender. "Though there's a rate of roundshot."

"That's no good. They'll just spread out. We'll be lucky to hit even one of them."

James grabbed his shoulder and pulled him round. "No good against what, Harry?"

The first torch flared at the bottom of the driveway. It was soon followed by others. The dogs, who attacked in that direction as soon as they heard the sound of movement, backed off quickly.

"If you care to turn round, James, you will see for yourself."

James did so, stumbling down the step in his haste. His jaw dropped at the sight of some twenty men, lined up in a row across the main entrance. Half had torches, the rest carried muskets. All had swords.

"Do you recognize the fellow in the middle?"

"I do," said Pender. "It's that bastard from last night."

James spun round to face his brother, pale and shocked. As he did so his feet scrunched on the gravel. The question he addressed to Harry fell on deaf ears, for it was addressed to the top of his brother's head. He had jumped down off the step and was on his hands and knees shovelling the small sharp stones into the muzzle of the brass cannon. Pender handed the slowmatch to James and grabbed the rammer and a thick cloth wad. When Harry turned his attention to the second gun, Pender pushed the wad into the mouth of the first, using the rammer to push everything as far down the barrel as it would go.

James decided that he was safer behind the guns, but he was hustled out of the way again as soon as Harry and Pender had finished loading, for they immediately set to elevating and aiming. Finally Harry tipped the powderhorn over the touch holes, pouring a slow stream of powder into the bore. James glanced at his brother-in-law, standing in the doorway in his nightclothes, looking incongruous with the long musket in his hands. For once in their lives they exchanged eye contact without malice, for their minds were too full of curiosity.

The men at the bottom of the drive had started to advance, their feet crunching on the gravel as they marched up towards the house in a line. Harry watched as their leader, his face still obscured by that heavy beard, lowered a musket and took aim.

"Inside, James. You too, Arthur," snapped Harry, for the crowded doorway presented a tempting target. Even an indifferent shot would find a victim. James might have protested, but Harry gave him such a shove that he was propelled into the hall just as the gun went off. A chip of brick flew off the wall where he'd been standing.

"The slowmatch, Pender."

His servant reached into the door and took the sizzling cord from James. Another musket went off, taking a lump of wood out of the door. Arthur, who was closest, didn't flinch. He lowered his own weapon, took careful aim, and fired. It didn't hit anyone, but the crack of a ball going past them stopped the men dead. The high-pitched voice rose up in the night air, with a screamed command to attack. The hesitation was minimal. A shout went up from twenty throats and the attackers rushed forward.

Harry stood at his gun, calling to his servant to do likewise. Then he lowered his match. There was a puff of smoke and a hiss. The powder in the borehole burnt through to the bag in the gun, setting it off. There were no breeches on the cannon, as there would be on board ship, with pulleys and rope to contain the recoil—these guns were only fired ceremonially—but they had a wad in them now, which contained and increased the effect of the exploding powder. A great shaft of flame shot out of the muzzle and the cannon recoiled dangerously, missing him by a fraction. Only the doorstep stopped it from going all the way down the hall to the foot of the staircase. The screams were already loud when Pender set off the second gun, and Harry, who'd been wondering how he'd find the time to reload, was delighted to observe that it wasn't necessary. The stones might take an eye, or embed themselves in very soft flesh: they wouldn't kill. It made no difference, for they were so numerous that every attacker suffered a wound. They dropped their torches, threw away their cans of turpentine, and fled, with their leader, who had lost his hat to either gravel or panic, well to the fore.

"How many men have we got that can use a musket?" asked Harry.

"About six," replied Arthur.

Harry looked at the party in the doorway. "That's ten including us. I don't think we're going to get much sleep."

James yawned in an exaggerated way. "Damn it, Harry, is this fellow going to keep us awake every night?"

"Will someone please tell me what is going on?"

They all turned to see Anne, in her nightdress, at the bottom of the stairs. Arthur was the first to respond.

"Madam," he cried. "How dare you appear in public in your shift. Return to your room this instant."

They found Tite, with a nasty lump on his head, still unconscious on the path and carried him back to the house. It was only when they'd revived him and they were sure the house was secure that James mentioned Wentworth.

"I cannot believe he has slept through the entire thing," said Harry.

"He managed to slumber his way through the commotion aboard the *Planet,*" James replied. "One can only assume his dreams are so boring that they keep him comatose."

CHAPTER FOURTEEN

ARTHUR HAD SPENT most of the night writing letters: to the Lord Lieutenant of the County, the colonel in command of the local Fencibles, Mr Magistrate Temple in Deal, plus another strongly worded missive to Lord Chancellor Thurlow. All detailed the events of the previous 48 hours, deplored the idea that such things could happen in a law-abiding nation, called for protection, and insisted on some form of law enforcement. They were sent off at first light, along with a note to Goodnestone regretting that their dinner would, yet again, have to be postponed. This was no time for social gatherings. All the neighbours with horses came together to scour the area for any sign of the men who'd attacked Cheyne.

The servants, well wrapped against the continuing cold, were set to watch the approaches to the house while the horsemen rode out. But try as they might they could find no trace of the party who'd come so far inland in search of their quarry. Nor could Harry advance a convincing reason why this had happened, unless their mere presence as witnesses to the murder of Bertles and his crew made them a target. If that was the case it would surely presage another attack; a worrying prospect, for it would entail a long period during which everyone would need to be alert.

There was no way that their leader could know that the passengers who'd been aboard the *Planet* had little to tell those in authority, besides a poor physical description, and the fact that he had an unusually high-pitched voice. And Harry's neighbours, for all their sympathy, soon grew impatient when their enquiries produced neither the name of a man, nor a ship, nor whence they'd come. In these troubled times, with the likes of Tom Paine spreading his venom from across the Channel, rumours abounded throughout the country of seditious societies, groups of the lower orders bent on revolution, who would fire a rich man's house to further their cause. Everyone had heard of such a case, though no one had witnessed it.

Surely all this talk of a party of armed sailors was so much stuff? And the numbers beggared belief. It wasn't far from that to the first hint that the whole affair was the figment of an over-heated imagination. What had started as an enthusiastic hunt soon lost its impetus, with an increasing number of Harry's neighbours begging off to return to running their own properties. Any evidence of the strangers' presence would have kept them at it. But it was as though the men had never existed. No one had seen them come or go. Finally Harry was forced to call off the chase, sure that they were back aboard ship nursing many a wound, and with the hope that they'd convinced themselves the game wasn't worth the candle.

"Perhaps the fellow now has a gravel voice, Harry," said James, attempting to lift his brother's obvious gloom.

"He has a name, James. With his voice and appearance so singular, I cannot believe his identity is not known."

"Perhaps Naomi Smith will know of him. I hear she has some contact with smugglers."

Harry shook his head violently. "I told you. He's not from around these parts. And as for Naomi, the rumours of her being involved in smuggling are as exaggerated as most other things about the lady."

"You would know better than I," replied James wickedly. "But with respect, brother, those two statements don't add up."

"Why not?"

"You say that he's well known with the same assurance as you say he's not a local man. If the latter is true, perhaps his identity is as much a mystery to others as it is to us."

"He knew Bertles by name," said Harry.

"You heard the way he gained information, Harry. I doubt that he'd have any difficulty extracting a name."

Harry turned away, leaning on the ledgers that would take up most of the rest of the day. There were ways that he could find out if he was right, but they were not something he could discuss with his brother. The attitude didn't fool James one little bit.

"As long as you yourself do not step outside the law, Harry, in order to bring this fellow to book . . ."

Harry spun round, trying to look innocent. "Me?"

The three men had been together a long time and it was a sad parting when James left, taking Pender with him. The only silver lining to that cloud was Wentworth's departure. Their unwanted guest had declined to assist in the search, and complained loudly about the lack of official interest while all the time declaring that he would bring the villains to justice. Even Arthur had lost patience with the man, enquiring sharply how he intended to do this with his backside stuck to an armchair.

Harry, despite the temptations of his own inclinations, now had to undertake those duties which fell to him as a substantial landowner, and visit his tenants, as much to thank them for their recent assistance as to look over their property, a task made more onerous by Arthur's constant presence. Regardless of how well he'd behaved on the night of the attack, the events preceding the assault still rankled. If his brother-in-law noticed his reserve, he gave no indication, no doubt putting it down to Harry's hatred of the task. So what little conversation ensued tended towards a list of the agricultural improvements he'd made.

These were long days, for his patrimony was not gathered in one compact piece, but spread around several parishes. Like most of the Kentish estates, it had grown over the centuries, through purchase and marriage, until one heir who'd put his love of cards before the care of his acres had been so reduced that he'd been forced to sell. The estate had not been in the family for long but his father had invested heavily, using his fortune well, so that now there was no part of the local agriculture in which Harry Ludlow wasn't involved.

Harry hated this, while Arthur revelled in it. Nothing pleased his brother-in-law more than the physical manifestations of the esteem in which he was held. There was, of course, the other side of his character, a genuine concern for innovation and people's welfare, which stood counterbalance. But Harry Ludlow knew it was easy to play lord and master, to delude oneself into thinking that as the owner one had power. But he was also well aware that such respect was a fine veneer, for these people were of English yeoman stock. They'd show respect as long as it was forthcoming, but any attempt to impose on them would soon lead to trouble. They were not above telling their squire he was a fool to his face if his actions warranted it. Besides that, they had methods of showing disapproval that required no words. Harry couldn't help but think it very much like a ship.

He was on the way back to Cheyne Court from some of his property around Eastry when he passed along the ridge overlooking the cemetery where Tolly Smith was buried. He could see Naomi as she knelt, tending to a small grave just behind her husband's. There were wild flowers aplenty around the huge Portland headstone, but the simplicity of the other grave, with its discreet stone and planted borders, was more appealing. Decorated covers kept off the frosts, and the winter pansies and snowdrops showed stark against the green of their stems.

He would never have reined in his horse if Arthur had been with him, but his brother-in-law had stopped off to visit at the former royal palace at Eastry Court, partly to take coffee and partly to bask in the sudden notoriety of his brothers-in-law. He sat watching her for an age, wondering how someone like her could possibly strike up a relationship with a dry stick like Arthur. The memories of his time with her flooded in, warm and disturbing, which made him kick his horse hard. She turned at the sound of the hoofs, gazing after the retreating figure as he thundered along the ridge, at a full gallop. Then she returned to her labours, singing softly to herself as she pruned and plucked.

CHAPTER FIFTEEN

THE DOGS' barking alerted them first. Then the heavy sound of the horse's hoofs, crunching on the wet gravel, drew everyone to the drive, not least Harry, sick of poring over the ledgers that had occupied him these last two days. The man on the horse clearly represented no danger, since he'd passed the men at the gate. He was well wrapped against the cold, and the drizzly rain streamed off his hat as well as his oilskin cloak. There was a tiny postillion platform added to the rear of his saddle, home to a small terrier, which seemed oblivious to the poor weather, content to sleep in spite of being soaked. The groom rushed out to take his horse and Tite was at the door ready to ask his business as the man dismounted.

Harry, delighted by this diversion, was already in the hallway before the visitor was shown in. His face was still hidden by his hat and muffler. The partially open cloak, dripping water on to the oak floorboards, showed high black riding boots over leather breeches, plus the hint of a uniform coat. The dog, still somnolent, was cradled in the man's arms. He swept off his hat with his free hand, then hauled his muffler free of his chin to reveal grey hair over a purple, craggy face.

"He's asking after you, Captain Ludlow," said Tite, who, having allotted himself an excessive bandage to cover his wound, looked more like a Turkoman than a household servant. He was now frowning at the puddle which formed at the man's feet.

Harry looked at their visitor enquiringly, forcing him to introduce himself.

"Joseph Braine, of the Preventative Service, enquiring after a Harry Ludlow, Esquire."

Tite gave him a sharp, unfriendly look, which was nothing to do with the way he said the Ludlow name, or the state of his hallway. He was not keen to welcome a member of that hated breed, a riding officer of the excise. Harry guessed that his visitor's presence must pertain to Bertles and the *Planet*. What had happened in the Channel would be common gossip by now. Perhaps he'd find out at last who and what he was up against.

"I am Harry Ludlow. May I suggest that you remove your outer garments, sir, and allow Tite to take them to dry?"

Braine put down the sleeping dog and did as he was requested, though Tite's reluctance to take the wet cloak was plain to see. He favoured the dog, which raised its head and looked lazily around, with an even less welcoming glare. His voice, for all the polite servant's delivery, was as inhospitable as his countenance. "You may leave your animal by the kitchen fire if you choose."

"Sniff goes where I go," growled Braine. "If needs be I can conduct my business here. It makes no odds." He was obviously a man accustomed to being unwelcome, and Tite's malevolent looks had no effect on him at all. "Happen I won't be here long, anyhow."

"You may fetch your dog into the drawing-room, Mr Braine, if he's not the type to lift his leg at any standing object. Otherwise, I must ask you to leave him outdoors."

Braine reached down and lifted the terrier up, scratching the animal behind the ears. "Never fear, he's an indoor creature, if'n he's cared for proper. Do you have a drop of brandy available, Mr Ludlow?"

Harry tried to contain his surprise at such a want of manners. The excise officer noticed his reaction.

"It's not for me, Mr Ludlow. It be for Sniff here, an' he'll need a bowl to take it out of."

Tite was about to make objection, by the look on his face. Harry spoke to cut him off. "That will be all, Tite. See to the gentleman's cloak and hat, and fetch me a bowl."

Tite's glare was turned on him, before the servant remembered himself and fixed his angry features into an expression more becoming to his station. He shambled off, leaving neither of them in any doubt, with his whispered grumblings, what he thought of this "gentleman." Harry turned and made for the drawing-room.

The exciseman had sat down close to the fire by the time the bowl arrived. Harry put a drop of brandy in it and turned to hand the whole to Braine. The creature's head was up and alert, and he was whining slightly as he struggled in his owner's arms. Braine put the bowl on the floor, with the dog beside it, and Sniff licked it up greedily.

"He seems partial to the brew, Mr Braine."

"He is that, sir. He goes mad when he's deprived of it. Which he is when we expect to check for contraband."

Harry had heard of animals being debauched by drink so that their keen senses could be used to find hidden spirits. But it was the first time he'd actually seen one and it made him exceedingly curious. He knelt to the dog and scratched its ears. Harry clearly had the flavour of the spirit on his thumb, for the dog licked it greedily.

"Don't go doin' that when he's deprived, or he'll take your finger off." Braine scooped Sniff up and returned him to his lap.

Harry stood up abruptly. "You've yet to tell me the purpose of your call."

"I doubt that's truly necessary, Mr Ludlow."

Braine reached into his coat and pulled out a large piece of folded paper. The look on his host's face threw him for a moment, for it was clear that Harry was completely mystified.

Braine's purple face took on an angry look, his thick grey eyebrows seeming to meet in the centre of his forehead. "We gets enough sticks and stones, sir, from all and sundry, not to mention the threats, without the likes of you taking to putting up posters."

"I'm sorry, Mr Braine. I don't know what you're on about."

Braine had the look of a man who felt he was being practised on as he held up the folded paper. His bitter tone made the dog growl slightly. "This, sir, which is not only damned lies and calumny, but as good as an invitation to riot."

"May I see what it is?" asked Harry, holding out his hand.

"Don't pretend you don't know," snapped Braine.

His demeanour finally made Harry respond in kind, but he kept his voice under control.

"I'm not much given to pretence, sir. Nor am I accustomed to being addressed so in my own drawing-room. Pray show me what you have brought."

Braine handed over the folded page. Harry took it from his hand and opened it out. It had a bold headline addressing it to the PEOPLE OF DEAL, as well as all RIGHT-THINKING ENG-LISHMEN, followed by the offer of a ten-guinea REWARD. The type below varied in size as the writer sought to emphasize the main points.

A call for the SEAS to be made SECURE, so that we may SAIL them without FEAR of MURDER and the DEPRE-DATIONS of the Excise. This very MORNING, Captain Tobias Bertles, a black-hearted VILLAIN, cast a party of INNOCENT souls adrift upon the open sea. This to avoid the exciseman. Said Bertles was then brought to, and horri-bly MURDERED with all his crew by a ship unknown. This SHIP pursued us, with DEADLY INTENT, to the very edge of the SANDS so as to DROWN our ability to WITNESS.

FOUL deeds in very sight of the ENGLISH shore. Where were the EXCISE? The name of that SHIP, and its PURPOSE, are at present a MYSTERY. Any information leading to the detection of SAME to Mr Harry LUDLOW, of CHEYNE COURT in the parish of CHILLENDEN!

Harry was shaking his head as he read it, for this poster explained a great deal. But this was hidden from Braine, whose voice sounded even angrier.

"Well, sir, do you still pretend ignorance?"

"I have never seen this before, Mr Braine, nor did I have a hand in composing it . . ."

Harry got no chance to continue, for Braine exploded. He was struggling to his feet, pushing the poster down to look Harry in the eye. "Never seen it, sir! A tract which near implicates the Preventative Service in a shipborne massacre."

Harry was still shocked at the mere existence of the poster, still trying to place it in the context of the attack on the house. So much so that his response was feeble. "Come, Mr Braine. I see no such words to imply that."

"Do you not, sir," snapped Braine, standing now, his outstretched finger stabbing at the poster. "Well it is there and plain to see. Where were the excise, it says? As if to make out they were aboard Bertles's ship!"

The name of Bertles, spoken out loud, brought Harry back to the matter at hand. The events of that day flashed through his mind, especially the insufferably smug air that Wentworth had adopted just before they'd left Deal, not to mention his continuing assertions while he was a guest at Cheyne Court. His voice was as loud as Braine's as he sought to calm the man.

"You may sit down, sir, and receive an explanation, or you may fetch your cloak and hat and depart without one." He waved the poster furiously. "I am not the author of this, and if you take leave to doubt my word again, I'll make you answer for it over the barrel of a pistol."

It would have worked on a man less accustomed to hatred and dissimulation. But Braine spent his life being lied to. Not believing protestations of innocence was now an ingrained habit. He stuck his face close to Harry's and positively bellowed. "It'll be you that'll answer, sir, upon my honour."

"What is this unseemly display about?"

Only the dog had heard him enter, for it had raised its head slowly to look across the room. Arthur's voice cracked out from the open doorway. Braine spun round to look as Harry's eyes flicked over his shoulder. "Who the devil are you?"

Arthur's voice was now like ice as his hand went out on his long walking stick. Harry had never seen such an aristocratic poise. "You dare to question me within these walls, sir. I find that exceeding offensive."

"Mr Braine is a Preventative Officer," said Harry.

The walking stick twiched abruptly, and there seemed an unusual moment of hesitation in Arthur's demeanour, as though he was shocked. Yet he recovered quickly enough, and he couldn't avoid the play on words which presented itself.

"With the customary manners, to boot, sir. If you wish to shout at the owner of the house, please do so from the very boundary of his property, not here in his drawing-room." He looked down at the dog in the exciseman's arms. "And there you may allow your creature to bark to your heart's content."

Arthur's interruption had taken the heat off the confrontation, his visitor being stuck for a suitable reply. Harry had time to mollify him. With some effort he strove to be conciliatory.

"Calm yourself and sit down, Mr Braine."

"To what purpose?" the older man growled, casting his eyes between them.

Harry waved the poster again, which assured his undivided attention. "Upon my honour, I had no hand in this. Yet I have a fair idea who did."

"Your name is appended."

"Without my permission, sir."

"What is it, Harry?" asked Arthur.

"A piece of mischief perpetrated by our recent guest, Mr Wentworth." He walked across to the centre of the room and gave the poster to Arthur, before turning back to face Braine. "Are you aware of what took place in the Channel, Mr Braine?"

"Course I am. The whole town is afire with the rumours."

"Then let me lay some of them to rest, sir, and appraise you of the facts."

Braine was persuaded to sit while Harry outlined what had

happened, detailing the response of Mr Magistrate Temple and the unwillingness of the navy to take action. Arthur moved to join him by the fireplace, to see the exciseman's face.

"And you were not there, Mr Braine, so we could not appeal to you."

"You catches smugglers by putting your arse in a saddle, not a chair."

"This is not a pothouse, Mr Braine!" snapped Arthur, looking up from the poster.

Harry spoke quickly, cutting off Braine's response. "In truth, I was at a loss to know what to do then. My brother and I resolved to come home, leaving the solution of that problem to another day. But the young man Wentworth clearly felt that this was inadequate. He was much exercised by the recent threat to his person. He's not a man accustomed to danger."

"Then he should bide his tongue," said the visitor sourly.

"How heartily I agree, Mr Braine," said Arthur. "Much tedium would be avoided if he took that advice. Harry, does this have anything to do with what happened the other night?"

"Everything, Arthur."

"And to think he slept through it all."

Braine was looking from one to the other, utterly confused. Harry decided that matters should be dealt with one at a time, so he concentrated on what had happened at sea.

"I cannot see that he has accused you of complicity," said Harry, indicating the poster, which Arthur still held in his hand, "even in the most jaundiced reading of the tract."

"That's not how they view matters in the town, sir. Why, they are practically saying we did murder . . ."

"Which would make you terribly unpopular," said Arthur softly, before Braine finished his sentence.

Braine entirely missed the irony, taking the words at face value. "Who cares about being popular, in my office? But we all cares about staying alive."

Arthur looked at the poster again. "It is this household which has suffered, sir. The same men who murdered this Bertles continued their depredations on land. They attacked this house, in strength, and it was only good fortune that led to their being discovered before they could do mischief. Surely this has not brought anything like the same threat to your person?"

That made Braine snort, for threats to an exciseman's person were an everyday occurrence, and he appeared entirely uninterested in what had happened at the house.

"Let's just say it comes at a bad time, sir. And the victim happens to be the wrong person, an awkward sod you might say. If Bertles has been done in, any hint that points to us will be believed. For it is known that we have cause."

He looked at the two other men, who were obviously curious enough to allow him to continue. "Do you know what we do on a shingle coast when we find untaxed goods in someone's cellar?"

Both Harry and Arthur shook their heads.

"Well, we takes shingle off the beach and fills it in. Stands to reason in a future search that a cellar full of shingle is not in use. Well, we did just that a few years ago, only to find that instead of bein' mad at us, the locals were laughing."

"Some bucolic joke, no doubt," said Arthur, implying thin skin.

"Oh, yes," said Braine, without humour, his eyes fixed on the flames. "One of our men had gone missing for a bit. We thought perhaps he was off chasing smugglers. Often happens. And he was young and keen, Charlie Taverner."

Braine spoke softly, head down, as though not wishing to be heard, so he didn't see Harry stiffen at the name. "Too keen, I reckon, the number of times he was nowhere to be found. Forever riding off somewhere, chasing hares . . ."

Then he carried on with his tale in a normal voice. "Chance comes up and there's no time to inform another officer." He raised his head and looked at Harry and Arthur in turn. "But it wasn't like that, at all. We got information, from an unimpeachable source, saying that this cellar was full of contraband."

"Was the information correct?" asked Harry.

"It was!" snapped Braine, as though that fact alone was enough to make him angry. "We cleared it out, arrested the owner, and filled the cellar in. Then, few weeks after, there was poster put up, just like the one in your hand, saying as how the excise had taken to fillin' in their own. An' the man who joked the most, the man responsible for that poster, was Tobias Bertles, though I can't be sure that he himself had a hand in what happened."

"What did take place?" asked Harry, who had a horrible feeling he knew the answer.

"They was laughing at us so much, we thought we'd missed summat. So we went back to that cellar and dug it out again."

"And had you," asked Arthur, coldly, "missed something?"

There was no humour in the laugh that followed, but there was evidence of tension in the way Braine stroked the dog's ears.

"Oh! We had that. They'd taken young Charlie Taverner and bound him hand and foot, with a tight gag on his mouth, stuck him in there, and covered him over when we was halfway through. Then we came along and filled the whole—finished the job. Poor bastard must have heard the sound of our voices as we worked. No wonder they was laughin'."

"Dead?" asked Harry.

Braine was looking at the fire again, as though the flickering flames held a picture of the event he had just described.

"Must have run out of air to breathe. That stands to reason. Mind, the rats had got through the stones and started on his eyes."

CHAPTER SIXTEEN

BRAINE HAD relaxed, like Arthur and Harry, now sitting back in his chair, as though the telling of the tale exorcised some private Calvary. Sniff was now curled in front of the fire beside his empty saucer, whilst his master outlined the odds against the service in which he was employed. What he didn't say, because he didn't need to, was that he was a mere deputy. Someone else had the excise sinecure, and therefore most of the income, from his position. But that person would stay at home in comfort, content to let another risk his life for far less reward.

"Stands to reason you can't prevent smuggling on a coast like this, not if'n you've got no ships of your own to speak of. To my mind these villains have got to be taken at sea. Once they've landed their cargo, it's ten times as hard to find." His eyes blazed angrily. "But what have we got? One cutter for the whole coast from Ramsgate to Rye."

Harry felt the burn of hypocrisy as he listened to Braine's tale of woe, and assumed that Arthur must feel the same. They were both purchasers of un-excised goods. Living in this part of the world, where the prosperity provided by war was temporary and tenuous, it was hard to see smuggling as a crime. Indeed the very title that the *contrabandiers* went by, the Honest Thieves, told you all you needed to know about the way they were regarded in the public imagination. He had never himself sat on a jury trying a smuggler, but he knew that people like Braine had no end of difficulty convicting them when the twelve good men were truer to their neighbours than they were to the law.

"We has our successes, mind, as the goods in Bertles's cellar testify. And we took another lot just yesterday, thirty hogsheads of best Genever gin. It all depends on our informers. If the source is unimpeachable, then we usually get a result."

His craggy face, which had lightened for a moment, clouded again as he turned to gaze into the fire.

"Not that we ever get the true miscreant, mind. They stick up some shaver to take the blame, with a promise of a place in the gang once he's served his time. If you looked at the contents of the gaols you'd reckon that smuggling was a game for lame-headed lads under eighteen."

Braine looked up, his purple, craggy, unfriendly face creasing slightly. He must have realized by their silence that these two men had little sympathy for his troubles. They'd let him relate his tale without asking a single question. They were proper gentry, a breed he despised; for it was their greed that kept the smugglers in business. He hauled himself to his feet and looked down at a slightly abashed Harry Ludlow.

"I want them posters stopped, Mr Ludlow, and that done this very day."

"You may set someone to take them down if you wish, Mr Braine."

"Tried that," he snapped. "They just keep appearing again."

"They can only be printed in so many places," said Arthur.

Braine glared at him. "Well, I ain't got time to go searching out no printing press. I've got more important matters to attend to."

"Like catching the man who murdered Bertles and his crew?" asked Harry.

The Preventative Officer looked him square in the eye, as if trying to make sure that Harry understood he was speaking the truth. It had the opposite effect to that intended.

"If he's local, and landing contraband, I'll do him for evasion. Far as I can see, smugglers killing each other only makes life easier."

"He wasn't local," said Harry.

Braine, who had a stern countenance anyway, like some bibli-
cal prophet, now looked at Harry with added suspicion. But it
had a stagey, unreal quality, which made him appear like the guilty
party, rather than attaching that to his host.

"How can you be so damned certain?"

Harry ignored the implication of the look, the idea Braine was
trying to convey, that he himself was somehow involved in the
trade. He also wondered if he should answer. After all, Braine
clearly wasn't prepared to reveal if he knew anything. By his attitude to the posters he was positively discouraging further enquiry,
and he had no interest in what had happened at Cheyne Court.
But pride forced him to speak, for he would not have this fellow
think that they'd survived by mere luck.

"Do you know the Kellet Gut, Mr Braine?"

He shrugged, as though it was of no account. "Course I do."

That angered Harry, who was now certain that he knew more
about the murderer than he was saying. "Well, whoever chased
us in that ship didn't. In fact I doubt he knew these waters at all.
Otherwise he'd never have let me lead him south of the passage,
landing him in a position where further pursuit was impossible.
He would have borne up to cut me off and I wouldn't be here to
answer your impertinent questions."

"Sounds like straw-clutching to me," said Braine, his eyes narrowing at the unexpected rebuke.

"Do you know the man who killed Bertles?" asked Harry.

"How could I," replied Braine, "since I didn't see him?"

"Perhaps you don't have to see him, Mr Braine. Perhaps he's
quite notorious. Not many people smuggle with a ship that size,
let alone a fleet. His name could be common knowledge to the
excise."

"That may well be true, Mr Ludlow," said Braine calmly. "And
I dare say if we ever lay him by the heels, with proof to put before
a judge, we'll call on you, along with the other so-called passengers of the *Planet,* to witness at his trial. Now, if you don't object,
I'll bid you good day."

Braine picked up his dog and was halfway to the door before Harry could reply.

"One of the grooms could do it just as well as you," said Arthur.

"No. It's better I go myself," replied Harry, stiffly. Providence had contrived to hand him an opportunity and he wasn't about to let it pass.

Arthur wasn't convinced, and for good reason. The idea of a man of Harry's parts putting himself to a task that any number of his servants could perform was ludicrous.

"It wouldn't have anything to do with looking at ships, would it?"

"Is that such a bad thing?" He waited, but since nothing was forthcoming he carried on, partly in the hope of forcing a response. "I will most certainly enquire, though I doubt there'll be much in Deal, for the navy will not chase French privateers and the locals lack the means. Besides, the ships are generally too small for what I have in mind."

"Which is?"

"Doing what I set out to accomplish originally, which is deep sea privateering somewhere like the Bay of Biscay. That's where the prizes come in from the Indies and the East, with cargoes worth the trouble. There's not much profit to be gained from raiding the coastal trade."

The look of dissatisfaction was now plain on Arthur's face. His thin ginger eyebrows were knitted together. Never given to a humorous countenance, he now looked as though he had bitten hard on a lemon.

"Is there something more than your usual disapproval, Arthur?"

His brother-in-law shrugged, as if he was trying to dismiss the suggestion, but it didn't quite come off.

"I shall not repeat myself, for I am as weary of expounding the argument as you are of listening to it. All I will say is that if it's profit you're after, you can make more in London than you can at sea."

"As a tradesman?" asked Harry, mischievously.

"You know very well I do not refer to trade. Nor do I merely refer to money. I allude to power and the wealth and station that flows from it. The government is the source of all patronage. We stand well in the eyes of Pitt and Dundas, who are grateful for our support. You are in a position to claim a share of that. If you'd consent to undertake parliamentary duty yourself you could well secure some form of ministerial office. From there you could lay claim to a title. I assume that one day you will marry and produce an heir. It would be a fine thing for your son to begin life as an earl."

"Or even better, a duke."

"If your heir began life as the son of an earl, and had one tenth of your brains, he could not help but secure a dukedom."

"I'm not attracted by titles, Arthur. Captain Ludlow will suffice."

Harry felt his mood lighten as he breasted each rise. The sense of freedom was immediate. From the top of the chalk downs, on horseback, he caught sight of Pegwell Bay, with the sea sparkling beneath a clear winter sky. The air was bitingly cold, the ground hard as a rock and slippery, so he dare not risk anything other than a gentle trot. He was in no rush to complete his journey. He would see the printer, call on Captain Latham and offer him dinner, perhaps even spend the night in the town if there was a room available.

And he was alone, at liberty to ask questions about his adversary. Harry had less faith in the law than either James or Arthur, though it was not a sense of incomplete justice that made him pursue the matter. The man who'd killed Bertles had come all the way to Cheyne Court to silence witnesses. Someone that determined didn't sound as though he would let matters rest. For his own safety, and that of his family, it made sense to find out who he was, where he came from, and what it would take to see him standing in the dock on trial for murder. Perhaps, for all

Wentworth's gall in using his name, some information would come from those posters.

His first real sight of the anchorage lifted his heart. Here was a forest of masts, with not less than three hundred ships. Deal luggers and Dutch flutes aplenty. Indiamen East and West, coasters designed to carry coal or grain. Baltic traders, whose cargoes of timber kept the navy afloat, convoys assembling before setting off to all the destinations in the known world. And then there were the warships, their masts taller than any merchant vessel, with the flag of Admiral Duncan flying in the hundred-gun *Venerable*. By the time the smell of the sea had been replaced by the less appealing smell of the town, Harry was resolved to seek out a ship and return to sea, regardless of his brother-in-law's opinion.

James sat with his attorney, looking at the papers he had passed to him. The voice of the lawyer, outlining his difficulties, seemed as dry as the parchment he held in his hand.

"I'm afraid the action looks indefensible, Mr Ludlow. There is a mass of evidence. Besides that, his cronies will swear the truth of what he says, even if it comes to perjury, just for a share of the largesse that will flow from his success. True, he will most certainly not get anything like fifteen thousand guineas. No judge will award such a sum. But he will burden you with his legal costs, for sure. So pursuit of the whole amount is something Lord Farrar can contemplate with equanimity."

"It cannot be allowed to come to court."

"I understand," replied the lawyer, gravely. "No man of parts would wish his reputation sullied in such a manner."

James lifted his eyes from the parchment scroll, his fingers playing idly with the red ribbon that was used to tie the brief. "I was thinking of Lady Farrar."

The lawyer opened his mouth to speak, to say that her reputation was already too tattered, but one look at his client's face stopped him.

"We will have to come to some accommodation," said James.

The attorney sat back in his leather chair. "Then may I counsel delay, sir. Lord Farrar's debts increase by the hour, as does the pressure from his creditors. It is only this case, and the prospect of payment, which prevents them from slinging him into a debtors' prison."

James smiled grimly. "I know the gentleman better than you. As his debts increase, so will his price. He spent his own inheritance, then married Lady Caroline with the sole intention of spending hers. Since he is being dunned by his creditors, that means he has succeeded."

The lawyer frowned, unhappy that his client intended to ignore his advice. But the forms had to be observed. "I will, of course, obey any instructions you care to give."

James just nodded. "I want you to offer Lord Farrar the entire sum."

Lawyers don't gasp with surprise, they're trained not to. But James saw the cheeks depress as his attorney sucked in a silent breath.

"It is conditional of his granting his wife a divorce, with another five hundred guineas if he will stand as the guilty party."

"He would be ridiculed for such a course of action!"

James snapped, his voice angry, for his patience was thin, both with the case and his lawyer. "There is only one form of ridicule for such a scoundrel, and that is the inability to lay a coin on a card table."

The lawyer did not recoil from this outburst, for he was trained to avoid that too. "You know the gentleman better than I."

"Good," said James quietly, his anger evaporating as quickly as it had surfaced. "I also want you to initiate discreet contact with Lady Farrar."

"I must point out that such a course would be most unwise."

James ignored him. "She will be more strapped for funds than her husband. Get hold of her bills, then contact her creditors and assure them that any debts directly due to her are safe, and that her credit is sound."

"That is bound to surface, Mr Ludlow. It will make negotiations much more difficult."

"I don't want negotiations, sir. I want conclusions."

It was as though he'd never been away. Ten minutes off the coach and Pender was back in that twilight world he knew so well, a world of narrow stinking alleys and grim hovels. Many an eye was cast at his fine boots, but the club he carried in his hand, as well as the direct way he returned their stares, told all who contemplated theft that the attempt would be a painful business. He was recognized, of course, by some people. But there were no shouts of welcome, merely discreet nods. They were as cautious as he. To call his name, which was known to carry a price, could send some rat scurrying to the Beak looking for a reward.

Pender weaved his way through the whole area. He kept going for two reasons. One, he wanted all those who knew him to be aware he was back. But he also wanted to be sure this area was safe. Pender was not the type to place two feet anywhere, even in his own backyard, until he tested the waters with a cautious toe. It was that attitude that had allowed him to survive this long free from arrest or pain in a world where a man could die and never be missed.

Satisfied that he was safe, Pender began to acknowledge those whom he'd recognized and started to ask questions. The answers he got showed that the earlier reserve had not just been discretion. Those who knew him were reluctant to talk, waving vague hands as he enquired about his wife and children. But he located their whereabouts eventually, and taking a firmer grip on his club he set off to find the spot where they now lodged.

"Captain Latham is not here, sir," said Cath Hogbin, leaving Harry in no doubt from her tone that she found it hard to bear. "But I expect him back for dinner."

"Then bespeak us a table, Cath, and dig out something special from the cellar, for I owe the good captain a princely feed."

Her eyes sparkled as she replied. "There never was a man who deserved it more, Mr Ludlow. He is indeed a prince."

The bustle in the street seemed greater than ever as Harry made his way along the Beach Street to Sandown Castle. The tide was high and the waves now cascaded against the fortress, hammering at the walls relentlessly, as if trying to dislodge them stone by stone. The battery of 42-pounder guns was still manned, but in a lackadaisical manner, without sentries. No one challenged him as he made his way through the postern gate. The artillerymen had appropriated the chambers on the inland side of the castle, leaving the outer rooms, where the sea pounded on the outside wall, for the Preventative Service.

Braine, well wrapped against the cold air and damp walls, sat at a desk near a red-hot stove, with Sniff curled up in his lap, writing in a ledger. His mittened hand stopped and he reached for his sword as Harry's footsteps echoed on the bare flagstones. It stayed on the hilt as Harry approached, and the look in the man's eyes was exceedingly unfriendly. Behind him, so tattered it was barely readable, was a poster offering a reward for information leading to the arrest of the men who'd murdered Charlie Taverner.

"I require a list of printers," said Harry. His voice sounded ethereal in the vaulted stone chamber, louder and more peremptory than he'd intended.

"You can get that anywheres," growled Braine.

"True," said Harry, nodding towards the grubby poster. "But since I presume you have some idea who owned the press, you will save me a great deal of foot-slogging if you point me in the right direction."

The sound of fresh, more numerous footsteps, reverberating off the walls, made him turn. Braine was looking past him towards the open door, his expression still grim. Two men, clad in ill-fitting worn blue coats, had come into the room. They had a skinny youth, in a tattered blood-stained shirt, manacled and bowed, between them. The boy had received some stout blows, judging by his posture, not to mention the bruises which covered his face.

"He won't admit to no more," said one of the men in the doorway. "Says he brought the brandy over hisself."

"See this specimen, Mr Ludlow," said Braine, pointing a mittened finger at the youth. "Name's Digby Cavell. This streak of piss, who couldn't lift his arse off a privy unaided, has owned to shifting thirty hogsheads of Genever gin all on his own."

Harry walked over to the doorway and lifted the boy's head. He looked about twelve years of age, though he was probably older. His listless eyes were blackened and his lips encrusted with dried blood. Lumps covered his face where he been slapped or punched. Braine was still listing his crimes in the background as Harry felt his anger rise.

"Shipped them in from Holland he says, in a rowboat, one at a time, and stored them in the cellar where we found 'em."

"This is an outrage," hissed Harry.

"It's a downright falsehood an' no mistake," replied Braine, who could not see the look in Harry's eye. But the men holding the boy could, and they stepped back a pace. "But it was ever the same. As I told you, the true culprits always stick up a shaver like Digby to take the blame."

"More than blame," said Harry angrily as he turned round. For the first time Braine saw the look in his eye and realized that his visitor was less than impressed with his methods.

"By what authority do you beat this boy?"

"None that you can question, sir," snapped Braine, half rising from his chair. The dog Sniff slipped off his lap, waking instantly and landing on all fours.

Harry's voice rebounded off the walls, adding to their effect. "What you are doing is contrary to the law, sir!"

"Don't you presume to come in here and lecture me, Ludlow," shouted Braine. "I suppose you'd have me feed this turd red meat while I question him?"

"You have no right to use violence, Mr Braine."

"Tell that to those who murder my men, sir!"

"It is your duty, once you've apprehended a felon, to hand him over to a magistrate."

"A magistrate. Let me tell you that Mr Temple treats me with no more respect than he extends to you, sir."

"If this is the way you present the accused, I'm not surprised," replied Harry coldly, before Braine's words had sunk in. "Besides, how do you know the way he treated me?"

Braine must have realized he'd stepped too far and said more than he intended. He tried to bluster his way out. "Temple treats everyone the same, sir, for he is hand in glove with crime."

"Then he must be hand in glove with you, sir," yelled Harry, who now had two good reasons to be angry, for he realized that he'd missed a vital point after the attack on the house.

Braine must know who'd tried to drown them. Perhaps Temple did too. Indeed, it was possible that every smuggler in Deal had an inkling, if not certain knowledge, of the man's identity. That attack on Cheyne Court had not been mere coincidence, nor could he mistake the leader, for he'd heard the man's voice as plain as day. Yet he wasn't local. A man who didn't know the Kellet Gut couldn't find his house without a degree of assistance. His earlier assumption that there was no local connection was being discarded as he spoke.

He'd already established in his own drawing-room that a direct enquiry addressed to Braine would produce no result. The man wouldn't even tell him the location of the printers. He realized now that he had to get those posters down, since he had no idea of how much their presence had contributed to events. Anyone wishing to inform would have done so by now. Leaving them could only add to his problems. But he had no intention of departing without the Cavell boy.

"I intend that you release this youth in my custody, for if you do not I shall be obliged to ask the officer in charge of this castle to afford me a file of soldiers."

Braine's mouth flew open, and he let out a great rush of air, which passed for a laugh. "Then you'd best send to Portobello

Court, sir, for that is his normal location. He's never out of the whorehouse." He sat down, looking at his ledgers as he continued, as if to inform him that he was of no more account than his sums. "You may accompany my men if you wish. I was just on the point of ordering them to take him to Temple."

Braine looked past Harry to his two ill-kempt assistants. "Do as I say, then get along to Farrier Street. I want that cellar filled to the brim."

"We 'as been up the whole night," whined one of the men.

"And by the look of you all the gin in them hogsheads wasn't poured away," growled Braine. "Get some rest if you must, but I want that job done sharp, so the bastards know we mean business."

CHAPTER SEVENTEEN

THE CROWDS that gathered along the beach road did not differentiate between Harry and the two guards as they marched Digby Cavell towards Mr Magistrate Temple's residence. They booed and hissed at him with the same fervour they aimed at the Preventatives. The mud from the side of the road, mixed with animal droppings, started to fly, causing the party to break into an ignominious trot. They hurried along, the youth stumbling in their midst, arms held up to ward off the worst of the flying filth.

Temple, fetched from his office, didn't seem the least bit surprised at the lad's physical condition. He had a cell for confining prisoners and the boy was despatched there with no ceremony. While he filled in the details of the charges in a great leather-bound book, Temple seemed far more interested in ensuring that the charge for transporting this boy to the Sandwich Assizes should fall on the Preventative Service rather than St George's parish. Having also recognized Harry as the man who had traduced him, he was very unforthcoming when the subject of printers and Wentworth's poster was raised.

"An incitement, sir, and nothing less. We have riots, murder, vice, and immorality, and now you add this. If I could find an offence with which to detain you, there would be two felons on the way to the Assizes instead of one."

Harry gave as good as he got, but he took good care that no one else heard him. "If you wish to fill a coach with crime, Mr Temple, you could do no better than secure your own passage." He was out of the door before the magistrate could reply, but the blood that suffused his face was satisfaction enough. The first of his posters greeted him on the wall by the house, pasted to the brickwork, almost lost amongst those from naval ships offering great rewards and much glory for signing on to take the king's bounty. He tore it off and began his search for the source. Using information he gleaned at the Three Kings to aid him, he struck lucky at the second business he visited. The printer cast his eye over the poster, as though he was checking for errors.

"I most certainly did print that, sir, an' I have a stack of the same in the back of my shop."

"Then do me the honour of burning them," said Harry.

"How could I countenance such waste, sir?" replied the printer. "Besides, it was a Mr Ludlow that instructed me, an' I can only accept an order to desist from him."

"I am Mr Ludlow," said Harry tersely.

The printer looked up at this. The doubt as to his visitor's identity was plain in his red-rimmed eyes.

"You may well be Mr Ludlow, sir, but you are not *the* Mr Ludlow who ordered these. Not only did he specify that they should go out in quantity, he bade me commission a lad to ensure that those torn down were replaced." He lifted an inky fingertip and pointed to his glasses. "A printer has eyes, sir, and a memory. Not that he would need to exercise it over such a short span of time. You are not the gentleman who represented himself to me."

"That was a Mr Wentworth," snapped Harry.

The printer blinked and his crabbed face showed a trace of anger. "That is a very hectoring tone, sir, if I may make so bold as to check you. Do not presume to name my clients to me. The order for these was placed by a Mr Ludlow of Cheyne Court, and that, sir, is where I've been instructed to forward the account."

"What account!"

"That seems to me a damned silly question, sir. Accounts are what people pay for services rendered."

"Mr Wentworth didn't pay you?"

The printer's hands were on his counter, and he leaned forward, poking his inky finger, in an aggressive way that sat ill with his slight stature. "I have already informed you, sir, that I do not know the name Wentworth."

Harry, in his frustration, had a sore temptation to grab him and fetch him a good shake, but it was Wentworth who was at fault. He'd obviously used his name and committed his purse to this idiotic venture. Patiently Harry explained, aware that the printer was suspicious. His earlier angry tone had not inclined the man towards him, but the information that he might go without payment really made the smaller man concentrate.

"Not paid, sir!" he yelped. "I cannot abide the expression, let alone the deed."

"Since I am the real Mr Ludlow," sighed Harry, "I will have to pay you."

The man's manner changed abruptly. All his aggression and suspicion evaporated. He reverted to the shopkeeper concerned for his bill, seeming to shrink to even smaller dimensions in the process. Two inky fingers tugged at his sparse hair.

"How is a man to tell, if'n a gentleman lays a shilling on the counter and says his name."

"I'm surprised he bothered," said Harry, wearily reaching for his purse.

The burly drunk tried to hit Pender the minute he came through the ragged curtain. But the club which he had behind his back proved its worth. Pender was not by nature an aggressive man, but his anger was so great that the swinging blow nearly took his opponent's head off, sending him crashing to the floor unconscious. His ragged children, their skin and protruding bones a mass of sores and bruises, had been softly crying from hunger when he entered. Now they added fear to their moans, and their thin voices rose in a piteous wail. His wife, slumped on the floor in a corner, looked at him through a gin-soaked haze, a stupid smile on her aged countenance. Her emaciated face had the look of a woman who'd suffered no end of beatings and her clothes were soiled with the contents of her own body.

He stood in the middle of the room, trying to make some sense of the scene before him. He'd always looked after his wife and children, indeed the advent of his first born had turned him to crime to feed and clothe the girl. Success at thieving and his habit of selling the goods back to those he'd robbed had ensured that his family never went without, just as it had also guaranteed that he suffered from little interference, for a good number of years, from the law. But success breeds jealousy: someone who lacked his skill had fingered him whilst he still had the goods in his possession. It did no good to plead that he'd never laid a finger on anyone, unlike most of the other local thieves, who delighted in assaulting their victims. British justice held that assault on the person was less of a threat to society than an assault on property. Nor would a plea of necessity evoke sympathy. Judges would rather see dead children in the street than condone theft. With what he'd done, and with the evidence on a table in the same court, he would have been dangled from a rope for sure.

He moved forward towards his children, who'd been pink-faced and healthy when he left. The shock as they cowered away brought tears to his eyes. They would not bear to let him touch them, so he turned to his stricken wife, pulling the stone jug of gin from her bony fingers and leaning forward to look into her face.

"How in the name of hell did this come about?" he croaked as he lifted her chin.

"Pour me some gin," she said. The voice was thin and he could see in her slack-jawed mouth that all her teeth had gone, from disease or the blows she'd suffered.

He kept his voice low as he replied. "You need an apothecary, Jenny Pender, not a jar of gin." But he knew that his wife was beyond any help that even a physician could give. If you lived close to the poor in King George's England then you lived cheek by jowl with death. The sight of it was no stranger. It was not love that made his eyes sting, for they had fought when he'd been at home. It was the sight of a woman who'd once been his burden, a well-boned spitfire, reduced to a skeleton who was so far gone she could not control her bowels.

A groan behind him made him turn round. The children had fallen silent while he'd examined their mother, yet they whimpered again as the drunk started to recover, rolling on to his hands and knees with his head between his palms. Pender was over him in a flash, his club raised, with murder in his heart. A blind man could see that the pain his family had suffered had been inflicted by this sot on the floor.

"Who are you?" the man groaned, lifting his head to look at the figure silhouetted above him.

"That's none of your concern," growled Pender. "But you better be telling me about yourself, or you'll get another swipe from this club."

"Ferdy Wood," said the man swiftly, one hand raised to ward off the expected blow.

"How come you're here," snapped Pender, his finger pointing towards his dying wife.

"God alone knows," Wood pleaded, "for she's no use to man nor beast."

Pender's club took him on the shoulder, causing the man to yell in pain. The words tumbled out of him, every one a whine, all accompanied with gestures to enforce the truth of what he was saying. But Pender was looking into the man's eyes.

"I took her and her brats on, out of the kindness of my heart, after her man ran for a king's bounty."

Pender poked him with the club, knocking him on to his back. "Did you take the bounty, as well?"

"Weren't it my due, mate, for offering protection?"

Pender's voice was hard as stone, and the spittle of his hate hit his opponent square in the face as he railed at him. "I bet you took your due, you bastard. What did you do with my pay warrants, sell them half price to a crimp so that you could afford to drink?"

Wood's eyes widened in terror. "Pay warrants? Christ Almighty, are you her man?"

The club was up above Pender's head. "You should bless your luck that I'm not Christ Almighty, for I'd despatch you to the hell you deserve."

"Ease off, mate!" cried Wood, his hands coming together in supplication. "I took her in and cared for her and your bairns. It ain't my fault she got sick. I did my best for her. She'll die full of gin."

"And my nippers, you sod. What did you have in mind for them?"

Confusion showed on Wood's face, evidence that the answer to that question would damn him more than silence.

"Strip," snapped Pender.

"What?"

"Your clothes. Take them off. Every stitch."

"Have a heart, mate, it's the middle of winter."

The club swung again, missing Wood's head by a fraction. "You can have oblivion if you'd rather."

He squealed like a pig, a sound echoed by the three children still cowering in the filthy cot. But he did as Pender had instructed, tearing off his clothes as quick as he could until he stood stark naked. Pender looked at the pale skin, the flabby but well-nurtured belly of a man who'd starved these children to feed himself. He lifted Wood's grubby stock and tied it round his mouth, stifling the words of protest and tied the man's hands behind his back, before spinning him round to look him straight in the eye.

"Right, you sod. It's out in the street you go."

The fear increased in Wood's eyes, for he knew what that meant. No one would untie him, even if they knew him. A naked man would find no sympathy. But he'd find pain aplenty, as both men and women, some who'd suffered and many who'd not, used him as an unexpected source of sport. If he had a brain he'd head for a church. But a crowd would gather, including street urchins, the cruellest of the lot, who'd do their best to ensure that if he reached sanctuary, and found a vicar willing to untie him, he would do so on his knees, begging for mercy, and in no fit state to let on who'd tied him up.

Pender spun him and booted him out through the filthy rag that passed for a door. The hoot, from a dozen throats, was as immediate as he could have wished. Pender followed him into the stinking alleyway, watched as Wood started his stumbling run, heading for the nearest square that contained a church. The first sod of mud hit him within seconds. Others followed, mixed with stones, forcing him to turn away from his course. The sound grew as more people joined in the pursuit. A hue and cry was up, as word spread through the streets that there was sport to be had. Baiting bears and bulls was one thing, but it could not compare to the rare pleasure to be afforded from baiting a naked man.

He turned and looked back into the hovel. His wife still lay in the corner, her head lolling to one side while she laughed at some private joke. The children remained in the stained cot, with no idea what to do. If they recognized him they didn't show it. But they'd been so abused and had become so cowed that he reckoned they only saw a man. And that, in the life they'd led since he left, only gave notice of pain, not love. They'd stay where they were, all of them. His wife because she could not move, his children because they had nowhere else to go. He dropped the flap behind him and went in search of a donkey and cart.

It was after six and night had fallen. It was bitterly cold, with the threat of snow in the air. James, having stayed too long at the Admiralty, saw that he was faced with a walk through the dark and threatening streets that stood between him and his lodging in St James's. He headed for Pall Mall, the lights of the Prince of Wales's palace, Carlton House, blazing on his left. It was easy to justify his wanderings and his feet needed no excessive bidding to follow the route to the familiar doorway. He would not seek to gain entry, for his attorney had expressly forbidden him to have any contact with Caroline. But he would stand beneath her window and look up, as he had done many times before, if only to wish that things could improve.

He had at least the satisfaction of having achieved something! Lord Spenser had promised to look into the attempt to murder the party that had sailed in the *Planet,* damning smugglers and their ilk in the process. He also had something he thought would mightily please his brother: a list of ships that had been submitted to the Admiralty for sale. As Spenser had so wryly observed, while the navy might be in a position to purchase one or two, the public purse would not run to so many, and Harry Ludlow could take his pick.

"He shall not foul my hawse, James Ludlow, as they say in the service."

The bustle of the London streets barely dented his thoughts as he made his way up the lane that bordered Hyde Park. The area on his right hand seemed to be one vast building site. This was seen as a fine location for a grand house. Londonderry had finished his, and Apsley House was at the gardening stage. But the Grosvenors and the Duke of Dorchester were still in the hands of carpenters and plasterers, working by torchlight to complete these princely palaces.

Within ten minutes he found himself in Hanover Square, outside the Farrar house. It would be mortgaged to the hilt, of course, and on the market for a new lessee before the spring. Not that he'd want to live there. First he must gain Caroline her freedom. Once he'd achieved that they could then decide what to do. If London found their liaison too difficult to swallow, then there was always the country. And if that proved tedious, then they could retreat to Italy.

He could not be so close and not call, despite his earlier promises. Almost without thinking, he stepped forward to pull the bell.

◆ ◆ ◆

She was at least clean now, clothed in a white shift. Pender looked into the still face, that had in death recovered some of the aspect he remembered from times past.

"You're not staying, then?" said the apothecary, looking at the gold coins that Pender had placed in his hand.

Pender shook his head without looking up. "See her buried decently, with a service said and a headstone over her grave."

"She can be interred by noon tomorrow."

"That would be too late for me, friend," said Pender, turning to look at the three children standing in a line, now neatly dressed and washed but still painfully thin and frightened.

The word was out on his name for sure. Perhaps the law wouldn't stir itself to act for days. But that was not a chance he could take. They might just recall how much they wanted to lay him by the heels before, remember by what a narrow margin they'd missed him, be smarting still from the ridicule they'd suffered when he slipped through their fingers. No purpose would be served by his taking a risk.

He looked back at the apothecary. "I have a duty to the livin', friend. Do as I bid you, please."

He leant forward and kissed his dead wife on the brow before turning round to hustle his children into the horse and cart that waited outside, ready for the long journey that would take them all to Cheyne Court and the start of a new life.

CHAPTER EIGHTEEN

"YOU WOULD seem to have a war on your hands, Mr Ludlow," said Latham.

Harry made a dismissive gesture and leant forward to pass the port to his guest. They'd enjoyed a superb meal, and Cath Hogbin had made sure that Harry Ludlow gave her "prince" only the very best from the cellar. Not that he minded, for Latham deserved every bit of thanks that Harry could give him.

"You're sure it was the same fellow?"

"I heard his voice, Captain Latham, just as plainly as I can hear yours now."

"A frosty night; perhaps your ears played tricks, sir?" Harry shook his head as the soldier ruminated, looking for reasons as to why what was obvious should not be so. "How did the fellow know where to find you, or even your name, if it comes to that?"

"Come, Captain Latham. If anyone was privy to the noises we made when we came ashore it was you. And as for my name and address, that miserable penny-pinching scrub Wentworth posted them all over the town. Not only have I had to pay for the damned things, I've been put to further expense having them removed. My only fear is that the names of the other people in the boat became known through gossip. I've already written to Major Franks, though living surrounded by the Shorncliffe Light Brigade, I doubt he's in any danger. My brother is safely in London and the house is now well guarded. But being so close to Deal, we were bound to suffer from his initial incursions."

Latham had a twinkle in his eye as he listed the last name. "And Wentworth?"

"Oh yes," said Harry wearily, for his anger with the young man had turned to that. "Though I was tempted to put up another poster with his address."

After dinner, Latham had an engagement to attend upon Mrs Elizabeth Carter, the famous blue-stocking writer, who had a house in South Street. He invited Harry to accompany him, with the assurance that he would be most welcome.

"She is fond of youth, sir, for all her venerable years. And such an entertaining gossip. She knows something disreputable about everyone who's been anyone these last fifty years."

Harry declined with good grace, saying that he wished to take a turn around the town to check on the posters. Latham left for his appointment, having secured a room for the night for Harry. Harry did want to check that his posters had been removed, but he was afire with curiosity. Dinner with the soldier had done nothing to damp his desire to find the man who'd sought to drown them; rather the opposite, for Latham seemed to be the first person he'd talked to for an age who was not advising him how to live his life.

The information he needed was known to a goodly number of the locals. Posters might not do the trick, but a direct question with the offer of an immediate reward might loosen the odd tongue. His mind went back to that first day in Deal and the confrontation they'd had just outside the Three Kings. The batman, Cephas Quested, who'd interfered with his attempts to converse with Bridie Pruitt certainly knew more than most, otherwise he would never have curtailed their talk. But Harry would stay well away from him. There was Bridie Pruitt herself, of course. She might have something to say. Perhaps if he asked about her first, to find out where she lived. And then there was Bertles. Even if he only had enough information to indicate where they might have met, that would help.

The streets were crowded: bustling taverns full to the brim with sailors, some fresh from foreign parts. A quarter of the merchant trade of England seemed to pass through Deal. Ancient statutes, and the liberties of the Cinque Ports, meant that press gangs were barred from operating in the Downs. But sailors, prime hands some of them, were taken for the navy by private contractors: crimps, who would fill the men with drink, or tempt them with a doxie, then lure them to a quiet spot and sandbag them before bundling them into a naval tender.

Care had to be exercised in the choice of victim, for the locals took it very unkindly if one of their number was so treated. But the crimps were Deal men, known to all who worked here. For the boatmen, pilots, fishermen, and smugglers, they were easy to avoid. Only strangers were taken, let ashore by their captain after months at sea. And since they had not yet been paid the full rate for their voyage, their captain would not complain if they failed to return. As long as he could get his ship to the next destination, the Pool of London, he would not miss his man. Besides, he would pocket the wages outstanding, sure that a man pressed for the navy would have little chance of redress. Outgoing captains, who needed their sailors, took greater care, and were exceedingly vocal when they lost a hand. Not that their protest counted for much. By the time a man was aboard a naval ship he was listed as a volunteer, had pocketed the king's bounty, and was lost to the merchant fleet for the duration.

The man would be replaced, of course, but at prime rates. The only hands available knew they were a scarce commodity and charged accordingly. And they were numerous. Harry knew that if he stuck up another poster, asking for hands to man an exempt privateer, he would find himself inundated with proper seamen. He was turning that thought over in his mind when he saw Cephas Quested enter one of Deal's most notorious taverns, the Paragon. Despite his earlier reservations, it seemed too good a chance to pass up, so he followed him through the door into the noisy room.

He had to peer through the pipe smoke to see where he had gone, finally spotting him whispering in someone's ear, hard by the musicians noisily playing their fiddles and flutes. Harry, moving closer, observed the way that Quested poked the man with the point of his elaborate club. He could see the look of fear in the fellow's eyes as he listened. Sense dictated that he stay away. It was none of his concern, but his feet seemed to take him in that direction without bidding. Harry found a spare seat at a table less than four feet away, just before the conversation ended.

Quested laid his carved club on the table and lifted his head slowly, like a man who knew he was being observed. But he didn't turn his head. Instead he jerked it at another fellow, who shot out of his chair, so vacating it for him. Harry knew the batman had him in the corner of his eye. He waved frantically to a serving girl, shouting loudly to order a tankard of ale, determined to give the appearance of a man relaxed, as well as one intent on pleasure.

Harry was at home in a seaport. But he could tell, by the occasional glance which was thrown his way, that this made little difference to Quested or those who sat with him. They had a stiffness about their demeanour which was very apparent. It was hard for Harry to avoid looking at their table, even with all that was going on in the room. He tried hard to concentrate on other people, imagining explaining to someone like James how each separate group represented an individual drama. There would be crime here aplenty, even if you left out smuggling. He could see men who knew their surroundings, local men in groups, sitting with the confidence of hard bargains, drinking their ale as they scanned the room for a likely mark. And they were not lacking in candidates. The Paragon was packed.

Up in the gallery that ran along two of the Paragon's walls the better class of whores were plying their trade under the watchful eye of the owner, who'd want his cut if they found a well-heeled customer in his tavern. A party of naval midshipmen, drunk as lords, were creating enough noise to drown out the fiddler, determined that all should know that they were as brave as lions. The gallery also contained well-dressed fellows, landsmen, who looked a cut above the clerks and shopkeepers down below. One of them, maybe more, would be a private contractor looking for hands to sell to the navy. Yet others were sleek-looking captains, with the East Indiamen's officers, awash with ostrich and gold lace, easily the best dressed.

But mostly, down here in the well of the tavern, the customers of the Paragon were pigtailed seamen. Harry, like any crimp who cared to look, could identify those sailors who were at the start of a voyage, as opposed to those who'd just come in, merely by their attitude. More than that, he could spot the others, the men who were for hire if the price was right, men who would not be fooled by a crimp's bookish appearance and his friendly ways. The whores at this level, who traded in copper, not silver, tended to be brutes. They were broad of beam, with rouged cheeks and forearms that would not shame a champion ostler. Most would service their clients in a darkened alley, that is, if they were sober enough to perform. Others, already drunk, who tended to paw their grotesque companions as an owner strokes a cat, would likely wake in the morning, breeches intact, shivering from the cold air, wondering what had happened to their purse.

Harry was so intent on his thoughts that he didn't notice that Quested was on his feet heading in his direction. He shifted his position quickly, ready to leap up if he was threatened, though he doubted even someone like Quested could do anything in so public a place. The man stopped before him, the carved club swinging easily in his hand. Harry, who had deliberately looked elsewhere, pretended surprise when he finally acknowledged Quested's presence.

"Are you tailing me?" Quested asked.

"Would that be necessary?" he replied, deliberately examining the man's square, scarred face and massive shoulders. "You don't strike me as a hard man to find."

"That's right, mate. Nor do I have much trouble catching up with them I seek. Not like some I could mention, who takes to larding the whole town with posters, despite a request to mind his nose."

Harry got to his feet slowly, one eye on the club. He knew that others were watching them, for all that the noise in the room had only diminished a trifle. Once erect he moved close to Quested. He was in a dangerous, isolated situation, one which required a degree of bluff to balance.

"I don't remember your warning being in the nature of a request."

Quested sneered, his lips curling in a mock smile. "Forget my manners, did I?"

"I don't suppose you did, not being in possession of any."

The smile disappeared and the carved club, with its elaborate snakes and dragons, came up a trifle. "Are you seeking a clout round the lug?"

It was now Harry's turn to smile, which he made sure was broad enough for all those interested to observe. "You'd never connect, friend, not even with that club."

Quested didn't blink. He had all the confidence of a true hard case. "I heard you was a gamecock. But so am I, mate. I can lay aside the club if you wish it so, an' I'll still box your ears with one hand."

"What happened to Bridie Pruitt?" asked Harry.

The question threw the other man for moment, for he had been expecting a different response. "Who?"

"Bridie Pruitt. The woman who lost her man in the *Planet*."

"Who says she did?" Quested growled.

"Anyone with half a brain, mate." Harry fought back the temptation to add an insult to that. He didn't actually want to fight Quested in a situation which was plainly not to his advantage. Even with the odds in his favour he would think twice about taking on such a brawler.

"You don't have much use for ears, friend, I'll say that. I already told you to mind your own."

Harry pushed his face a little closer, aware that the noise in the

Paragon had diminished even further, as more people became aware that there was the chance of a fight taking place. Those closest, who realized earliest, and who stood to suffer accidentally, had already edged their chairs away.

"Listen, Quested. I didn't put up those posters. Not that it's any of your business if I did. But the man who carved up Bertles and strung up Bridie Pruitt's man also tried to kill me the other day, by sailing right over the boat Bertles put us in. I don't take very kindly to that, but being in no position to do anything I let it pass. But hearken to this. By sheer chance I came across an armed party getting set to attack my house, in the middle of the night, and it's only by luck that I saw them off. It was the same man. You might not know much about me. But if you care to ask around, I dare say there are enough people who know the name of Ludlow who will tell you that's not something I'll sit still for. So you can warn all you like, friend, I'll set my own course, and if you foul my anchor, I'll not back off. Raise that club to me, just once, and I'll lop off your arm."

Quested looked down at the sword Harry was wearing. There was no fear in it, just the act of a man checking the odds. Then he looked back up, his eyes boring into Harry's. They stood like that for a few seconds, each of them tensed to move at the first hint that his opponent meant to attack. Harry could feel the tingling sensation he always had before an action, as though his blood lacked patience.

"So you've a mind to tangle with this fellow?"

"I'll not wait till he attacks again," Harry replied. "And if you know who he is, I should tell him so."

"What makes you think I know?" Quested growled.

"I won't insult either of us by answering that."

For the first time the batman blinked, as though the mere act of thinking strained his ability. Harry saw a slight chance to take the initiative. Asking him would be as useless as questioning Braine. But a threat might do the trick, however slight. "I'll find him, mate. And if in the process I ruffle a few feathers, or interfere with other people's ability to trade, then so be it."

"You'll wait here, Ludlow," said Quested suddenly, backing off slightly.

"Why should I?" asked Harry, completely thrown by this unlooked for response, for he could hardly believe that his threat had produced such an impact.

"I need to find out how much trouble you're goin' to be. When I've smoked that, I might decide to aid you." The batman frowned. "I had no time for Tobias Bertles. He had too big a mouth for his chosen game. But the man who killed him overstepped the mark. Not in skinning Bertles. That was fair. But he shouldn't have hung the crew."

"You do know who he is, don't you?"

"Happen I do, Ludlow. But I might not say. I might just work out that you're full of piss and wind, an' set my mind to decanting you on to the floor."

"I just want a name."

"As I said, Ludlow, stay here. I'll send someone to fetch you if we want to do business."

"We?" asked Harry.

"Just wait."

"And if you don't return?" asked Harry.

"Then I'll make sure everyone in Deal knows it. Which means you can ask till your ears are blue, you'll get nowt."

CHAPTER NINETEEN

HARRY SAT nursing his tankard of ale, wondering if he'd chosen the right course. He'd been tempted to follow Quested. He might send someone, a lure for a trap; but Quested was the type, if roused enough, to use his club in the market place on the day an Assize was sitting. That was his job as the Aldington gang's chief batman. He was a man who would kill with ease, using his trade-mark club, with its delicate carving, or any other weapon to hand. He also behaved as if he had near immunity from punishment. He walked Deal town fearing no man, including the law. That had been plain from the way he'd warned Harry originally. He was known to all and sundry as a dangerous rogue, a man it would be fatal to cross. Harry doubted if even Braine, who could not be in any doubt about his occupation, would dare to try and accost him without a troop of well-armed soldiers in attendance.

Surprisingly, it was Quested himself who returned, beckoning to Harry from the doorway to join him. He kept a weather eye on the other tables, making sure that none of Quested's previous companions stood to follow, but was reassured by their undisguised curiosity as he passed. If they'd intended to follow him they would surely have pretended to ignore him.

He walked out on to the hard crust of mud that covered the road outside the Paragon. Quested was waiting at the bottom of the street, his round leather hat shining in the glow cast by the lantern above the Paragon's sign. Harry joined him and they turned the corner in the roadway known as Middle Street. Respectable houses and businesses existed cheek by jowl with less salubrious concerns, like the hogs' slaughter house, but in the main it was a

street of numerous noisy taverns. The lanterns on these provided
sufficient light to make the whole thoroughfare a place of activity, with groups singing and the odd fiddler providing the music
for people to dance. Hawkers called to the pair trying to entice
them to cock-fights, and bare-knuckle boxing bouts.

As they approached Portobello Court, a narrow dead-end alley,
the number of whores increased till they could not take a step
without a proposition, and the girls were not the type to let those
who ignored them walk by without an insult. The Hope and
Anchor was on the corner of a wide square, which by the debris
that littered the street appeared to be a daytime market. Now it
was home to bear-baiting, dog-fighting, and the like. Quested
stopped before entering the tavern, examining the square as if sniffing for danger. Satisfied, he pushed his way into the tap-room. It
was crowded to the door, but the crowd found the space to part
as he led Harry through to a table at the back.

Every chair was full. The man at the rear, in the largest chair,
a leather affair with an intricately carved frame, leaned forward
to make a point, exposing some faded gold lettering. His long,
fine silver hair gleamed in the light from the lantern directly above
his head. The motions of the crowd interrupted him, and he
glanced up as they approached, holding up his hands to still the
conversation of the others. The face was sharp featured, lined, and
grey, as though gone to seed through over-indulgence. It was not
the face of a healthy man and the small consumptive cough that
he emitted added to the impression of a creature near death's door.
Huge black rings framed his pale blue eyes. The lips were thin and
wet. With his shiny silver hair and his sober grey clothes he looked
like a proselytizing evangelical parson who drank as much as he
preached, and was close to meeting his maker.

He addressed Harry in a gentle, well-modulated voice, deep and
attractive, which was followed by another small cough. "If you'll
forgive me, sir, I have a small amount of business to conclude.
Pray let Quested know what you would like to drink."

"He'll drink brandy and lump it," growled the batman, with a scant display of respect, before he turned and elbowed his way to the hatch from which the drinks were served.

Harry had a chance to look at the four other men at the table. They were scruffily dressed and pigtailed, and clearly made their living on the seas. Despite their precautions in speaking quietly, the odd word floated up to register in his ears. One of them mentioned a cargo of silk. Judging by the silver-haired man's smiling response, which exposed long yellow teeth, he was not to be disappointed in his attempt to secure a sale, the only problem obviously being the price. They haggled away quietly, before striking a bargain. A final shake sealed their arrangements, and they stood up to leave just as Quested returned with two goblets of brandy.

The silver-haired man leant forward again, gesturing for Harry to sit down. The gold lettering at his back was exposed again: IN NOCTE POSSUMUS. Harry read the inscription as he complied with the request, taking a chair at the side which would afford him a view of the room. Not that he could see much. Once the sailors who'd been dealing at the table left the noisy crowd closed behind them, with much grinning and playful jostling, leaving Harry and his hosts in a space cocooned off from the world outside. Quested took a chair as well, sitting opposite Harry, his goblet of brandy untouched in front of him.

Weighing the odds, Harry could be content, for they'd not invited him to a quieter spot. Here, in the open tap-room, he was relatively safe. No one in their right mind would lay hands on him with such a crowd to witness it. Their host looked anxiously over his shoulder, wet his lips, then favoured him with a benign, thin smile, which contrasted sharply with the glare he was getting from Quested.

"It was good of you to accept my invitation, Mr Ludlow."

"I find myself at a stand, sir, for I cannot reply without knowing your name."

The thin smile again, a second anxious glance, this time at Cephas Quested, followed by another slight cough. "You have an overweening curiosity in that direction, I find. Cephas here tells me that you're after another name."

"I will accept yours as first step, sir."

The man looked at Quested, who nodded. Then he turned back, fixing Harry with his pale blue eyes. "Temple."

Harry's eyebrows shot up. "Are you in any way related to the magistrate of the same name?"

"We are half-brothers, sir, sired by the same father, but different mothers. He is, of course, somewhat younger than me."

Harry looked at Cephas Quested, adding what he could surmise to what he knew. There was no doubt that he was dealing with one of the most powerful smuggling gangs in the town, just as it was plain by his occupancy of the chair that this man was the leader. Yet the fellow lacked stature. It wasn't just his physical dimensions, which were slight, nor his lack of good health. There was no air of command about him, no feeling that those around him either respected him or feared him, one of which would be absolutely essential to hold the loyalty of such a hard-bitten crew.

But it was the name that filled his mind. Smuggling might be common in this part of the world, but it was still crime. To have the leader of a notorious gang closely related to the man charged with upholding the law argued a degree of acceptance above the norm. There was no guarantee that they cared for each other, of course. It was as if this Temple had read his thoughts, for when he spoke he answered the question uppermost in Harry's mind.

"We enjoy a good relationship." Temple flicked a hand towards the glowering presence of Cephas Quested. "Indeed my brother relies on me to keep order in the town. It is so much simpler for me to persuade someone against wrongdoing, since I am not constrained by legal procedure. A word from Quested here usually does the trick."

"I dare say he returns the compliment in some way," said Harry, with a degree of deliberate irony.

"Oh, he does, Mr Ludlow," said Temple, leaning forward and laying a gentle hand on Harry's sleeve, an act which exposed the faded gold lettering again. "We find the petty restrictions that affect most men are not applied to us."

He glanced past Harry again, but the anxious look was gone. Harry took a sip of his brandy, giving himself a moment to think. The buzz of conversation had died behind him, as though the whole tap-room was hanging on their every word.

"Did you command Tobias Bertles?"

Temple shrugged. "At one time. But he was an unreliable cove, given to the kind of pranks that make life warmer than I would like. When he found himself a patron willin' to stand him the money for a ship, I was pleased to see him go."

"Who was this patron?"

The grip on his sleeve tightened a little, and Temple looked slightly confused. Then his grey face took on a shifty look. He gave Quested another glance, as though seeking approval. Harry guessed that he was unlikely to find out the name he was after, never mind the identity of the man who'd backed Bertles. "What did you think when Bertles was murdered?" he asked.

"Only that he very likely brought it on himself."

"And his crew?"

"Few were local. Deal is full of hands for someone willing to pay prime rates."

"Bridie Pruitt lost her man. Was he local?"

Temple looked confused. Quested cut in quickly, with an authority that contrasted strongly with his supposed superior's.

"Never you fret about Bridie Pruitt, Ludlow. She'll find another to buy her bread. Perhaps if Bertles's funds had run to long contracts, he might have had more local men."

Harry's mind went back to the scene of the deck of the *Planet*, to the crew that Bertles had been so eager to impress. What Quested said made sense. There had been no hint of loyalty in the crew, more the air that their captain had got them into a situation for which they hadn't bargained.

"From what I saw, his money didn't extend to buying contraband either."

"Is that so?" said Temple, patting his wrist.

"He was in the process of stealing another man's goods. That's what started the trouble in the first place."

Harry was surprised by Temple's lack of curiosity. It was almost as if he knew what had happened and didn't need to be told.

Temple gave him a sly smile, as well as another gentle squeeze on his lower arm, and spoke almost jokingly. "That sounds like Tobias Bertles all right. And from what I hear, he and his backer chose to rob one of the most hard-hearted bastards in the trade."

"That's the name I'm after."

The eyes flicked towards Quested again, as if seeking permission to continue. "I'm forced to enquire why."

"I should think if you've spoken with your brother the magistrate you'll already know the answer to that. The 'hard-hearted bastard' tried to kill a group of people, including me, who had nothing to do with Bertles and his games."

Temple sucked his teeth. But the sly smile soon returned. "Fellow didn't succeed. Why bother?"

"A party of armed men came to my house last night. The man that led them was the same person who tried to run us down in his ship. It was only by the merest good fortune that we stopped them from doing what they intended."

"Which was?"

"Given his previous behaviour, I doubt it was anything less than murder."

"Now why would he want to murder you, Ludlow?" said Quested with a sneer that made his scar stand out white on his red face.

Harry ignored the tone of sarcasm. "I can take care of myself. But it's not just me. It's my brother as well. I cannot speak for his attitude to the other people in the boat. But if he's prepared to go to those lengths to find us, for we were all witnesses, I must also assume he has them down for mischief too."

"So, given his name, you'd turn him in."

There was a stirring in the silent crowd. But Temple had his eyes locked on Harry, which, despite the obvious commotion behind him, stopped him from turning to look.

"I most certainly would. That is, if I didn't kill him personally."

He'd seen Quested pick up his goblet for the first time, just as he felt the pressure on his forearm increase. But Harry was not prepared for the vice-like grip that Temple took, nor was he ready for the stream of brandy that hit his face, momentarily blinding him as he spun sideways to avoid it.

Hands grabbed him. Little of the brandy had actually managed to get into his eyes, but it was enough to make opening them a painful business. The gag was round his mouth before he could protest and he felt the ropes cut into his wrist as his hands were lashed behind his back.

"I think after last night this'll cheer you up," said Quested.

Harry's heart chilled as he recognized the voice that replied, so high and girlish.

"And I thank you kindly. It was mere luck you found me, for I was to sail on the ebb. So this is Ludlow."

"The very same."

"Then all I require now is some help to dispose of him."

It wasn't Temple who replied, but Quested, and there was a definite hint of tension in his voice. "I've no mind to bring trouble on my head. I think the rest is down to you."

"I didn't request a present, mate," he squealed. "I told you that I wanted redress. I've no mind to carry this bastard down to the beach, scratching and biting, for all this hellhole to see. Anyway, from what I've heard, you've got things set up a treat. A nice cellar all awaitin', from that bone you threw the excise. Don't tell me you're afeart. What's one more buried body to the Smuggler King?"

The high voice turned to an ugly cackle and repeated the expression, which he clearly found amusing. "Smuggler King!"

Harry tried to turn round, to open his eyes to see. He was denied the former by the hands that held him, the latter because he couldn't bear the stinging sensation of the alcohol. There was a pause, which in his blinded state seemed to last for an eternity. Finally Quested spoke, his voice even. "It makes no odds. Better safe than sorry."

"Let's use the tunnels," the other man piped.

"That'll cost," said Quested.

"No!"

Quested spoke like a man who had all the good cards, including those that should have belonged to the gang leader. "Take it or leave it, friend."

There was a metallic crash, like the sound of a purse being dropped. Harry heard the sound of a trap being opened, then he heard that voice again, as high pitched and merciless now as it had been when he'd first heard it in the middle of the Channel.

"You were clever in that damned jolly-boat, mate, never mind your pretty trick with the gravel. My men have been picking bits of stone out of themselves ever since. But it's time to pay the piper. You're about to learn that stealing another's cargo is a death sentence. And just as Bertles died special, so will you, to serve as a lesson to all. With what you've got comin' your way, you'll wish I'd tipped you into the drink."

CHAPTER TWENTY

HARRY COULD feel the air change as he was unceremoniously dropped through a flap in the floor, crumpling in a heap as he landed. It was cool and smoke free, in stark contrast to the air in the tap-room above. The thud of feet on the stone floor told him that several of his captors had followed him through the hatch. He was roughly hauled to his feet and pushed into a stumbling gait. At that point he risked opening his lids a fraction. Several of the men around him had lanterns, which bounced off the chalk walls to emit a glowing light. His eyes stung as the brandy mixed with the cool air, but he could see well enough, through the slits he'd managed, that he was in a long narrow tunnel.

"You must think I was born yesterday, Ludlow," said Quested, who stood just behind him, "coming in 'ere with your cock-an'-bull tales, as if you didn't know what Bertles was about."

Harry couldn't reply, but he shook his head in a vain attempt to let Quested know that he hadn't the faintest idea what he was saying. The other man continued, his angry voice echoing off the walls.

"He didn't have two ha'pennies to rub together one day, then he's walking out to purchase a ship."

Harry's eyes were wide open now, though still smarting. They had just entered a large chamber that appeared to have at least a dozen exits. The spaces between the feeder tunnels were lined with wooden caskets and piled-up barrels of spirits; great bales wrapped in sackcloth sat on top. The air was dry, without that smell of damp that usually pervaded a cellar, which argued a proper supply of air. There was nothing temporary or gimcrack about this.

These tunnels were well dug, properly ventilated, and obviously led to any number of entrances and exits, so that the smugglers, when taking the contraband inland, had a varied choice of places to exit above ground. Too many for an overstretched Preventative Service to watch.

Harry was spun round to face Quested. "You and that damn fool Bertles nearly started a smugglers' war. An' then what do you do, you slimy bastard? You go an' suck up to the Preventatives, and take a hand in the beating of young Digby Cavell."

Harry shook his head violently, which made Quested even angrier, and he swiped him around the head with a clenched fist. It hurt, but Harry knew that the batman had put little effort in to the blow. He looked like the type of brute who had the kind of punch that would fell a bull.

"Are we about to stand round here all day?"

For the first time Harry realized that the smuggler with the choirboy's voice was with them. He tried to look past Temple, to get a view of the real source of his troubles, but he was looking down one of the tunnels, with his back to the men around Harry. Quested glanced over his shoulder too, and kept talking, almost with a spirit of defiance.

"Bold as brass, you was, marching along the street like God Almighty. Showin' away like them other useless sods. There was no cause to beat the lad, unless you paid him. He didn't know nowt. An' then you come and play the innocent with me. Just who in the name of hell do you think you are, an' just how stupid do you take us to be?"

Harry shook his head again, but wearily, for he knew that even ungagged words would fail to deflect Quested's anger.

"You financed Bertles and plotted with him to pinch another's goods. Well, he's paid his price for thieving, an' now it's your turn to pay yours."

Harry's mind was caught between his impending fate and the false impression everyone seemed to have that he was Bertles's employer. The face was an inch from his watering eyes now, still ablaze with anger. He could feel Quested's spittle cooling on his face. But it was the other smuggler, hidden behind Quested's bulk, who pronounced his fate, the piping voice made more eerie by the resonance of the tunnel walls.

"You know how Bertles died, I'm told. I dare say you think that was horrible. But you'll die worse. How long will he last, Quested?"

Harry had to shut his eyes. The batman's breath brushed over his cheeks as he replied. "It ain't been proved, but they reckon a well-fed man can last two or three days buried in shingle. They say he can even hear the rats tunnelling through the stones to get at him. Perhaps, tied hand and foot, they'll start to eat him before he's gone."

The other smuggler let out a squeal of laughter. "I hope so, Ludlow, for by the trouble you've caused me, teaming up with that damned arse Bertles, you damn well deserve it. An' when they've done the maggots'll come along and pick you clean."

The smuggler had no mercy in his voice, at all. It was the same as two nights ago, in the Channel. He was enjoying himself. Harry, fighting to avoid panic, latched on to the mention of two days. He was trying frantically to think who would miss him. Latham might, but then the captain had his own concerns. He would assume that Harry had either returned home or decided to spend the night at somewhere like Portobello Court. Arthur wouldn't even begin to worry for another 24 hours, and given Harry's wandering nature perhaps not then. The man he needed most, Pender, was away in Portsmouth collecting his family.

"An' the beauty is, Ludlow, you'll never be found. At least not until someone decides to pull down the houses fronting the beach. And those who seal you up will never even know. A fittin' end to you, I say, since Cephas Quested tells me you're so well in with the Preventatives."

The laugh that followed, like that of a boy whose voice was yet to break, had an ethereal doom-laden quality as it bounced off the chalk walls. "Enough talk. I want to get out of this damn place."

Harry had all the pieces of the puzzle now. In his mind he heard Braine telling his tale again, just as he recalled the orders he'd given to his men as they left Sandown Castle to take the Cavell boy to the magistrate. As they grabbed him and forced him down one of the feeder tunnels, he managed to get one arm free and turned to kick his captors. The strength that he ascribed to Quested was borne out when the batman fetched him a clout that lifted him bodily off his feet, before sending him crashing to the ground in a heap.

"The pity is, Ludlow," he said, straddling his inert body, "that we don't have time to make sport of you. If I had my way you'd be goin' into that cellar without a single bone whole."

He turned to one of the other men, who was holding a lantern aloft. "Go up into the street and make sure it's clear. We don't want those Preventative bastards coming back from their dinner too early."

The man hurried off as they pulled Harry back to his feet. His head was ringing from the blow, making his movements sluggish. Quested's foot caught him in the rear. "Move on, Ludlow, or I'll break your legs and have you carried."

The man who'd gone ahead with the lantern came hurrying back down the tunnel. "Coast's clear, Cephas. The pigs are at their trough. I've slipped a nipper a penny to keep his eye on them."

Only one of Braine's men saw him enter the Ship Inn, but his reaction was enough to tell his companion who had arrived. Both dropped their tankards with a thud, as though the idea of taking a sip of ale was the last thing they would want. But their attempts at innocence were wasted on Braine. His voice cracked across the crowded room, chilling more than their blood.

"You no-good lazy buggers. I told you to do that job right off, and here you are teasing your gullet with beer."

The two men were up and halfway to the door before he'd finished his sentence, their heads down like badly behaved children expecting a blow. No one remarked on the shaver who slipped out of the door just ahead of them.

"Here," said a gruff voice from behind the hatch, "who's paying for their victuals?"

Braine raised his angry glare towards the voice. Then he lifted Sniff and pointed his snout towards the hatch. "Do you want me and my dog to have a look in your cellar, mate? I seem to recall that you're only licensed to dispense ale on these premises."

There was silence, not only from behind the hatch and from the patrons in the tavern. Few had a cellar, larder, or loft that didn't contain unexcised spirits.

"That's right," barked Braine at the owner, "you stow your whistle, an' just accept that some of the funds you've dunned out of King George are being repaid."

It didn't bother Braine at all that everyone in the room, man and woman, cursed him for a no-good bastard as he left. His men were waiting for him in the street, an act which earned them another angry rebuke. They rushed ahead, making for Farrier Street and the seat of their night-time labours. Braine hoisted Sniff a little higher and strode after them.

The youngster shoved his head through the flap into the cellar. Quested, who was standing closest to it, raised his club in alarm. But he dropped it when one of his companions recognized the nipper they'd set to watch over the Preventatives.

"Get a move on, lads," said the child urgently, gesturing to the men who stood, with shovel in their hands, before the great pile of shingle that filled half the cellar. "Braine has booted them out of the Ship. They'll be here in no time."

The voice was faint in Harry's ears, too faint to make out the words. But the crunching sound of more shingle being piled on him had stopped. He lay, in darkness, aware that the only thing that prevented the small stones filling his mouth was the gag. The cloth was fairly thick, but he had to breathe through it now, because the shingle blocked his nostrils. The metallic clang as the shovels were thrown down was as clear as the vibrations of pounding feet coming to him through the stone floor where he lay. His eyes, still smarting, were closed because they had to be. Even if they'd been open he would have had nothing but darkness. Harry was filled with despair, filled with the knowledge that finally his sanguine temperament and his belief in his own ability were going to cost him his life.

He'd watched them dig his grave, making a dent in the work that Braine's men had already done to carve out a hole for him. He fought them, of course, but his feeble attempts against such odds had provoked amusement rather than annoyance. Getting him on to the floor had been a struggle, and keeping him there while they piled the first heaps of stones on had put a stopper on their grim humour. But it returned as the shingles covered his body first, the weight of his tomb pressing down on his legs and chest, leaving his face till last. Cephas Quested came forward then and took the shovel for the last act of Harry's life. But he crouched to say goodbye.

"Happen there'll be a warm bed going spare, with you gone," Quested gave him a cruel grin. "I will say it's a long time since I came across someone not afeared of me. I hardly ever gets to have proper bouts these days."

Quested looked at the fluid that was still streaming out of Harry's reddened eyes. He put forward a finger and touched it as it ran down his cheek. His face took on a look of mock horror, the same as the voice he used to call to the men behind him.

"Look at this, lads, poor bastard's blubbing."

That voice barked out its impatience again, so high that Harry was sure he could feel it bounce off the floor.

"Bury the sod, for the sake of Christ, so's I can go about my business. I've got near two hundred tons of cargo waitin' for me."

Quested stood up and raised the shovel. For a moment Harry

wondered if he was about to bash his brains out. But it swung down into the shingle beside his head, and he had to close his eyes in a hurry as the heap of stones hit him painfully in the face.

The two men struggled back from the beach with their barrows full of shingle, tipping them in through the cellar door to add to the pile already there. Braine stood in the road, with Sniff in his arms, watching them.

"Best get down and shift some o' that further in," he said.

The two men dropped down into the cellar. Braine put Sniff down and followed them. The dog, not happy to remain above his master's head, jumped down on to the floor and immediately raised his leg to mark the territory.

Braine lifted a lantern and peered around what was left of the room with exaggerated care. The two men, plying their shovels, looked at each other with that air of mute impatience subordinates use when their betters can't see their faces. Braine then tapped and poked the shingle before finally moving away to let them work. Sniff was around the diggers' feet, getting in the way as he always did. One of the men made a mock swipe at the dog. But he was careful that Braine didn't see. The man was fussy about his animal.

The crunching sound of stones being added to his tomb was faint in Harry's ears. Hope had faded. The gag was too thick for any sound to pass. There could be no rescue, or at least none that would come in time. The cold from the damp shingle was chilling him to the marrow and he could smell the salt water that clung to it. He doubted he would live long. In some respects it was like being immersed in cold water. He'd known a man die in minutes after going overboard in northern seas. He prayed that he would be gone before anything started to feed on his body.

He couldn't actually stiffen his body for the weight of the stones on top of him. But every muscle contracted as he heard the first of the scrabbling sounds. He tried to pretend he was imagining it, but with every nerve stretched to breaking point it was difficult.

He also fought hard to put another interpretation on what sounded distinctly like small claws scraping at stones.

Harry hated rats. He'd never loved them as a youngster on his father's ship, but he'd learned to live with them and even, in his later life as a young midshipman, to fatten them up for eating. But ever since he'd had to take them on with his bare teeth, they induced a form of terror in him. Easy to fight during daylight, it was often the stuff of his nocturnal dreams, and he'd often woken in a streaming sweat at the thought of them feeding on his flesh.

Now they would smell him, even through the salty stones that covered his body. Their sensitive snouts would pick up the heat from his body to find him. Animals that could gnaw their way through an oak plank in search of food would not be deterred by loose shingle. He could hear the scrabbling getting louder and louder as they came closer. He prayed to a God he rarely acknowledged to let him die, for he could imagine the rodents starting on his exposed face, rather than his body, covered in clothes.

The first scratch, as a claw scraped his face, just below his eye, heightened the terror to a point where Harry felt he was about to burst out of his skin. Another scratch, firmer this time, as the rodent sought to clear the stones away from his face before it could feed. He waited, his breath trapped in his lungs, for the first of the teeth to sink into his face. The tears that came out of his eyes now had nothing to do with brandy. He was crying from sheer panic.

The first cold touch of the nose made him stretch, despite the weight that covered him. Then the paws went to work again, cutting into his cheek as they burrowed to push the stones back. He could hear the sound of the rat sniffing, right by his ear, as it sought to gain room to bite. The heat of its breath was plain on his cheek. Then that cold nose touched him again, just below his eye.

The warm wet tongue was a shock, nearly as great as that of the anticipated bite. The paws were still going, scrabbling noisily, but beneath him now, as the animal fought to get at the brandy

that had soaked into Harry's clothes. He could hear a voice calling, indistinctly at first, but more clearly as the stones were dug
out from around his ears. The name was burned into his brain.

"Sniff, damn you, get your arse out of there."

The dog was pulled away, whining in protest, and Harry, who
could now open his eyes, found himself staring into Braine's angry
purple face.

CHAPTER TWENTY-ONE

TO SAY THAT Harry wasn't popular was an understatement, and his suggestion that he stay in the cellar while the Preventative Officer fetched him a disguise only made matters worse. It was, of course, an absurd request, made on the spur of the moment. Braine might hold his tongue about Harry's survival, but it was doubtful if the two men filling the cellar could be trusted to do the same. Yet he had to do something. Once word surfaced that he was alive, he had to believe there would be another attempt on his life.

Harry was sitting on the pile of stones that had so recently been his tomb, picking pebbles out of his clothes, while Braine's men fetched yet more barrow-loads of shingle from the beach. His hurried explanations of how he came to be there had singularly failed to dent the exciseman's angry demeanour. In fact Braine had curtly advised him that he had only himself to blame, and he'd be better off minding his nose and sticking to farming.

The reference to farming stung, for Harry hated it, proud as he was of his reputation afloat. He spoke when he should have remained silent. It was clear that he could not count on Braine as an ally. Why this was so he couldn't say. But it was a fact that had been plain from the first time they'd met.

"I think I can hand you the King of the Smugglers on a platter."

Braine snorted contemptuously. "It will take more'n you to nobble Temple, sir."

"You know who he is?" asked Harry wearily.

Braine mistook his tone of voice, seeing Harry's recognition of reality as some kind of criticism. He barked back defensively.

"What do you think I've been about all these years? I've known who he is since I came here. Not that it be much of a secret. But knowin' don't help, for even if I haul him in for something I'm sure he's done, he'll have a dozen men swear that he's innocent, as well as a local jury packed with his half-brother's mates."

"And if he was tried in another court?"

"Magistrate Temple would make sure he weren't, not for smuggling at any rate."

"What if the charge was attempted murder?" asked Harry slowly.

"Never mind murder attempted, Ludlow. He's killed any number of people. Who'd you think put the black on young Charlie Taverner? The same rules apply. Temple don't do his own dirty work. He leaves that to others. Say you can get him before a Quarter-sessions court. He might not be able to get the jury he wants, but neither will you get a conviction. Why? 'Cause you'll never come up with the proof. Temple sits like a spider at the centre of a web, only the strands are dug out of chalk."

He saw the look on Harry's face and gave a ghost of a smile. "Aye, Mr Ludlow. We know about them tunnels an' all, though we're stumped when it comes to where they run."

"At the risk of a rebuke, I am forced to ask if you are at all interested in curtailing smuggling."

Braine frowned, as though the answer to the question was obvious. It didn't make him angry, as Harry intended it should. After all, he'd only just escaped with his life and he felt entitled to a degree of pique that redress was seemingly impossible. The exciseman indicated the pile of stones in front of them, which now filled three-quarters of the cellar.

"I grant you that this shocks me to the marrow. It goes against the grain, an' no mistake. But as to smugglin', you can't stop it, Ludlow. Leastways not with what I've got to hand."

Harry was, if anything, even more sarcastic. "Then why bother with Preventative Officers?"

That needled him. The purple, craggy face, thrown into relief by the lantern at his side, went two shades darker. "We contain it, sir. If it wasn't for us every man on the coast would be engaged in the trade."

"And murder," said Harry coldly. For after the previous two days that seemed just as prevalent.

Braine didn't reply. He merely shook his head, as if mystified. Harry felt there was no point in pursuing matters further, for the truth was obvious. Braine and Temple had some kind of unwritten, probably unstated pact. The exciseman accepted he could not get a conviction against Temple, while the smuggler knew that provided he kept matters within bounds, throwing Braine the odd small success like Digby Cavell and his hogshead of Genever, they could live side by side. Should Braine prove over-zealous the fate of young Taverner could be waved in his face. In some respects Braine was like a partner in Temple's enterprise, making it difficult for anyone else, smaller in stature and lacking protection, to engage in the business in any serious way.

Bertles, by his ill-fated enterprise, had upset their neat arrangement. Both were happy he was gone, so that they could now settle down in peace. Perhaps Braine had been a more energetic officer once. But he had been taught a telling lesson. Harry recalled the way he had related the story about his fellow exciseman's fate, one he'd so nearly suffered himself. But Harry suspected that long before Braine discovered that Preventative Officer's body in the cellar he was aware that Temple could kill him at any time he chose. For what he was getting, acting as a surrogate for a man who took the lion's share of the money that went with his occupation, it wasn't worth dying. Better to live, draw his stipend, turn in enough small fry to convince those in power he was diligent, and leave Temple to get on with his nefarious trade.

"What if I were to bring a charge against Temple myself?"

Braine looked at him, his face registering neither enthusiasm nor displeasure. "You can do that, for sure, Ludlow. But you've seen the lengths they'll go to for what seems, to my mind, a trifling thing. I reckon you'll be dead before you get halfway home."

"What's to say that won't happen anyway, Mr Braine? After all, I've survived one attempt on my life already. What happens when they discover they've failed?"

Braine looked at him from under his heavy brows, contemplating his response for a long time. Finally, as if acknowledging that there was no other way to say the answer, he spoke.

"I've already said I find it hard to believe that Temple would do a thing like this. Not that he ain't capable, mind. I know he is. It's just . . ." Braine waved his hands, as though the word he needed eluded him. The one he finally used sounded, to Harry, wholly inappropriate. "Odd."

The sound he heard in the tavern, of a heavy purse landing on the table top, came back to mind. "There's no nobility here, Braine. He was paid."

But Braine looked as if he hadn't heard him. His eyes were fixed on the beams that held up the roof.

"As I say, a trifling thing. What you was about . . ."

"I wasn't about anything."

Braine turned his gaze on Harry, with an expression of pity on his face. "If you lay low, Mr Ludlow, with the air of a man contrite, I think I can square things so that you'll be left in peace. After all, it was no skin off his nose, and Bertles is gone."

Harry balled his fists to contain himself. Even justifiable anger would serve no purpose for there was a more important aim to be gained. Braine might speak for Temple, indeed believe that he could persuade him to leave Harry be. Perhaps he was right. But the Preventative Officer had not been present when Bertles died. That man, whoever he was, did not have an ounce of pity in his frame. If ever Harry Ludlow had heard the utterances of a man who enjoyed killing for its own sake, it was when he sat off the *Planet*'s quarter.

Perhaps Temple could be stopped, seeing that further action could sorely affect his business, since it could force Braine to do his job properly. But would the real culprit desist? That was where the root of the problem lay. All he needed was the man's name, and some idea of where to find him. Braine knew who it was, and it was worth trying, just once more, to find out.

"And the man who paid Temple, who tried to run me down in the jolly-boat. The same man whom I caught skulking around my house the other night . . . ?"

Braine shrugged but interrupted, clearly not wishing to wait for Harry to ask him to identify the man. "Why did you help a fool like Bertles purchase his ship?"

"Where has this absurd idea come from? I first met Bertles in Flushing, when he already had a ship."

"That's not what I heard."

Harry glared at him. "I shall spare you the need to explain where you acquire your information, sir. But I am speaking the truth, and what's more I can prove it, beyond a shadow of a doubt."

Braine's lined face took on a more positive look. "Then we have here a misunderstanding, Mr Ludlow. If that's the truth, it's just a case of convincing another party it's so, and things can return to normal."

It wouldn't do, not by a long chalk, but Harry composed his face, seeking to appear as if he accepted Braine's statement at face value. This was a problem he'd have to deal with himself, though how he was to go about it was as much of a mystery as any other. But if he couldn't have the Preventative Officer on his side, Harry certainly didn't need him as an enemy. It was more instinct than logic that dictated his reply.

"You wish me to leave the matter in your hands, Mr Braine?"

They could hear the metal wheel of the barrow trundling along the hard-packed earth on the street. This private conversation would have to end anyway. It was a measure of Braine's caution that he nodded rather than spoke, even though it would have been impossible for his men to hear him.

"Captain Latham, I would be obliged by the provision of an escort. I need to get back to Cheyne Court and I have good cause to believe that there are a number of people who would like to stop me."

The elegant soldier looked at Harry's soiled, salt-streaked clothes, his eyes lingering at the point where Harry's sword should have hung, and his eyebrows rose in a quizzical expression. "Have you been set upon again, Mr Ludlow?"

Harry nodded curtly. Latham gave him a little smile but said nothing, being far too polite to enquire about the details. He gave an explanation which was brief and decidedly inaccurate, for he left out mention of Temple and of being buried alive, as well as Braine's offer to mediate on his behalf, confining himself to the fact that an attempt had been made on his life. Even if it sounded feeble in his ears, it was clearly sufficient. The captain turned and pulled the silken cord that would summon a servant to his rooms. Then he turned and opened a large chest. "I shall accompany you myself, sir. And in case we do meet trouble, I shall furnish you with these."

Latham turned round and presented Harry with a box containing a brace of pistols. A servant appeared at the door and he issued a stream of instructions: his riding boots to be fetched from the kitchen at once; both horses, his and Harry's, to be outside the door, saddled and ready to leave, in fifteen minutes; a note to rouse out his sergeant with an order to get an escort party ready, with a corporal in charge, light marching order plus muskets and bayonets. Harry was impressed by his evident efficiency. Latham gave a deliberate impression of studied languor in all his doings. He couldn't help wondering what someone so obviously competent was doing here, building barracks, while the armies across the Channel, retreating before the enemy, so clearly lacked proper officers.

"It is good of you, sir," said Harry. "I would not ask if I thought it unnecessary."

Latham, putting on his sword, favoured Harry with his most engaging grin. His dark brown eyes positively twinkled, which with his olive cast of skin gave him the look of a Barbary corsair.

This impression was enhanced when he pulled the weapon out of its scabbard, obviously relishing the sound it made. He held it up before his eyes, twisting it to catch the light.

"Why, Mr Ludlow, you have quite made my day. You cannot comprehend how bored I am. Not that I would have you set upon for the world, but . . ."

The sword swung through the air, whistling in a quick cut and parry. "May God forgive me for saying so, but I hope whoever attacked you tonight tries again."

"You'd be better off with these," said Harry, holding up the freshly loaded pistols.

The sword whistled through the air again in a repeat of the previous motion. "They do not provide the pleasure of a blade, sir. And I have observed that cold steel terrifies the enemy more than the prospect of a ball."

The horses were ready and outside the door of the Three Kings in the required fifteen minutes. Cath Hogbin, ignoring the baleful eye of her father, watched her hero as they made their way out of the door, her eyes gleaming as she took in Latham's martial bearing. They mounted swiftly and the captain gave her a slight wave. Then he turned to face Harry. "You fear these ruffians will try again, Mr Ludlow. It strikes me, sir, that your survival will be common knowledge soon. Deal is mighty porous in the article of rumour."

"I dare say it is known in the wrong quarters already," replied Harry grimly. He had contemplated sneaking away, but had put that aside on the good grounds that had he done so he would have been on his own and extremely vulnerable to a determined pursuit. Since his survival could not really be kept a secret, then it mattered little how quickly it became public. Latham had obviously come to the same conclusion.

"Then, once we have gathered up our escort, let us parade through the town. Those who mean you harm should be made aware that you are now under the protection of the army."

"You do not fear a riot, Captain?"

Latham shook his head slowly. He knew, as well as Harry, how much a file of soldiers could incite the local populace. "I think I told you that one of my men was shot on the beach last month. I was constrained then by that very consideration, ordered to do nothing. It was an error, Mr Ludlow. It never does to be pusillanimous in the face of a threat. So as to the possibility of a riot, I desire one more than I fear it. Nothing would give me greater pleasure than to turn this den of iniquity on its head."

Harry grinned at him. "Let us make it so, Captain Latham."

The soldier gave his horse a gentle nudge and they cantered off past the naval yard, riding round the dark mass of Deal Castle to the tented encampment in the paddock at the rear. Harry could see that everyone was awake, for lanterns bobbed about the place as the sergeant called out his orders to prepare their escort. As soon as he saw his officer approach he detached himself from that duty and ran to report.

"I want the pickets doubled around the barracks site, Sergeant. I dare say what I have in mind will cause some people to seek vengeance by liberating more of our bricks."

The men had formed up, their capes buttoned against the cold, their muskets at the ready. Latham rode to the front of the troop and turned his horse before giving the order to proceed. Harry came alongside him at the head of his men, excited himself by the noise of their boots crunching on the hard earth.

"Damn it, Mr Ludlow, all we lack is a fife and drum!"

A crowd gathered, as it always does when soldiers march. Latham led his men along Lower Street, sunk below sea-level. The lights of the Old Play House danced on the polished metal of the soldiers' accoutrements, and, since the customers were of the better sort, the detachment was favoured with a huzzah.

Harry shouted above the noise. "I am minded to pass the Hope and Anchor, Captain Latham."

The officer nodded and swung his troops up one of the narrow streets that led to Middle Street. They marched past the innumerable inns and taverns, bursting with customers, their heavy boots crashing in time on the new-laid paving, and echoing off the walls of the tall, narrow houses. The whores of Portobello Court, still working hard, jeered them as they passed. No one stood outside the Hope and Anchor, nor bothered to come and look, even though Latham slowed his men to make the point.

The detachment marched all the way along till the buildings ceased, leaving just the outline of Sandown Castle and the corn mill against the dark, starlit sky. Harry knew as they'd passed the Hope and Anchor that for all the apparent indifference he'd been observed. That pleased him. He wanted to give those who'd wished him harm ample opportunity to observe that their attempt at murder had failed. Let them worry about what he would do next.

"I must of course return to my post. But I can leave the men here for a day if you wish," said Latham.

"I doubt that's necessary, Captain."

"Do you think your servants are sufficient to protect you?"

Arthur shook his head, but Latham was looking at Harry, who nodded emphatically. He didn't enjoy telling Latham a deliberate falsehood. The man had come to his aid in the most timely manner. Mind, he felt he had little choice, for what he planned was likely to lead to a serious breach of the peace. Since its maintenance, under the orders of a magistrate, was part of Latham's responsibilities, it would be best for him to be unaware. Harry doubted that the captain would forbid him to act if he knew. But he dared not risk that possibility.

"The countryside is as close as the town, once alerted. No strangers will be able to get within a mile of Cheyne Court without my knowledge."

Latham looked at the ground and frowned, giving Harry just enough time to gesture to Arthur, bidding him to say nothing.

"You will have seen how long it took us to get here last night. I cannot come to your rescue in time if you are attacked."

"Never fear, Captain Latham. I have any number of neighbours who will be only too happy to assist."

"Then I'd best get my men on their way, lest they become over-familiar with the contents of your larder. They will not take kindly to their rations if exposed to proper cooking."

He turned to face Arthur, giving him a small bow. "May I thank you, Lord Drumdryan, and your wife, for you have treated both me and my men most handsomely."

"It is the very least we could do, sir," said Arthur, returning the bow. "And I am sure I speak for Mr Ludlow when I say that you will be welcome at this house any time your duties permit."

Latham lifted his head and sniffed the air, which was full of the smell of fresh-baked bread. "That is an offer I may be tempted to accept in very short order . . ."

All three men spun round to attend to Anne as she bustled into the room, her cheeks flushed with happiness. She'd taken the escort in hand as soon as Latham arrived, ushering them into the area of the kitchen where they could be warmed and fed.

"Your soldiers' pouches are full, Captain," she said, with a slight air of breathlessness. "If they can be brought to stay their hunger on your way back to Deal, there should be enough to feed your entire detachment."

"Most kind, Lady Drumdryan," replied Latham.

Anne looped her arm through Harry's. "Nonsense, sir. It is poor recompense for your bringing my brother safely home. It would not be remiss to observe that you have probably saved his life."

Harry looked at her closely. She had not been privy to the tale he'd told Arthur. She smiled up at him, though it was accompanied by a creasing of her forehead.

"You need not think I do not know what happened, Harry. Hospitality has its compensations."

"The soldiers?" Harry asked, trying to hide his amusement at the look on Arthur's face. The idea of his wife conversing on equal terms with lowly infantrymen was anathema.

"I have had to allow for a degree of exaggeration. No one made of flesh and blood could sustain themselves, if the captain's men are to be believed." Anne beamed at Latham but said no more.

They all escorted him to the door and watched as he led his men out of the gate, all rosy cheeked from the hot cider punch they'd consumed. Tite, his head still swathed in his theatrical bandage, was standing below them, muttering imprecations against red-coated "bullocks," a breed of men who never rated very highly to a sailor. Anne gave him a very hard look, then led the way back inside.

"I wonder if you could leave Harry and me alone, my dear," said Arthur.

Anne looked from one to the other, then finally settled on her brother, fetching him a look that made him very uncomfortable. "I cannot pretend to understand why you refused his offer of help, Harry."

It was natural to try and bluff, for he could only assume that his sister was guessing. "What offer?"

"Dear brother, I was standing outside the drawing-room door when Captain Latham made it."

"Anne!" exclaimed Arthur.

"I am aware that it is ill mannered, husband," she snapped, in a display of temper she rarely showed in Arthur's presence. Her hand rested on her swelling stomach. "But you will accept that I have other considerations, which are above those of our own safety."

"You have nothing to fear, Anne," said Harry softly.

Her face, which had displayed nothing but strength, collapsed. "I cannot believe that. The people who tried to kill you, in such a barbarous manner, will not spare anyone if it suits their needs. We have ample evidence of that."

Harry wanted to ask what the soldiers had told her, but decided not to, since that might force him to tell the equally horrifying truth.

"I shall provide ample protection for you and your unborn child."

"How? These people are bound to be more numerous than us, even if we can engage our neighbours to help."

Harry half turned to include his brother-in-law. "Arthur. I need the ledger that contains the names of the men who served with me on the *Medusa*."

"Whatever for?"

"I want them here, at Cheyne Court. I have no intention of waiting to see if these people intend to try again. I am about to go on the offensive, and to do that I don't need soldiers to guard my house, I need a party of my own sailors at my back."

CHAPTER TWENTY-TWO

ARTHUR HAD a sheaf of mail from those in high places promising immediate action to curb the lawlessness he'd reported. But both he and Harry knew that to those in power the word "immediate" had a very different construction to that given in Johnson's dictionary, and it could be weeks before such intentions were translated into concrete action. There was private mail too, including a cheering packet from James, enclosing a list of ships presently on the stocks that might be suitable for privateering, with their designs and specifications.

Nothing was more guaranteed to raise Harry's spirits. He was particularly taken with a ship under construction at Grisham's yard in Blackwall, built to a new design by a naval architect called Steppings, specifically for the opium trade. Opium cargoes, destined for China, were compact and highly prized, so they required a vessel with minimal cargo space, great speed and manoeuvrability, accommodation for a reasonable crew, and a good number of cannon to ward off Malay pirates. Harry spread the drawings out on the table and examined them minutely. Flush-decked, the design shared some of the characteristics of an old-fashioned 28-gun frigate, especially in the height of its masts. Though smaller than a proper navy vessel, with the capacity to mount fourteen guns, it was undoubtedly suitable for use as a warship, which was why it had been offered at a premium price to the Admiralty. If the claims of the builders were to be believed, it would combine speed with firepower to make a formidable instrument.

Such a vessel would be a touch larger than anything else he'd ever had, which would present problems in manning and increased

exemptions. But the nature of the war had changed his require-
ments in the last two years. Easy pickings were a thing of the past,
even in the Bay of Biscay, now crowded with British warships and
a host of other privateers. It might be necessary to consider going
further afield, and this ship, properly armed with twelve-pounders
and a couple of cannonades, might just answer for such a task.

There was little gaiety in the accompanying letter, none of the
gossip about those in and out of power and fashion which normally filled his brother's communications. The lawsuit would be
bearing down on him, of course. Harry did wonder what James
would say of recent events. No doubt he would give his older
brother that look which relayed his firmly held view that most of
Harry's troubles were entirely of his own making. He wrote back
immediately, but confined himself to a request that James should
take a trip down to Deptford yard to get some impression from
the builder as to when he expected to launch the ship, and an idea
of the price, ending with a promise that he himself would come
up to London in the near future.

Pender came back along the road to Cheyne Court, with his wide-
eyed children sitting upright in the back of a donkey cart. Two
days on the road, first in coaches, now in this cart, had created
the beginnings of a bond between them, something approaching
their relationship before he fled to join the navy, though the eldest
girl, named Jenny like her mother, was still withdrawn. She was
old enough to understand everything that happened. Looking at
her thin face and blank eyes her father could not but wonder just
how much she had suffered. The boy, Peter, was of an age to see
only pleasure or pain. Once he was released from one, he cheer-
fully accepted the other. Charlotte, the youngest, named after the
queen, was barely walking, her growth and development stunted
by lack of proper care.

If they grieved for their mother it didn't surface, and there was
no hint from any of them that they missed their familiar surroundings. He tried not to make it sound too magnificent, this

new home, for he could not tolerate their disappointment. Yet the closer he came, the more he detailed its grandeur. He pointed to the six brick chimneys, just showing above the trees, as if they alone would underline how warm they would be within the walls. He would have to leave them there, motherless, in the care of others. When Harry Ludlow left, as he must, Pender would go with him. But his children would have a home, he was sure of that, a place where they would be well fed and properly raised.

Tite's musket, which came out of the hedgerow a second before he did himself, had his children, who'd been full of curiosity, diving for the floor of the cart. Pender hauled hard on the traces himself, his heart in his mouth, for he'd been taken by surprise, which was not something he normally allowed to happen.

"You're back, are you?" said Tite, his weapon aimed steadily at Pender's chest. "About bleedin' time."

Pender was angry, still reeling from the shock. He indicated the thick bandage that showed clearly below the brim of the old man's hat.

"I didn't think it was that bad. Or did somebody give you the kind of clout you deserve?"

"You won't be so cocky when you've seen the captain."

The musket twitched slightly, as though Tite was contemplating pulling the trigger. Then he walked forward and looked into the cart, plainly not pleased with what greeted his eyes.

"More useless mouths to feed."

The urge to respond violently was tempting. But he did have the children to consider. Pender didn't want their first experience of Cheyne Court to be the sight of their father booting an old man all the way back to the house. They'd witnessed enough violence recently to last a lifetime. He flicked his whip and forced the donkey into motion, leaving the old man to his solitary duty by the roadside.

Tite gazed at the back of the cart, cursing the driver. The cocky young sod had got off on the wrong foot with him, instead of being a bit humble and accepting that he was older and wiser. Pity, because Tite would have loved to ask him a few things about the captain, not least if he had another lady-love stashed away somewhere; for Harry had, to Tite's knowledge, been nowhere near Naomi Smith, which was a damn shame, because it made the information he had about Drumdryan worthless.

Pender was cursing too. He'd made an enemy of that old man, who would be here when he was gone, able to take out on his children what he could not on their father. Now, in sight of the house, he wondered if he'd done the proper thing bringing his children here. And Tite's words were still with him, too. He had the feeling that something else had happened in his absence. Something damned unpleasant.

He found out soon enough, for Harry did not spare his servant the details. The children were put in the care of Mrs Cray while Harry, plainly delighted to see him, dragged him off to his rooms. Pender watched as he excitedly paced the floor of his office, ticking off what he knew and what he didn't, especially about Bertles's murderer.

"They've got hold of the absurd notion that I financed Bertles. God only knows where that comes from. But even when I convince them otherwise, it won't stop our real enemy. I need to know who he is and where he hails from. Once I've got that I can work out a way to take him. Since nobody wants to volunteer the information, we'll have to find a way of persuading them."

Pender hadn't missed the piratical gleam in Harry's eye, which boded ill for somebody. "Would I be permitted to observe, Captain, that it's a time for clear thinkin'?"

Harry stopped his pacing abruptly and looked at his servant sharply. It was all there, in the look and the bearing, as well as the soft way he'd spoken the words. It was as if Pender was saying, "There you go again, charging in like a bull at the gate, as if such a thing hadn't got you into enough bother already." Harry Ludlow did not take to being checked. Yet he sought in vain for the words that would rebuke this man, who looked him square in the eye with an expression which, on another's face, would qualify as downright insolent.

He tried hard to make his response sound like some kind of censure, but it didn't come off. "You're not suggesting that I sit still and do nothing, are you?"

Pender grinned. "I'm not one to fly direct in the face of nature, your honour."

"Damn you," said Harry, but without rancour.

"If we're to have a war, Captain, we need some men to support us, especially since we'll be working on another's patch."

"I've sent for the men who were listed on the books of the *Medusa*."

"That don't amount to more'n twenty."

It was Harry's turn to grin. "Which is just about the number of men I'd take in the longboat if I was raiding an enemy shore."

"They've got more," said Pender.

Harry was still smiling, the prospect of action having its usual effect on his outlook on life. "They always have."

But it was clear that Pender's questions were having some impact, forcing Harry to examine his plan. What it revealed to him, as he paced up and down, was that he didn't have one. He was operating on instinct in a situation that needed something more definite. Instinct, plus a wealth of experience, might work for him at sea, where most of the factors that ensured success unfolded slowly. But would it do for his present difficulties? This was not his natural element. That was an advantage enjoyed by his enemies. He grinned at Pender again, glad that his servant had made him concentrate. He recalled his earlier words about needing the name. That was paramount. And until he had that he could not get a clear picture of what would then need to be done.

Braine wouldn't disclose it. Temple certainly knew, but he was safe in his tavern, surrounded by his henchmen. An army could attack the Hope and Anchor without success and, even if they could force their way in, Temple would be long gone down his chalk-lined tunnels. And what if he had the name? The man who murdered Bertles wasn't local. He had seen that in the Kellet Gut and nothing anyone had said to him since had questioned that supposition. Quite the reverse, for the brandy in his eyes had not stopped him from hearing of his assailant's desire to get away from Deal. He had two hundred tons of contraband to collect. Where did he land it? It was one thing to know, quite another to do something about it. Wherever he hung out would be just as well protected as the smugglers' hideouts in Deal. His mind turned back to the night he'd woken, as the *Planet* hove to off the French coast.

Bertles had stolen a cargo. But he'd known where to go to steal it, which pointed towards a regular landfall at an appointed time. He needed the name right enough. But more than that he needed the location of the spot on the coast of France where the smuggler picked up his cargo. For if he was going to take him, he would do so in his own natural element.

"How we doing, Captain?" asked Pender, who had been patiently watching Harry as he sorted out his thoughts.

He didn't reply for a moment. Pender's observation about their lack of hands had struck him forcibly, as well as his remark about "having a war." With the best will in the world he could not contemplate that. For a start he had no idea of the odds he faced. How numerous were the smugglers in a place like Deal? Dozens, hundreds? What he had on his hands now was bad enough. More than that, it would be days before the men he expected would arrive. Could he just sit here and wait for that, with the risk that Temple would come to try and get him? Not Temple, perhaps, for he had not struck Harry as the energetic sort. But Cephas Quested might. The batman had required little bidding to do murder. Merely the contents of a purse.

That relationship was not as clear cut as it should be. Quested was more than Temple's right-hand man. In that tavern, he'd sounded very much as though it was he who was in charge. Maybe Temple wasn't such a force after all. He didn't look healthy and didn't sound like a man who took pleasure in his authority. It could be Temple was just tired, and needed someone like Quested to stiffen his backbone. Or it could mean that the balance of power in the gang was shifting to the younger man.

Harry, schooled as he was in the idea that attack was the best form of defence, knew he must do something, if only to give the smugglers pause. Perhaps, with the batman out of the way, he could achieve his aims by talking. Might Temple, bereft of both his protection and influence, and made plainly aware of the trouble Harry could cause, consent to compromise? But he knew instinctively that Quested would never agree to that. And if his voice in the gang leader's councils was anything like as strong as he suspected, he alone could kill any hope of peace. So getting rid of him made sense. He didn't have to die, but perhaps if he could be neutralized . . .

"Do you remember that fellow we ran into in Deal, the batman, Cephas Quested?"

"I'm not likely to forget an ugly sod like him," said Pender.

"How many men would you say it'd take to capture him?"

Pender raised an eyebrow, clearly not content to continue speculation without more idea of what his captain was on about. It was typical of Harry Ludlow that even with someone he trusted completely he was not prepared to go into the complete details of what he thought he should do. Partly he wasn't sure. But there was a real element of revenge in going after Quested, which had nothing to do with his true object.

Harry looked his servant square in the eye. "I think he has possession of the information I require."

"Is he the only one?" asked Pender swiftly, making Harry wonder if his own look had betrayed some of his inner thoughts.

"No," he replied, forcing himself to smile. "But one of them I can't touch and the other, if he has it, won't say."

"And this Quested?"

"He won't volunteer. But he walks about alone, sure that he's untouchable."

"Capturing him won't be easy, but it can be done if you can get him alone. Mind, getting a heavyweight like him out of Deal might be a mite more troublesome still."

"How would you take him?" asked Harry, whose mind was on the batman's club.

"I wouldn't," said Pender. "'Cause I don't see how you could do without near killin' the sod."

Harry looked at Pender again, but this time his eyes were diamond hard. "Would that be so bad?"

CHAPTER TWENTY-THREE

HARRY INSPECTED Pender's children after they'd suffered from the attentions of the cook. They were still painfully thin and clearly terrified, having been scrubbed from head to toe. Their hair was clean and dressed, still damp from the washing. But the two eldest stood to attention at their father's bidding, while the nipper tried to hide her face in her father's shoulder. The cook, Mrs Cray, stood to one side, her eyes fixed on the children.

"Welcome to Cheyne," said Harry, slightly awkwardly. For him, children were generally difficult to talk to. Pender's were no different. If anything they were slightly worse. They had that way of looking at him, with a direct, open countenance, that made Harry think they'd recall every word he said, ready to repeat it back to him should he fail to remember.

"Since your father now works with me, you will stay here. I have asked Cook to sort you out a room at the top of the house and she will also take you under her wing, using you to help in the kitchen. We shall either have a schoolmaster here or you will attend the Charity School in Deal. You will be put to your tables as well as learning how to read and write, for so I promised your papa. Attend to your lessons, carry out the tasks that you are set, and your life here will be happy. But . . ."

Harry had rarely felt such a humbug as he stood there with his raised finger, implying by his stern look that punishment would be swift if these half-starved mites failed in their learning or their duties. Mrs Cray was nodding sagely, her round face cast in a serious mould. But Pender, trying to avoid a smile, did little to help. Harry sighed inwardly. This domestic formality had to be gone through, yet he would rather have quelled a mutiny than lectured these children. If it had been anyone other than Pender, he would have left the task to Arthur.

"They need feedin' afore they can be set to any task," said Cook.

"Then make it so, Mrs Cray," said Harry, happily turning his mind to more pressing matters. "Feed them up."

He couldn't just leave without saying anything. Indeed, after what had happened it made sense to ensure that Arthur knew his destination. Not the details of course. But if Harry had hoped to avoid an argument, he was soon disabused.

"Since the law won't do anything, Arthur, I must."

"The law will do something if you give it time, Harry," said his brother-in-law sharply. He'd spent most of the day writing even more irate replies to everyone in authority, calling on them to act swiftly and put an end to the mayhem. "I am forced to observe that you are displaying your customary impetuosity. What you propose lacks any sense."

Harry stiffened at the rebuke, for no one, however close, had the right to address him in that manner, and Arthur, for all his disapproval, had never dared to talk to him in such a way. He had also, for once, completely lost his natural composure, accompanying the words with a black look, which made matters worse. When Harry added to the list what had happened with Naomi Smith, his brother-in-law was lucky not to be called out for his temerity.

"I am inclined to allow you a degree of liberty, Arthur. But I would not like you to assume that you had *carte blanche* to abuse it." There was no reply, for Arthur had lost the capacity to speak, alarming in a man so naturally urbane. "I shall leave the house well guarded if that's what troubles you."

"You forget that I was a soldier," he snapped, angrily. His voice rose to a near shout. "I don't require you, or anyone else for that matter, to tell me how to set a picket!"

What was amiss? Arthur never allowed himself a display of temper. It wasn't fear, for Harry knew that he was a man as brave as he needed to be. It was another manifestation of the change in their relationship since his return. It couldn't be guilt: Arthur wasn't the type. He resolved to talk to Anne. But that would have to wait. If he was to get to Deal in plenty of time to achieve his aim, he would have to go now.

"Say goodbye to Anne for me, Arthur. Tell her to expect me for breakfast in the morning."

Arthur just turned his back on him.

But Lord Drumdryan watched them depart, half an hour later, with a deep frown. His expression had little to do with Harry's intentions, more to do with the piece of paper in his hand. The letter reminded him that interest was due on his loan. If he defaulted the whole sum was forfeit, an amount of money he could not raise. It would mean going to the money lenders. Only they would accept him now, for he'd pledged all his credit elsewhere in his bid to achieve financial independence. He recalled the day when, upstairs at the Griffin's Head, he'd committed himself to this venture, and wondered, not for the first time, whether impending fatherhood had not pushed him into an unwise decision. Oddly enough, the song "Tom Bowling" came into his head. They'd been singing it downstairs when he left. Not the true version, of course, which had vexed him. He'd met Dibdin the composer, and knew the song well. One line sprang to mind now:. "*But mirth is turned to melancholy.* Dear God," he said aloud, his head raised to the ceiling. "Can I have nothing in this life that does not come from a Ludlow?"

"It makes sense to assume that they have a watch on the road from Deal, so we'll take the roundabout way and approach the town from Sandwich."

Pender just nodded as they made their way out of the gate and turned north-east. The sun was setting behind them, a red ball in the cold evening air as it sank somewhere to the west. They rode through Eastry to the village of Worth, then turned south-east till they met the road that linked Sandwich and Deal, coming into the town on the landward side of the corn mill that stood behind Sandown Castle. Darkness had fallen and with it the temperature. Harry pulled his hat low and his greatcoat collar up, then added a thick muffler to hide the lower part of his face. It was a suitable precaution against the cold night air and he stood little chance of being recognized. But there was an element of display in even this manner of dress, for if he stood still in one place too long, he would, in a suspicious town like Deal, attract a degree of attention.

Pender took their horses to the stables behind the Royal Exchange Hotel, telling the lad to leave them saddled and paying an extra coin for the use of the stall nearest the door. The boy, who seemed a touch dim-witted, watched as he took a musket from the leather holster and headed back out into the street. He walked up to the beach to join Harry, handing over the weapon and the cartouche containing the powder and balls. Harry handed him a piece of chalk in return. "If you're forced to follow him to some place we haven't thought of, try and leave a trail with this. I shall do the same."

Pender, no stranger to low life, had never been in a place with so many drinking dens. Every second doorway seemed to offer the prospect of spiritous liquor or ale. If he'd had a drink in every one he couldn't have sandbagged his youngest daughter, but with a man the size of Quested a look through the door sufficed. And in every place he stopped eyes were on him, some guarded, some curious. But Pender knew a footpad as well as he knew a crimp and it must have showed, for no one tried to engage him in genial conversation, or tried following him out into the street hoping that he'd head for somewhere dark.

Harry, with the weapons well hidden under his greatcoat, took up station on the corner nearest Portobello Court. Despite the cold the streets were as busy as ever, with blue-nosed whores swathed in shawls importuning equally frozen customers, offering warmth as well as gratification. Those who accepted were whisked into the alley behind to reappear in a remarkably short time. Those who declined were exposed to a high degree of ribaldry. Since the latter far outweighed the former, Harry was regaled with a raucous cacophony of highly amusing insults directed at the members of his impotent sex.

Engrossed in this street theatre, he nearly missed Quested. The batman, with his carved club slung over his shoulder, walked right past him, marching towards the beach. It was only the crunch of his metal-studded boots that made Harry turn to look. The batman returned the stare but passed by without stopping, having no idea whose face lay behind the thick muffler. Harry took his lump of chalk and drew a quick H on the wall, added an arrow, and waited until Quested was halfway up the street before setting off in pursuit.

Pender was in the Paragon, which was as crowded and smoky as the night before, when Quested entered. He might only have seen the man once, and that briefly, but there was no mistaking the bulk and the ugly face. He watched as his quarry took a chair at a crowded table. A drink was placed before him and he engaged in earnest conversation. It was always bound to be a difficult choice if this happened, to stay and watch or go and inform. Try as they might, neither Pender nor his captain could think of a set of rules to govern every eventuality. But Quested's settled air decided him, and he slipped out of the door in a manner designed to draw the minimum attention.

"Pender!" cried Harry from across the road. Wreathed in deep shadow, Pender had to look hard to see him. "Over here, man."

He walked slowly across to join him, for there were enough people around the entrance to observe any haste. He turned and looked back at the doorway, his back towards his captain.

"What do you reckon, your honour?"

"We take him at the first chance," said Harry.

"How?"

"We have to lure him up one of these dark alleyways."

"I hope you've got a plan for that, Captain, 'cause I'm damned if I have."

"Cephas Quested," said Harry. The walls, close to on either side, made his voice sound loud and hollow.

The batman stopped and turned slowly towards the darkness. "Who's 'at?"

"Don't tell me you don't recognize my voice, Quested."

It was a measure of the man's confidence in his own abilities, as well as his feelings of absolute security, that he took a step towards the alley, ignoring the drunk that lay slumped beside a wheelbarrow at the entrance. "Don't fuck me about, you swab. Step out where I can see you."

"I don't want you to faint away, Cephas Quested. After last night, you might reckon you've seen a ghost."

"Holy Christ!" Quested snapped. The club was up in the air, but he wasn't stupid enough to leave the safety of the street.

"You said you wanted a bout, I recall," said Harry, stepping forward and pulling down the muffler just enough to show his face. "Now's your chance."

Pender, no longer slumped on the ground, pushed the musket up under the batman's chin. Harry had to speak quickly to stop Quested reacting violently.

"Stay still!" he snapped. "That is, if you want to keep your face attached to your head."

His speed was amazing. The carved club was flying at Harry's head a split second after he swept aside Pender's musket, hitting him with a sideways blow. Harry was saved only because the club hit the wall before it hit him. He fell backwards, dropping on his knee. Quested dived into the alley, arms outstretched, striving in the darkness to get hold of his invisible opponent.

Harry took his full weight as he fell on top of him, which emptied every ounce of breath out of his lungs. In the confined space there was no room to wriggle free, but neither was there room for the bigger man to swing his arms properly. Instead he fumbled about looking for Harry's throat. He'd almost got a grip when Pender hit him with the stock of the musket. His head shot forward, taking Harry on the bridge of his nose. Blood flowed immediately, filling his nostrils and mouth as it gushed out. He could hear Pender's voice calling urgently, a sound interspersed with the thud of something hitting flesh and blood.

Whatever Pender was doing slowed Quested down, but it did not entirely stop him. Harry pushed a hand into his face and felt Quested's teeth sink into his thumb. The gun going off was like the day of judgement in the alleyway, but it illuminated the scene enough for Pender to take proper aim with the stock of the musket and he fetched Quested a blow around the ear which was hard enough to stun even this giant. That didn't afford Harry much relief, for he now had Quested as dead weight on top of him.

"Quick, Captain," called Pender.

Harry wanted to swear at him, to tell him he could not comply: he had little breath, blood streaming out of his nose, a damaged hand, and a cart-horse astride his chest. But his anger helped, and with his servant's pulling and his pushing they managed to raise the inert body enough to allow him to wriggle free.

"Murder! They're doing murder!"

The voice was high-pitched and female, so it carried. Pender, appearing suddenly from the darkness, earned a scream to add to the words. But he'd forced the women to run away, giving them a little time. He ran back into the alley. There was no time for niceties. He made sure that his heels did some damage as he scrambled over Quested's head.

"Get an arm, Captain, and heave him upright."

"No time," gasped Harry, still holding his nose. "We'll have to leave him there. Let's hope you hit him hard enough to keep him out of action for a while."

The noise was getting louder as a crowd gathered at the bottom of the alley. Harry stubbed his toe on Quested's club, which made a ringing sound as it hit the stone wall. He picked it up quickly and the two men ran towards the seaward end, emerging into the street near the Three Kings. Harry ran on, down the alley to the beach. The sound of the surf on the shingle drowned out all the other noises as he bent down close to the water, cupping his hands to wash the blood off his face.

CHAPTER TWENTY-FOUR

HARRY TURNED to find himself alone. There was no sign of Pender, yet he had definitely followed him through the alleys that led to the beach. Gently he touched his nose, which was luckily intact, wincing as his finger made contact with the swollen bridge. Then he saw the barrel of the musket glinting on the shingle, with Quested's carved club lying beside it. He bent down to pick it up, grabbing the cartouche that lay beside it so that he could reload. The light wasn't good, but the phosphorescence from the surf helped, and he was performing a task he'd completed a thousand times. The weapon was reloaded and ready for use by the time Pender returned. "Where have you been, man?"

"Had to find out how we'd got on, your honour, so I joined the crowd that got Quested out of that alley."

"Are you mad? What if you'd been spotted?"

There was a slight note of asperity in his servant's voice. "Who's goin' to spot the likes of me in a crowd?"

"Did you find out anything?"

"Quested is out cold, with a lump on the back of his neck the size of a goose egg. And there's blood aplenty. They carted him off in a barrow to the Hope and Anchor. It's my guess, from looking at him, that he won't be upright this age. That is, if we haven't killed him, which I truly hope is the case."

"It won't bother me, Pender."

"This is England, your honour. Not someplace foreign."

Harry barely heard that remark, his mind being fully occupied in finding a way to take advantage of Quested's absence, temporary or permanent. He had to find a method of bringing his involvement in this event to Temple's attention, but in a manner that would not initiate a violent response. It would help if he could disperse the rest of Temple's protection, as well as dislodge him from that damned tavern.

"We need a couple of bottles, a lantern, some rags, and turpentine," said Harry, casting around the beach for a big enough stone.

The Hope and Anchor boasted of its supremacy as a tavern by having large windows made up of thick glass in eighteen-inch panes, something which cost a great deal of money, even without the imposition of a window tax. It was a way of saying "damn the expense" as well as damn the authorities, for any man who stood close enough could see through the panes and make out what was going on inside, which should have been anathema to a place engaged in covert trade. Harry Ludlow remembered that glass from his previous visit and prepared to make the man who owned the place pay for his arrogant display.

They went first to the stable, replacing the unwieldy musket in its case, taking instead a pair of pistols from Harry's saddlebags. Pender kept Quested's club well concealed from the stableboy. Anyone from Deal would recognize it instantly. Then they went shopping. In buying the things he needed Harry had been tempted by the idea of knocking up a ship's chandler and purchasing some powder, but much as the idea appealed, he didn't want to blow the place up, or even destroy it. His intention was to demonstrate that he was capable of causing a great deal of trouble: so much trouble that he would be better accommodated than harmed. On their way back to the beach to make their preparations Pender had helped himself to a metal-topped boathook, which he'd lifted out of the hands of a drunken and indifferent longshoreman.

"Better than stones, I reckon," he said, to Harry's enquiring look.

"Greatcoats off, Pender," said Harry. "Otherwise we won't be able to move properly. We can hide them in one of the boats."

"Hats as well, your honour, I'd say." He held up Quested's

decorated club. "And this too. It might bring on unwelcome attention."

Harry whipped off his tricorn hat. Pender rolled everything neatly around the club and stuffed it under the thwarts of one of the fishing boats, then picked up one of the round pieces of wood that the boatmen used to get their boats well up the beach out of the water. After a final check of their inventory they headed towards the Hope and Anchor, ducking through alleys to avoid any unwelcome attention.

There was an open-air cock-fight taking place in the square. Harry and Pender stood on the edge of the throng, waiting while the bets were placed. As soon as the fight started the crowd edged forward, leaving the two men some clear space. They turned towards the tavern and made ready. Pender slipped the round pole from the beach into the two handles on the door, barring it.

As the noise behind them rose in a crescendo, Harry knelt by the tavern wall and opened the lantern, poking the turpentine-soaked rag in the bottle into the flame. It caught slowly and he put it aside, following up with another bottle. As soon as the second one was alight, Pender swung the boathook as hard as he could, choosing a square pane which looked as though it already had several faults.

The first blow merely cracked the glass, and no doubt caused a few of the customers to jump away in alarm. Certainly someone was trying in vain to pull the doors open. The second blow shattered the glass completely. Pender poked at the pane to make the gap larger, while Harry stood back from the wall, both flaming bottles in his hands. Pender, satisfied that he'd done as well as he could, turned towards the tavern door, the boathook raised to take on the first man to force his way through. This action was none too soon, for the piece of beach-wood, which had been soaked so many times it was extremely brittle, cracked in half. An angry face appeared at the broken window, the mouth open, ready to yell abuse. But the sight of a flaming bottle coming straight for his head made preservation his priority.

He heard it shatter as he threw the second. It missed its mark and broke on the frame, but most of the contents went through, spreading a fine quick blaze. It looked as though the second was going to be more impressive than the first. His yell to Pender came just too late, for men were beginning to pour out of the Hope and Anchor, to run full tilt into a swinging blow. The vicious metal hook, surmounted by an equally dangerous spike, cut towards their heads, catching their leader across the face. Pender jabbed at the others, forcing them back through the door.

The crowd behind was yelling its lungs out, encouraging one cock to go for a clean kill. But the flames had attracted the attention of those closest to them and some of the crowd had turned towards the tavern. Harry grabbed at Pender's arm to haul him away. More and more of the crowd were turning to face them. Harry took out both his pistols and pointed them. The mere sight of these did wonders to kill curiosity and they ran for safety, heading for the beach and darkness.

Behind them the yells of panic grew as the blazing turpentine started to work on the paint, and those who might have chased them were taken with containing the fire. They disappeared easily, running through alleys and doubling back on themselves to fool any pursuit. They got back to the beach and hauled out their greatcoats. With those, and their hats crammed on their heads, their appearance was entirely altered. Pender stuffed the club inside his coat and they returned to the tavern to see the results of their efforts.

Mr Magistrate Temple had got a water engine on to the scene in double-quick time, though a line of water buckets had done most of the work. He stood in his heavy black coat directing a stream of water on to the smouldering wood around the window. The actions of the pump were clearly excessive since any fire inside had already been contained. Harry, edging close, saw that the magistrate had an air about him, as though he was using a toy that saw too little daylight. He was encouraging the two men on the pump to push harder, while others had an endless stream of instructions to clear the heavy canvas hoses to avoid kinking. One of the men pumping, no doubt suffering from a degree of exhaustion, must have said something about the excessive nature of their efforts. Mr Magistrate Temple, his eyes ablaze, turned on the poor fellow, his temper more heated than the dying fire.

"Pump harder, man. Let the people of the parish see that their rates are not wasted."

"Belay that pump!" shouted a voice from the tavern door. "You're flooding the fucking cellars."

"I will not risk the town for the sake of your stock, sir," shouted the magistrate.

"If you keep that a-pumpin' you'll flood the blasted town!"

"Go on," came a voice from the crowd, "let him have his fun. Cost a fortune an' it's sat in his backyard since he bought it."

The magistrate spun round, if anything even angrier. "Fun! What fool termed this fun? You'll call it fun all right when there's a real blaze and I decline to use my waterpump. We'll see how much fun it is when the whole of the Middle Street is ablaze from end to end!"

A female voice called out next. "I like a man who pumps long and hard."

Another female, probably one of the whores who wandered along from Portobello Court to watch the event, joined in the ribaldry. "Especially if it's long and thick."

"Here, try this for size."

The two women whooped as a man at the front of the crowd, definitely drunk, spun round. Ripping open his breeches, he exposed himself to the whores and those around them. The whole crowd now seemed to cry out at once, with one droll remark drowned by the next, all overborne by the cries of the more staid women. Temple, his square face bright red with anger, yelled in vain, trying to persuade his fellow citizens that they were witnessing the triumph of his municipal foresight. His men seemed to sense that the whole thing was over, for they stopped pumping without orders. Eventually their leader noticed this and with a nod gave them the command to rehouse the hoses.

"Secure the engine and take it back to my stable," he said. Harry and Pender were close enough to see that he was dejected. As he walked off, heading back to his house, Harry nudged his servant and set off in pursuit.

Mr Magistrate Temple, who'd opened his front door before he realized he was not alone, looked hard at the front of Harry's greatcoat, which was liberally spotted with dark blood-stains, then at the swollen nose, both illuminated by the light from the hallway. His words were as unwelcoming as his look.

"If you wish to see me, sir, then I suggest you return in the morning. I am just about to retire."

No one had laid a hand on Temple for years. His eyes nearly popped out of his head when Harry grabbed his stock and pushed him unceremoniously backwards, Pender following him in, shutting the door quickly. Harry forced him back into his drawing-room, pushing him towards the blazing fire.

"You will see me now, Mr Temple, or you'll find yourself retiring to Maidstone gaol."

There was surprisingly little strength in his small, stocky frame, but the voice didn't lack power. "Unhand me, sir!"

But Harry wasn't finished with his threats. He tugged hard at the linen bunched in his hand. "Or it might even be the end of a rope, for being a party to murder, robbery, and smuggling."

Temple opened his mouth to speak, to protest further, but Harry held up the intricately carved club he'd taken from Quested, and he stood, mouth open, as he tried to make sense of this object being carried in another's hand.

"This club is familiar, is it not?" said Harry. "It belongs to the man you rely on to keep order in the town, the man who works for your half-brother, the self-styled 'King of the Smugglers.'"

Temple's mouth was opening and shutting as he sought to speak, but Harry, in his anger, had taken such a tight hold that speech was difficult. The man's face was now very red.

"You'd do well to remain silent, Mr Temple, while I explain to you just how much deep water you are in."

"I think you're choking him, your honour," said Pender calmly. If anything Harry tightened his grip, which produced a gratifying reaction in the protruding eyes. "It's no more than he deserves, Pender."

"I would not make so bold as to doubt it, Captain. But I would observe that with the magistrate dead we'll be no further forward."

Harry relented just a little, enough to allow the man some breath. Temple looked set to protest again, but Harry held up a stern finger to stop him. "Say nothing, sir, and listen. I know of your arrangements, how you set about keeping the peace. I know what your brother does and where he stores his contraband. I dare say that you both have tidy fortunes. If you wish those maintained, intact, you will do exactly as I say. Otherwise I will beggar you, and drown your peace in such a degree of trouble that the foundations of the town will tremble. Your brother tried to murder me last night, and it was only the hand of Providence that caused him to fail. If you wish to protect him from my revenge, then you will summon him here forthwith. You will pen the note as soon as I release you, and say nothing till he arrives." He tightened his grip again and shook hard while waving Quested's club, with its snakes and dragons, before his terrified eyes. "Otherwise you won't live to see the sun rise. Your brother is to come here, and alone."

Whatever regard existed between the two Temples did not extend to self-sacrifice. The look in Harry Ludlow's eyes, coupled with the behaviour he'd already shown, could only leave one impression: that he intended to kill. Yet the man before him sat down and penned his note with such haste that Harry could only surmise one thing: if a Temple was to die, the magistrate was intent on ensuring that it would not be him. As soon as he was finished Harry took the note, read it quickly, then handed it back to Temple to be sealed. Then he gave it to Pender.

"Find someone to deliver this."

"I can do it myself, your honour."

"No," said Harry. "I want you here."

Pender went out. The pause, while Harry's attention was elsewhere, seemed to have restored some of his composure.

"I remember you, sir, from the other day. How dare you come into my house and manhandle me? You won't get away with this, Ludlow!"

Harry had been inspecting a small door, one of two situated on either side of the fireplace. "Is that a cupboard for dressing wigs?"

"Yes," said Temple.

"Then I suggest you wait in there till your brother arrives." Harry opened the door and beckoned for him to get to his feet and go in. Temple waved his hand, as though the dust from the wig cupboard was already in his nostrils. Then he pointed to the door on the other side of the grate. "I would prefer that one."

Harry shook his head and passed him a candle. "Powder your wigs while you're there."

Temple gave him a sour look, but a twitch of the club made him scurry to comply. A chair under the handle of the door secured it. Pender returned after a few minutes to find his master seated comfortably in a wing chair at the other side of the fire, the carved club by his side and the pair of loaded pistols on his lap. He handed one to his servant.

"What now, Captain?"

"We wait, Pender."

His servant nodded, took a high-backed chair, and sat down behind the open door.

"They're taking their time," said Pender.

"You don't reckon he will come alone then?" asked Harry, smiling.

"Would you?"

He just shook his head and held up his pistol. "I must talk to him, Pender. Even if he arrives with an army at his back."

They heard a creak as the front door opened, felt the draught around their feet as the blast of cold air entered the building. The footsteps were slow and measured as they crossed the bare oak boards of the hallway.

A man, tall and stocky, dressed from head to foot in black, stood in the doorway. Harry couldn't really see the face, for he had a wig on under a broad-brimmed hat. But the height and girth made him curse, for the last thing he needed now was someone calling on the magistrate to enlist his services. Whoever he was, he must have sensed Pender's presence, for he used his cane to push the door open till it knocked against the servant's chair.

"My brother?"

"Your brother," said Harry, lamely.

The man reached into his pocket for a piece of paper, looking at it before he turned his eyes back on Harry. "Are you the one who sent this?"

"Temple?" asked Harry, his voice betraying his uncertainty.

He didn't even nod, as though to answer in the affirmative was superfluous. Harry, still confused, threw the carved club at the man's feet. The stranger stared at it for a while, then raised his head to look at him. "There's been a spot of mayhem in the town tonight. I dare say you're the fellow who smashed my window and chucked in a couple of bottles of turps."

"I was tempted to use grenadoes. Nothing would give me more comfort than to blow the place apart and line the Hope and Anchor's walls with blood."

The mention of blood made him recall his first question. "My brother?"

"Are there three Temple brothers, sir?"

He looked at the paper in his hand again. "An odd question."

"I met a Temple last night, sir, at your tavern. He was not remotely like you."

The voice had been even and cold, but now it took on a different, dangerous quality. Harry was left in no doubt he was dealing with a man who had natural authority in abundance.

"I require news of the magistrate."

"He is safe," said Harry. "Unlike some people I know, I find the murder of a defenceless man difficult to contemplate."

The man frowned at this, as though Harry was levelling some false accusation at him. The magistrate must have heard the voice, for he started knocking on the wig-cupboard door, calling to be set free.

"Am I to be allowed to see him?"

Harry nodded to Pender, who made his way across the room to remove the chair and open the door. The squat figure emerged dustily from his temporary cell, brushing furiously at his clothes. The man in the doorway didn't move, but his head jerked towards the magistrate, as if to reassure him.

"You have yet to answer my question," said Harry.

"Which is?"

"Who you are, for you are not the man I met last night. He claimed to be the magistrate's brother. Another member of the family perhaps?"

"The only two members of my family are in this room, sir."

"Then who was it sitting in King's chair in the Hope and Anchor last night?"

"I have no idea, sir. I was not even in Kent last night, let alone Deal. I returned from Sussex this afternoon, after an absence of two weeks."

"But your name is Temple?" asked Harry, still uncertain.

The man waved the note. "If it was not, why would I be here? Now you will be so good as to oblige me with some explanation. For instance, you could begin with your name."

CHAPTER TWENTY-FIVE

"HARRY LUDLOW." He looked for a reaction. There was none. "And you, are you indeed the Temple who terms himself the 'King of the Smugglers'?"

"Only a fool would answer the second part of that question."

"You are the magistrate's brother?"

The man waved the note again. "I am Jalheel Temple, and this was addressed to me at the Hope and Anchor."

"I would like you to come in and sit down," said Harry. He did his best to disguise the confusion that the reply had engendered. The man glanced at the edge of the doorway, as if to indicate that the present position afforded some protection. Then he shook his head and waved to his brother to move away from Pender and his pistol.

"I think not."

Harry smiled as he glanced behind him, for Pender didn't have to move his gun far to ensure that the magistrate stayed rooted to the spot. Then he turned his attention back to the brother.

"How many men did you fetch along?"

Temple didn't blink. "Enough."

"Enough for what, sir? Your safety or my disappearance?"

"I find myself at a stand, sir. For I have no idea what you're talking about. The nature of this note, asking me to meet my brother alone, made me curious. It also made me cautious. But I will not move one more foot till I have some notion of why I'm here."

Harry, when he finished explaining what had happened in the cellar, as well as the Hope and Anchor, was convinced that the real Temple knew the man he described, and despite his efforts to avoiding showing anything, the impersonation had annoyed him. But he would not name him, despite a request to do so. The whole tale of this incident had clearly affected him deeply: his body became tenser as Harry related his tale. He did acknowledge Cephas Quested, who was, according to his employer, still out cold in an upstairs room at the tavern. As to the identity of the other smuggler, the cause of all this mayhem, getting that name was simplicity itself. But Temple observed that it was important to this man with the gun, and used the information to trade. He gestured to Harry, then to Pender, still threatening his brother.

"I cannot consent to continue with these pistols at our heads."

Harry lowered his own weapon and indicated that Pender should do the same. The magistrate collapsed on to a chair in a sweating heap. His brother walked over to him, interposing himself between Pender and his prisoner, to reassure himself that he had suffered no harm.

"He's suffering from fright," said Harry, impatient for the name.

"Trench," said Temple at last, turning. For the first time, free from the shadow of the doorway, Harry had a good look at him. The face was pale skinned, with high cheekbones and a slightly hooked nose. The lips were thin and unsmiling above a square jaw and the blue eyes held Harry's in a steady gaze. "The man's name is Obidiah Trench."

"He is a smuggler?" asked Harry.

"I thought you knew that?"

"I wanted it confirmed."

Temple raised his voice, as though talking to someone other than Harry Ludlow. "At least my brother is safe now."

The slight draught on the back of Harry's neck alerted him first, Pender's sudden attempt to threaten both the Temples second. But the older Temple swung the head of his metal-topped cane, catching Pender on the wrist. The pistol, now pointed at the floor, discharged itself with a loud crash. Pender didn't drop it, but it was clear, as he spun away clutching his wrist, that his hand was temporarily useless. Harry's raised pistol brought the first smile he'd seen to the other man's face. Given that it had a gloating quality, it did nothing to reassure the recipient. The words were even more chilling.

"There is a pistol about three feet away from the back of your head, Mr Ludlow."

"And mine is pointed right at your chest," replied Harry.

"Ten feet to three," said Temple. "I would say the odds are in my favour."

Harry now smiled, partly to bluff his opponent, but more at his own failure, for he been given an earlier clue. Now he knew why the magistrate had wanted to be placed in the opposite cupboard. There was a secret passage, no doubt connected to the underground tunnel system. One of the smuggler's men had used that to get behind him, waiting till his employer had got close to Pender before opening the door. His near shout had been the signal.

"Well, Mr Ludlow?"

Pender was looking over Harry's shoulder. He nodded to his captain to confirm the danger he was in.

"You are relying on two erroneous suppositions, Temple."

The thin lips actually parted as the smile deepened. "Am I, indeed?"

"The first is that I am an indifferent shot, and the second is that I will submit to the possibility of another attempt to bury me alive."

The smile disappeared. "I have no intention of trying to bury you alive, sir."

"You will forgive me," Harry snapped. "On such a short acquaintance, I do not feel able to rely on your word."

"It is that or a bullet, sir."

"Be assured that you will survive me by less than a second."

It wasn't true, and Harry hoped to God that Temple wouldn't see the flaw, for there was no way a man who took a ball in the back of the head could aim his own weapon. Did Temple know that you could only hear a pistol ball after it had passed you, that it would be lodged in Harry's skull before he even knew the trigger had been pulled? They stared at each other for several seconds. Harry wasn't the only one in the room holding his breath.

"Why did you come here, Ludlow?" asked Temple.

"To talk."

Temple waved his hand, not only indicating what was taking place in the magistrate's drawing-room, but the whole town of Deal. "You could have achieved that without all this."

The reply to that was difficult, for Harry knew he had to pacify him. The man who stood before him was nothing like his impersonator. He had natural authority, seemingly abundant personal courage, and plainly a high degree of self-esteem. Being threatened offended his pride. Involving his brother, notably less stalwart, probably incensed him. He might well seek to resolve matters in a way that would satisfy his anger, rather than his interests. So his voice, when he spoke, was devoid of bravado.

"Permit me to ask what you would do, sir, if someone buried you in shingle?" Temple didn't reply. Harry pressed home the advantage the pause gave him. "Hardly the stuff of polite conversation. Indeed I doubt if most people would seek an accommodation at all. My calling card should not have been an insignificant bottle of turpentine. Indeed, I had good cause to use several barrels of powder."

"Then why don't you?"

"I am quite capable of going to war with you, Mr Temple. And I could set the whole of east Kent alight in the process, which would certainly make your present trade difficult, if not impossible. On the other hand I have property close enough to Deal to be vulnerable . . ."

He didn't finish the sentence. Temple was quite capable of working out the situation for himself. He jerked his head to acknowledge the threat to his rear. "Matters have come to a head sooner than I anticipated. But they must be resolved. The threat of death hangs over me still, and for reasons I do not understand, discounting a sheer love of murder. Until that threat is removed, I have no choice but to act aggressively."

Temple stared hard at him, then raised his eyes to the man behind Harry, jerking his head in dismissal. "Close the door!"

The cold stream of air, drawn into the hot room by the blazing fire, ceased. Pender's eyes, which had never left that weapon, swung back to Harry's, providing double proof that the threat was removed.

"It is now your turn to demonstrate a little good faith, Mr Ludlow," said Temple.

If he was going to get out of danger, Harry had to go now, before a message could be got back to the Hope and Anchor. Temple's companion, whoever he was, would be scurrying through those tunnels to alert the rest of the gang. Five minutes from now the whole place would be surrounded by armed men—if it wasn't already. Temple must have smoked his dilemma, for he favoured him with that cold smile again.

"It is never easy to drop an advantage."

"It could cost a man his life," replied Harry enigmatically.

Temple shook his head. "No, Ludlow. If you were intent on killing me, my brother would have been dead by the time I arrived, and I would have followed very swiftly. And if it's any comfort to you, this house has been surrounded for quite some time."

Temple whipped off his hat, jerked at the tails of his coat with both hands, and sat down in a chair next to his silent, shivering brother.

"You can put up your weapons."

"Have you heard of the Hawkhurst gang?" asked Temple, who'd seen his shaken brother off to his bed before resuming his seat. He glanced at Pender, who'd moved to block the door that led to the tunnel, but if he bothered him he didn't let it show.

Harry recalled that notorious bunch of rogues. He himself had barely been born when the Hawkhurst gang had been at their most active, but at their peak they had terrorized the whole of southern England, becoming more than mere smugglers as they raised their trade to unprecedented levels. As business had increased so did their numbers, and with it their propensity for violence. Such an enterprise could not be hidden from view. It therefore became essential to ensure that what was plain to every eye was never mentioned by any mouth.

Entire villages were burnt to terrorize the inhabitants of Sussex. Pitched battles were fought with the excisemen, who could not fail to intercept a fair proportion of such an abundance of contraband. Eventually things had got out of hand, and the authorities, who usually favoured a benign attitude to the trade, had to acknowledge that the Hawkhurst gang were more than "Honest Thieves." They had become a government in their own right, threatening the stability of an entire region of the state. The army was called in, the gang rooted out and destroyed.

"It is not commonly known that the information used to destroy the gang, the location of their hideaways, was provided by their fellow smugglers," said Temple.

"For their own self-preservation, no doubt."

Temple nodded, acknowledging that Harry's remark had saved him a great deal of explanation. "Precisely, Mr Ludlow. Everyone's operations were affected by the Hawkhurst people. The larger they became, the more they pillaged our trade."

"This was all a very long time ago," said Harry.

Temple nodded. "I was young myself then, but I can remember the anger my father directed at their activities. He was a close associate of Aldington, and a prime mover in the notion that the Hawkhurst excesses should be curtailed."

"What has all this got to do with Obidiah Trench?"

"He comes from that part of the world, Mr Ludlow. He is, in some respects, a successor to the Hawkhurst gang."

"He certainly shares their taste for blood," said Harry sharply.

"I grant he lacks gentility," said Temple, with a fine degree of understatement.

"And Tobias Bertles?" asked Harry.

Temple frowned, though whether it was the name or the way Harry was forcing the pace of the conversation wasn't plain.

"Imagine, for it became common knowledge after a time, what attitude the Sussex men have for their fellow smugglers in Kent."

"I doubt it's warm."

"You are right, Mr Ludlow. Competition ensures that there is little love lost anyway. But history conspires to make them even more suspicious."

"So when someone like Bertles, so clearly a Deal man, starts purloining their contraband . . . ?" Harry left the conclusion up in the air.

Temple wasn't pleased. He gave Harry a suspicious look. "I find you know a great deal more than I suspected, Mr Ludlow."

"You forget, Temple, that I was aboard the *Planet*. I saw Bertles at his labours."

"How many times?" snapped Temple.

"Just the once," replied Harry evenly. "I was returning home from Flushing after eighteen months abroad."

Harry could see that Temple wanted to pursue that line, for reasons that he neither understood or cared about. He posed a quick question, beating Temple to it. "Did your being in Sussex have anything to do with Bertles's activities?"

There was anger now, along with a decided mistrust at the pace of Harry's thinking. "It had everything to do with it, sir. I went there, personally, to reassure Trench and his people that we knew of Bertles, what he was about, and that we would take care of him ourselves."

"What did you have in mind?" asked Harry, softly. "The fate of that young exciseman, Charlie Taverner? Burial in a cellar?"

Harry felt he had hit home. Temple bit his lip in an effort not to react. Instead he fought to keep his face from betraying his feelings, and waved his hand in an uncharacteristically fey gesture. "That is academic now, is it not?"

It was then that the truth started to dawn on Harry. "Did you see Trench?"

"Of course."

"When?"

"What difference does that make!"

"You said that you have been away two weeks, sir. Yet you saw Trench, who was off the coast of France seven days ago. That means you met him at the start of your visit. It follows that if you did, you gave him your reassurances. Yet within days Obidiah Trench found Bertles trying to steal his goods. Are you sure you didn't alert Trench, and give him *carte blanche* to kill Bertles, in any manner he chose?" Temple was silent, which Harry took as an acknowledgement. "I've seen him and heard him, Temple. The man is as mad as he is dangerous. The way he murdered Bertles and his crew was sheer barbarism. Did you throw him the crew, or was he supposed to leave them be?"

"I think I have made a mistake in underestimating you, Mr Ludlow," said Temple coldly.

The way that Trench and Quested had talked to each other came sharply back in to focus in Harry's mind. Not friendly, for sure. But for the two men to be dealing with each other at all, behind the gang leader's back, argued that Temple was far from secure in his own backyard. "Have you underestimated Trench, as well?" he asked.

"That is my concern, sir!"

There was a hint of self-satisfaction about that, as though the subject, like the late Bertles, was academic.

"I take leave to differ. Trench has attempted to kill me three times. I cannot believe that he will stop trying."

"If your presence aboard the *Planet* was, as you say, an unfortunate coincidence, then this can be remedied. Trench hoped that he would find the owner of Bertles's ship at the same time as he found his thief. Perhaps he thinks you are that person."

"I begin to see. You offered both Bertles and the man who financed him as peace offerings."

Again Temple declined to acknowledge Harry's statement,

merely repeating Braine's reassurances. "If there has been a mis-understanding, it can be remedied."

"Would there be any point in my asking whose name you gave Trench?"

Temple dismissed this. "I didn't give him a name, Ludlow. The information we had came from an unimpeachable source, but it didn't run to a name. But when Trench pressed me, which he did, most emphatically, I gave him what information I had."

"For some reason he has confused me with this fellow. I really think that I too should be privy to that information. I too would like to locate him."

"To warn him, no doubt. No, Ludlow. If Trench wants him, let him have the fool."

"How much faith do you repose in Trench?"

The sudden change in direction rattled him. He reacted sharply. "That, if I may say so, sir, is truly none of your concern!"

"Perhaps not. But he hails from the same part of Sussex as the Hawkhurst gang. He certainly shares their taste for violent solutions. When we were off the coast in Bertles's ship, I saw three sets of masts, all somewhat larger than any lugger or the twelve-oared cutters you use. He's working on an industrial scale, Temple. That might present a worry to a man who could remember what things were like in the sixties."

Temple's eyebrows arched, making him look like a character in the drama, a man playing the part of a patent liar. "Mr Ludlow, for the life of me, I cannot see what you are hinting at."

"Can you not, sir? I think you can. You saw Obidiah Trench two weeks ago. You gave him your message, whatever it was. Yet you didn't return home when he sailed to intercept Bertles." Temple's face was like a mask, but his blue eyes were blazing with anger. "You see, sir, I was wondering what it was that detained you in Sussex."

"I do not answer to you for my social life, sir."

"Could it be that you saw Trench, with his uncontrollable

nature, as a threat? A revival of the Hawkhurst days? That you stayed around to see if there was another who might consent to help dispose of him?"

Temple stood up abruptly. "Your speculations are useless, Mr Ludlow."

"Are they, sir? As useless as your attempts to replace Obidiah Trench with a more amenable gang leader?"

Harry stood also, moving closer to Temple. It was guesswork, he acknowledged. But it was, judging by Temple's irate reactions, close to the mark. The concerns of warring smugglers didn't worry him at all. But it so happened that this particular conflict, if there was one, suited his needs perfectly.

"What would concern me, sir, if I were you, is the possibility that Trench may discover your attempts to oust him."

Temple tried to smile as he replied, tried to stare Harry down, but the worry was there in those eyes. Not fear, for Temple wasn't like that, but trouble perceived. "You have an over-endowed imagination, sir."

"Do I, Mr Temple?" Harry was close enough now to let Temple feel the warmth of his breath. And it was warm for his words were full of passion. "Your right-hand man does business with Trench, without informing you. How can you doubt that Trench knows of your activities? I am probably going to kill Trench. I am going to take a ship to his rendezvous on the French coast, emulate Bertles by thieving his goods, and invite him to pursue me. Once out of sight of land, I will turn and destroy him. Then I shall come ashore and crow about the fact that I have nailed a notorious smuggler. There is, I believe, a reward for such a thing." It was now Harry's turn to smile, as he dropped his voice to a more normal tone. "I cannot be sure what your plans are, sir. But should mine fall in with yours in any way, then you must inform me."

"Why?"

Temple didn't realize it, but with that one word he confirmed all that Harry had been saying. "There could be repercussions which would affect matters in Deal. If you were to assist me, that could be avoided."

Something in Harry's look must have alerted Temple. "You merely seek assistance."

"No, sir, I do not. There is also a price to pay."

"Which is?"

"Two people tried to murder me last night. There were others, but they were mere pawns, so I must let their presence pass. But the man who assisted Trench, who set up the whole subterfuge, such as your impersonation, the man who took the money as payment for my delivery—"

"Quested," said Temple, interrupting impatiently.

"That's right, Mr Temple. He also has very likely betrayed you to Trench, so that he can succeed you as the leader of the Aldington gang. I don't want Quested to disappear. I want him harmed. You can throw him to the Preventatives if you like, as a feather in their cap, to make up for Bertles. As to the crime he's accused of, choose for yourself. I don't care if he hangs, spends the rest of his life in a lead mine, or ends up transported. But I want him paid out, for if you don't do it, I most certainly will— but in my own manner!"

Temple had to step back in the face of Harry's anger. "You ask a great deal."

"I offer a great deal in return. You cannot doubt that Trench knows about your manoeuvres, just as you are aware of the type of man he is. You sort out Quested, and I assure you that I will take care of Obidiah Trench."

Temple stood for a moment, ruminating on Harry's offer. He bent over and picked up his hat from the table by his chair, then, standing erect, put out his hand. "It seems we are to be temporary partners, Mr Ludlow."

CHAPTER TWENTY-SIX

THEY CAME BACK to Cheyne Court before first light, entirely unmolested, calling in the pickets that Arthur had set on their way to the house. No one was up at that time of the day. Arthur, as a precaution, had made himself a bed in the hallway. He lay there in his cot, snoring gently, the stubble of his thick ginger hair exposed for once, with a loaded musket and a pair of pistols by his side. In repose his face had none of that hauteur which seemed so natural when he was upright. Harry and Pender, having removed their boots, made their way to the kitchen, stole some of Mrs Cray's fresh bread, covered it with dripping, ate hungrily, then went gratefully to bed.

That morning, with their captain still sound asleep, the first of Harry's crew started to drift in. These were proper sailors, clearly identifiable by their dress and pigtails, men who had served in a man-o'-war before they ever took Harry Ludlow's money. They knew how to hand, reef, and steer, and could carry out their tasks without any of the shouting and starting so common on a king's ship. Any naval captain, in the present shortage, would give his eye teeth to have them on board. They would be a prize catch for the numerous press gangs. Yet these same sailors could walk the length and breadth of England and not be taken up.

And, it transpired, Arthur had only to contact one and the rest followed. Whatever method they had worked out to communicate with each other operated better than the postal service. They arrived in twos and threes, slung their hammocks in one of the barns, and set to with a will to turn their temporary home, to them so full of animal filth, into something more habitable. Within two days the barn was scrubbed clean, with hammocks slung and all the men Harry expected fully mustered.

Tite was as pleased as Punch, swapping yarns and informing all and sundry that he was a true blue-water sailor, as well as boring them to distraction about his years of service. They listened politely to his boasting but held him as a person of no account, a mere servant by land and sea. But this Pender fellow, with whom they'd never served, so obviously close to the man who had been their captain, was a different number altogether. The man was not a proper sailor, bred to the sea, even if he did seem to know his stuff; or at least he didn't dress himself like one. But he had an air of confidence which under normal circumstances might have commanded respect. So they were unsure how he fitted in. Harry Ludlow took great care to issue his orders through him. Not that there were many of those, for they were a crew without a ship.

Yet hints to the man that he should relate something of his background were met with silence, for Pender, though friendly enough, was not slack-mouthed, and certainly not the type you could ask to explain himself outright. So they pressed Tite for details, and given the old servant's natural malice, were not overly impressed with what they heard.

"Fit to fetch and carry in the victuals line, I dare say," was the old man's verdict, delivered with a loud and derisory sniff, relishing the attention such enquiries afforded him. He was unaware that he was describing, very accurately, the general opinion the sailors held of him. He let his eyes run over the men assembled round the red-hot stove, so out of place in the timbered barn. "Pender's poor-quality canvas to my mind, fair-weather stuff that's apt to split in any kind of blow."

Harry read the letter from James over a proper breakfast, fighting to keep a straight face as his sister watched, hungry for news of her "little" brother. The first news was disappointing. Grisham, the master builder at Deptford, was sure that the ship could not possibly be ready for six months. But that was not the problem.

It was the second part that made him fight to keep a straight face.

. . . For in spite of the strictures of my attorney, I could not avoid paying a personal call on Caroline Farrar. In the past her husband kept an entirely separate establishment. But for reason of economy, no doubt, he has actually taken to living with his wife. That he turned up there while I was visiting was unfortunate, for it of necessity involved a unpleasant scene. But despite the threats he made that night to my person I did not take him seriously, otherwise you would have been appraised of this affair earlier.

But the demon of his life, drink, reached his addled brain, as it always does. In a fit of inebriated anger he actually issued a public challenge. Indeed it was so public, in the gaming room at Brooks, that he is at a stand when it comes to withdrawing. I am sure he regrets all this, for if he puts a ball in me (I have chosen pistols!) then he will be killing the goose he needs to lay a golden egg. And if he fails and I survive, he cannot, in all honour, continue with his court case after a duel. Not that he has much honour, so I will suspend judgement on that possibility. Who knows, for the sake of *Caroline*'s honour, I may end up settling with the rogue, financially, on my deathbed.

I cannot ask you to attend, for you have your own concerns. But if you feel that you would wish to be present, we have appointed a time four days from the above date, at dawn, by the high pond at Hampstead Heath. Please convey my regards to Anne, and keep from her the latter part of this letter.

He sat looking at the signature, his eyes slightly misty as he contemplated the letter's contents, embued with James's characteristic understatement. None of the passion of the encounter was allowed to intrude. It was as though none had existed. Harry knew better. He'd spent a great deal of the last eighteen months in James's company. He knew that he had a temper, that he was just as likely to be the cause of the duel himself. Added to that, he was no fool. All his regard for the lady in question had not kept him chaste. He had returned to the bachelor state, taking opportunity with relish as it presented itself.

And while they'd been away, James had allowed some of that passion to seep through into his art. He had eschewed portraiture, with its calm and studied composition, on most of their journey, taking instead to marine painting, forever asking his brother's advice about the trim of a ship's sails as it tossed about in tempestuous waters. And in doing so he had revealed a great deal of himself, for he could never be brought to paint a calm sea. It was as though the swell of the waters reflected his own turmoil. Chided about this, James had merely replied that Reubens, in his marine works, was a more troubled soul.

"Is James well?" asked Anne, cutting through his thoughts.

Harry gave her his most reassuring smile, through his swollen nose sounding like a man with a cold. "Perfectly. And he sends his love to you."

Arthur raised his eyes slightly. No action of James's elicted praise, even a correct one. "He is fanciful with his words. He uses love in place of regard."

"That is just your dour northern way, husband," said Anne. "Here in the south it is quite in order to name the true affections."

The mask of the *grand seigneur* re-asserted itself on Arthur's face, a sure sign that he was preparing a rebuke. "Whatever you say, it is clear that the effect of your brother's regard ensures me little at my own table."

Harry coughed softly, for his brother-in-law had quite forgotten the table was his. Anne covered the embarrassing silence. "All the news in James's letter cannot be happy, Harry. I quite distinctly saw you frown."

"The ship," said Harry quickly. "James went to look it over for me. I think I mentioned that I had asked him to."

"Indeed you did," she replied, ignoring Arthur's impatient glare, which appeared at the merest mention of a ship. "Is it not suitable?"

"It is not ready, nor likely to be for some months."

"Are we to have your tars about the place for ever?" asked Arthur, who considered Harry's crew a disreputable bunch who were shirking their proper duty to the nation. Normally he would not have mentioned it, but he seemed to be in an exceedingly bilious mood this morning.

"You cannot say that they are not clean, Arthur," said Harry.

"In their habits, yes. If we shifted them from barn to barn they'd be doing the estate a service." He gestured towards his wife. "But I am glad my child is not yet born, and so is not about to witness their language."

"They have been exceeding courteous to me, husband."

"So they should be," he said sourly.

Anne looked at him for a time, but there being no clear way to cheer him up, she turned back to Harry. "And what other news does he send?"

"Who?" said Harry, whose mind was quite definitely elsewhere. Was James asking for his support? Did he need it? Not normally flustered, he was now, as he searched for something to say that would avoid relaying the truth. "The usual things, tittle-tattle from the town."

It was Arthur who saved him. "It must be a fine thing to lead such a useless existence."

The remark made Anne's rosy cheeks turn bright red, but she fought to control her voice, so as not to embarrass her husband in the presence of her brother. "If you had one good word to say about James, husband, it would lend some credibility to those you use to complain of him. One thing he is not is useless."

Arthur stood up angrily, then collected himself lest he allow his standards to drop. "It is not a subject that you and I should discuss, since it always makes you forget where your duty and loyalty should lie."

For all Anne's self-control, family tensions were never far from the surface. Harry wondered why he was the only Ludlow not to have such a temper, and since it was a thought, there was no one to disabuse him of this patent fallacy. His sister's tone was clipped and biting.

"They have always lain with the truth, husband. Something you have often had cause to remind me is a higher duty."

Harry turned away, ashamed to be forced to witness this public quarrel.

"I see I am to have my words twisted then thrown in my face."

"You leave me no choice, husband."

"Please do not fix your lack of proper behaviour at my door, madam." Arthur bowed slightly to Harry. "The mere mention of James Ludlow seems to diminish me in my wife's eyes. I shall leave you to discuss your paragon in peace."

"Arthur," said Harry.

Now Arthur lost his temper. His voice rose as much as his eyebrows. "Allow me the freedom of following my own dictates, Harry. To be at the mercy of one brother-in-law is bad, but two is intolerable."

Harry could have checked him, reminded him of his situation, as well as the fact that no one was permitted so to address him. The matter of Naomi Smith still rankled unresolved; perhaps that was the reason for this display of spleen. His return could not have been entirely welcome. But it would never do to say anything in front of Anne. Besides Arthur had turned to leave. Harry looked down the table at his sister's face, set hard, determined not to even glance at her husband as he left the room. She sat still long after the door closed. Then she raised her eyes from the table to look at her older brother.

"Do you know what is amiss?" asked Harry, gently.

Anne smiled, but it had a bitter quality. "I was just about to ask you the same thing."

"I don't follow."

"James, when he was small, used to lie to me. All boys do and it is in itself nothing to remark on. But he rarely succeeded, for he could not carry it off. I knew him too well. For the first time, this morning, I realized how much like him you are."

Harry lifted the letter from the side of his plate. "He is having his usual misfortunes with Caroline Farrar."

"That is all?"

Harry nodded, quite prepared to test Anne's theory that she could tell when he was lying. But he spoke quickly, just in case, turning the matter back to Arthur and wondering how much Anne knew, for the Griffin's Head was mighty close to Cheyne Court. He doubted that his liaison with Naomi had been a secret to her. Did that apply to Arthur as well? Caution demanded that he avoid enquiring, but even as he formed that thought his tongue had embarked on a dangerous course.

"I'm more concerned with your husband. I've never known him more morose. And as for displaying a temper . . ."

"Am I permitted to scold you, Harry?" asked Anne.

That remark, given his train of thought, shocked him. But he fought hard to keep that hidden and forced himself to smile. "You, sister, and you alone."

She didn't respond to that, her face remaining grave. "How do you think Arthur views his situation here?"

She gave the impression of someone about to confess. Harry didn't want to know, didn't want the responsibility that would follow disclosure. That made him a little sharp in his response. "Is that what is making him so difficult?"

"I am with child. I think impending fatherhood has concentrated his mind somewhat. Things which appeared rosy in the past have taken on a different hue."

Harry's mind could not avoid the image, even though he was aware that the drift of his thoughts was wrong. He found himself comparing his sister's rosy cheeks to the ashen ones he'd seen at the Griffin's Head. That was a different hue, and no mistake. But Anne was talking about something entirely different. He coughed to cover his mild embarrassment and said the first thing that came into his head. "I know that I have abused his good nature."

Anne laughed, this time with real pleasure. "Good nature. What a strange expression to use about Arthur."

It was with some relief that Harry continued, for the conversation seemed to have moved to safer ground. "You know what I mean, Anne. I have gone off on my travels and left him here to carry a burden that's rightfully mine. I must say though that up until the present I always thought that Arthur enjoyed the arrangement. That it was mutually convenient."

"He has never hidden the fact that he feels you irresponsible."

Arthur had said the same thing to him, many times. He shrugged that off. But somehow the words in his sister's mouth stung him more. "And what, sister, do you think?"

"Is a woman's opinion worth asking for? That seems a mightily modern notion."

"Don't tease me, Anne," said Harry with a frown. "Arthur and I have always enjoyed a degree of friendship. I have also to observe that I've rarely met a man with more self-control. Yet both seem breached. If you have an explanation for what has changed your husband, I'd appreciate it, for I'm at a loss to know how to respond."

A note of desperation crept into her voice. "Have you asked him, Harry?"

"Of course I have, Anne," said Harry softly, leaning forward to emphasize the point. "But I'm afraid his Versailles manners don't assist him in such a case."

"Versailles manners? That's James's expression." It was hard to tell if the words in Harry's mouth pleased or disturbed her.

"Do you know what he wants?"

"Freedom," said Anne.

"Arthur is under no compulsion from me to stay here."

Anne rubbed her burgeoning stomach. "Perhaps this is the cause. The baby makes something which was once acceptable feel suddenly like a constraint."

"Why?"

She smiled to take the sting out of her words. "Being a sailor debars you from so much, Harry. Being wealthy takes away the need to consider the rest."

"Such as?"

"The child's future. Arthur does not want his dependence on you to extend to his son." She laughed slightly. "He is so sure that it is a boy. A girl will quite crush him, I fear."

"Then I wish him the right of it. A son will be a fine thing."

"He wanted you to go to London, Harry."

"He has told me that many times."

"Arthur longs for London. Not long ago, indeed just before your return, he had some hopes of a *coup* that would allow him to do so."

"A *coup?*"

"Strictly financial, I assure you. And don't go asking me what it was. He does not confide these things to me. I only know that he has engaged himself to some enterprise which is designed to free him." Her face clouded over, even though her cheeks stayed rosy. "Yet I cannot believe that everything has gone according to plan. Arthur has stopped mentioning society, and, as you have observed, has turned fractious."

"He wishes to give up his responsibilities here?"

"Not entirely, that is, unless you wish to assume the burden yourself. He adores Cheyne Court, for all he's forever carping on about improvements to the house."

Arthur was afire to face the house in stone, in a desire to bring it up to date. Harry rather liked it the way it was, but out of fairness had consulted James. His brother's reply had all his customary anti-Scottish venom: "He just seeks to line the pockets of the Adam brothers, Harry. I should leave the house be." He brought his mind back to the present. "Am I being particularly insensitive, Anne, in what I'm missing?"

She shrugged. "If you had a residence in London, he would be happy there, too. Happier than he is here, for it would afford him the chance to make his own way in the world. After all, he has the proper degree of interest."

"Dundas?"

"The Secretary for War esteems him, and despite what James says it is not merely for his Scottish blood. Arthur is clever, Harry. Given even a moderate opportunity he would do well. But that is not a course he can undertake from east Kent. He needs a proper residence in town. Then, instead of being dependent on his wife's family, he could stand on his own two feet, plan his own future and that of his unborn child, without reference to anything other than his own conscience."

Harry fingered the letter, thinking that Arthur had some strange methods of easing that conscience. "He has your portion, Anne. Would that not suffice for him to move?"

Anne dropped her head, making Harry regret that he'd posed the question, for if Arthur had been speculating that was the likely source of his funds.

"That is a question only my husband could answer. Perhaps he does not feel that such a sum provides him with security."

Harry recalled the settlement his father had made. It had been sufficient, without being overly generous. As a man who'd started poor and had to make his own fortune, their father had not been spendthrift with his daughter.

"I am going to see James, after I've been to Blackwall Reach, Anne . . ."

"Whatever for?"

Harry lied smoothly, taking the second part of his statement only, proving beyond doubt that he was very different from his brother.

"I cannot leave decisions about ships to James. If anything he knows less now than when I first took him to sea. You would not credit how ignorant he is in that line. There are ways of hurrying shipwrights . . ."

"Bribes?" asked Anne.

Harry laughed. "Not always, sister. But the man could easily be holding out on a lubber like James, just to secure a better price. He will find me a harder bargain."

"What has that to do with our conversation about Arthur?"

Harry looked down at his empty plate, unwilling to meet his
sister's eye. He knew what he was doing was for his own advantage, which engendered a degree of guilt. He cared a damn sight
more about his own freedom than he did about Arthur's. And a
brother-in-law in London was no use at the Griffin's Head, if Harry
decided to pursue the matter. He could not countenance Naomi
Smith's preferring Arthur to him. Indeed the more he dwelt on it,
the more he realized that with his unexpected homecoming he'd
merely caught the lady unawares.

Their loose relationship, with no questions asked, had worked
well up till now—anything else, for Harry, would have been
another unwelcome tie to the shore. Thus she was free to behave
as he had on his travels. That she'd chosen to do so with his
brother-in-law was damned irritating. But it wasn't enough to ter-
minate the connection entirely, even if Arthur wasn't around to
gloat or feel traduced. Nothing was guaranteed to make Harry
feel more of a scrub at a time when he was appearing generous
whilst in reality merely being selfish.

"Don't you know, Anne? While I'm in London, it will give me
a good opportunity to find a place to live."

"But you don't want to live in London, do you?"

That made him look up. "No more than I wish to spend my
life here. But I own the house nevertheless."

Anne went bright red again, but the embarrassment was mixed
with a feeling of joy. "Harry!"

"I cannot say to Arthur that I do not need him here. And I
hope he will forgive me if I choose to extend his responsibilities
to looking after my house in London as well."

She was on her feet and heading his way before he'd finished,
to envelope him in the kind of sisterly hug that she usually reserved
for James. Given what he was about, it was surprising how good
that made him feel.

CHAPTER TWENTY-SEVEN

TEMPLE'S MESSAGE reached Harry just as he was leaving. He cursed softly as he read it and marched back into the house, calling Pender in after him, ignoring the curious enquiries of his sister and his brother-in-law. The Deal smuggler had sent to Sussex for information on Trench. The reply had been swift. He was planning another trip to pick up contraband, with a landfall expected in seven days. There was a slight hint of desperation in the part that followed. Temple informed Harry that Obidiah Trench was overheard talking of stopping off in the Downs again, of "sorting matters out once and for all." He tried to make this sound like a threat to Harry, but it was clear from his words that he perceived Trench's imminent descent on Deal as more of a threat to himself.

Now, as he made his way towards the library, trailing Pender in his wake, he regretted not including Arthur in his plans; it was something he'd avoided, partly out of pique, but also to spare himself another lecture on his supposed irresponsibility. Harry had to get to London, to stop James if possible, to assist him in some way if he couldn't. Nothing counted for more than that, not even the idea of waylaying Trench. But to ignore this letter from Temple would negate all his previous ideas of the best way to tackle the murderous swine. Only at sea, in a well-manned ship, could Harry guarantee himself an advantage. And he had no intention of relying on anyone but himself. As for Temple and his Deal smugglers, since their leader was plainly terrified of Trench, and his recent second-in-command, Quested, had already shown himself willing to be suborned, he placed no reliance in any support which would come from that quarter.

Numbers were the key. He had to overwhelm Trench with a stronger crew. And they had to be men willing to fight. Those in the barn were of that stripe, but they were too few for the task at hand. He had hoped to man his ship from the men who hung around Deal, and given even a few days with him he was sure he could impart some degree of fighting spirit.

"Shut the door, Pender," he said as he entered the room.

His servant did as he was asked, and as usual waited till his captain said something before offering either a question or an opinion. The contents of Temple's letter provided meat for both.

"As you know, Captain, I'm no great shakes in the article of ships. But if this here barky which you've had your eye on is anything like you've described it to me, a sod like Trench wouldn't come within ten miles of it."

Harry smiled, taking the worried look off his face and replacing it with a gleam of anticipation. "On a dark night, with the ship well disguised to look like a merchantman? He'll come after us all right, especially if it's loaded to the gunwales with his contraband."

But Pender wasn't convinced, which was made obvious by the frown on his normally cheerful face. "If as you say, it's a matter of more men, why bother with a disguise?"

"Because you're right, man," replied Harry, with a trace of asperity. "If we don't disguise a ship like that, he'll take one look at her gunports and head for safety."

"This ship ain't ready?" asked Pender stubbornly, refusing to be cowed by his captain's display of impatience.

"I've told you, I have only my brother's word for that. And when it comes to being no great shakes in the article of ships, you lead him by several cables."

"Even Mr James would be able to see if it were ready to float."

"What are you saying, man?"

Pender grinned, quite taken with the way Harry was glaring at him. "I'm saying that it don't make no difference to the present case if it's not to be ready for six months or one. If you want to take on Trench, right off, you need another ship. And since you're intent on disguisin' the barky anyway, you might as well get hold of one that don't need it."

"A merchantman?"

"That's right. There's bound to be a few goin' in the Downs, with all them ships anchored there."

"And men?" asked Harry.

"Deal is awash with 'em, you know that as well as I do, Captain. Let's get some on our books, fetch them back here so's they can mix with your old crew. Then when we have a boat, we can ship them aboard and put to sea without anyone givin' away what we're about. I don't know about you, but I ain't got much faith in that Temple."

"We have to include him, Pender, for we depend on him for information."

"Is there any way it could be just him, Captain?"

Harry slammed the wood panelling with a balled fist. "I've got to go to London, Pender. You know why?"

"I do, your honour. But I can recruit the hands if you leave me here."

"And a ship?" asked Harry.

Pender shrugged, for he could not provide an answer to that.

"Temple could get one," said Harry. "No one would question his buying a ship. They would just assume he'd decided to smuggle in a proper merchantman instead of using luggers and pinks."

The trap that shot out from the lane took Harry by surprise. He'd been lost in thought, allowing his horse its head, and it was the animal's shying away from the sudden apparition which first alerted him. By the time he had a firm grip on the reins he was face to face with the driver. Naomi, the hood of her cloak thrown back to expose her fine blonde hair, was hauling on the traces, trying to bring her skittish pony under control. She swung round in an arc, as though she was searching for deliverance from this embarrassing encounter. The lines of concentration and effort were still there when she looked up at Harry. He, at a loss for anything to say, merely raised his hat.

"How very formal," she said, after an awkward pause.

Harry was impressed by the steadyness of the look in her grey eyes. The cold air had reddened her cheeks slightly. But there was no hint of the usual mocking smile that sat so well on her beautiful face. He wanted to smile, to take the stiffness out of his expression. Such proximity to a woman he knew so well, and admired so much, produced an odd sensation. His heart was beating a little faster and the blood coursing through his veins made his skin tingle. But there was also a part him that wanted Naomi to speak, to explain, perhaps even to apologize. That feeling, and the thought of Arthur, dictated the tone of his reply.

"Perhaps I'm surprised that you reined in your pony. You could have carried straight on."

Her frown deepened to an expression he'd seen often enough before. It was the look of a woman to whom no one could condescend. He'd been exposed to it himself in the past, on those occasions when his attitude toward Naomi had been a little too cavalier.

"It's a fool who takes things for granted."

"I took it for granted that I would be welcome on my return. Clearly I was wrong."

That brought a hint of anger to Naomi's voice, yet to Harry it seemed forced, rather than natural. "If you think you're due an explanation, Harry Ludlow, you will wait in vain. I run my own life. I'm not any man's chattel."

He felt such an accusation unfounded and was stung into a hasty reply. "I have never thought of you as such, Naomi."

"Have you not? You looked, and behaved, very like a man crossed the other night."

That too was forced, as though Naomi was determined to keep her dignity. So be it. Having been a little foolish he would have to be the one to bend. He smiled suddenly and pulled his feet from the stirrups, preparing to dismount.

"I know. And the thought of that affects me deeply. But my pride was sorely dented."

There was no corresponding smile from Naomi. In fact her tone became a bit sharper. She flicked the reins to put her pony in motion, just as Harry swung his leg over the horse, leaving him half in and half out of his saddle.

"Stay aboard your horse, Harry. I've no time for your pride. I have more important business to attend to."

He sat on the road, watching as the cart disappeared, turning away from the Griffin's Head, not towards it, along the road that led through Northbourne to Deal.

By the time Pender got to see Temple in his private chambers Harry was in Canterbury, taking the coach for Rochester, still wondering how he'd so mishandled his chance meeting with Naomi Smith. The Smuggler King was in the process of changing his clothes, discarding his black outfit for a splendid military uniform. He read Harry's letter in his shirtsleeves, ignoring the servant's anger at the way he'd been kept waiting.

"A ship," he said, looking up. "Who's going to pay for it?"

"Captain Ludlow," said Pender quickly, for this hiccup was something they'd not foreseen. Both men had assumed that Temple, in order to nail Trench, would be happy to help them acquire a ship.

Temple flicked the letter at him and began to put on his thick red uniform coat. "It doesn't say that here, man."

Pender knew he didn't have the kind of stature that would allow him to either browbeat or impose on Temple. Harry Ludlow did, but it was no use crying for what you couldn't get. His sole advantage was that he'd never spoken in Temple's presence, even to Harry, so the smuggler had no notion of what he was like or how he stood with his employer. If Temple, to his mind an arrogant man, perceived him as a humble servant, a mere messenger, then that would be the part he'd have to play. He would need a mixture of guile, and that natural disloyalty inherent in hired men, which someone like Temple would take at face value. Pender steeled himself to the kind of grovelling tone which came hard.

"Typical of the captain, sir, an' it was ever so. Rush and more rush, with nothing finished proper. He was in a hellfire hurry to get to London, Mr Temple, an' I dare say he forgot to append that part, but he said to me, clear as day, that he was going to buy the ship hisself."

"I smell stinking fish," said Temple, suspiciously.

Pender looked cunning, adding a slight look over his shoulder, as though what he was about to say was not to be overheard. "'Tween you and me, he reckons he'll get his money back on Trench's brandy and silk, so he won't want to share ownership."

Temple's eyes narrowed, and his chiselled face became stern. He turned to look in the long pier-glass as he did up his shiny brass buttons. When he finally spoke, it was as if he was talking to himself. "Does he, by damn!"

"And I reckon 'e's right, your honour. You should 'ave seen the stuff Bertles had aboard, an' he was disturbed long before he'd finished his thievin'. That there Trench is shipping his goods in by the million."

Temple waved away the absurd exaggeration, but it was clear that he was pondering the situation. He rubbed his forehead with his fingertips. Pender watched him warily, waiting for the seeds he'd sown to increase his doubts. You could almost see the man's thoughts in his reflection as he admired his outfit: of the profit implicit in taking Trench's goods; of the possibility that Harry Ludlow, once introduced to the smuggling game, might consider it a profitable way to do business, competing with the Aldington gang . . . "I shall purchase a ship," he said suddenly. "I hate to disappoint your master, but the goods he takes will belong to me."

"With shares," said Pender, in a slightly hurt tone.

Temple gave him a wolfish smile. "Of course. For the master and the crew."

Pender coughed loudly. The subject of a crew was not something he wanted to discuss. Temple would want to man any ship he bought with his own sailors, something Harry Ludlow would never tolerate.

"By the way, your honour, what happened to that cove I clouted with a musket, Cephas Quested?"

Temple was putting on his belt, a wide buff affair. He turned and looked him square in the eye. But with only the evidence of the previous conversation to go by he made the mistake of talking to Pender as a clever man does to a dolt.

"Still out cold. You hit him too hard, friend, he may never wake up."

"Is he still here, your honour?"

Temple snapped impatiently, which only increased Pender's suspicion. "Of course he is, man. He'll not leave here till he's answered for his actions to me."

Pender left the Hope and Anchor, wondering where Quested was. He might be dead, for Temple had the right, after his batman had betrayed him. But Pious Pender had spent his life smoking out other people's lies, and given the life he'd led, with the constant fear of a sheriff's hand, he had a hound's nose for betrayal. The way Temple had said those words about Quested had made him uneasy.

"If the bastard ain't dead," he said softly to himself, "I hope to God he's well away from Deal."

The four boatmen pulled hard as they weaved their way through the myriad ships which packed the Pool of London. It took skill to cope with the treacherous tides of the Thames, with strong currents running round numerous sandbars making manoeuvring difficult. But these boatmen had been doing it all their lives, and not knowing that Harry had anchored here a dozen times they took care to show him the sights on their way upriver, pointing eagerly as they passed Greenwich and the like, one certain way to turn a silver tip into gold.

That certainty was sorely dented when their passenger, hitherto silent, curtly commanded them to pull for Blackwall Reach. The shore was lined with dockyards. He scanned the slips for his ship, which was a vessel of some hundred feet in length, and spotted what he was looking for in no time. First the lower masts, almost too big for the hull, stout oak trunks that would have to bear the high upper masts, then the line of gunports, seven a side. But the grace of the design counted for just as much. No other ship on the shoreline had anything to match it. He gave more precise directions, so that the boatmen would pull close by her.

The ship was in the water, riding high with clean copper showing, her hull complete. It was being fitted out internally, judging by the sounds of hammering and crashing emitted through the open ports. Men were working at the bows and the stern, carving and fixing the exterior decoration. Harry felt that the ship was a lot closer to being finished than the six months quoted to his brother. It all depended on what needed doing between decks. She required her standing rigging, but that was easily achieved, in weeks rather than months, with a crew of his own to assist.

"Haul away for the Savoy Steps, lads," said Harry. But he didn't look at the men. He was gazing at the ship, mentally cautioning himself not to fall for her too easily, lest he pay the shipbuilder more than she was worth. But she was undeniably beautiful, with sleek lines added to formidable firepower. In his mind's eye he saw her at sea, canvas spread aloft, smoke billowing from her guns, in full chase after fat and profitable prizes. As he turned, his boatmen saw that piratical gleam in his eye, and mistaking its aim, mentally downgraded him to a man who'd be lucky to part with sixpence.

"The gentleman is well known, Mr Ludlow, and I must say does not enjoy an unblemished reputation."

For Benedict Cantwell, normally the most discreet of men, to make such a statement was to damn Lord Farrar more than a hundred vicious oaths from less careful sources. A mere ten years Harry's senior, he looked much older, with his parchment skin, sharp features, and greying hair. His family had been Admiral

Ludlow's bankers since Harry's father had a penny to spare. It had swollen to much more than that by the time Harry's father relinquished the highly profitable West Indies command. Now Benedict, the head of the family concern, was a trusted adviser to the son and heir, though more accustomed to dealing with Lord Drumdryan than he was with his principal.

"Do we have any reports on his competence with a pistol?" asked Harry.

"Able, sir, if not more than that," said Cantwell, examining the report he had before him. "He has been out on many occasions, mostly in disputes over gaming, and has caused great distress with wounds that have on two occasions led to a death."

His thin finger, with an almost flesh-coloured nail, searched along the lines of the report Harry had requested, seeking the rest of the information. "Ah! here we are. 'Though it must be said, of late, his want of sobriety has interfered with his aim.'" Cantwell looked up from his papers, his lips pursed in distaste. "He is termed a rake, sir, though his sins tend to be bets or bottles, rather than beds."

If the banker, who was now smiling thinly at his own alliteration, wondered why Harry Ludlow, whose nose seemed somewhat swollen, wanted this information, he didn't ask. Perhaps he already knew, for James had said that the news of the duel had travelled. Given the furore that James's affair with the man's wife had caused two years before, it was likely that these latest happenings were common knowledge.

"Is he a creature of habit?"

Cantwell looked at his report again. "He is, if you can term recurring sin such a thing, Mr Ludlow. Lord Farrar is a denizen of St James's, well known in all the clubs, and is refused entry at White's. His most common haunt is Brook's, since the stakes at the tables there tend to be higher than those elsewhere."

Harry stood up, obviously preparing to leave, though ready enough to thank Benedict Cantwell for his work. The banker looked shocked.

"You are not leaving yet, sir, surely?"

"I did intend to, Mr Cantwell."

"But we have things to discuss, sir."

It was now Harry's turn to be surprised. He sat down abruptly, feeling like a child who'd just been reprimanded. "Have we? I looked over the accounts at Cheyne Court, and I have to say that everything seemed to be in perfect order. More than perfect, in fact. I was amazed at the increase in the value of the family stocks."

"That is the past, Mr Ludlow. We need to speak of the future," said Cantwell, managing to adopt so doom-laden a tone that Harry wondered if the future existed.

"You are aware that I leave all these matters in the capable hands of Lord Drumdryan."

"Of course," said Cantwell, his thin eyebrows arched. "But there are some burdens that should not be placed on intermediaries. The war progresses indifferently, sir. The government has chosen to follow several different strategies in the hope of success. The simplest intelligence knows this to be folly. Men have been sent to Flanders, as well as the West Indies, with similar results, though yellow jack has killed off more in the Caribbean than enemy action. Admiral Hood has been pitched out of Toulon and now there is talk of a landing somewhere near the mouth of the Loire River."

"Are you sure about Toulon?" asked Harry, who had an interest, since he'd just returned from that part of the world, having at one time been a guest of Admiral Hood aboard the *Victory.*

"Certain. And he has failed to eliminate the French fleet, though apparently the fault lies in Spanish inefficiency. It is not yet confirmed, I grant you. We only have private intelligence on the matter. No official dispatch has yet arrived. What I am trying to say, sir, is this. That though your stocks have shown considerable gains, should the war deteriorate into stalemate, which is likely unless it is more vigorously pursued, I need your permission to liquidate those stocks and move into more stable areas such as gold."

"What would be the result?" asked Harry.

Benedict Cantwell thought for a moment before replying, his thin lips pursed in concentration, as though he was a man who found he needed to impart bad tidings, but didn't know how to begin. Yet when he spoke his words had little connection with the expression on his face.

"You will incur a certain loss if we are wrong and make a fortune if we are right."

"A certain loss?" asked Harry.

For the first time Cantwell smiled. "Nothing that could not be repaired by a couple of stout prizes."

"Then it seems I have little to say. Do you wish my consent in writing?"

Cantwell nodded, pulling a prepared paper from under his report of Farrar. "A simple signature, Mr Ludlow, so that there can be no doubt as to your wishes."

Harry took the proffered quill and signed quickly, once he'd read the note. He did wonder at the necessity, since Arthur would have taken the advice just as readily as himself. Still, bankers worried all the time, it was in their blood. He handed back the note and turned to another subject entirely.

"This may be outside your area of competence, Mr Cantwell, but I have a mind to acquire a property in London. Somewhere reasonably fashionable, and big enough to entertain on a decent scale." Cantwell's eyes had been blank since Harry had misused the word competence. To him there was nothing outside his competence. "Would it be better to buy or lease?"

"I do not have your portfolio to hand, Mr Ludlow. But I believe you own a fair tract of land by the river in Chelsea. In that case it would be better to build."

Harry thought of Anne and the impending birth, of the joy it would give her to see Arthur settled and in pursuit of his own fortune.

"If one was in a hurry?"

"That is never advisable, sir," said Cantwell sharply, before he arched his fingers and adopted a pose of deep thought. "A short lease, to cover you while you built, would be best," he said finally.

Harry was halfway to the door when he replied. "Thank you, Mr Cantwell, you have been most obliging." The banker stood up, but Harry was through the door before he could come out from behind his desk. He sat down again as the door closed, wondering if he should have told his client the real reason why he'd asked him to sign that paper. Yet he could see no way of not breaching his confidentiality if he did so. He could hardly tell Harry Ludlow that his brother-in-law, another customer of the bank, was up to his ears in debt. Lord Drumdryan had not only speculated with his wife's portion, but he'd also in the last few days been borrowing from Nathans, the Jewish bankers. This piece of intelligence had come through one of Nathans's employees who had a stipend from Cantwell's for that very purpose. As Cantwell's was excluded from the transaction, he had no idea where the money was going. It had become imperative to have the power to overrule Lord Drumdryan in writing. Men in such a parlous situation, regardless of their apparent personal probity, could not always be relied on to make the right decisions.

CHAPTER TWENTY-EIGHT

"I TAILED HIM to the edge of town, an' waited till he was out of sight from the top of Sholden Hill."

Temple, in full-dress uniform, sat in his high-backed chair in the tap-room. He flicked a finger to dismiss the man he'd set to tail Pender. He had said he intended to return to Cheyne Court, to await his master's return, but Temple was a cautious man, apt to worry, something which had kept him alive and rich in a dangerous occupation. That lie about Cephas Quested had come instinctively. The crack on the head had left his batman with a goose-egg bump and a nasty cut, but his thick skull had saved him serious injury. Quested had overstepped the mark in obliging Trench, then compounded the error by failing to tell him of the attempt to kill Ludlow on his return. Temple smelled treachery, though Quested, given the proof he had of Ludlow's complicity, claimed he'd merely made an understandable error of judgement.

Temple rarely made anyone privy to his innermost thoughts, including his right-hand man. Quested had shared the little information he'd gleaned about Bertles, just as he knew where it came from, but he had no inkling of his leader's machinations in Sussex. He'd tried to persuade the Romney Marsh and Hastings smugglers, who bordered on his territory, that Trench, with his violent nature and uncontrollable ambitions, should be removed, since he threatened them all; not one of them would stir, even although he'd already poached a fair amount of their trade. Trench, safe in his east Sussex hinterland, with a web of family connections that included a lord lieutenant, local magistrates, and several members of the judiciary, inspired too much fear. Now Temple was faced with the fact that his attempts to unseat him would become known. If they were, then he was in grave danger.

Things had gone too far, and now threatened to get completely out of hand. Bertles had been a damn fool, forcing him to act at the first hint from Trench that a Deal man was involved in stealing his goods. He'd given up Tobias Bertles to Trench's revenge willingly enough, which should have been enough. Yet he could not blame another, for it was his own admission of Bertles's endemic poverty that had alerted Trench to the fact that the man must have a backer.

He'd said it innocently enough, almost as an aside, for he had drawn the same conclusion. It had never occurred to him that Trench would want the identity of this person. He assumed that he would be content with the man who was stealing his goods. Not so. There was the hint that he himself might be involved, one which he'd managed to stifle. But Trench was adamant about the need to find out. The memory of what had happened to the Hawkhurst gang, and the role of the Deal men in that, ran too deep. He was determined to root out the entire connection as a warning to others tempted by rich pickings to "shear off." No doubt that was his reason for hanging the *Planet*'s crew.

The memory of that conversation made him angry, for Temple prided himself on his standing. He was acknowledged, and feared, as the leading smuggler on the east Kent coast. Through his connections, and his brother, he damn near controlled Deal. He was the warden of the Deal pilots, which gave him power, a ready source of information on incoming cargoes, and control of their community chest. On top of that he was an officer in the Volunteer Fencibles. He'd felt a damn fool when Trench had demanded the information about a matter relating to his own backyard and he had been unable to provide it.

And now it seemed, if Quested was to be believed, that the man who claimed innocence and offered a temporary partnership, a marriage of convenience, was none other than the man who'd backed Bertles. Quested claimed to have seen the written evidence with his own eyes. But had he? He had high hopes of finding out the truth this very day. But if it was Harry Ludlow, what was his game? Perhaps, having used Bertles as a foil, he'd seen what the trade was worth. Was he out to get rid of Trench, just to take over the Sussex man's trade? Such an act would oblige more than the Aldington gang. But Harry Ludlow would be operating from around Deal. Temple had expended much effort to reduce the local competition. Through a combination of threats, bribes, and the odd piece of information, he had Braine eating out of his hand. Now he was faced with a new danger from Harry Ludlow. That thought was even less welcome than the idea of a successful Obidiah Trench.

His mind turned back to the third part of the conundrum. Had Quested betrayed him? Was he in league with the Sussex man? He'd sent him to see Trench, ostensibly to strike a bargain: Temple would cease his attempts to remove Trench and give him Harry Ludlow in return for peace. If Quested was reliable, Trench would probably accept, since a war with the Deal smugglers would do them equal harm.

But if there was treachery in the air he could reverse the situation and betray Trench to Ludlow. That still left Quested, of course. His next thought made him smile. He picked up his sabre, which was lying across the table. His face looked long in the narrow reflection of the silver scabbard, accentuating his dark, sharp features. It really didn't matter about Quested. His batman, even if he was reliable, was getting ideas above his station. He was expendable. And he'd be much safer with Trench out of the way as well. Which only left Harry Ludlow. That turned the smile to a grin, with his teeth now huge and menacing in the mirror of his scabbard. In his mind he could see a way to scupper them all. The means to do so were close at hand, and his to command.

He stood up and hooked the long, curved, cavalry sabre to the thick buff belt that had gained the regiment its nickname, "the Buffs." It was a source of great pleasure to him that he had gained a commission in the local Volunteer Fencibles. He'd subscribed handsomely, of course, to the fund set up by Billy Pitt. The locals had enjoyed many a laugh over a drink at the prime minister's expense. Pitt, Lord Warden of the Cinque Ports, had initiated the idea of the Fencibles as a militia to protect the coast against invasion, with the unstated hint that they might take a hand in suppressing the smuggling trade.

William Pitt prided himself on being known as the scourge of the contrabandiers, the man who'd ordered all the boats on Deal beach to be burned. Clever he might be, in the ways of government and the like. But it was counting-house cleverness that blinded him to the obvious. Quite simply, he wasn't local, for all he had a residence at Walmer Castle. Temple, along with all the others on the coast who had an interest, had immediately signed up for his regiment. The best way to make sure that they never interfered with smuggling, in any major way, was to be the ones responsible for its suppression.

"I'm expecting company," he barked to the man behind the serving hatch. "A lady. Show her up to my rooms as soon as she arrives."

He would have been a damn sight less pleased with himself if he'd seen Pender at that moment. He would have cursed himself for not asking his man how he'd managed to follow someone on a horse so easily. Pender had spotted the tail right away, and set off on foot to make his way out of Deal, reasoning, rightly, that Temple's man would not follow him all the way home. As soon as he dropped out of sight in Mongeham village, he turned and retraced his steps, actually following the other fellow right back into the town.

He was now touring the hostelries, like the Ship Inn and the Albion, cautiously approaching the more obvious sailors, and offering them prime rates to join an unnamed ship. They were suspicious, of course, for this was a favoured ploy of the less talented crimps, who would lure a tar to a quiet spot with the promise of a merchant wage then have him knocked on the head and handed him over to the press. To all, his message was the same.

"Meet me behind the mill near Sandown Castle. If you have a mate who's a proper seaman, bring him along as well. Now you can't approach that spot without being seen for half a mile, so you'll have the chance to leg it, if'n you smells a rat. I will meet you there before sundown."

"An' what then?"

"Then you'll find out who seeks to employ you, friend."

"Merchant rates?"

"More'n merchant rates, friend. You'll be sailing under a captain who knows how to make men rich."

They took the coin Pender offered in different ways, but all posed the same question. "Who is he?"

"In good time. First step is to be at the back of Sandown Castle, with any kit you've got, at the right time."

"Thank you for coming, Harry," said James.

He looked pale and drawn, like a man who hadn't slept or eaten for days. Harry restrained himself from remarking on his brother's appearance, made worse by the loose paint-streaked coverall he wore.

"I presume the encounter is still on?"

James nodded wearily and made his way backwards through the pile of packing cases that filled his narrow hallway, all the *objets d'art* he had purchased on their travels, including bronzes and sculptures. Harry pitied the poor souls who'd had to manhandle some of the objects up the steep stairs.

Harry had never been in an artist's studio which wasn't a complete mess. Even James, fastidious in his dress and manners, was no exception. As a breed they seemed incapable of confining their paints to the canvas, nor the canvases themselves, finished or bare, to anything other than untidy heaps. No wonder they donned hats and smocks to protect themselves. The private rooms at the rear were altogether different. Equally well lit by a large skylight as well as large sash windows, they showed James off to better advantage, being tastefully and expensively appointed.

Portraits adorned the walls, and Harry reasoned that many were of women with whom his brother had been romantically involved. Yet he could not see the one of Caroline Farrar, which on his last visit had occupied pride of place above the mantel, and that surprised him. It had been replaced by one of James's more preposterous seascapes, of a ship on its beam ends in a mass of foaming water. He was there, in one of his brother's earliest efforts, resplendent in naval lieutenant's uniform. It was a portrait that he'd always disliked: it did scant justice to his brother's talent while reminding him of his chequered past, and James had caught a look which made Harry uncomfortable. Not evil exactly, but avaricious, with just a hint of a man who would kill lightly.

Classical statuary filled the alcoves between furniture, a mixture of old and new, with dark, heavily carved Jacobean oak mingling with the more colourful mahoganies and plain simple lines of the newer pieces. The light from above glinted off silver and crystal. A polished box, its interior lined with deep red silk, lay open on the Sheraton sideboard. Harry walked over to look at the pistols it contained, a gift he himself had given his brother.

"You must be fatigued after your journey," said James, throwing off his paint-streaked smock. He took up a decanter and poured two glasses, one of which he handed to Harry. "There are biscuits in that tub by your hand."

"How long have you had these pistols, James?" asked Harry, knowing the answer perfectly well. His brother, sipping some wine, didn't reply, but the look in his eyes said all that was needed. Harry picked one out, rubbing the silver and gold filigree work which adorned the stock. "Have they ever been fired?"

"No," said James.

"Do you have others?"

James merely shook his head, well aware of what Harry was driving at. "I have never felt the need to practise with such weapons. I know how to use them, Harry. That will suffice for what needs to be done."

"That is clearly nonsense, brother. They need to be used, to have the sights checked and properly aligned. If you do not do that you could well find your aim off by several feet, quite apart from the mere advantages to be gained from firing them a few times."

"A fine sight I'd be, in Green Park, blasting off with pistols. With poor sights I could remove some very famous people."

Harry resolved to see to the pistols himself. For some reason James appeared like a man resigned to a terrible fate, one that he could do nothing to avoid. It was evident in his face and his demeanour.

"You have to tell me what is amiss, brother?"

James finally laughed, but it emerged as the cackle of a slightly deranged man. "Is it not obvious, Harry? I am about to risk everything."

"That wouldn't bother you, James," said Harry flatly.

"But it does, Harry. Eighteen months in your company, despite our adventures, has not made me bloodthirsty."

"You didn't need to be with me. If I had a guinea for every time I've heard you curse Lord Farrar, I'd have enough to fund the National Debt."

"That is true," James replied.

"So now you are about to be afforded the chance. A clean shot, a rival disposed of, money saved, and Caroline a widow. What could be better?"

James smiled weakly. "Imagine the scandal if Caroline married the man who shot her husband."

"You're no more afraid of scandal than you are of facing her husband," snapped Harry, finally losing patience. "I have come a long way, James, at your request. Please oblige me by informing me why you're behaving like this."

"You are striking a very elder brother pose, Harry."

That made him even angrier. "Eyewash. Just answer the question, for I have no intention of standing still to watch you approach a duel in this frame of mind."

James, who'd squared his shoulders to tease his brother, let them slump again. "How much would you say I have sacrificed for Lady Farrar?"

"A lot. But the true answer to that is something only you could know. It would also be worthwhile to remember that she too has made sacrifices."

James's eyes dropped to the floor. "True, brother, true."

Harry walked slowly over to James and laid a hand on his shoulder. "What could I say that would press you to speak?"

He looked up. "Nothing, for no man likes to be seen to be a fool, Harry. But you, of all people, deserve some explanation. That night, I should not have gone anywhere near her house. It was a foolish thing to do." Harry nodded in agreement, well aware that he would probably have done the same. "I was readily admitted, Harry, and Caroline was delirious with happiness when she saw me. We were locked in an embrace when he entered unannounced." James rubbed his eyes, as if to hold back tears. "I've held that woman many times, Harry. I've felt that rush of blood that makes my skin seem like a burden."

"There's no need—"

James cut across him, and the life had returned to his eyes. "There is, brother. That feeling was entirely absent. There was nothing. We were like two old friends exchanging a chaste kiss. She felt it too. I could tell. Whatever passion we had has cooled if not evaporated." James's voice had risen to a near shout. "I am about to face a man across a pistol for a woman I no longer care about because I lack the courage to ignore this ridiculous convention! How can I possibly kill him?"

They were thirty strong, on edge, talking amongst themselves and casting anxious glaces in all directions. They didn't cease to be wary when Pender was sighted, trotting along from the edge of the town on horseback. If anything their anxiety increased as he approached. He dismounted early, to ease the tension of the assembled group.

"So we're here, mate," said one of the men, less patient than his fellows. He was a hardcase, with all the evidence in the scars on his swarthy face.

"Tell me your name," said Pender.

"Flowers," the man replied.

It was so inappropriate that Pender nearly laughed. "Well, Flowers, you done the first part an' now it's time to do the second."

"Which is?"

"A walk, friend. Quite a long one. At the end of it you'll be fed and housed, and get a chance to talk to men who served with the captain before. Then you can decide if you want to stay or go."

"What captain?" called a voice from the back.

"In time, lads," said Pender, glancing towards the round walls of Sandown Castle. "If you want to eat you follow, if not, you'll stay. But I suggest we get on our way, for if anyone spies a crowd like this from them castle walls they'll think we're likely Jacobins talking sedition."

Pender remounted his horse and hauled its head round with difficulty, for he was not yet a competent rider, even on a peaceable mare. He looked down at the assembled sailors.

"There's no more words to say. Either you come or you don't."

"If we don't?" asked Flowers.

"Then I look elsewhere, friend, and leave you to hear them boast in the taverns of how much money they've pocketed."

Pender knew it wasn't words that decided these things. It was an indefinable mixture of his personality and their curiosity and greed.

"Nowt to lose, I reckon," said Flowers, surprising Pender, who had marked him out as a potential troublemaker.

"No, mate," said another man. "We only stand to gain."

"Gain what?" said Flowers suspiciously.

"Sore fuckin' feet, mate, that's what. I 'ates walkin'."

That made them all laugh, and overbore any doubts that they had about following Pender.

, , ,

Harry was losing steadily, watching his pile of gold diminish as it made its way from his side of the table to the other. He was far from dismayed. He wasn't losing any more than normal to everyone at the table, only to the man he wanted to. Lord Farrar, his purple, drink-sodden face alight with pleasure, scooped the coins towards him, fixing Harry with a black-toothed grin.

"Mere luck, sir. I do assure you," he said, for the last thing he wanted was for this "mark" to lose heart and take his wealth elsewhere. If he'd smoked the physical likeness to his wife's lover in this man across the table as Harry sat down to play, it hadn't shown. Not that Harry had made it easy. For one of the few times in his life he was wearing a wig. He'd also powdered his face to hide his ruddy sailor's cheeks.

Farrar kept talking, intent on reassurance. "Most uncommon, why I am more often in your shoes than my own. My companions know me as a loser."

"Hear him, hear him." The chorus of agreement was added by Lord Farrar's friends, a dozen of whom had gathered to witness this uncommon good fortune.

Again Farrar had missed what he sought, which was the right expression to ensnare his fellow gamester, for the word "loser" was out of place. He sought to cover it, as a gambler does, by doubling it.

"Though it is one, sir. Winning and losing, as any man of sensibility knows."

Harry looked at Farrar, now refilling his crystal goblet with claret. If ever any man lacked that vital ingredient of the age, it was he, for Lord Farrar had a quite singular grossness of character. You could see he'd been handsome once, but now his puffy flesh allowed only the remains to show. He'd been drinking all the time they'd been playing cards, never sipping once. Any glass presented to his lips was immediately drained. Harry replied with a foppish giggle, having allotted himself the role of the country fellow up in London for some sport who aped town manners.

"How I agree, sir, for only a poltroon would care one way or the other."

The watery, red-rimmed eyes narrowed slightly, but Farrar added an insincere laugh in a bid to cover his patent curiosity. "Thank God you're the type to lose with good heart. I trust, as well, that you are cooper-bottomed enough to withstand the loss."

Harry shrugged. "Oh, easily."

"It is the very thing to play cards with a man of parts, sir."

Harry effortlessly matched the insincerity, measure for measure. "As you are yourself, my lord, I am sure. A loss at the table would not embarrass a stout fellow like you."

Farrar let out a booming laugh and drained his glass. "Well spotted, sir. But here we are, near boon companions, and you've not yet furnished me with a name."

CHAPTER TWENTY-NINE

THE WHOLE conversation, up till now, had been carried out in the loudest tones. But now Harry dropped his voice. Though he rarely visited London, let alone the St James's Street gaming clubs, there was always the chance that someone might know him.

"I did not presume, sir, but I will do so now if you request me."

"Indeed I do."

"The name is Temple, sir. Jalheel Temple."

Farrar, already more than a little drunk, had a blank look on his face, for he'd asked the question without even considering the nature of his response. And being a name that meant nothing to him, it left him beached. Harry, to stop the feeling of *bonhomie* diminishing, raised his voice again to its previous booming tone. He also raised his glass of claret, which he'd managed to empty once in the same time as Farrar had cleared a bottle.

"This is a thin brew, sir," he cried. "Can I call upon you to join me in a man's drink?"

Farrar had raised his glass with Harry, but it hadn't stopped in midair. He gagged slightly, caught between a swallow and a response.

"Brandy," cried Harry, loud enough to make a great number of heads turn. "Lord Farrar wants brandy, and so do I."

"Please, Mr Temple," said one of his companions, who Harry knew to be Viscount Trafford. He was a tall fellow, so thin and powdered he looked like a taper. "Lord Farrar has a meeting in the morning, one that requires a clear head."

The allusion was obvious and Trafford emphasized the word "meeting" to ensure complete understanding.

"Then he will need to stay warm, sir, and there is nothing guaranteed to warm the blood more than French brandy."

"We must return to our game, sir," said Farrar, indicating the scattered cards.

Harry adopted a slightly petulant tone, pushing against the table as though about to depart. "I must have some brandy first, my lord, for I know it immeasurably improves my game. However if you do choose not to join me . . ."

These last words were delivered in a throw-away fashion, but left no one in any doubt that if there was no spirit to drink, there would be no cards either.

"I'll stand a glass with you, sir," replied Farrar, his eyes dropping to the pile of coins that lay in front of Harry.

"Farrar," said Trafford, leaning forward.

Farrar's purple face took on a deeper hue, as he rounded on his friend. "Do not dictate to me, sir. You do not have the right."

"I am your second."

Farrar positively spat in his companion's face, so great was his anger. "You are *second,* sir. Not a second. It is the tale of your life to forever be at the back of better men."

Trafford's cheeks, not full to start with, seemed to retreat further, as he sucked on the insult, leaving his face skeletal. "I have undertaken a duty, Farrar, which I shall conclude. My honour demands it."

"Honour, Trafford!" spat Farrar. "You speak to me of honour, a man who crawls nightly into a Jewess's bed so that he can dun her father for the price of a drink!"

The timely bottle arrived at the table, as the two men looked as if they were about to exchange blows. Harry picked it up and pushed it between them.

"Come, gentlemen, a drink, then some cards."

Farrar's anger was like a snuffed candle. The mention of cards reminded him of his main purpose. He turned back to Harry, thrusting his goblet forward, giving him a full view of every bad tooth in his head as he smiled. "A capital notion, sir. Fill me a bumper and let's drink to lady luck."

Harry obliged, taking care to fill Trafford's glass next. By the time he'd filled his own, Farrar had already emptied his and held it out for a refill, accompanying the gesture with braying laugh. "Never could wait for a toast, sir."

Harry raised his glass with one hand, as he filled Farrar's with the other. "Then let's have it now, my lord."

Harry kept his voice loud, to maintain the impression of being drunk, and the way he was forever picking up the third bottle backed up his claim to be overfond of brandy. But an acute eye, one that was not taken with the money changing hands on the table, would have observed that he sipped little and added less, so on those occasions when he did extravagantly drain his goblet, there was little to consume. Farrar, matching him glass for glass, showed a quite astonishing capacity for drink. But Harry knew he was being sustained by the continued excitement of winning. The change registered very quickly, when Harry won his first hand for an age.

"There we are, sir," he cried. "Luck has turned at last, as it ever must."

"It is near two o'clock, George," said Trafford. "We must get you to your rest."

"Nonsense," cried Harry, showing his first trace of spirit. "I win one hand and you call adieu."

His words had the desired effect. Not even this disreputable crew could gainsay that remark. Farrar drained his goblet again. Harry filled it up immediately. The cards flowed across the green baize of the table and the game continued. The steady tide of Harry's gold now ebbed, heading back across the table to him, as he won hand after hand. Farrar drank more on a losing streak than he did when he was winning, not deigning now to wait until his brew was poured. Harry kept a steady supply near the man's elbow, watching as the few muscles left in the face slackened through drunkenness. By the time he called a halt it was past four o'clock and all the good humour had gone out of his hosts, for most of the gold now stood piled in front of him.

"Well, I thank you, Lord Farrar," he said.

"What for?" slurred the other man.

"Why, for that toast, sir, to Lady Fortune. I don't doubt, but for that, I'd have been going home a pauper."

Farrar was rocking slightly, unable to sit upright. Nor did he have much luck with his sentences. "You take cog . . . you take cog . . . You believe such things, sir."

"Why after tonight, my lord, only a man bent on destruction could deny it."

Harry didn't wait for a reply, which given Farrar's state could have taken an age. He swung round and called for the man who'd been serving the table all night. "Two more bottles, my man, if you please. For I shall take one to bed, and I'm sure Lord Farrar will too."

He might have been careful, but even Harry knew, as soon as he hit the fresh air, that he'd had more than was good for him. He had to grab at the railings to remain upright. The club, knowing he was carrying a goodly sum, and guessing at his probable condition, had offered him an escort. He had declined since his destination would identify him. But he was not about to walk, or more likely stagger, even at this time in the morning. He decided to take a chance, called for a carriage, and had himself driven the few streets to James's studio. One thing he could do was to take off his damned wig; he hated wearing them with a passion. It afforded him great pleasure to send it spinning out of the coach window.

"Are you drunk, Harry?" asked James.

Harry pulled himself upright, for James could never be allowed to guess what he'd been about. "I have had a drink or two certainly, brother."

James walked up to him and peered into his face. If he wondered at the powder on Harry's cheeks, he didn't say. But he did gently ease the brandy bottle from under his arm. "And you're not finished, by the look of it. It is customary, brother, to conduct a wake after someone is dead, not before."

"Not much fun for the corpse," said Harry, slumping into the chair that James had guided him towards.

"No," James replied coldly, for the first time taking in Harry's clothes. "Whatever are you wearing, brother? You're clad like a rake."

Harry, drunk, was no more immune to sudden truculence than Lord Farrar. He positively snapped at his brother. "Can a man not go out on the town once in a while?"

James, in a less depressed state, would have made much of that, but his voice was sad, devoid of the languor he normally used to such devastating effect. "He can go to the devil four times over, Harry. But I do reserve the right to comment when you behave out of character."

"What time have you called the coach?"

"Five of the clock, which by my reckoning leaves you fifteen minutes to sober up and get that powder off your cheeks."

"You don't think I suit it?" asked Harry.

There was just a little flash of the old James now, which lifted Harry's spirits. "What I think is of no account. But it does render you ghoulish in the light of a lantern. We can't have you alarming the horses, can we?"

"Wake up, Harry," said James, gently nudging his snoring brother. The effect was instant, for after a life at sea Harry could pack what looked like a night's sleep into half an hour, and be completely awake as soon as he was roused. But he had a head that reminded him of what he'd been up to as soon as he moved. If that hadn't done so, the raging thirst and thick foul-tasting tongue would have sufficed.

The coach bounced along the hard, rutted land towards the high pond, with the horses slithering on the ice. The other party was already there, along with the doctor, huddled in their coaches, round lanterns, to try and keep some warmth in their bodies.

Harry was grateful for the extreme cold. It allowed him to don a thick muffler again, which, with his hat, made him virtually unrecognizable.

It would be an early dawn. The sky was devoid of cloud, so the first hint of sun would suffice for their business. Again this suited Harry, for full daylight could render him recognizable. If he saved James's life but in the process totally destroyed his brother's reputation he doubted he would be in receipt of much gratitude. James might claim that he didn't care about honour, but he could not live with the accusation of cowardice, of the idea that he'd used subterfuge to extend his chance of life.

Farrar looked ghastly. He stood, shivering under his cloak, with the hunched shape of a man who could barely remain erect. His eyes watered copiously in the chill air and he had a line of thick white saliva drying on the bottom of his lip. Being unshaven added to his air of destitution, which contrasted with James, who would have given everything to be elsewhere, but at least looked every inch the determined duellist.

Harry spoke with the doctor, forcing the man to lean closely to hear what he had to say through the thick muffler. There was a tense moment when Harry approached Trafford, offering the ritual right of withdrawal. The tall viscount looked at him keenly and Harry waited for comprehension to arrive. But what interest the man had faded quickly and he turned to look at Farrar. A wiser, or perhaps a less wounded, second, looking at his principal, might have accepted the offer on his behalf. But Trafford let the opportunity pass, and as the sky grew grey enough to allow them to see, the two opponents took up their positions.

They stood back to back, listened to the litany as the doctor explained the rules, marched their ten paces, and turned on the command. The edge of the world had gone blue now, lit by a sun still well below the horizon. Farrar stood, feet splayed apart, swaying back and forth, with his pistol barely raised. James lifted his gun, aiming down the barrel at his enemy. Harry watched as the finger started to squeeze on the trigger, his heart in his mouth. It

seemed, at that moment, for all that James had said, all that he
had believed, his brother had it in mind to kill Farrar. All Harry's
subterfuge was a waste. Worse, he'd multiplied the odds for a man
who might have won anyway. The drop of the wrist was so imper-
ceptible that Harry missed it. But the ball sent a great spurt of
dust rising out of the frozen ground between Farrar's legs.

That, and the sound that accompanied the passing ball, seemed
to aid his concentration. He raised his own weapon, steadied his
body and fixed his eyes. James stood, looking at a point above his
opponent's head. So he did not see that Farrar's pistol was moving in arc, as the drunken nobleman failed to control his hand.
The pressure was showing on his face, as his remaining black teeth
bit into his whitened lower lip. The point of the pistol swayed still
further. Farrar jerked it back. It was again over-corrected. No one
could interfere. James had fired. His opponent had all the time he
needed.

Harry was watching his eyes, for that would tell him the moment
he intended to fire. His whole being was concentrated on the one
spot. Everything else had faded to nothing, the scenery, the sounds
of the horses shaking their harness did not intrude. He saw the
twin trickles of fluid running over the wrinkled bags under Farrar's eyes, spreading out on the tops of his cheeks.

The moment came as the pistol swayed again. Harry had
stopped breathing as he prayed for the shot to miss James, for
even a drunk could be lucky. Farrar jerked his hand to bring his
aim back to true, over-compensating massively just as he squeezed
the trigger. Harry's hat flew off his head and he felt the searing
pain as the ball removed a layer of tender skin. He spun round
and retrieved his hat in what looked like a show of insouciance.
The other men by that Hampstead pond would never know how
close their drunken principal had come to exposing him.

For all the pain under his hat, Harry was laughing inwardly.
James, who'd aimed to miss, was alive. So was Farrar, if he could
bear the state of his head for the rest of the day. All the debts
were settled and clear, with honour satisfied, even if purses and

hearts were empty. But the unexpected bonus was not something even he could have foreseen. Lord Farrar would now, and for the rest of his life, be a laughing-stock. He would always be the man who, on Hampstead Heath, on a winter morning, took careful aim and shot his opponent's second. He could challenge all he liked in future. Anyone, with even the dullest wit, had good reason to turn him down. After all, what gentleman, happy to risk his own life, would readily imperil the life of his second?

CHAPTER THIRTY

IT WAS curious to watch, the way the new men refused to mingle with the old. Even in a landlocked barn the conventions of shipboard life were observed, with those who considered themselves old Medusas, and thus a cut above the others, shying away from contact with the men Pender had brought in. He had hoped that the older hands would inform the newcomers of their profits, to persuade them that sailing under Harry Ludlow was worth a good deal more than a mere merchant wage. But contact was kept to a minimum, with growls exchanged instead of words. Another factor which militated against an easy transition was his own lack of authority, for Harry had not formally given him any office. And Tite, who seemed to have nothing better to do, was always there to undermine him.

Pender would fight as readily as the next man, but he hated to do it without purpose. He could not easily convince himself that it was necessary now. But his main worry was simple. If his captain's information was correct, they would be going into action against Trench and his men in a matter of days, with only this scratch crew to back them. Right now, with their petty disputes about hierarchy grumbling below the surface, they were as likely to assault each other as attack anyone else.

The old Medusas were less of a worry. They knew Harry, and once he was here to command them would follow wherever he led. Perhaps the same could be said of the others, for the captain had the rare gift of attaching men to his cause. Only someone like Pender, close enough to see him without his public mask, knew how much concentration went into that seemingly effortless air of confident leadership.

Flowers was the obvious candidate amongst the new men. He was a big, swarthy fellow, scarred from many encounters. Both his nose and his jaw seemed slightly out of turn, and his habit of talking out of the corner of his mouth gave his whole head a slight crescent shape. He was vocal about the small slights Harry's old crew delivered, and moaned incessantly about being berthed too far away from the stove. And his effect on the Deal men was clear. He was turning them into a fractious mob, biting at each other with as much venom as they displayed for the older hands.

Flowers had, as might have been expected, hogged a place by the stove, turfing out one of the other sailors. That hadn't satisfied him though and he launched into a barely disguised attack on the Medusas, who were ranged around the other side. Pender only heard the exchange by accident, having come in to organize some small-arms practice. A quick word would have silenced both men. But it would also leave them disgruntled, with their quarrel still simmering, plus the added resentment from being checked by him. So, aware that they hadn't spotted him, he held his tongue.

"Will you leave off with your gab," said Peacham, one of Harry's topmen. "You don't need a fucking stove, mate. You've got enough hot air coming out of your gob to melt Polar ice."

The other man spat into the open stove, producing a loud hiss. "I don't recall askin' for your opinion, mate."

"It's easy to avoid my opinion. Just stay quiet, an' at your end of the barn."

Flowers pushed his head back, sniffing the air loudly, vaguely waving his arm towards the Medusas's hammocks. "There's a rank smell here, an' no error. Now it ain't straw, 'less it's been pissed on, but it's plain enough where it's coming from."

"Your nose is too close to your arse, old son," said Peacham, a remark which was greeted by laughter from his mates.

"No, it's not that. Smells like someone has fouled their nest to me. Can't say I fancy sharing a lower deck with someone that can't hold their water."

"Then you knows what to do, mate. The road back to Deal starts right outside the barn."

As the other man stood up from his seat, Pender said, "Shut up, Flowers."

He spun round to face the voice, determined to deliver the reply he'd already worked out. "Happen I will take that road. An' if I do, I dare say most of the lads will go back with me."

The Deal men growled and nudged each other. But Pender's next words soon put an end to that. He was as aware as anyone that this was the moment of truth. "You've failed to spot that I'm astride the road, Flowers."

"If I want to go, Pender, you won't stop me."

Pender stepped forward and slowly took off his outdoor coat, then his pea jacket. The murmuring had stopped and the eyes of all the men flicked between the opponents in this new dispute. Flowers didn't need telling what was up. A man didn't take off his coat in that manner unless he had a fight in mind.

"Is it just you and me?" he asked, glancing at the Medusas.

"Square goes, Flowers," said Pender, looking in the same direction. "You got naught to fear from them, they don't rate me any higher than you do."

The man spat on his hands before raising them in front of him. He also crouched slightly, with the eyes narrowing in his scarred crescent face. "Then let's be having you, mate."

"Not in front of the stove. If we knock that over the whole barn will go up." Pender indicated the empty space at the far end. "You come over here, Flowers. And never fear, for I intend to keep you warm."

"Do you want to set some rules?" said Pender.

"I don't."

Pender shrugged. It would be a dirty bout anyway, if it went any time, with scratching, biting, kicking, and gouging. He had survived more than one of those in his time, and all because of his own speed. Besides, he didn't know any other way to fight. The streets in which he'd been raised allowed for only one aim. Win, whatever it takes, for there's no nobility in losing. Flowers might be twice his size, but the man moved slowly. And given their relative weights, the bigger man would expect Pender to stay away from him. He was wrong.

There is a coldness that comes over a good fighter. He can see clearly, hit hard, and in the right place, all the time keeping a dispassionate watch on his opponent. There is also that ability to bury any feeling of pain, so that he ignores whatever his enemy is doing to him, until he achieves his own aims. Pender was like that. Flowers caught him twice before he was inside the bigger man's guard, but his determination carried him onwards. Flowers tried to bear-hug him then, to squeeze the air out of his lungs, but Pender head-butted the man's already bent nose. Within the space of a few seconds he kneed him in the groin, punched him in the guts, pushed both his thumbs hard into his eyes, then sank his teeth into the man's ear.

Flowers had already started to retreat under this assault. Pender, letting go of his bleeding ear, allowed enough daylight to come between them to swing both hands and feet, something he did relentlessly, landing blows that had little actual weight, but a profound effect. Once you are going backwards, it is hard to reverse it. And a man intent on protecting himself is not retaliating. Pender increased the gap and his heavily booted foot took Flowers under his knee. The man dropped slightly, enough to equalize their differing heights, and then Pender caught him. The fist, right at the point of the chin, jerked Flowers's head back. Already off balance, he fell. Pender's swinging boot took his head just before it hit the floor.

"I smoked you right off, sir," said the doctor, an elderly gentleman by the name of Milliard. Harry winced as the physician dabbed at his head with the raw spirit, wondering if he was ever, in his life, to be away from brandy used in one form or another. But the doctor had pronounced it efficacious and there was no gainsaying medical opinion.

"Your brother has that portrait of you in his drawing-room, has he not?"

Harry couldn't nod, so he grunted, hoping by doing so to state his displeasure at the mention of the piece, but the doctor had turned his attention to James, clearly intimate enough with the younger Ludlow brother to feel confident in giving him a wigging.

"Duelling, sir. I though at least you had more sense."

"So did I, Dr Milliard."

The old man pushed hard at the long raw wound on Harry's head, which may well have served to show his displeasure, but his victim felt aggrieved. James, not at all put out at the tone of the doctor's strictures, continued smoothly, with a sense of detachment quite alien to the subject. "I cannot say how I would act in other circumstances. There is an element of the romantic in all this. My soul was engaged. So perhaps I required myself to seem heroic."

Harry, still being stung by regular daubings of spirit, cursed James under his breath.

"Soul, forsooth," spat Milliard. "The only emotion attached to duelling is stupidity."

"Then we are a tribe of fools, for Harry has been out too."

The doctor sniffed loudly, and his ministrations immediately became more intense. His next words were preceded by a very painful jab at the very seat of his patient's discomfort. "That does not shock me. I have looked on your brother's face often. You caught him well, for he would not hesitate to kill."

"Damn it, sir," snapped Harry, throwing back his head to get away, "if you're not more gentle with your daubing I'll be tempted to prove you right."

The raised voice, the glare, and the threatening manner didn't affect Milliard at all. He looked at Harry, his head cocked slightly to one side. "Oh, yes, James Ludlow, you caught him well."

"You must come with me, James. How can you miss being there when we catch up with Obidiah Trench?"

James waved his hand languidly, for he was truly stuck with a good reason to deny Harry's wish. The primary cause of his early return to London was now a painful memory. He had commissions that had already waited eighteen months. They would not suffer for another week. And, in truth, he wasn't sure, in his present frame of mind, if he could face being confined in the studio with a subject.

"It will mean staying at Cheyne Court," he said finally.

"For one or two nights," replied Harry. Then his face took on that devious look that James had caught in the portrait. "What if I could get Arthur away from the house?"

The thought of Arthur brought colour back to James's cheeks.

"He won't go when I'm there. He'd be too afraid that I'll undo all his meddling."

"Meddling," said Harry, "what meddling?"

He was still getting the reply to that question, and a lot more besides, in the coach that took them down to Deptford, with James displaying a rare passion in the process.

"It amazes me that you cannot see these things, Harry. If you had talked to Tite, he would certainly tell you. He has made that poor old man's life a misery."

The "poor old man" tag jarred with Harry, who knew Tite better than James supposed, but he let it pass.

"The man even scolded you the night we got back. Scolded you for being late for dinner in your own house."

"He has acquired the habit over the years of considering it his own."

"It is not acquired, brother. It is a national trait. From Bute downwards, every Scotchman who's held high office has behaved as if he owned England. Dundas is the same, wrapping Billy Pitt round his little finger."

"The king is content to term himself a Briton."

"I have nothing against the Union, brother. Indeed some of the Irish are amusing. I don't know that we've gained much from the Welsh connection, except a lot of lawyers and doctors who poach English clients."

"Well, I thank God for it," snorted Harry, finally stung into a derisive response. "We are in the midst of a war with the French, and the Union will survive because we have a few amusing Irishmen, some very rapacious Scotchmen, and a lot of Welshmen of the middling sort."

"Now if we'd united with the French, Harry," said James, with a twinkle in his eye, "that would have been just the thing, for it would have been the blending of two cultured nations, both raised by Rome. We have flown in the face of our classical heritage and not only taken down the walls, but we have permitted the barbarians to enter."

"Am I being practised upon, brother?" asked Harry.

James laughed and nodded. "We are approaching the dockyard, Harry. It would never do to have you in that benign frame of mind when you look over the ship. If I cannot rouse you to parsimony with tales of Arthur, then I must stoop to other means."

Harry looked out as the coach swung through the narrow dockyard gate. The shed itself was already occupied with the frame of another vessel, but through the skeletal timbers Harry could see the ship he was after, riding on the oily waters. He nudged James and pointed.

"That's the one."

"You forget that I've already been here, brother. I know that is the one."

"She has a neat trim about her, don't you think?"

"I fear I've failed to put you in the mood to haggle," said James, doubtfully, for if Harry had looked at a woman with the naked affection he was demonstrating for this hulk he'd be confined by a magistrate.

But haggle he did, for over an hour, and that after an inspection which had taken even longer. The Blackwall shipbuilder, Grisham, had as many dodges as Harry had answers. First was the price, then there was the small matter of what that included. Each dockyard luxury was Harry's absolute necessity. . . . The discussion was too technical for James so he turned away. The winter sun started to set over the river, full of every kind of sailing craft.

The sunset colours, shot through with the smoke from countless chimneys, formed the most extraordinary background.

The chill air kept the warm smoke from settling, and it lay like a strand of diaphanous grey in a wide stripe about five feet above the water. The sky was tinged azure blue, silhouetting the ships' masts, stark and black. The moon was well up, a narrow crescent of white. In the foreground the filthy water rippled, picking up the dying rays of the sun. The horizon was indigo here and orange there, with the wispy clouds hanging like black veils.

It had been a bad day for James Ludlow, indeed a bad week, ever since his return to London. But looking at that setting, which made him itch to have his paints, did more to restore him to peace than anything Harry could say. He knew that he was bored with portraits. He would not promise never to do another, but he was determined that his next foray would be by personal choice. But this, with the ships and the light; surely his heart would lift to paint scenes like this.

"I shall inspect the copper bolts at random, at least one in ten, on the day of purchase," said Harry, emerging from the ship-builder's tiny office.

"Then you must pay to have them replaced, sir, as well as removed, for they have been set in tight. So tight I doubt you'll shift them. We do not furnish gimcrack work in this yard."

"You will pay, Mr Grisham, not I," replied Harry, without the slightest hint of rancour. "And you will not lose by it, if you exclude time, for I have no desire to change the bolts, merely to inspect them."

"Only time, sir," cried Grisham theatrically. "Have you been asleep these last five years? Has no one told you how the price of labour has risen? Why, the men who work here rob me blind."

"It is your blindness that worries me, sir, for if they are robbing you, they may well be robbing the ship."

Even James knew that dockyard trick. The scullies who worked there would cut both ends off the bolts, some as long as four feet, and hammer them home on either side of the join, leaving nothing in the middle. The copper purloined was sold as scrap. Since these same bolts were the very thing that held the main ship's timbers together, it did not need Providence to endanger the crew. A hefty blow and the ship would just disintegrate.

Harry had all the cards and he knew it. The original buyer for this novel design had failed to complete the transaction. Grisham would be well aware, by now, that the navy was unlikely to take her. What he couldn't guess was that Harry had that information too. In the shipbuilder's mind, as he looked at this potential purchaser, he rated him a difficult customer. This was hard bargaining, and for all that he was conceding points, he was enjoying the game. There was a final loud shake of the hand, and the business was complete.

"Four months, Mr Ludlow, an' there's my hand on it," said Grisham.

"Fourteen weeks," replied Harry, opening up an earlier dispute.

"We've been through that, sir," said Grisham with a sigh. He was a man who'd not shake hands lightly.

"So we have, Mr Grisham, so we have. I shall instruct my attorneys to draw up a contract."

The light was fading as they left, with the moon more powerful than the sun. Harry lay back on the padded seats of the coach. "Why, I am quite done up, James."

"But happy?"

Harry jerked upright. "I know she looks a mess to a landsman's eye. But she's a beauty, James, and no mistake."

"Then I wish you joy of her."

Harry looked James right in the eye, gripping his arm with one hand. "And you, brother, how are you?"

James laughed, which was answer enough.

CHAPTER THIRTY-ONE

"I CANNOT open my purse further, sir," said Temple, observing Harry's patent disappointment. He put his hands to the lapels of his long black coat, taking on, with the pinched look on his face, the appearance of a lawyer pleading in court.

The men rowing the bumboat stared straight ahead, ignoring their passengers' conversation. Instead, they concentrated on the third man, wondering where he'd got those two livid black eyes. Pender, had they asked him, couldn't have told them. He'd been convinced that Flowers hadn't laid a hand on him. As far as the crew were concerned, they helped, giving everyone still berthed in the barn an excuse to gently rib him. Pender knew from long experience, that people didn't do that unless they esteemed you in some way. And it had also reassured Flowers, and dampened his desire for revenge, when he observed that he'd done some damage. The atmosphere, by the time Harry returned, was well on the way to being everything his servant had hoped. Tite had been advised to shove it when he moaned about him, and told, in no uncertain terms, that his so-called wound was a scratch and he'd be better off getting back to the kitchens, where he belonged.

As they climbed aboard and stood over the open hatchways the smell of rotting timber rose to greet them. The rigging was as bad as the filthy deck. Untidy, with loose ropes everywhere and blocks that looked as though they hadn't been greased since Creation. Temple was correct. Harry was disappointed. He had not anticipated anything special. But Temple had managed to find a vessel that looked at first sight unfit to cross a river, never mind the English Channel. It was a ship of the same size as the *Planet,* a Dutch trading flute, broad-beamed and slow by the very nature of its build and previous function.

"You would have been hard put to open your purse less, Mr Temple. This kind of ship can be had for the coins that slip through your floorboards."

"It will do for the task we have in mind."

"We?" said Harry, regarding the smuggler with a raised eyebrow.

Temple adopted a lofty tone, like man whose dignity brooked no argument. "I cannot allow you to set out on this adventure on your own, sir. If my interests are threatened, they can only be properly safeguarded by my presence."

"That was not the arrangement, Mr Temple," replied Harry coldly. "We distinctly agreed that Trench was mine."

"You may have him, sir, to skin alive if you wish."

Appraised of Temple's conversation with Pender, Harry didn't need to enquire as to what interest Temple had in mind. Had he anticipated such an outcome he would have bought a ship himself. But it was too late for that now. He had to get his crew aboard, get the ship into some form of order, and get to sea, or he would miss Trench.

"Follow me, Pender," said Harry, making for the hatchway.

"Where are you going, Mr Ludlow?" demanded Temple, who was not pleased to be left alone on the deck.

"I'm going to inspect the ship, sir, something I suggest you might have done before you paid for it." The smuggler opened his mouth to protest, but Harry cut him off. "I cannot believe you bought this, Mr Temple, especially since you intend to accompany us. You put all our lives at risk, including your own."

Temple went pale, for he was a man unused to ships of this type, more at home in a small lugger, or one of the large, fast cutters with twelve oarsmen that could make the journey to France in three hours on a calm night.

"You judge her unsound, sir?" he said to Harry's disappearing head.

Harry bobbed back up again, maliciously indulging himself with a spot of exaggeration.

"She is somewhat more than unsound, sir. If you feel we are keeping you waiting too long, Mr Temple, I would advise against stamping your foot with impatience."

He went back down the hatchway again. The timbers on the maindeck were merely damp. It was when you went below, especially to the spaces under the holds, that mattered. The bilge was foul even by normal standards and the cross-bracings that could be seen above the damp ballast all had mould on them. Harry poked his finger into one of the main supports, dismayed by the way it went in to the rotten wood without effort, almost up to his knuckle.

"That's bad, Captain," said Pender. "Even I know that. Trench'll have us over, no bother, in this tub."

"We can withstand Trench, Pender. But if it comes on to a blow, then this thing could be a death trap. Mind, it may not be as bad as it looks. It's impossible to tell the true state of her timbers without shifting the ballast."

"How will the men take to berthing aboard this?"

Harry turned and looked at Pender. "The Medusas will accept whatever I tell them. You will have to swear for the Deal men."

Pender grinned, then touched the corner of one blackened eye. "Well, Captain, I feel they'll follow me. Happen it's time to find out if I'm right."

"I want some tubs of sulphur down here, right away. The smoke will cover the smell of rot. All the stoves to be lit and kept going full blast as well. We'll throw off all the hatchways and get a couple of windsails rigged. Who knows, a bit of heat and a touch of fresh air can work wonders."

"What's this barky called, by the way?"

Harry laughed. "You'll never believe this, Pender. It's called the *Dragon*."

"The *Dragon*," said Pender, his teeth gleaming. "God strike me, but if St George had come up against a dragon like this he would have been drenched, not singed."

They went back on deck, to find Temple pacing the windward side like an admiral. He looked at them enquiringly as they emerged, filthy and damp, but Harry declined to respond.

"When will you bring your crew aboard?" he asked.

"What crew?"

Temple gave him a thin-lipped smile. "Come, Mr Ludlow. Do you really think you can have your man recruit over twenty seamen in the town of Deal without it coming to my notice?"

"I wasn't trying to avoid your notice," said Harry. But it lacked conviction and he knew it.

"I take it you have no objection to my putting a few of my men aboard. After all, the more we outnumber Trench, the better."

"I cannot see how that squares with your intention of remaining aloof in this affair. You can hardly deny involvement if you are on the deck of the ship that takes Trench, surrounded by your own men."

Temple was not a smiler, unless you termed the merest stretch of his bloodless lips by that name. But he smiled now.

"Never fear, Mr Ludlow. If the prospect vexes you, my men can go ashore before we sail. But I cannot leave this vessel unattended. Some villain might steal it."

"That's precisely what we're going to do," said Harry to the assembled crew.

"It'll make Deal a bit warm for us, Captain," said one of the new men. A few of the Medusas growled at him, content, as their commander said, to follow wherever Harry led.

Pender answered the man gently, for it was a reasonable observation. "You won't be goin' back to Deal, mate. Captain Ludlow has bespoke a brand-new ship, fresh off the stocks at Blackwall Reach. Once we've seen off this Trench character, it will be all aboard for blue water and French gold."

"My brother has already left for Sandwich with a list of what we need. We'll take on our stores there. Not much, for we're not going far. We must, at all costs, get away before anyone can get a message to Temple that we are tied up at Sandwich Quay. I looked at the tides on the Stour and we can be back at sea, at the very latest by tomorrow night, if we put our backs into it. The rest of the work, like the rigging, will have to be done in deeper water."

Harry looked at the men. Some demonstrated profound scepticism on the venture, that was plain. But none of them made any further moves to protest. He made for the barn door, telling Pender to carry on.

"We need to get started soon," added Pender, "if we want to be arriving at the anchorage just after dark. So get your dunnage together and put this barn back into a fit state for cattle."

Arthur was coming up the drive as Harry made his way across from the barn to the house. He was dressed for hunting, though still elegant in an immaculate buff coat over dark corduroy breeches. The man carrying his guns had several brace of birds to contend with as well.

"A successful day," said Harry, pointing to the hanging carcasses.

Arthur glanced over Harry's shoulder. Two sailors, having lifted the stove between two poles, were heading for the rear of the house. Nothing, at this time of year, could have more clearly underlined that they were all about to depart.

"What about you, Harry, have you had similar good fortune?"

"My hunt is only just beginning."

Arthur smiled. Harry had avoided giving him any real information about his intentions. Anne had obviously been right about what troubled him. The merest hint of a London house had raised his spirits.

"Then I wish you joy of it. I shall hang these pheasants in anticipation of your speedy return."

"Thank you."

Arthur looked over his other shoulder, and this time he frowned. Harry turned to find Tite standing there. The old servant touched his forelock, but whatever words he wanted to say wouldn't come. Harry couldn't know that it was Arthur's presence which troubled him, for on hearing of the planned expedition he'd set his heart on going, willing to trade disclosure of Arthur's misdemeanours for a place on the ship. Not that there was much to tell. Still not sure how the land lay, he'd gone down to the Griffin's Head to drop a hint or two. That had earned him a flea in his ear, as Naomi Smith lashed out at him in a manner she normally reserved for drunken strangers.

"Do you want me, Tite?"

Harry's question unlocked his jaw, for he'd get no second chance. "I hear you're planning to take the admiral's brass four-pounders."

Harry frowned as well. He had no desire to hold this conversation in front of his brother-in-law, either.

"I am."

"Saving your presence, Master Harry, I's looked after those guns since they was first brought here, that bein' when your father struck his flag."

"I know that, Tite."

"Well, I feels that where they go, so should I."

Harry's look softened, he could hardly do otherwise looking at the bent old man, wrinkled, frail, and with no teeth. Only the eyes, for all their watery quality and poor range, still had their potency. Tite knew they were going off to fight, and he wanted to be part of it. But Harry couldn't expose this old man to such a risk. Besides he'd be more of a hindrance than a help.

"Your duties are here, Tite."

"We will happily spare him from those," said Arthur coldly. Tite was amazed, for he was so determined to succeed that he'd geared himself to speak out even in front of Arthur. And now this "damned Scotchman" was aiding his cause. For probably the first time ever, he smiled warmly at Lord Drumdryan. It was not returned and he looked back at Harry. "There you are, Captain."

Harry was in a quandary, undermined by his brother-in-law's remark. He didn't want to tell Tite the truth, that he was too old, more likely to get in the way than add anything to the expedition.

"You may supervise the dismounting and loading of the guns on to the cart. You may accompany them to Sandwich. But you will not sail with us, d'you understand?"

Tite had pulled himself upright at the tone of command in Harry's voice, wondering whether "half a loaf" would suffice. His mind made up, he answered crisply enough, even if it was slurred by his lack of molars. "Aye, aye, Captain."

"May I enquire as to your destination?" asked Arthur.

"I should have thought that was obvious. Mind, if anyone calls, I would rather you told them we've gone to London."

Arthur half turned, indicating the top of the windmill that stood on the hill that led to Eastry.

"It may interest you to know that there is a man watching the house. He's a low-looking cove, but bold. He made no attempt at concealment when I passed close."

"Pender!" shouted Harry.

"He's chosen that spot well," Arthur continued. "He can see who comes and goes, and also observe anyone who gets near enough to threaten him. I doubt that your man Pender will get as close to him as I did."

Pender was already hurrying towards the two men. He was abreast by the time Harry asked why.

"Because he has been set to watch you. He saw me as an innocent, merely someone out hunting. I took the precaution of coming in through the woods, so I doubt he's even connected me to this house."

"Are you offering your services, Arthur?"

"Why not? You and James whispering half the night, making your plans. My wife and Mrs Cray baking ship's biscuit, and now Tite volunteering his services. If the entire family is to go to war, I have no less desire than Tite to be included. I suggest I retrace

my steps, taking these birds with me, and make my way past the
windmill again."

"Only a little closer this time?"

There was something of the soldier in Arthur now. His eyes
didn't exactly gleam, but they certainly held an expression that
made him look less of a courtier.

"I can then enquire as to what the fellow is about, and since I
am armed, I doubt he'll refuse me an answer. I take it you want
him kept alive."

"Of course," replied Harry. "And I want him confined until
nightfall tomorrow. After that you may release him."

They made straight for Deal, moving quickly so that they stayed
ahead of any news of their whereabouts. Harry led them past
Sandown Castle as darkness fell, and on to the beach without
pause. The moon was out, in a clear frosty sky, providing ample
light. There was no shortage of boats, nor did the men whom they
hired enquire about their numbers or the fact that Harry's men
were armed to the teeth. They took the fee and did their job, being
as close-mouthed as the rest of the inhabitants of the town.

If Temple's men had any intention to resist, the sheer number
of men coming aboard the *Dragon* soon dissuaded them. The
whole ship reeked of sulphur, a distinct improvement on the smell
of rot. It was pleasing to see the way that his Medusas, who all
knew their place, went right about their duties. Pender's Deal contingent were less sure of themselves. But they were sailors, so once
directed to their various tasks they set to with a will.

There was little to rig in the way of sails, but they didn't need
it. The greatest danger, once they'd unmoored the *Dragon,* was
the sheer quantity of shipping, all firmly anchored head and stern.
There was also the force of the current. Deal might provide a safe
anchorage, but it also had a very large tidal rise and fall, which
in certain circumstances had a riptide quality that could drag a
ship's anchors out of the soft sand below.

They had to manoeuvre their way, with only a sliver of moon, through a veritable cat's cradle of ropes, with the tide making fast and hurrying them on. There was no end of shouting from other craft as this mad bugger, who didn't know the time of the clock, was rudely told to sheer off. They removed the paint off one Indiaman, which led the captain of that ship to apoplectic rage. Harry ignored him, refusing to name his vessel when called upon to do so.

The shipping thinned as they cleared the anchorage and opened Pegwell Bay. Harry, grateful for the moonlight, however slight, put up the helm and drifted in slowly towards the deep-water channel of the Stour. He needed the rising tide, as the *Dragon,* deep-hulled, would navigate this river with difficulty. The long approach to Sandwich, which meandered through thick reed beds and foul marshes, was silted up. Once a thriving port, and the premier naval base of England, the town was now confined to small ships plying the coastal trade.

James, having bespoken them a berth, was waiting on the quayside surrounded by carters' wagons bearing heaps of naval stores. Miles of cordage, bolts of canvas, some already stitched together as sails, tubs of tar and turpentine, nails, blocks, pulleys, water barrels, pork and beef barrels, hogsheads of biscuit, cheese, butter, firkins of beer, and a barrel of rum. Harry had lanterns slung in the rigging and they worked on through the night to get everything loaded. What they were about could not be concealed. It had, indeed, excited a fair amount of attention. The traffic between Deal and Sandwich was constant, and given that Temple had his ear to the ground, the chance of his hearing about the *Dragon's* whereabouts was better than fair.

Tite appeared with the ship's biscuit and the two brass cannon. Harry set the old servant, and the men who'd accompanied him, to fixing breechings forward on the poop. James, with nothing else to do, had hot food fetched from a local inn, with his brother ordering the men to work and eat at the same time. By dawn everything was aboard, but as yet unstowed. The *Dragon* was much deeper in the water now, and for all that Harry Ludlow liked a tidy deck, he also wanted the option of unloading some stores in the narrow channel. For if the ship stuck there he could bid farewell to any idea of getting away to sea without Temple.

During the hours of darkness he'd spoken to the locals, who knew the channel best. He asked them about the tide and decided, despite the unholy mess on his decks, to try and get the *Dragon* out on the morning tide, a time when the wind was more likely to be favourable. He could then anchor in the bay and complete the work. Having hired several local boats, and shifted his crane from the main mast to the mizen, he bade them follow him and cast loose. His own boats, full of sailors, were out ahead, ready to take over the tow from the horses when the animals ran out of hard ground to haul on.

The wind was light enough, though in the twisting channel it was often dead foul. Harry was in the bows, listening to both the leadsman and the water below, his ear cocked for that tell-tale grinding sound of his keel striking sand. The most treacherous part of the river was at the mouth, where the silt, eddying round an old wreck, formed an underwater bar. Harry anchored, trying to gauge the height of the flood, then set all the sail he could, bracing his yards round to catch the wind. He could feel the *Dragon* straining on the single anchor. He called on his boats to haul the ship's head round and tow hard, casting off the cable with a float, so that it could be fetched later.

James watched his brother in the pale morning light. If Harry disliked the expression James had captured in that early portrait, he would have hated to see himself now, for he was glaring at the dark swirling water below the bows like a demon intent on mischief. Harry closed his eyes as he heard the keel hit the bar. The way on the ship slowed, the ropes to the tow becoming taut. Ahead James could see the men, red faced as they nearly pulled themselves upright by the pressure on the oars. The *Dragon* was nearly dead in the water, but suddenly the bows dipped.

"She floats, the old barky floats!"

James turned to see old Tite, his watery blue eyes ablaze with pleasure. Harry didn't have time to be pleased at the words, or angry that the old sod was still aboard. He was too busy calling in his boats, telling one of them to fetch that anchor before it was stolen by one of the Sandwich watermen. He turned back to look down the deck, his face still set in that devilish cast, not sparing James in the general glare.

"Now let's get the deck tidied up, otherwise we'll be the laughing-stock of the English Channel."

CHAPTER THIRTY-TWO

THE CROSSING, with the wind in the north, took some twenty hours, for the *Dragon* lived up to what was expected of her, wallowing along at a snail's pace, yards braced round and pumps clanking. The crew worked hard to improve matters even as they sailed her and by the time they made the crossing the ship was a little less temperamental. Once in sight of the shore, Harry put his helm down, steering south with the wind nearly dead astern. Sailing easy, he had the crew fed and sent them to sleep by turns.

It was with a tremendous sense of *déjà vu* that Harry sat off the French coast. The night sky was almost identical to the last time he'd approached this place, with clear patches interspersed on occasions with cloud, which plunged the whole scene into Stygian blackness. There was less moon, but the mass of stars helped when the sky cleared. With more of a sea running in the confined waters, the *Dragon* rolled alarmingly as she lost steerage way. Harry hauled his wind as soon as he spotted the array of ships' topmasts against the skyline. If Temple's information was correct, it had to be Trench. The rendezvous was exactly right as well as the timing. The Sussex man never loaded at night. Working on an industrial scale, he waited for first light to transfer his goods aboard. That had given Bertles his opportunity. It would now do the same for Harry Ludlow.

There were no cliffs around here for him to hide against. The coastline of this part of France was low and marshy, ideal smuggling country. Not that the locals who supplied Trench had much to fear from authority. Few in France, these days, could afford to buy the goods they were trading. Their worthless Revolutionary *assignats,* printed by the million, barely purchased enough to feed them. Besides that, anything that brought in English gold, which helped to pay for the Revolutionary war, was more than welcome. Those in authority actively participated in the trade, even, it was rumoured, some of the regicides themselves.

He had towed his boats in towards the coast, so they were already over the side. No noise disturbed the quiet night as Harry led his Medusas over the side. Not wholly trusting their new captain, the Deal contingent showed no jealousy at being excluded. They were content to leave the dangerous tasks to others. Muffled oars took them silently in towards the long sandy beach, the line of which was illuminated by the strip of white water lapping the shore. All the orders had been given aboard, so those detailed to guard the boats took up their station without a word. The others followed Harry inland.

They'd laid fascines to make a path over the dunes and across the sandy beach, so finding the barn where Trench's contraband was stored presented no great chore. It was even less difficult to get inside, since those left to guard the hoard, in the presence of all that drink, had not mustered the power to resist temptation, and lay back on the great bolts of silk, snoring loudly. Harry had them taken and secured anyway, treating them with a roughness that they scarcely warranted. But it was all grist to his mill. He wanted Trench angry. In that state he was all the more likely to commit errors when he set off in pursuit of the *Dragon.*

The barn was near a hundred feet long, with contraband piled all the way to the rafters. Every known commodity was catered for, from spirits to perfumes. But mostly it was French wine, brandy casks bearing the marks of both Cognac and Armagnac, high-quality Holland gin, and great bolts of plain and printed silk. But there were spices too, and trading goods that had come in from all over the globe, the private ventures of ships' captains, excisable goods sold to the smugglers who operated small boats in mid-Channel then brought their cargoes here to be taken to England in larger vessels.

They moved as much of it as they could; not to the shore, because that was too far and they were too few to make an impact. But the sandy dunes of the coastline presented ample places to make it look as though they had been at work for hours. If Trench came to look, before he spotted the *Dragon,* he would believe her to be well laden with his property, making a chase certain.

The whole area was devoid of human habitation, more a home to birds. Harry's crew moved about without the need for great caution, helping to crystallize certain thoughts that their captain had been harbouring for days. However much Temple demurred, Bertles had been rumbled because he'd been expected. It was betrayal, allied to the greed of a man who fed at this forbidden trough once too often. Harry's presence would, as far as he knew, come as a complete surprise. But he didn't entirely trust Temple. He could not afford that anything should go wrong. He would get one clear shot at confronting Trench. After that, should he fail, all the advantage would lie with his enemy.

So he had to make it look like he was a serious thief, just in case the smuggler came ashore early. His true intention was to wait until first light, to allow Trench's men and his own to see what appeared to be the last boats, well laden, putting off from the shore. At all costs he must entice the smuggler to pursue him into deep water. Harry, showing only a third of his available men, and keeping his guns well hidden, would let Trench board. Then, having raked the deck with grape, he would attack those still upright with half his crew, the Deal contingent, while the Medusas boarded Trench's ship and took care of the men the smuggler had left behind.

Back on the beach, with the boats loaded to the gunwales with stolen goods, they waited, ready to shove off at a moment's notice. Harry could see by the light of the great stern-lantern that some of Trench's men from the ship closest to the beach were getting ready to come ashore. Against the reflected starlight the silhouette of the first boat pulled off, followed by several others. The men waded ashore and started inland. Harry tried to count their footsteps to the barn, tried to calculate the point at which the first shout of alarm would split the dawn air.

This was the critical moment. He did not want to be attacked whilst stationary and close to the shore. Nor did he want too many of Trench's own boats in the water, threatening to cut him off from the *Dragon*. He also had no idea if Trench had a gang of French tubmen available to load his cargo. Those tubmen would make short work of his men if they were trapped on shore. Worse than that, if they were brought aboard Trench's ship to take part in the fight they could nullify his slim numerical advantage.

The first faint shout came as the earliest hint of daylight tinged the eastern sky. Softly, he ordered his men to cast off. The shouting increased in volume as Trench's men came running back towards the shore. Once his boat was under way, and out of the surf that lapped against the shore, he took out his pistol, aimed it carelessly at the beach, and fired.

"Shout, lads, and some of you make it sound like you're Frenchmen."

The cacophany of sound that erupted around him fixed the attention of those on Trench's deck who had frozen at the crack of the pistol shot. Men came running on to the beach, waving their arms to alert the ships' crews. All hell broke loose as the shouting across the still water matched that in the *Dragon*'s boats. The first ball from a musket slapped into the sea some ten feet away. Harry shouted for his men to pull harder, glad to see that, with exquisite timing, Pender had slipped the anchor on the *Dragon*, and was setting sail to make good their escape.

Sails were also coming out of Trench's ship, as his men ran up the rigging to release the bunts that held the canvas to the yards. Harry and his boats came alongside the *Dragon*, throwing their barrels and bolts to waiting hands on the deck. They came scrambling aboard themselves with frantic haste. It was not entirely play acting, for the amount of musket fire from Trench's men, coming from all three ships, made the low boats distinctly perilous. Harry was on his quarterdeck in a trice, taking over the wheel from

Pender, and giving the commands to set more sail. He also ordered the Medusas below, where they would remain hidden from Trench's gaze, ready to take to the boats through the sternlights and board the enemy on his unprotected side. The *Dragon* picked up speed, though scarcely enough to satisfy Harry. James had a glass on Trench's ship and as the light increased he called to his brother to come and have a look.

"Not now, James," snapped Harry, busy giving vital orders to his crew.

James did not respond to Harry's sharp tone. His voice was calm as he replied. "I think what I have to show you will interest you, Harry. It might even cause you to alter your plans."

He pushed the telescope into his brother's hand. Harry raised it, twirling the frontpiece to adjust the focus, automatically looking to the prow to see if the enemy was moving. Trench had also slipped his anchor, though as yet he had no way on the ship. But they were not far apart. In ten minutes, when the sun came up, each deck would be clearly visible. But now, in the grey, pre-dawn light, the telescope was necessary. He raised it from water level. It threw Trench's quarterdeck into sharp focus. It also threw up the round, scarred face of Cephas Quested, leaning over the rail, his finger pointing directly at Harry Ludlow.

"What in God's name is he doing there?"

"A good question, Harry, since Temple told Pender that the man was still upstairs in his tavern, yet to recover from the blow he'd administered."

Harry spun round, pacing up and down quickly. What did this development portend? Behind him James called to Pender, handing him the telescope. His servant's single coarse expletive only served to underline the shock of seeing Temple's right-hand man on Trench's ship.

"I didn't believe the bastard I knew he was lyin'."

"Why have they allowed us such licence?" said James, indicating the stolen goods that littered the deck. "Quested must have known we were going to show up here."

"No," snapped Harry. "If they'd wanted to trap us, they'd have taken us at anchor, certainly when I was ashore. And they would never let us raid their store of contraband."

"But it must be a trap, Harry."

Harry looked right through his brother. "Yes, James, a trap. Set by Temple. But for whom?"

"All of us, your honour," said Pender. "I think Temple hopes we'll cancel each other out."

Harry shook his head violently. "If that's his aim, he's taking a hell of a chance. If I fight Trench, one of us has to survive. And Quested on Trench's deck means that . . ."

Harry paused, shaking his head violently again. Then he grabbed the telescope from Pender's hand and made for the rigging. James looked at Pender, hoping for enlightenment, only to see that he was equally mystified by this behaviour. Harry raced up to the cap, then carried on up to the crosstrees. Once he settled himself securely, he took out the telescope and swept the horizon. The clear night had given way to a dawn of low grey cloud, but there was a strip of clear sky to the east between land and cloud, which the sun edged into. He waited while it rose, lifting itself to light an increasing horizon.

The sail on the horizon was only a speck of white and it disappeared almost as soon as he spotted it. If anything served to increase his suspicion, it was that act. No innocent merchant ship would take in its upper sails at dawn, for the very simple reason that they would not be set during the night. Only someone who wished to remain unobserved would do such a thing. But they'd been too slow, for Harry had spotted them. There was only one problem. He didn't have the faintest idea who "they" were!

He turned to look at Trench's ship. No need for a telescope now. The bright red sun was behind them, high enough to throw everything in sharp relief, like one of those Dutch paintings James was so fond of. He could see Trench supervising the issuing of arms to his men, and the red flash of metal every time one of the smugglers swung a blade or a pike.

He called to one of his sailors to come aloft, gave him the telescope and the position of his sighting, and bade him keep his eyes
peeled. Then he slid down a backstay to the deck, still littered
with the contraband that had been so hastily slung aboard. James
and Pender watched him closely. He'd stopped to look at this
cargo, his face creased in concentration.

"I want that stuff over the side," he snapped. "The barrels will
sink on their own, but the silk will float if it's not weighted."

Pender gave the orders. Though the men obeyed, some of the
Deal crew were clearly reluctant, since the silk alone was worth
a mint of money. Harry glared at them, and for the first time they
saw the black face, the reverse of the good-humoured coin, that
those who sailed with him before knew so well.

"I want it over the bows, so that Trench cannot see it go. And
if any of you are tempted to hide a barrel or two, let me tell you
that there is a revenue cutter just below the horizon, which is just
waiting to come aboard and clap us all in irons."

"You've seen it?" asked James, quickly.

Harry looked even angrier, not wanting to have to explain a
guess. James could hardly fail to catch the glare, which made him
spin round to look back at Trench's ship, rapidly overhauling the
Dragon. The voice from the masthead only added to the tension.

"I've got her, Captain," the sailor shouted. "Can't see her deck,
but she's fore-and-aft-rigged."

"And well armed," said Harry to himself. Then he raised his
voice so that the Medusas, crouching just below the hatchways,
could hear him too.

"We proceed as before, men. That ship isn't going to come anywhere near us till we engage Trench. Once we're locked in battle,
they'll come up hand over fist with their guns run out. We can't
fight them and I, for one, don't want to."

James coughed loudly at the look in Harry's eye, which gave
the lie to that statement. His brother grinned at him to acknowledge the observation, before throwing out his arm to indicate this
unexpected threat.

"What it does mean is that we have to finish with Obidiah Trench before they come up. We are all innocent merchant sailors, going about our business, when we're attacked by this villain. Don't anyone so much as breathe a word about contraband, or being ashore in France last night, for if you do, we'll all end up in Maidstone Gaol."

Harry was glaring again, but it was an imposed look. He knew that nothing pleased a sailor more than lying to authority. These men would do it willingly, embellishing the tale with such colourful additions that nothing short of the personal thanks of Farmer George himself would suffice to reward their unselfish valour.

He called to the Deal contingent, still on deck. "Now ease those braces a touch, then arm yourselves. I want Trench alongside us a mite quicker than we originally intended. I'm hoping he won't run out his guns, since he doesn't think we've got any. But if he does, get below until I call you back on deck."

It was gratifying to see these men, new to his ways, obey so well. No one rushed to ease the ropes that held the yards, bowsed tight to take maximum advantage of the wind. They sauntered, with the majority gathering round those doing the work to ensure that they were unobserved from the enemy deck. And it was nothing sudden either. They eased the ropes inch by inch. The *Dragon* wasn't doing much in the way of speed, and she slowed gradually. But it was subtle. Trench would believe he was overhauling them due to his superior seamanship.

Harry half wondered about issuing further orders to avoid killing anyone. He had no desire to be taken up for murder. But he put the thought out of his mind. They wouldn't carry any weight in the heat of a fight, where a man was intent on his own survival. And it might take some of the spirit out of his crew, which would only make the task harder. Besides, his whole plan hinged on surprise, on the use of the two small cannon on an apparently unarmed ship. He turned round, glad to see that James had made his way to the poop. Tite was there, grinning like a gargoyle. His brass four-pounders, still well covered, were loaded and primed and he'd lowered the tub with the slowmatch into the skylight of the main cabin so that the tell-tale smoke would not give the game away.

The Medusas would be crowding into that same cabin now, ready to haul in the boats being towed behind. If the Deal men did as they'd been ordered, and retired towards the cabin door before the assault of Trench's men, then Tite could fire off his guns. They'd been unable to purchase metal grape-shot, so the guns were again loaded with shingle, but this time carefully selected for size. It wasn't the true answer and it wouldn't do the same amount of damage. But given the present circumstance, where a dead body could be classed as murder, that was all to the good.

Trench was close now, with his guns run out, his great bearded face set in an angry glare. He'd set his ship to take Harry's wind, a manoeuvre that his enemy fully expected. Cephas Quested was yelling insults over the narrowing gap between the ships, leaving no one aboard the *Dragon* in any doubt of their forthcoming fate. The Deal men, who knew him and his reputation well, ignored him. It was too late to send them below, but they maintained their positions without orders, ready to obey any instructions their new captain issued. Pender stood with them, clearly pleased at the way they behaved. He put an arm on Flowers's shoulder, giving him a gentle shove of encouragement. The other man, so recently willing to fight him, and even more bruised than his late adversary, opened his swollen lips and grinned in reply.

"Let fly the sheets," yelled Harry, as soon as he saw the sails flap. He spun the wheel to bring the *Dragon*'s head round, pointing his bows right across those of Trench. The smuggler had to spin his own wheel to avoid a collision, and his guns, clearly with untrained crews, went off uselessly, their shot landing harmlessly in the sea. All his careful preparations were thrown into confusion. He had to order armed men, waiting to board the *Dragon*, away from the side of his ship to tend to his own flapping sails. The gun crews, in total disarray, left their cannon for the same purpose.

Harry spun the wheel again, using what little way was left on his ship to put her on a parallel course. The gap between the two vessels closed rapidly. His own sailors, freed from all other duties, rushed to the side, yelling at the enemy. Trench's men, much more numerous, with Quested the most vocal, eschewed gunnery and responded in kind. Pikes and swords jabbed across the gap as the two ships ground together. Harry looked aloft. A few of Trench's topmen were up there, casting the ropes that would lash the two ships together.

The roar from the enemy deck increased in volume as they started to climb on to the *Dragon*'s side. Harry looked beyond them, disappointed to see that Trench, their captain, was content to watch the action from the safety of his own quarterdeck . He cursed, for he was the man he wanted. Yet he could not leave his own deck to follow the Medusas who were at this very moment lowering themselves unseen into the boats. Harry pulled out his sword and fixed his eye on Cephas Quested. If he couldn't have Trench, then Temple's batman would do just as well.

The level of sound had risen. Yet even above the noise Harry could hear the man he'd left aloft, shouting down to tell him that the ship he'd spotted earlier was coming up fast, with everything set. It was an armed cutter, the *Nimble,* with a dozen 12-pounders, six of which were run out on the larboard side, ready to rake both ships if that should prove necessary. At the news Harry turned his attention away from the forthcoming fight. He could see the revenue cutter's sails from the deck now. Had he left himself enough time?

Quested helped, seemingly eager to prove himself braver than the others, acting as if he was the captain and not Trench, who stayed by the wheel. He was the first to leap on to the *Dragon*'s deck, his booming voice raised for the others to follow. They did so readily, for Harry's men fell back slightly, leaving them space. Swords clashed and pikes jabbed, with the batman waving a huge nail-studded cudgel. This alone seemed to be enough to drive the Dragons back. They retreated towards Harry, still by the wheel.

Trench must have seen something. His girlish voice screamed across the water as Tite whipped the covers off his guns. But Quested was too busy trying to kill Harry's men to respond. As soon as they'd cleared the waist of the ship, the Dragons, who had given a good appearance of contesting every inch of the deck, melted away before them. The clear space before him allowed Quested to lift his eyes, allowed him to see the danger they were all in.

"Now, Tite!" yelled Harry.

There is a gap in the firing of a gun, a moment between the point when the slow-match is put to the touch-hole and the flaring powder ignites the charge. Tite, being poorly sighted, added another half second as he fumbled around. For most of the bemused boarders, it wasn't enough. But Quested had time to throw himself to the deck, so that the bags of shingle, bursting from the cannon's mouth, flew over his head. It decimated the rest, and the Dragons, rushing forward as the guns went off, were amongst them in a flash, with Harry at their head, slashing right and left as he tried to fight his way towards Quested.

He barely saw Pender flash across his eyeline. He had leapt up into the rigging, grabbed a loose rope which hung down from the maincourse, and launched himself at Quested. His feet were out in straight line before him. As the batman struggled back on to his feet, Pender's boots took him right on the side of the head. Harry was close enough to see the ear burst open, close enough to see the look of shock fade to unconsciousness as Pender, letting go of his rope, landed on the falling body.

Both men disappeared into the mêlée. Harry was halfway towards Pender, ready to cover his back, when the fight went right past him. His servant was crouched over Quested, a marline-spike raised, with the clear intention of smashing the batman's brains out. Harry grabbed him just in time, then recoiled quickly as Pender, his eyes full of hate, turned to attack him. The look faded as quickly as the aimed blow. Harry hauled him to his feet and threw an arm round his shoulder, partly in affection, but mostly to show him the result of their action.

Most of Trench's men were cowering in the scuppers now, their arms up to protect themselves from the blows being rained on their heads. Just then the Medusas burst over the unprotected side of Trench's ship. The smuggler, with few men to protect him, didn't behave well. Harry would have expected him to stand and fight, at least to ensure that if he was taken it was by force. But Trench threw away his weapon at the first hint of danger, then fell to his knees, hands raised in supplication, his high-pitched voice pleading that his life should be spared.

The boom of the guns took everyone's attention. Harry yelled at his men to make all secure before rushing to the far rail. The *Nimble,* which had swung round broadside-on to the two ships, fired off another salvo. It whizzed through the *Dragon*'s rigging, holing the sails and smashing one of the yards. But it wasn't that which made Harry mad. It was the sight of Braine, with Sniff in his arms, standing behind the cutter's wheel, issuing instructions to the captain.

Braine looked as though he had no intention of coming aboard. Instead he seemed content to stand off and bombard the defenceless ships. Harry still had his sword in his hand. He ran to the mainmast and slashed at the halyard holding the *Dragon*'s scrap of a flag. He'd never struck to an enemy in his life. It afforded him little pleasure that he was now forced to do so, and to someone who should have been a friend.

CHAPTER THIRTY-THREE

THE *NIMBLE* came alongside, sandwiching the *Dragon* between herself and Trench's ship. Harry's Medusas, ignoring the arrival of this unforeseen development, had carried on with their task of securing the captured ship. Those who'd surrendered to the Deal contingent were shepherded back to their own forecastle. Not all of them, for Tite's cannon had done terrible damage. Men lay everywhere, mostly groaning wounded intermingled with the odd still body, perhaps dead, with the inert bulk of Cephas Quested the most obvious. Trench, who now stood alone on his quarterdeck, had his hands tied behind his back. He'd apparently recovered some of his venom, for he spat at everybody who came near him, his own men as well as Harry's, mouthing curses at those whom he suspected of letting him down.

Braine came across in the company of several armed men. He stood for a moment surveying the carnage on the deck, before turning towards Harry, who stood by the mainmast with Pender and James just behind him. Braine made a gesture with his hand and the armed men fanned out behind him, their weapons lowered to cover those of Harry's crew who lined the opposite rail. One or two of his men raised their weapons in response.

"Belay that!" cried Harry sharply, indicating that they should adopt a less threatening pose. He wasn't sure what was afoot here. But one thing was absolutely certain. No good would ever come of an assault on a group of revenue men. Their leader indicated that some of his men should go below, no doubt to search the ship.

"Well, Mr Ludlow," said Braine coldly. "You have done us a

service by concentrating on your fight. Here we find that we have taken two smugglers for the price of one."

"Two smugglers?"

"You will surely not pretend to be otherwise engaged, sir, despite all your previous protestations of innocence?"

He stopped as he observed his men return to the deck. One of them gave him a surreptitious shake of the head, and Harry thanked the gods for the instinct that had made him throw Trench's contraband over the side. It was clear that Braine was annoyed, for all that he sought to disguise it. Harry couldn't keep the malice out of his voice, nor the smile off his face, as he drove home his advantage.

"Perhaps if you were to search the other ship, Mr Braine, you would have a mite more luck."

A single sharp command drove his men into action. They rushed over to Trench's ship, pushing aside those members of Harry's crew who'd come to the rail to listen. Harry curtly ordered his Medusas back aboard the *Dragon,* before turning once more to confront Braine.

"I should be well satisfied, sir. I will make you a present of Trench and his crew, with a pious if unfounded hope that His Majesty King George will see some of the profit from the cargo. As to myself, and your unwarranted suspicions, I would advise you that half a cake is better than nothing."

Braine was having difficulty maintaining his self-control. He walked up close, so that their noses were nearly touching, his voice a soft hiss meant for Harry's ears alone.

"Stay out of these waters, Ludlow, and stay out of my way. More than that, take that smirk off your face or I'll clap you in irons, regardless, just for the inconvenience it will cause you."

Harry kept his voice low too. He had no desire to publicly threaten Braine. But the anger was evident, as well as the fact that he was deadly serious.

"Try it, Braine, and I'll throw you and your men into the Channel. You exceed your authority."

Trench's high voice cut through the air, pealing angrily. "Why ain't you searching his ship, you swabs!"

No one aboard the *Dragon* could hear the words the sailor guarding Trench said, but they made him puce. His thick beard trembled as he squealed his response.

"Don't you fall for that. He's as guilty as Cain. He's a smuggler all right, even if he and his type only steal their goods."

"Stow it, Captain," cried one of his men, "we're in enough of a trough already."

For once Trench's voice seem low enough to be normal. "You'll pay with the skin on your back for that remark."

The call from the hatchway unlocked their mutual glare. Braine, hearing the call, pushed past Harry and climbed over the rail to inspect some of the contraband they'd begun to fetch up from the hold. Harry quietly ordered some men aloft to cut the lashings that held the yards together. Pender already had others standing by the braces. Tite's voice, loud and hissing through his gums, made everyone turn.

"Guns loaded and run out, Captain."

Harry turned to face the grinning servant. James stood beside him, equally smug, for they'd trained one of the loaded cannon, unobserved, on to the revenue cutter, and another on Trench. The evidence of what those guns could do was still lying on Harry's deck. Braine had turned at Tite's shout, and his face went pale, for the old man was standing with the slowmatch just above the touch-hole, while he was standing right beside Trench, totally unaware that the old servant probably couldn't even see them.

"There are at least two more smugglers in the bay due east of here, Mr Braine. I suggest you would be better served attending to them, rather than preventing me from going about my lawful business. I have already observed that you've exceeded your authority. I am quite prepared to test the matter in the courts, even if, by some unfortunate accident, you're not around to witness it."

Braine fought to keep control, his craggy purple face shaking with the effort. "You may go, Ludlow, but steer for the Downs. I'm not finished with you yet."

Harry had already turned away before he finished speaking. "Get these bodies off my deck."

"What I cannot understand, James, is that no matter what I say, no one will believe I'm not engaged in smuggling!"

"It must be your pure and innocent nature, brother."

Harry smiled, but the jest didn't break his train of thought. "I was sure I'd convinced Braine, but he just accused me again."

James looked back over the aftrail, to where Trench's ship and the *Nimble* were still wallowing on the swell. "He's Temple's man, remember, you said so yourself. If the King of the Smugglers tells him to believe you're in the same game, he won't argue."

Harry was looking at the same view, wondering why Braine wasn't going after the other ships. "But why does Trench believe it? I thought he was after us because we witnessed Bertles's murder. But he doesn't seem to care about that. And if we're right about Temple, then he thinks so too."

"I should go home and settle down to a life of farming."

Nothing could make Harry Ludlow groan more than that remark. It made him want to put the helm down and head for blue water. Instead, he set his course for the Kellet Gut, standing off from the wreck-littered sandbanks until he was sure the tide was high. His course through the anchorage took him past most of Admiral Duncan's squadron. He felt as though every eye at the side of these warships was eyeing his men, with a view to pressing them into the Fleet.

Temple, in his Fencibles uniform, complete with feather-trimmed hat, had himself rowed out, having waited anxiously at the Hope and Anchor for news, with men placed on the shore to fetch him as soon as his ship, or the *Nimble,* was in the offing. His face, as he approached the side of the vessel, was a picture. The *Dragon* had clearly been in a fight. But with the Ludlow brothers, in the company of their servant, leaning over the side, and none of the other pieces in his chess game in sight, he didn't know whether to be pleased or furious. He clambered aboard awkwardly, his sabre causing him no end of trouble.

"The gentleman has an exceeding martial bearing, brother," said James quietly. "Should we be all atremble?"

"Well," he demanded of Harry, as soon as his boot hit the deck. "Were we successful?"

It was James who replied. "Perhaps, Mr Temple, it would be best if you tell us what to your mind constitutes success?"

"It may well be that our survival is not in that category," Harry added.

Temple glared at James, but he latched on to the important word which Harry had used. "Survival. That must mean you found Trench."

"Not only Trench," said James. "We also found your man, Quested."

"Who the devil are you?" demanded Temple, glaring at James. It was impossible to tell if his anger was genuine, or an attempt to avoid the question.

"James Ludlow, sir." Temple shrugged, as though the name was meaningless, which made James furious. "I am another one of those people Trench seemed intent on murdering."

"Why would Trench want to murder you?"

"You'll get your chance to ask him yourself, Mr Temple. Braine is bound to fetch him back to Deal."

Temple's pale face lost what little blood it had. His hand fiddled nervously with the hilt of his sabre. "He's not dead, then?"

"Nor is Quested," said Harry. He didn't know if that was true, for Pender had hit him hard with his boots, so hard that he'd nearly taken his head off.

"So, Mr Temple," asked James, his tone full of languid irony, "you must tell us. Are we successful?"

There was a long pause, while Temple weighed the odds. Neither brother could tell what he was thinking, but no genius was required for that. He'd sought, by using Braine and the *Nimble*, to take care of all his perceived enemies. Braine had two of them, but the other one was standing before him, free to come and go as he pleased.

"I'll thank you to vacate my ship, gentlemen." He gestured to Pender and the rest of the crew. "And take these scruffy rapscallions with you."

Harry sucked his breath in hard, then released it slowly. James had turned to glance at him, wondering what he would do. Temple was a dangerous man, perhaps too much so to cross. And he knew that his brother could, if required, take the long view. But Harry Ludlow the privateer won out easily over the pragmatist.

"Pender," he said softly. "See Mr Temple over the side."

The smuggler never got his sword out of its scabbard. The men who lifted him over the rail missed his boat by a mile, and since Temple couldn't swim, all that was left on the grey surface was his feathered hat. His boatmen fished him out, dragged him into the bottom of their wherry by his wide buff belt, and headed for shore lest they suffer the same fate.

"Mr Magistrate Temple is at this very moment preparing orders for me. I am to arrest you, Mr Ludlow, for smuggling."

"I had hoped to welcome you back to our house in more pleasant circumstances, Captain Latham," said Lady Drumdryan. "And my husband will be mortified to have missed you. He is out visiting tenants."

The soldier gave her a small bow, but he also managed to convey how sad this development made him. But his soft brown eyes never left Harry's face.

"How long?"

The speed at Latham's reply showed that he had worked everything out on the way to Cheyne Court.

"He will issue the warrants to me as soon as I return. I have told my sergeant to inform him that I'm out hunting, an excuse which is valid till nightfall. I can, legitimately, refuse to march in darkness, just as I can delay my arrival here till at least noon tomorrow, by resting my troops on the way. But you must understand, given orders by the civil power to bring you in, I have no option but to obey. If I do not, they will muster the Fencibles.

They, sir, are a crowd of criminal rascals masquerading as soldiers. I would not wish to leave your fate in their hands."

"We find we are once more in your debt, Captain Latham," said James. "It would be good, for once, to see the shoe on the other foot."

The entire family murmured their approval at that. The soldier had taken a most serious risk in coming to warn Harry.

"I am included in this warrant?" asked James.

"No, but your man Pender is."

"What about my crew?"

Latham turned to Harry. "They are to be put aboard Admiral Duncan's flagship, for him to spread amongst the fleet as he sees fit, even those who have exemptions."

Harry gave a small laugh. "Would that it was another commander."

"You know Admiral Duncan?" asked Latham, with just a trace of hope, for someone with Adam Duncan's connections could move mountains.

"Yes. My father and he were professional rivals, but not friends."

"Ah!"

"And Duncan is, of course, a Scotsman," said James, taking advantage of Arthur's absence. His sister gave him a sharp elbow in the ribs. Latham raised a dark eyebrow at this, but said nothing.

"Pray be seated, Captain," said Anne, pulling at the bell. "You must be fatigued after your journey. You must dine with us, before you begin the long journey back to Deal."

"Most kind, Lady Drumdryan," replied Latham, with a bow so courtly and old fashioned it would have mightily pleased her husband.

"Trench has been carried off to Maidstone, charged with murder and evasion of excise duty. The murder charge won't stick without witnesses, so you will be called for that. The goods he fetched in are due to be auctioned on the morrow, at the Three Kings."

"What about the other two ships?" asked Harry. Latham looked at him without comprehension, forcing him to explain. "It would seem that Braine and the older Temple had made themselves a tidy sum. They are smuggling goods that they have not had to pay for."

"Will they allow that they got the idea from Tobias Bertles?" said James.

"A man who casts a long shadow," said Arthur sourly.

Harry was sick to the back teeth of the name Bertles, sorry that he'd ever heard it. The man had enveloped his whole household in trouble. "What about Trench's ship?" he asked.

"That's being auctioned as well," replied Latham. "Having been caught full of contraband it is naturally forfeit."

"Where is it?" James noticed that Harry's voice had changed, but no one else did.

"Lying off the Three Kings, hard by the public quay."

Harry seemed to sit up suddenly, as though his muscles had become tensed for action. "You have no idea how grateful I am, Captain Latham. I shall, of course, be well away from Cheyne Court tomorrow."

Latham raised his glass. "I sincerely hope so, sir. But do not, I pray, tell me where you're going, lest by my countenance I betray the fact that I have some knowledge."

"You anticipate trouble, sir?" asked Arthur.

"Questions will be asked." His handsome face clouded over, the first sign of anger that anyone at the table had seen on the young officer's face. "But since I am moving at the same pace as our commander-in-chief, the Duke of York, I don't feel that any-one will dare remonstrate with me."

It was James who picked up the undertone. "Has he failed yet again?"

"He has, Mr Ludlow. He has retired to Hanover, with his tail between his legs, his army broken. They have even penned a song about it."

➤ ➤ ➤

Latham was still singing verses from "The Grand Old Duke of York" as the groom led his horse to the front door. He had had too much to drink, masking his anger at events in the Low Countries by over-indulgence. He rubbed the brass cannon, back in their rightful place, before mounting his animal. Harry had the groom lead him down to the gate, with instructions to stay with the captain until he was sober enough to stay in the saddle unaided.

"So, Harry," said James, "what's the plan?"

Harry looked at him oddly, as if preparing to deny that he had one. But he smiled instead. "I think I'm spending too much time with you, James. It's becoming impossible to keep a secret."

James and Arthur stood well in the background while the contraband was auctioned, content to let others buy up the silks and spirits. Braine sat to one side, his face glowing with pleasure, for some of the money coming in would be paid to him as a reward. But the smile vanished as the two men stepped forward, which they did at the first mention of the ship.

"Now, gentlemen," said the auctioneer. "I don't have to tell you seafaring types that she's a sound vessel, a ship-rigged barque, going by the name of *Miranda*. I dare say you've spent the morning looking her over. Old Prospero himself would be proud to have her. Now we can go about this two ways. I have here an inventory of all the stores in the hold. I intend to start by putting the whole lot up for one price. But be warned that I have a reserve. If'n I don't get to that, I shall sell the stores piecemeal, cask by cask, and nail by nail, and the man that wants the ship will still be here when the sun goes down."

"Why is it," said Arthur, "that every auctioneer you meet, quite pleasant fellows in normal life, are prey to tricks and chicanery as soon as they raise a gavel?"

James was so unused to being addressed in normal tones by his brother-in-law that he could not frame a reply. Braine had left his seat and come towards them. Both men turned to face him just as the bidding started. "What are you about?" he said, harshly, pushing his purple face close.

Arthur's reply was loud enough to stop auctioneer and bidders alike. "How dare you talk to me in that manner, sir. I will not have it. Do not assume that your uniform gives you the right to address a gentleman. You are a low and crooked piece of scum, for all your airs. I shall discover who has your sinecure, and ensure that he finds himself a more amenable deputy."

Braine went an even deeper shade of purple at that. He knew that the Ludlows had power in Westminster. But his own certainty soon reasserted itself, for he was on what he saw as his own patch.

"We'll see if you're so cocky when brother Harry is taken up." If he'd expected consternation at this remark, he was sorely disappointed. James actually yawned in his face. "He'll be behind bars before noon, an' up before the Quarter-sessions in Maidstone come Lady Day."

"He must talk to you if he desires to plead guilty," said James. "After all, Mr Braine, you will be able to tell him exactly what to say."

"The bidding, James," said Arthur.

Braine's eyes opened wide as soon as James raised his catalogue. He looked from one man to the other, then at the auctioneer, his mouth open as he sought to make sense of their interest. James bid again and the Preventative Officer ran for the door, pushing his way angrily through the crowd.

No one could outbid James Ludlow, for Harry had been quite specific. "Whatever it takes, James." Tite, at the window of the Three Kings, right behind the auctioneer, turned and waved as soon as he saw James bid. Harry and the crew ran for the nearest boats. They were aboard before the auctioneer's gavel hit the block for the last time. Never had going, going, gone, had such a truthful resonance. They were working on raising the anchors by the time James was signing for possession.

James and Arthur, with Tite, were on the beach by the time the magistrate arrived. He was puffing madly, out of breath, and

Braine, who was behind him, was in an even worse state, for he'd run both ways.

"Stop that ship," gasped Temple, trying to shout, though to whom was unclear.

"Whatever for?" asked James.

"It is being stolen!"

"I hardly think so, sir. I have just purchased the vessel. If anyone has the right to say it's being stolen, it is I."

Harry kept his head down behind the bulwarks, as he'd promised to do. But in observing the comedy being played out on the shingle of Deal beach, he was sorely tempted to stand up and wave farewell. Both Temple and Braine were dancing around James, waving their arms in protest.

"Thick and dry," came the cry from the bows.

"All hands to make sail," said Harry, in a voice that would not carry to the shore.

Harry sailed north to fox his pursuit, purchased some powder and shot in Yarmouth, then retraced his course, heading for the coast of Normandy. The Channel was dangerous for him and Biscay too far away. Obidiah Trench would be tried, and if Arthur did his work in Whitehall, Harry's pardon would allow him to be witness at his trial. For all the natural pleasure of being at sea, there was too much left unfinished ashore for him to be really happy. But for the first time, as they sailed south in search of prizes, he had time to hark back, and examine the causes of the trouble which had put him at sea in Trench's ship.

It was still not entirely clear why Temple and Braine thought he was a smuggler. Trench could only imagine such a thing because he'd been given false information. It was clear that he'd come after Harry for that reason, not, as he'd previously supposed, to stop him facing a charge of murdering Bertles. Escape from that may have been previously arranged with Temple's brother, the magistrate, which would explain his laggardly way of dealing with the matter. But even if they'd thrown him Bertles, they had surely not included the entire crew?

It was when Harry was looking at the papers aboard the *Miranda* that he remembered the manifest he'd signed for Bertles. He tried hard to recall the details of that fateful dinner. Much came back: Polly Franks's endemic gaffes; Wentworth and the way he'd behaved towards her; Bertles, filling their glasses to ensure they had a good night's sleep. That leather folder that he'd opened, plus the details he'd filled in, could have provided the information that had led Trench to both his erroneous conclusions and his house. Perhaps Wentworth's posters had not been the cause of the attack on Cheyne Court, after all.

Try as he might, he could not recall if anyone else followed suit. Perhaps that was it. James had followed him out on to the deck of the *Planet*. It was doubtful if he'd had time. And there had been an unfriendly atmosphere between Franks and Wentworth that could easily have distracted them. If his name was the only one on the manifest, especially with what he'd added as his occupation, then it would be easy for Trench to assume that he was no passenger, but the owner. He'd need to talk to James and the others before he could know if these suppositions were true.

But that didn't square with Temple's behaviour. He had claimed, in his brother's parlour, that he'd given Trench some information about Bertles's backer, long before he'd ever heard of Harry. An "unimpeachable source," he'd said. That had to point to someone other than him. Yet the King of the Smugglers had clearly put that aside in favour of the notion of Harry Ludlow. Why? It was clearly in Temple's interest to remove the man, for he disliked competition, even if only to mollify Obidiah Trench. Had Trench shown him the manifest, with Harry's name and address appended, a piece of written evidence that overbore whatever other information he had from his unimpeachable source?

Nothing but questions, with precious few answers, plus the nagging suspicion that he'd missed something. He needed to place Bertles, still convinced he'd seen him before. Once ashore he could pursue that. And there was still that girl, Bridie Pruitt, whom he'd never had a chance to question. Harry needed the answers to all these things, and not out of curiosity. The only way he could ensure that Temple, powerful and unassailable in Deal, left him and his family alone, was to find the true identity of the man who'd bought Bertles's ship!

Harry put the ship about and sailed north, penning his letters in the cabin while the *Miranda* made for the seaward edge of the Goodwins. He dare not go ashore himself, but he dispatched Patcham in the pinnace, his task to post his two letters, one to James and the other to Major Franks. They backed and filled all day until the pinnace returned, bearing a poster with his name, his alleged crimes, and the price of a hundred guineas for his capture.

Harry could not consider the implications of that now. He had a ship to sail, an imperfect instrument with a mixed crew. He turned his mind to that at the moment he aimed his bowsprit to the south, and left the other matters to ferment. He was in no position to resolve them at present. They would have to wait till he'd seen Trench swing from the gallows.

CHAPTER THIRTY-FOUR

"IT HAS ARRIVED," said Arthur, reading the letter to his wife over the breakfast table. "Trench is to come up before the judge at the Midsummer Quarter-sessions in Maidstone."

"What happened to Lady Day?"

"I suspect there are too many trials outstanding to attend to first. His has been postponed till the summer session. Besides, this suits us. We should have managed to see off the charges against Harry well before then."

"There's still no word from Major Franks," said Anne.

Arthur frowned. "Perhaps we should send someone to Hythe to find out why."

"Anything, husband, rather than that dreadful creature be acquitted."

"He has James to witness against him, plus Wentworth."

"That scrub!" snapped Anne, earning a look of rebuke from her husband for a very unladylike expression. But he could hardly call on her to withdraw, for the young man from Warwickshire had agreed to attend the trial only if his fare was paid and accommodation provided.

"Perhaps if we can find Major Franks, Wentworth won't be necessary."

"It should be Harry who is at the trial. That creature Trench is not even accused of trying to kill my brother."

Arthur pursed his lips. He'd already insisted they draw a veil over the events at Cheyne Court during the months of October and November. Any mention of that time tended to anger him.

He adopted a soothing tone, unaware that his wife, who knew him too well, saw it as transparent and false.

"Harry will be there, dearest. Dundas will see to his pardon long before that. Besides, he will be pleased by the delay. He can stay at sea until the trial, by which time his new ship will be ready."

That didn't mollify her; it made her even more irate. "Grisham is another man whose honesty does not stand the test."

Anne was right again. The shipbuilder, without Harry to push him, had put other work before the completion of the ship. Not that his purchaser seemed to mind. He was enjoying himself off the Normandy coast, taking quite a number of prizes. Nothing like his previous success, for they tended to be smaller ships with less lavish cargoes. But enough to more than pay his expenses. There was one off the Downs now and Arthur could conveniently send the message he'd just received back with the returning prize crew.

He pushed back his chair and headed for the library, making for the large chart which his brother-in-law had left on the wall before he'd fled from Deal. His finger went automatically to the rendezvous that Harry had arranged. To Arthur it looked simple. Cap de la Hague seemed a mere stone's throw from the south coast of England. The dates were written on the wall by the side of the chart.

There were grubby finger marks all over it. This upset his fastidious nature and he rubbed at them furiously. It would be Tite, who'd become even more irascible since the action with the *Dragon*. No doubt he'd been in here, still imagining himself a sailor, and playing with the divider as though he had the ability to set a course for an interception. Arthur, even less of a navigator, was prone to the same himself, so the chart, at the rendezvous point, was peppered with holes punched through the parchment.

Arthur rubbed at a particularly troublesome stain, wondering what Tite was doing with tar on his fingers. Then he had another thought, which made him frown angrily. Pender's eldest girl, who asked after her father constantly, might have come in here to seek his whereabouts. Never mind that it was strictly forbidden. She was a bold girl, getting more so as she absorbed her lessons.

Harry Ludlow would be off the Cap de la Hague on the second Sunday in every month, weather permitting. That also looked simple, for he was hunting along the coast, intercepting ships making for Le Havre and Honfleur. Only a sailor could tell him how difficult it was to guarantee a rendezvous. Arthur would never understand that you needed the wind to get you to the right place. The prevailing westerlies could not be guaranteed. He could never comprehend why anyone trying to meet Harry should wait a whole week before bearing up for a second rendezvous in St Peter Port in Guernsey. There Harry, should he be forced away from the first, would wait out the month before putting to sea again.

He sat down to write to James and Wentworth, resolved to go to Hythe himself to find out what had become of Major Franks. As he did so the other letter crackled in the pocket of his watered silk coat. Arthur was avoiding the banker Cantwell. He put all thoughts of his own troubles behind him and concentrated on what had kept him occupied all these years: his job of managing the Ludlow estates.

February was a terrible month to be sailing these waters, and the *Miranda,* having already gone through the winter, was beginning to show signs of requiring a thorough refit. She was the only ship that Harry had ever bought blind, and though basically sound she'd had her faults from the very first day. She shipped too much water through the planking, which tended to open up in any kind of sea. Worse, from Harry's point of view, she disliked guns going off, prepared to spring a sudden leak if he dared even a small, two-cannon broadside. He was reduced to one gun at a time, with a pause to allow the vibrations to settle before he could fire off another. If he ever met a French warship, or even a well-armed privateer with nationalist sentiments, he would have to run. Not that he was in much danger from privateers. Their prey was merchant shipping, not him. He was equally thankful that his patriotism had not been challenged, never having seen an English merchantman in danger.

The crew were now working smoothly, all the divisions which existed initially submerged by time and the storms they'd been through. Harry had raised Patcham to take a watch. Pender, whose brain was as nimble as his fingers, was learning at an astonishing pace, so that Harry, while he had the watch, was only called to the deck in emergencies. They'd become much closer through necessity. At times he would eat his dinner with Pender, though such intimacy tended to make the man uncomfortable.

"Sail ho!" cried the voice of the lookout. "Ship's cutter fine on the larboard bow."

"Letters!" cried Harry, leaping up from his desk, where he'd being helping Pender with his navigation.

Pender had long since stopped asking how Harry Ludlow knew things without looking. He accepted without question that it was the *Miranda*'s pinnace approaching, and followed Harry out of the cabin on to the deck. The sky was grey and overcast, with a stiff breeze coming in over the quarter. The ship was under topsails, with just enough set to keep her sailing slowly round her rendezvous. He saw the glee in Harry's face, something he couldn't share, for there would be no letters for him. And he could read, thanks to a kindly cleric in the village where he spent his first ten years. That made him think of his father, who had been forced to seek work in Portsmouth after the land around the village was enclosed. The city had killed both his parents, and he had survived only because he had enough cunning.

The boat came bumping alongside and the men, fresh from home, were hauled aboard with their sacks of provisions and their bag of mail. Ropes were slung from the yards and the boat was hauled out of the water, with twenty men round the capstan, then set inboard above the waist. Harry had retired to his cabin to read his letters, but he came on deck and called to Pender, who was supervising this operation, insisting that he come back into the cabin.

"Here," said Harry, handing him a sealed letter. "It's addressed to you."

Pender took it as though it was a writ, turning it over in his fingers before bending to read it. The writing was as crabbed as his own poor efforts, but it plainly stated that it was addressed to P. Pender, aboard the ship *Miranda*. He looked at the sealing wax, but being plain there was nothing to identify the source. He tore it open. The writing inside was no better than the address, with many words scratched, and to his mind misspelt. But it was from his Jenny, giving him news of herself and the other two children. Pender reckoned he was immune to emotion, but he turned away from his captain, lest Harry see the tears in the corners of his eyes.

Harry had opened James's letter first, and the contents of that only served to underscore his own impression of the seat of his problems. There was much about doings in town, fashions, fads, the war, and who was bedding whom. But it was the section referring to events on the *Planet* that engaged his total concentration.

Signing Bertles's manifest was not something I saw as requiring urgent attention. After all, we did not anticipate being slung off the ship in the middle of the night. I would have heartily complied next morning, but that was not to be. As to the actions of our fellow passengers, I am as much in the dark as you.

Harry then turned to the letter from Arthur. "Damn!" he cried, dispelling all thoughts of home and beauty. "They're not going to try Trench till the summer."

"What about pardons?" asked Pender, which to him, was much more to the point.

Harry scanned the letter before looking up. "They are yet to come, but Arthur seems confident. I had hoped for the Lady Day quarter-sessions. The *Miranda* needs a refit."

▸ ▸ ▸

Arthur shot out of his chair, with a look on his face that quite terrified his wife. "They've brought Trench's case forward to Lady Day."

"That's next week," said Anne.

Arthur bit his lip to avoid telling her that he was well aware of the date. "And the trial has been moved from Maidstone to Lewes."

"Why?"

"I cannot be certain. But it would be safe to conjecture that a Sussex jury will be more sympathetic to Trench than one from Kent. I must write to James, at once."

He was out of the room before Anne could say a word. She felt the child move in her belly, as though it too was alarmed by the news.

"No jury from around Lewes will convict him of smuggling, Arthur, any more than twelve Deal men would send down some-one like Temple."

"He is charged with murder, James."

James looked grim, with good reason. "Which will only bring him down if he's positively identified by more than one person. With Franks in Gibraltar we are stuck with one hope."

"Wentworth!"

"He's not someone I'd want to rest my case on."

Arthur hit the mantelpiece with the flat of his hand. "Harry could not possibly get here on time, even if his pardon was through."

"Send to Wentworth. Tell him that we will pay him to attend."

"How much?"

"Whatever he asks, Arthur. We can't risk Trench walking free from the court. If he does, all our lives will be at risk."

"Can Temple help?"

"Never in life, sir," cried Temple, leaning forward to reveal the lettering on his chair. IN NOCTE POSSUMUS. James read it as the Smuggler King continued. Being "Motto Latin" it was not a phrase he was familiar with, but he translated it as "In possession of the night." "I'm surprised you dare to walk through the door, sir, let alone demand my assistance."

"It was not a demand, Mr Temple, but a request."

"Two demands, sir. The answer is no to both. I will not go anywhere near the Lewes Assizes, and I will most certainly not ask Braine or the magistrate to withdraw the charges against your brother."

James discarded his polite demeanour, for it was getting him nowhere. "He is no more a smuggler than I am, Mr Temple, which you know very well."

Temple's eyes narrowed and he pursed his thin bloodless lips. "I cannot fathom why you deny it. We had an inkling where the money came from to buy Bertles's ship before he ever set sail, though I grant you we lacked an actual name. Your brother tried to put us off the scent but Trench himself produced written evidence."

"You saw this evidence?"

"No, sir."

"Was this evidence, by any chance, written on the *Planet*'s manifest?" The smuggler's eyes narrowed, as though the information was secret. "Mr Temple, I would point out to you that had we not been put off the ship my name would have been listed there, along with several others."

"I have other information, sir," Temple replied loftily.

"If your information points to my brother, then it is clearly false."

"You would not say that if you knew its source. Unimpeachable, sir, is scarcely a strong enough expression. A man should be careful whom he beds."

"Beds?"

"If you do not know the answer to that, then I should question your brother, for I will answer no more on the subject."

"I cannot contend this with you, sir, since you will not listen
to either truth or reason. Nor will you speak plain. But mark this.
If Trench is free, you stand in as much danger as we do."

"Never fear, Mr Ludlow. I can take care of myself." Temple
laughed deep in his throat and his hand went out to tap the creature beside him. "I might even set old Cephas Quested on him."

James turned to look at the former batman, whose head lolled
on his shoulders, while a thin stream of spittle dribbled from his
slack mouth, running into the base of his great white scar. Temple was still chuckling as he patted the man, who'd never recovered
from the effect of Pender's boots. The shoulders were rounded
now, instead of square, and the eyes roved far away.

"I thank your brother for this. He's much more scarifying than
a dead man. If anyone even thinks of betraying me, I tell them
they'll end up like Quested . . ."

The court was full to the rafters, echoing with ceaseless chatter-
ing, making the case for the prosecution difficult. Not that it
mattered, for no one seemed inclined to listen. Wentworth was
bellowing his evidence in an attempt to make himself heard. The
judge, Lord Justice Aspinall, was paying scant attention. Trench
wasn't even present and the dock was empty, a privilege that
should never have been extended to a man on a capital charge.

That had led to the first argument between Aspinall and Crown
counsel, Emerson, since the barrister from Lord Thurlow's depart-
ment had seen fit to complain at the absence of the accused. The
judge, who had a ferocious beaked nose, the only feature promi-
nent enough to protrude from his full-bottomed wig, held up his
hand. Immediate silence ensued while he asked if counsel required
his permission to invite a friend to dinner. Emerson shook his head.

"Then kindly do not tell me who I should have in my court,
sir," shouted Aspinall, to tumultuous applause. "Proceed with the
case."

The hand went up again when Wentworth mentioned money,
this time to defence counsel. The court fell silent as Aspinall leant

forward, his wig nearly touching his bench. The voice was silky
and wheedling, like a man who distracts your attention while he
raids your purse.

"Am I to understand . . ." Aspinall waved his hand in a help-
less way. "What is your name, sir?"

"Wentworth, milord."

"Well, Mr Wentworth. Tell the court again, in the same words
you've just used, how you came to be here."

"My presence was requested by Mr James Ludlow, with the
promise that I should be paid for any expenses I incurred, or losses
I suffered in my business."

"Paid, sir. You say you are here to send a man to the gallows,
and that you were paid!" The judge threw his head back, so that
all could see his gaunt face, with the eyes wide open in disbelief.
The court erupted in a cacophony of abuse. The hand went up
again and silence fell. "I must say, Mr Wentworth, that the jury
will know full well how to take the testimony of a man who was
paid!"

James and Arthur exchanged glances. It was clear that Aspinall
was directing the jury. Emerson threw up his hands in despair as
the noise started again, making the task of refuting that direction
impossible. Finally, after several attempts, he gave up and dismissed Wentworth. The young man gave James and Arthur a filthy
look as he went by, as though they were the authors of his ordeal.

James was called next. The mere mention of his name was occasion for another bout of yelling. As he was swearing the oath, a
rotten cabbage hit him on the back of the head. He spun to look
at the judge, only to find that Aspinall was looking the other way.
Jeers followed this, but the noise died away as he gave his evidence. He recounted meeting Bertles and what had happened off
the French coast. The judge's eyes rolled in theatrical disbelief at
his claim of innocence in the matter of smuggling. Emerson carried on bravely.

"Now, Mr Ludlow. It is common practice in a court of law to
call upon a witness to search the court and point out the man

accused. I cannot ask you to do this, since the man is not present. But the information laid against him makes him quite distinctive. Please be so good as to describe him to us."

The court went totally silent. No one even whispered. "He is about the same height as I, but much broader. He has an unusually high-pitched voice and a great black beard which covers most of his face."

"What," snapped Aspinall, his wig quivering. "Is this man you describe supposed to be Obidiah Trench?"

"He most certainly is," said James emphatically.

It was timed to perfection, as though Emerson was as much a part of the charade as the judge. A man stepped into the dock. He was clean shaven, with a non-existent chin. What passed for that appendage seemed to slip straight from his lower lip to his neck, giving him, with his protruding top teeth, the appearance of a particularly stupid donkey. The skin was scarred and pink, evidence that there had once been a serious wound to the face and neck. James wondered if that accounted for the voice.

"A great black beard, you say." James nodded uncertainly. "That covered most of his face?"

"Who is the man in the dock?" demanded Emerson.

"There's no pleasing some people. First you complain that he isn't there, now you're upset because he is. That, sir, is Obidiah Trench."

Whatever sound had gone before was as nothing to what came now. Every voice in the court was raised in screeching, derisive laughter. Then Aspinall raised his hand again, bringing silence, his eyes, shaded by his wig, fully on James.

"And what, sir, do you have to say now?"

James knew it was hopeless. The whole thing was rigged. He'd never get Trench for murder. He felt his temper rise, and though he fought to control it, he did not succeed.

"I think, sir, that you are a disgrace to the robes you wear. It may be in order for lawyers to suffer your taunts, but I will not, for one minute longer. You are corrupt, milord, and when you meet your maker, He will exact retribution for your sins."

"You do not lack foolhardiness, Mr Ludlow. Has anyone ever told you that it is dangerous to insult a judge in his court?"

Arthur was waving his hand, trying to get James to shut up. But his blood was up, and nothing would silence him. "It is more dangerous to insult justice, sir, which is the course you've set."

"I agree that you will not have to suffer my taunts a moment longer." The voice rose suddenly, and Aspinall's finger shot out accusingly. "You will suffer them for 24 hours. In the stocks, sir. And may the good people of this town still your impudent tongue."

A great cheer rent the air. Two court ushers rushed forward and pinned his arms to his side. Arthur and Emerson were on their feet, protesting violently, but neither could be heard over the din as James Ludlow was hustled out of the court. The ritual was played out, with the prosecution admitting they had no more witnesses, while the defence produced none. The summations were brief and noisy, but quiet came when Aspinall asked the jury if they wished to retire to consider their verdict.

"Retire, milord," said the foreman, standing up. "I see no need for that. The accused is a man of some standing in this town, an honest citizen, falsely accused. Obidiah Trench is plainly innocent, and I would enter a plea that the warrants relating to smuggling could bear examination, since they were clearly as malicious as the capital charge."

"The warrants have been cancelled," replied Aspinall, picking up a paper and reading it. "Withdrawn by a magistrate named Temple, and an exciseman called Braine."

There was a lengthy pause while the judge looked round the court. Finally his eyes came back to the foreman. "Do you find the defendant guilty or not guilty?"

"Not" was the only word Arthur heard, as another yell rent the air, this time full of hats thrown in jubilation.

Arthur stood beside James at one end of the town square, using his hand to deflect the odd object thrown by a passer-by. His brother-in-law was bent over, his head and his hands through the holes in the wood.

"Temple has bought Trench off by cancelling the charges of smuggling. The man is free to go where he pleases."

James had his eyes shut as he replied. "I doubt it will be long before he heads this way."

"I'm sorry, James . . ."

Arthur didn't get a chance to finish, for James cut across him. "I'm here because of my tongue, Arthur, not yours."

The swelling noise spoke of a crowd heading their way. James twisted his eyes as best he could, but it was Arthur who first spotted Trench. The man hadn't even spoken in court. That means of identification had never been put to the test. But he spoke now, his high-pitched voice full of venomous humour, which lost none of its impact for his ridiculous appearance.

"Well, now. Here we have a man that wanted to see me swing." He turned to the crowd. "Do you think I should have sport with him, lads?"

The square filled with affirmative shouts. Trench held up his hand. "I find, lads, it don't do, to take on the stocks on an empty stomach. Nor should we chuck at cocky here what we might want to eat. So I says we have our celebration first, then deal with this turd later."

He had to hold up both hands to silence them now. "Then we are agreed. Dinner first, sport after."

Trench turned round and leant down till his face was at the same level as James'. "You've quite a pretty face, cocky. But it won't be much longer, for when my mates are full of drink, I doubt they'll just be throwing cabbage. They'll cut you open with stones and fill the holes with dung. I doubt you'll keep your eyes, so I should pray that one of them uses a stone too big to stand, one that splits your brains."

Arthur put a hand on Trench and pushed him back. Some of his cronies started forward at this, but he restrained them easily. Then he tugged at Arthur's silk coat.

"You don't count, mate, for all your silk."

"I count enough," said Arthur, struggling to sound suitably aggressive. "Harm James Ludlow and I will kill you. That is if his brother doesn't beat me to it."

"Oh, yes. Mr Smuggler Thief himself."

"He's . . ."

"Dead, mate!" shouted Trench. "He has my ship, an' I'm going to take it back off him."

"You won't," said James, from beneath them. "He'll find you, long before you find him."

Trench crouched down again. "Is that a fact? Well, I have my bargain with Temple, which I shall keep. Second Sunday in every month at Cap de la Hague, ain't it, with St Peter's Port as a fallback."

Arthur almost squeaked, he was so shocked. "How do you know that?"

Trench stood up. The man was grinning at him, and nodding, his top teeth a good two inches further out than his lower lip. And Arthur was thinking of those marks on the chart in Harry's study. Not Tite, not Pender's girl, but one of Temple's men, with tar on his fingers.

Trench turned and called for his band to follow him.

"Come on, lads. Let's eat and drink. And no pissin' in the yard, either. I want you save it up so's we can see how we're doin' when we come to deal with Ludlow here. Got to have somethin' to wash the blood away!"

CHAPTER THIRTY-FIVE

ARTHUR, now back at the inn, sat in the wing chair, his mind racing to find another way out of this dilemma. Living at Cheyne Court these last years had made him soft. Everything had come too easily and the ambition which had driven him as a younger man had evaporated. Now he was on the brink of breaking the mould. Fatherhood was imminent and that fact had spurred him to reconsider his position. London beckoned, with all the associations of wealth and privilege which that image conjured up. He was sure of that, even if he arrived penniless. Dundas would help him to prosper. The road would be hard but he would have freedom, the liberty to undertake only those burdens he wished to shoulder. That might include the Ludlow patrimony, but if it did, it would be voluntary.

Did he like James Ludlow? Arthur wasn't sure, because he was old enough, and wise enough to see their past bickering for what it was, the resentment of two men competing for the same territory. But was James worth jeopardizing everything for? His wife, his child to be, and his potential future, a prospect made all the more desperate by his present financial plight. Neither of the Ludlow brothers understood what it was like to be poor. His mind went back to his wedding. He'd had to borrow money to buy a decent suit, a debt pledged against Anne Ludlow's portion. They would not comprehend the shame attendant on that.

Normally a cautious man, he had, for once in his life, taken a major gamble, prompted by the desire to look people like Harry Ludlow square in the eye. That, supposed to be the route to freedom, had become a burden even more difficult to carry. He was sinking deeper into the mire by the day, to the point where he might be forced, against all his instincts, to go cap in hand to his brother-in-law. That was an unpleasant prospect, if for no other reason than the fact that Harry would probably understand, forgive, and proffer help. That such an attitude would stem from a natural kindness didn't make it any easier to bear.

He'd often wondered what Harry Ludlow really thought of him. Most people wonder how they are perceived and Arthur was no exception, though James's opinion concerned him less. He despised modernity with as much passion as James Ludlow embraced it. The "spirit of the age" had led to murder, mayhem, and regicide, to a society where men of mediocre background and dubious lineage, trimmers with no manners and opinions for sale, prospered at the expense of public funds. Arthur Drumdryan could not embrace that. He was determined to remain true to the tenets of his upbringing, even if, he suspected, people laughed, behind his back, at the constant insistence on proper standards of behaviour.

"Versailles manners," he said softly, as he pushed himself out of the chair and propelled himself towards their luggage. Whether he liked or disliked James was an irrelevence, just as his financial difficulties, and the potential need for Harry's understanding, could not be allowed to impinge on his response. There was a matter of honour at stake, and if Arthur Drumdryan believed in anything, it was the maintenance of his personal honour.

No one had touched James. Not even a piece of stale bread had been thrown at him since Trench had spoken. They were saving him up for later, leaving him to worry at his future, more difficult to bear than the fate itself. Arthur brought him something to drink and they spoke quietly for less than a minute. Then Arthur stood to leave.

"I have a duty to resolve this, James. I shall do so, or die in the attempt. At the very least I shall put a ball in Trench before he casts his first stone."

Forced by his situation to look at the ground, it was hard for

James not to take that as pure braggadoccio. But he never got a chance to say so because his brother-in-law was gone. He heard his feet echoing up the alley, as he headed back towards the courthouse. Arthur, shaking like a leaf, crept to the rear of the building, to the part that housed the judges' quarters. The pistol in his hand was far from steady. Whatever his background or his standards, Arthur Drumdryan was not cut out for this type of behaviour.

But it was what Harry would do. Indeed, he would set the whole town alight rather than let James suffer a scratch. Threatening a King's Bench judge with a pistol would seem inconsequential. He'd tried to think of a way to break in, but it was not something he was familiar with. So, for the want of another method of entry, he lifted the trembling pistol, and with his free hand knocked hard on the door.

The speed with which it opened nearly gave him a seizure. He stepped back quickly as Emerson emerged. The prosecuting counsel looked at the gun, then at the owner. The shock on his face—for he was as surprised as Arthur—faded before a wicked grin. He held up a piece of folded paper which he had in his hand.

"I dare say you have come for this. Had I known of your intentions in advance, Lord Drumdryan, I would have let you have the first attempt at persuasion."

"Aspinall?" asked Arthur.

Emerson came out through the door, closing it behind him. The lawyer then took his arm gently, to lead him away from potential murder. "This is a warrant to release Mr Ludlow from the stocks."

Arthur, who disliked being touched, detached his arm, though without violence. "What did you use to persuade him?"

"His own self-interest, sir, which is all he cares about."

"Was it self-interest that caused that charade in the court today?"

"Yes. But whether that was done by means of a bribe or a threat, I cannot say. Trench has powerful protectors, men who are tied to him by blood or profit, or by his activities. Aspinall may be one such person. But he is such a disgrace to the office he holds that he is subject to pressure. There is no vice to which he is a stranger."

"Then why has he been allowed to continue?" asked Arthur.

Emerson sighed. "You will find, Lord Drumdryan, that government finds malleable judges a positive advantage in such troubled times. The letter of the law is sometimes insufficient for their needs."

"So Trench goes free."

"He does. And he cannot be tried again for the same offence. That is enshrined in Magna Carta." The barrister shook his head slowly, then held up the paper again. "Still, we have saved James Ludlow from his fate, let us be content with that."

Arthur doubted if that was wholly true, but he had no desire to engage Emerson in a lengthy discussion. Besides, the lawyer, who'd kept talking, didn't provide him with an opportunity.

"The release of Trench will raise an eyebrow in Whitehall, but no action will ensue. James Ludlow is a different case. A man of his station, maimed or killed, would cause a scandal, especially since I would report the matter to the Lord Chancellor myself. I doubt that his behaviour would bear too much scrutiny. Subject to a thorough inquiry, he'd be lucky to escape the gallows himself."

Arthur trembled slightly as the tension eased out of his frame. "I thank you, sir. It must have taken a great deal of effort to change his mind."

Emerson snorted derisively. "He has a twelve-year-old virgin in there. The old goat's sole preoccupation is to be at her deflowering. He was salivating with desire. I cannot even be sure that my strictures affected the man at all. James Ludlow means nothing to him, sir. I half believe he gave me this to be rid of me."

The barrister handed him the warrant, pointing to the pistol with his other hand. "Here, you take it, for it is better that you should release Ludlow. And put away that pistol, sir, for if you do not, I fear I shall be prosecuting you on a capital charge, given the number of tempting targets in this town."

▸ ▸ ▸

The clerk was unhappy about being dragged from his dinner. The turnkey from the gaol was even more unhappy about having to go out. But neither questioned the instruction, written above Lord Justice Aspinall's own seal. James was out of the stocks, and he and Arthur were far from Lewes, before the drunken mob arrived back in the square. Trench let out a scream, where another man would have bellowed. He cursed and he raged for an age. "He's not the one. It's the brother I want. And I knows where to find him . . ."

CHAPTER THIRTY-SIX

"DAMN AND blast the fool!" shouted Harry. "I've a good mind to leave him to drown."

He looked at the chase, a merchant ship, labouring in the heaving seas. He'd been after that prize, in deteriorating weather, for twelve hours. And now, just when they'd practically overhauled her, he'd have to call off the pursuit. The crew were already fighting their way to the braces and the shrouds before he gave the order to shorten sail. He watched as his quarry disappeared into the flying spray which the gale was ripping off the top of the waves. Then he had to grab hold of a stay as Pender eased her round a touch, till she had maximum speed before the north-east wind. He was by the wheel as quickly as the pitching deck would allow, for with the *Miranda* in her present state this was a manoeuvre he wished to oversee himself.

It was difficult, in such a storm, to come up into the wind. Up till now he'd had it ten degrees off his stern, a point of sailing dictated by the merchant ship he was after. Now, to rescue the fishing smack that was wallowing in the water, he had to run before the gale, then spin in the trough created by two waves, one of which would take the wind off his lower sails. The men below would have to loosen the sails at just the right time, haul round on the yards, then bowse them tight again, while the men aloft fought the canvas of the mizen-topsails to reef them in, leaving the main-topsails, hauled right round, to draw. Men could die trying this, but the crew of Harry's ship trusted him. Besides competence, there was Providence and luck. What other privateer captain would pass up a potential fortune to rescue a couple of poor fishermen?

The *Miranda* was shipping a lot of water in this gale, with the pumps clanking continuously, and she came round slowly. But she took the wind right and as the next wave ran under her counter, her sails billowed out and carried her forward on the starboard tack. He couldn't get to them on this heading, so he handed over the control of the wheel to Pender, who had two other men to assist, and made for the bows, ready to shout the order that would bring her on to a larboard tack. He considered sailing past the fishing boat and coming round again, for the bulk of his ship would provide shelter for them. But this was no sea, and no ship, to be playing games in.

Harry yelled as hard as he could, a cry that was taken up by men all the way down the side, carried to the wheel by the wind. They were at their stations, well aware of what to do. Pender timed it well, calling the orders in another trough. Slowly, groaning but not griping, the *Miranda* swung round on the other tack. The ropes flashed out from her side to the near-wrecked fishing boat. They missed the first time and had to be thrown again. Pender was holding the *Miranda* with little way on her, using the rudder and the leeway to slow her progress. He couldn't maintain it for too long, since she was in danger of being broached by a sudden gust of wind, or a freak wave.

The ropes flashed out again towards the three men clinging to the boat, this time one of them going to hand. Freezing fingers lashed the thin rope, then started to haul in the heavier cable. Pender eased his rudder and let her drift, taking the *Miranda* towards the fishermen, making the job of getting the cable aboard that much easier. As soon as it was secured, Harry called for all available hands to man the capstan, which proved difficult on a pitching deck, with men slipping and falling as they turned the great gear, coiling the rope around it, before it disappeared, dripping water as it was stowed below.

"Never mind the paint, lads," shouted Harry, who was pushing on one of the bars himself. "That boat could go down any second."

They hauled like heroes until the scrape of wood on wood told them she was right alongside. Hands holding loops were over the side and the near-drowned fishermen shoved their arms through to be hauled aboard. Harry grabbed the first one and turned him over without ceremony, pounding on his chest to force him to pay attention.

"How many aboard?"

The man just shook his head, uncomprehending. Harry shook him again, for he needed to cut that cable and set the *Miranda* free. If he didn't, that special wave that all sailors dreaded, twice the size of its predecessors, with the wind to aid it, would arrive and drown them all. Three times he asked without success, until he suddenly realized the reason.

"*Combien de personnes dans le bateau?*" he screamed.

"*Trois,*" croaked the fisherman, holding up three frozen fingers.

Harry turned, saw another two inert bodies on the deck, grabbed an axe from one of his crew and swung it hard at the cable. As soon as it parted, and he'd seen the wreckage spin away from the side, he gave the orders to bring his ship back round on to its original course to continue his chase.

"I think if he apologizes to me once more, I'll sling him back over the side."

Pender grinned, glad that he couldn't speak French. The three men, father and two sons, were from Alderney, the rockiest and most inhospitable of the Channel Islands. They had the odd English word, enough to get them watered and fed. But they could only talk to Harry. The weather had moderated, the wind swinging round to the west, and since they'd run out of conversation some time since, they were thrown back on gratitude, plus endless submissions that Le Bon Dieu would reward him, in heaven, for the loss of that fine French ship.

Patiently, Harry had explained that he would take them home once he'd made his rendezvous. Privately, to Pender, he admitted that the *Miranda* was becoming too risky a vessel for such a dangerous stretch of water. That last blow, and his efforts to catch the Frenchman, had done the ship few favours. Not that the other man was surprised, for he had to detail the men to man the pumps.

"God knows what would happen if we fired off the guns now," said Harry glumly. "Let's just hope our pardons arrive with the next contact. If not we'll have to sneak ashore at Deptford and take the new ship in whatever condition she's in."

A sailor entered the cabin. "Mr Patcham's compliments, Captain. We've raised the Cap of the Hog."

"Any sign of a sail?"

"Nothing yet, your honour."

"I'll be on deck presently," said Harry, giving Pender a meaningful look. But he was not the type to blackguard any ship he sailed, even one taken blind. "She's getting on, that's all. Given a proper refit she'll be as sound as a bell. Damn it, I don't even know when she was built. Odd, for all the conflict we've had, that I never even exchanged one word with Trench. Not that he would tell me much about his ship."

They made their way out of the cabin. The changing weather had brought drizzly rain in sudden squalls. But the swell from the storm was still apparent, with the current running south-east. The combination of that and the wind set up a choppy cross sea which made the ship pitch unpredictably. Harry could hear the slight groans of the timbers as they moved beneath his feet.

"Sail fine on the starboard bow," called the lookout. He called "two sail" before Harry had the glass to his eye. He'd just got the focus, and picked up the first ship's topsails, when the lookout called three.

"Sitting right on our rendezvous," said Harry tersely. In the corner of his glass he could see the granite bulk of the Cap de la Hague. "Which is damned inconvenient, whoever they are."

Pender waited. There was no one better than Harry Ludlow at this guessing game. He seemed to have a sixth sense when it came to telling if someone was friend or foe. The silence lasted for several minutes as Harry shifted his glass down the line of ships. Then he called to the masthead.

"What do you see?"

"Two schooners and a barque. Two masts apiece, with great lanteens on the schooners."

"Can you see any gun ports?"

"Not yet."

Harry turned to Pender, his lower lip stuck in his teeth. "Steer due north. Let's see what they do. But stand by to go about, as well."

"Danger?" asked Pender.

Harry shook his head slowly. "If we change our course and they hold theirs, no. But if they try to intercept . . ."

"First one's got ports, Captain, though that don't mean it's armed."

"He's a talkative soul, that lookout," said Harry, who liked things done navy fashion. "He would do us all a favour if he confined his opinion to the facts."

Pender put his head back to yell a rebuke, but Harry's hand stopped him. "It's all right, Pender. I'll tell him myself."

A vicious combination of wind and water took the *Miranda* as he started to climb. Harry heard the groan of protesting timbers again, and prayed fervently that the slight tightness in his chest was misplaced. His feet slipped from rope to rope of their own volition. As he climbed he tried to work out what to do if he had a fight coming. There was only really one option against three ships. He'd have to run and hope like hell they were poor sailers.

"Are they flying any flags?" he asked the lookout.

"None, Captain," the man replied, with pleasing brevity.

He knew that he was wrong about their sailing qualities after five minutes in the crosstrees. The ships were well handled and coming on, close-hauled, at a fair speed. But they were making no attempt to intercept. He felt decidedly uneasy. Those topsail schooners looked like fast boats. If he'd had them, Harry knew that his tactics would be the same. He'd seek to get the weather-gage by coming round to the south of his quarry, then come about with the wind just right and crack on in pursuit. The longer he waited, before taking a decisive step, decreased his chances and increased theirs.

"Come round four points to larboard," he called down.

The men below, who looked like ants from above, rushed to trim the sails as Pender swung the wheel. Harry trained his glass on the three ships. It was one schooner captain who gave the game away. The ship's topsails had shivered as she started to swing round in pursuit. Harry heard the faint boom of a signal gun as she swung back round on her original course. But he'd seen the smoke much sooner, a few seconds after he'd noticed the change of course. He didn't know who they were, but they were very definitely after him.

Harry, who'd edged away, made his preparations well in advance of his turn, making sure that when he let out his sails he would do so quicker than the pursuit. He questioned the Alderney fishermen closely, before offering them the cutter and a chance to escape, which brought back to his mind what had happened in the Channel. They did not understand why he broke off and looked suddenly over the side, with a strange look in his eye, nor did they comprehend the words he said.

"Trench? It can't be Trench."

It was the lack of flags to identify them. Without those, it could be anyone. Trench, warships, or other privateers—even ships hired by the Revenue come to take him in. Harry shook his head, as though to clear it, and continued with his explanation. The oldest of the three men, Gaston, answered for himself and his sons; he declined his offer on the grounds that since they owed him their lives it was their duty to assist him to escape from this threat. They were stout men, strong-limbed and weatherbeaten. But with nothing to do they'd get in the way on the deck, because they'd not be able to comprehend any of the orders.

Then Harry realized that each one of them could steer and would have, in these waters, a feel that easily surpassed his own. They had to know them well, since they fished them for a living. That would be especially true if he got close to any of the smaller islands, a thing he normally tried to avoid because of the treacherous, unpredictable currents. This stretch of water was a graveyard for ships that surpassed even the Goodwins, with a tidal rise and fall that sometimes exceeded fifty feet. Precise navigation could mitigate the hazards, but if he was involved in a running fight that was a luxury he'd be denied.

"Pender, I'm going to put our fishermen on the wheel. They can con the ship under my instructions. We're going to have a stern chase so you might as well knock the windows out of my cabin and set up some breechings for a pair of nine-pounders. Get the four-pounders up on the poop, with plenty of powder and shot."

He turned to Patcham. "I want extra stays set up on the mainmast. You'll have heard that grinding from down below. She's suffering in the kelson and with the top hamper we'll need she could rip the mast right out. Make sure everybody eats before we fire a shot and get the cook to make up plenty of food we can take cold."

Then Harry called the crew aft and explained to them what he was going to do. "From what we can see we are faced with three well-armed ships, all marginally better sailers than us. I can't run away before the wind because the two schooners would eat off the distance in no time. Nor can I just head into the Atlantic. It's got nothing to do with out-running the pursuit. It's more to do with the *Miranda* groaning like the morning after a night in Fiddler's Green.

"If I can reduce the odds to a single-ship action we'll try and board. But until then, I don't want any of them to touch the paint on our side, regardless of how close they come. It's one shot at a time, she won't brook any more. Every one of those has to count. Stand by to go about, and make it so neat, like a crack navy frigate, that they'll think they'll never beat us."

The turn into the wind was all he could have hoped for, though it had taken half an hour to prepare. They wore round like a pinnace, with the new sails flashing out the minute she was on her new course. The three pursuing ships gave up all pretence of uninterest and altered course to chase. They too had new sails going up, and it was with some despair that Harry saw the effect this had on the two schooners. They shot ahead of the barque and started to close the gap at an alarming rate.

"Pender, I want slowmatch amidships and ten barrels of biscuit."

No one stopped to ask why. They were all too busy, tightening every brace and fall to ensure the most speed. Harry trimmed a sail here and took a turn on a yard there, with his ear constantly attuned to the groaning of the ship. If he overpressed her, she would definitely spring her mainmast, and then he might as well cut down his flag.

The barrels of biscuit were brought on deck, becoming the subject of much amused conjecture. Harry had sorted out the two strongest men in the crew. He put them at either end of a hammock just in front of the wheel. For all that his men were concerned with the progress of the chase, they turned to see what Harry Ludlow was up to now, for he was patiently explaining to his two brutes what he wanted. With many a wry sideways glance at their mates, they laid a barrel of biscuit in the hammock and took a turn on the cords at the hammock's end. Harry stood by the mainmast shrouds, with his watch in his hand. At his shouted command, the two men ran towards the side and heaved the small biscuit barrel into the air. It flew over the bulwarks and landed thirty feet from the side of the ship.

Harry set them up again. This time they were less successful, going for distance rather than height. The barrel clipped the rail and tumbled into the water by the *Miranda*'s side. Harry favoured his two volunteers with a glare, and sharply informed them that they'd just blown a hole in the side of their own ship. That ensured the third attempt was more like the first. Harry had them work at the rest of the barrels till they had it right every time. Pender, afire with curiosity, could stand it no longer.

"I know you hate to be questioned on your own deck, Captain Ludlow. But what in the name of hell is going on?"

Harry grinned at him, not least offended by the question. He held up his hands, palms out, then squeezed them together.

"Those two schooners will probably take us between them, Pender. If they get far enough ahead of that barque we can fight one side, using one gun at a time. That's not going to hold them both up. It won't even do for one. But if we can pepper one with grape, just to keep her away, and let the other one come close . . ."

Harry lit a short piece of slowmatch and watched it burn down. Some of his crew had wandered closer, to see what he was up to.

"This is too slow, but I'm going to make up some gunpowder fuses ten seconds long, with some saltpetre in the middle. I light the fuse, it burns for five seconds, ignites the saltpetre so that it flares, which is the signal for my heroes to chuck it over the side."

"That's not going to kill anyone."

If Pender had seen James's painting of Harry he would have recognized the look in the eyes right away. It was there now.

"Didn't I say? These fuses will be attached to a barrel of gunpowder. If they go off too early they will totally ruin the rigging. If they go off on time, they'll blow a hole in the deck big enough to sail through."

"And if they're late?" asked Pender.

Harry spun round to include the crew assembled round him. "Then they'll kill all the men who've gathered round to see what's going on." He grinned again as the men backed off. "Stand by to lighten the ship."

They pumped the bilge out at a furious pace, then started the barrels of fresh water so that it ran into the holds, where it was picked up by the hoses and dumped over the side. His men worked fiendishly, fetching stores from below and chucking them into the grey sea, leaving a trail of jetsam in the *Miranda*'s wake. It was not the only thing in her wake. The two schooners, as Harry had predicted, had left the barque for dead and fetched his wake very quickly. Closer now, he could make out the differences. One had an all-black hull, while the second ship was blue, with a white checker along her gunports.

They'd also smoked his heading, south-west, and they were edging down to force him to turn. They made no attempt to disguise their aim, for they signalled to the barque, which immediately put her bowsprit further to the north so that when they forced Harry round, as they must do, it could close the gap by cutting the arc of his course. Harry consulted his charts and looked at his chronometers as the schooners edged to the south, ready to come up on his starboard side.

They were trying to force him to head for the open Atlantic, where time would be on their side, weather permitting. Harry wanted the safety of a port, preferably one like St Peter's in Guernsey, with guns at the harbour mouth to protect him. And if he was going to fight them, which looked increasingly likely, he didn't want them in line ahead, where they could stand off and fire broadsides at their leisure, while he could only fire two guns per minute in reply.

They'd surely want to compete for the honour of taking him and he had to try and use that to split them up, to bring them close on either side, so that they would fire just enough to clear his decks before boarding. Harry was worried about the effect of sustained fire on the *Miranda*'s hull. He went back on deck, looked at the pursuing ships, and after a short conversation with Gaston gave orders to his fishermen that would bring him round a course towards the northern tip of Alderney. That was tempting fate, as well as reposing a great deal of trust in his locals. The riptides and currents around that rocky, barren island were the worst in this part of the Channel.

It was no place to be taking the *Miranda*, unless he counted the greater danger which threatened. There was an anchorage at Braye, on the north-western coast, a bay which provided shelter from the prevailing westerlies, but apart from that he would be left with isolated fishing villages. If the worst happened and he was damaged but could still float, he'd run her aground in one of the bays. But first he would see what he could achieve by hugging the shore. Perhaps if he got close enough to the island they'd give up the chase, rather than risk their vessels in such deadly tides.

The schooners came round immediately, an action which split them up, putting blue water between their sides. And they started to race each other for the honour of catching him, with *"Blue Checker"* having the legs of *"Black Hull,"* which was exactly what Harry wanted. The boom of the signal gun came to him across the water. He turned to look at the distant barque, then back at the schooners, dismayed to see that *Blue Checker* had eased her braces to stay on station with her consort.

"Everyone fed?" he asked quietly.

"Aye, aye, Captain," Pender replied.

"We're going to have to fight," said Harry.

"Guessed as much, Captain." Pender paused before continuing. "Do we know who they are?"

Harry just shook his head. Pender's speculations would be as accurate as his own. Pender indicated the men sitting amidships, knotting ropes to make a bigger catapult for Harry's powder barrels. The gunner sat beside them making up fuses, all three under canvas so he could stay out of the occasional bursts of rain.

"Are we depending on those?"

"You don't like the idea?"

"I'd be happier with boarding nettings rigged."

"Good God, Pender," cried Harry, with mock horror. "How are we ever going to board the enemy if we've got nets rigged?"

"Land ho, dead ahead."

Harry saw his three fishermen elevate themselves. He relieved them at the wheel and let them go aloft. When they came back on deck, they were jabbering away in a local patois so dense that Harry couldn't understand a word. There was much pointing to the sea and the grey, overcast sky. Finally, the father, Gaston,

approached him. Speaking proper French, he began to inform
Harry of some of the peculiarities of the tides around Alderney.
There was much about time, the tide, and the season, with hints
of possibilities rather than certainties. Harry nodded sagely as they
talked, pointing towards the island himself, which could now be
observed from the deck. It didn't look inviting, merely a deeper
shade of grey than the surrounding sea.

Harry put them back on the wheel. Such local knowledge as
they had, the accumulated wisdom of generations, was priceless,
and it might just prove enough of an asset to redress the imbal-
ance in the coming fight. He prayed that his opponents were using
charts. These men would not need a chart to sail these waters,
indeed they would be at a loss to read one. But it was clear, from
his conversation with Gaston, that they had knowledge of every
submerged rock, every current and tidal race by day and season.

"Douse the galley fire, Pender, and issue a tot of rum to all
hands."

"Shall I start the casks when I've done that?" asked Pender
softly.

Harry just nodded. They both knew the temptations for sailors
when they thought they were close to death. They'd do nothing
to save themselves or the ship, but they'd go to any lengths to get
hold of the means to get drunk. Harry made his way to his windowless cabin. The two nine-pounders had been set up across the
stern and he bent to look through the gap at the two schooners.

"Run her out," he said to the starboard gunners, for they were
already at full elevation. "Let's try the range."

The men hauled on the breechings that held the gun to the deck,
pulling them so that the gun ran out, with the muzzle protruding
beyond the woodwork. Harry stepped round, taking a handkerchief and tying it about his ears. The noise of a gun going off in
this confined area could be deafening. Then he lowered the slowmatch into the touch-hole.

A great spurt of flame leapt from the muzzle. The cannon shot backwards until its movement was arrested by the restraining tackles. Bending low, he could see the ball arcing towards the enemy. It landed in the sea between them, sending water over both bows. The two ships immediately drifted further apart, which caused Harry to curse under his breath, though he was far from displeased. With one ball he'd achieved the very thing he'd been trying to do all morning.

"Right, lads. You've got one ship each. See what you can do. If they show signs of coming into line abreast, try to prevent it."

"Can we fire together, Captain?"

Harry mused, then nodded, reasoning that a ship was always stronger in its length than its beam, so even the *Miranda* could stand the strain. He went up to the poop, to oversee the work of the four-pounders, which he wanted to play on his enemies' rigging. From there he could supervise all the guns, with a messenger to relay his orders to the cabin.

They were close now and they opened up with bow chasers in answer to his guns. But the swell had increased, and the water was more disturbed, the effect caused by being on the edge of the Alderney currents. Neither side could do much damage, unless luck attended their aim. Harry left the poop to go forward to the quarterdeck. He had another quiet conversation with the old islander, who took him to the bows and pointed out the course he should follow. Harry relaxed as he listened, for what the old man was saying could produce an answer to part of his problem.

They went back to the wheel and Gaston started a very gentle edge to starboard, so infinitesimal as to be barely noticeable. His pursuers must be wondering at his course. He was sailing right into the wind, as close-hauled as she would bear, with the sheer rocks of the coastline dead ahead. They suspected a trick, no doubt, but they obeyed their leader's instructions to stay abreast. They were at least spread out, planning to take him on either side, swinging wide to ensure that they could descend on the *Miranda* at a sharp angle. Harry looked at Gaston. The

Alderney fisherman was smiling and nodding, as well as pointing a finger to the grey sky, to convey to Harry that whatever they'd cooked up was going according to plan.

Harry ran for the shrouds and started to climb. There was little time, but he wanted to see for himself. He didn't have to go any further than the cap. Dead ahead, he could see the line of gulls that swooped before the tidal race that swirled round the head of the island. Surging down the rocky shoreline, it produced a counter-eddy a mile off shore.

He returned to the deck as his enemies came abreast, *Blue Checker* to larboard, with *Black Hull* to the south. They'd head-reached a fraction before putting their helm down, so that they came in to the arc of his fire at minimum risk to themselves. Once close, they'd swing back on course alongside and start their broadsides. Harry smiled grimly. If only they knew how little he had in the way of firepower. Then he looked at Gaston. The gnarled old man was staring past him, at the swooping line of approaching gulls, his tongue stuck between his lips in concentration. He glanced once at *Blue Checker*, then back at the tidal race which had passed their bows, and finally called to Harry.

The men were ready. They eased the braces holding the yards as Gaston put the helm down. The *Miranda* picked up speed as she took more of the westerly on her sails and shot towards *Blue Checker*. *Black Hull* had over-reached but was coming round to pursue just as her bows hit the overpowering coastal current. The effect must have ripped the wheel out of the helmsman's hands, for the schooner spun into the race and was headed further south, with the birds swooping through her rigging and the sails flapping uselessly.

For a precious moment, Harry had only one enemy to fight, an enemy he was bearing down on at high speed. The bow chaser spoke out and at this range, aimed to fire on the downroll, they took chunks of wood out of *Blue Checker*'s bulwarks. The captain, who could see that he was at a disadvantage, was no fool. He put his helm hard down and spun in near his own length to remove himself from danger. It was an impressive piece of seamanship.

As Harry sailed by the unprotected stern, he cursed his want of firepower. A broadside would have done great damage. He took off some of the decoration, but he could achieve no more than that, and the jeering yells that came from his enemy depressed him, first because they were audible, and secondly because they were in English.

Blue Checker came round in pursuit. For the first time in an age Harry looked for the barque. His heart nearly stopped as he saw her. She'd ignored his manoeuvres and held her course, and was now threatening to head him off before he could weather the northern tip of the island. He watched, holding his breath, until he was sure that the wind, favouring him on this heading, was putting him ahead of his opponent. It would be a close-run thing, but he would just make it.

He also had two enemies still in his wake, one close and the other a good two miles to the south, heading out to sea to escape that current, before turning north again. He could clear the headland before the barque, but he might never get another chance for a single-ship engagement, a chance to reduce the odds. He took possession of the wheel from old Gaston and called out his orders.

"Mr Pender. Stand by to go about, then all hands ready to board."

They were sick of running, fed up with being hunted. They cheered at the thought of initiating an attack. Wearing round, the *Miranda* hit the coastal current at the right angle and, with the wind on the beam, took off like a greyhound. Harry had his ship under complete control and used that current to close on his enemy before they had time to prepare. He rattled out a stream of orders, then came out of the tidal race, using the counter-eddy of the opposite current to swing his ship right round, so that it drifted into the side of the schooner.

Blue Checker's captain sheered away, leaving half his paint on the *Miranda*. His gunports, which had been raised, were now smashed shut. For a moment, he couldn't clear his guns. But he was away from his attacker, with an increasing amount of sea between them and good reason to feel pleased. The boarders got out of the way. Harry shouted to the gunner to light the fuse poking out of his barrel. It spluttered as the "brutes" took a grip on their catapult, until it reached the saltpetre. The flare of that was the signal to spring the catapult.

The barrel spun through the air, with Harry yelling for his men to get down. Fascinated, they didn't obey. He spun the wheel in the hope that his rudder would do what his crew would not. The barrel hit the very edge of *Blue Checker*'s bulwarks and fell towards the sea. As its lower rim touched the water it finally exploded. The great fount of water made his men duck down, so they didn't see the hole that appeared in the planking of the schooner, right on the waterline.

The ship lurched to one side, as if in the grip of a huge hand, and started to settle forward. Worse still, she spun round, bows on to Harry's stern, the way on her carrying back into the fierce coastal current. If she fouled the *Miranda*'s rigging they might both go down. It was old Gaston, and the enemy helmsman, who saved the day. The old man grabbed the wheel out of Harry's hand and took the ship into the riptide deliberately, opening up an immediate gap between the two vessels. On board the schooner they knew that current spelt certain doom to their stricken ship. They used wind and rudder to stay clear and the gap increased. The *Miranda*'s sails, still set as they had been earlier, began to draw again and she was once more under control.

CHAPTER THIRTY-SEVEN

HARRY EASED her back out of the tide and brought the *Miranda* in a wide arc round the schooner. *Black Hull* had hauled his wind when he'd seen what happened and was standing off, trying to make sense of the fate that had befallen her consort. *Blue Checker* was down by the bows, taking water, with every chance that she might sink. Harry ignored them both and headed north, straight for the barque, which now stood across his escape route. He didn't want a fight if he could avoid one. If she moved over he would sail on. If not, he'd probably end up ramming her.

The barque was bearing down on him simultaneously, so the gap closed rapidly. Her master was edging away from the island, trying to force Harry to take the inside course. He declined the invitation to endanger his ship and followed suit till both ships were well away from the Alderney tides. Suddenly, while still out of range of his bow chasers, his opponent went about, sailing on a parallel course.

It was a clever ploy and increased the danger to the *Miranda* tenfold, since anything that delayed him increased the chance of the black-hulled schooner joining the fight. Harry had no choice but to hold his course. Even in a running fight he'd weather the headland in pole position, then, with open water on his starboard quarter, he could put up his helm and try to escape.

Things settled for a spell, so Harry had a chance to assess what had happened. The ships, or at least the crews, were English, which was puzzling. They were not navy, that he did know. Could they be hired by the Revenue to catch him? But that didn't make sense either. None of the ships flew any kind of flag to identify them.

Nor had they made any attempt to signal him to surrender, although he'd scarcely given them the chance.

The barque eased her braces and took in her courses, reducing to topsails only, which stopped his peregrinations. She was getting ready to fight. The lettering on her stern sprang into focus. Harry spelt it out, but the name *Rother* meant nothing to him. He followed suit in the matter of sails, for he wanted to give the impression of welcoming a scrap. But he made sure all his crew knew that the minute they came abreast he wanted every stitch set again, so that he could steal a march on his opponent, and get some way ahead.

They approached each other in complete silence, the *Rother* holding her fire through choice. Harry envied that. He was doing the same thing so that he could mask his weakness. Then he saw him, standing by the wheel, and all the questions about these ships, and their purpose, were answered. He could not know that the beard was new, that it had grown again since his farcical trial. He only registered that it was shorter. But there was enough of the face, with its piggy eyes, to leave him in no doubt at whom he was looking. The gap had closed to hailing distance, close enough to hear a shout, but too far to catapult a barrel. Trench, with his memorable voice, took advantage of it.

"Prepare to meet your maker, Ludlow," he screamed. "And I hope when you see Tobias Bertles you say sorry for ever buying him that ship."

Harry wasn't really listening to Trench. He was trying to stem the anger that seemed to consume him. For with his enemy here, instead of in gaol, it could only mean one thing. Trench had cheated the gallows. And if he'd done that, he'd also been free to take his revenge on Harry's family and property.

"Man the guns," he shouted. "All of them!"

"Captain," said Pender, who was equally shocked but less alarmed.

"Do as I say!"

"The barky won't stand it, you know that!"

Harry spun round, his eyes blazing. They were nearly abreast now, nearly to the point of commencing battle. It wasn't Pender who brought him to his senses, but Trench. "Time to pay you out," he screeched. "In like coin."

"Everybody down," yelled Harry, throwing himself to the deck. Old Gaston and his sons were a mere second behind him, so they felt the rush of air and heard the innumerable cracks as the grapeshot swept across the deck. Harry was back on his feet right away, counting off the time it would take them to load again. He only had one of his own guns ready to fire. He grabbed Pender.

"Load every cannon, then see to the sails." He could see the worry in Pender's eyes, the fear that his captain was so maddened by the sight of Trench that he was blind to common sense. "I know what I'm doing. I want to give him something to remember me by. But more than that, I also want to live."

The side of the *Rother* erupted again, much quicker than Harry anticipated. But it was round shot this time. Bits of the *Miranda*'s bulwarks flew in all directions, dangerous splinters that could kill and maim, as the well-aimed broadside took its toll. Harry managed two shots before Trench paid him out again. Near point-blank, the *Miranda* shook with the impact as the balls hit her hull, making her timbers groan like a sea monster.

Pender, who knew which orders to obey and which to ignore, had sent most of the men aloft to tend the courses, leaving only a few to load the guns. They were drawing ahead, but only for a moment, for the *Rother* increased her speed as well, keeping abreast. And they were still a full mile from the point at which they could turn away. The next broadside was fired too late, on the downroll, and most of the round shot ended up in the water. Harry was making his way up the side, black from head to foot, firing each gun in turn, doing his best to reply to the onslaught. But it was feeble stuff by comparison.

Trench reverted to grape again, this time aiming into the rigging, trying to kill Harry's crew; only a miracle kept them all in one piece, for the sails were riddled with holes. He turned to round shot , and a pounding continuous fire that made the *Miranda* stagger each time she was struck. Harry wasn't so engrossed in his weapons that he couldn't hear the sounds from below. And what he heard did nothing to make him feel more confident. And even deeper down, on another level, he wondered what would befall him if he landed up at the mercy of Trench. It didn't bear contemplation. And his crew would suffer the same as those on the *Planet.*

"They're preparing to board, Captain," shouted Pender, whose mouth had to be close to Harry's ear, to penetrate his captain's near deaf state. Harry stood upright. He looked at the approaching headland, the northern tip of Alderney, and calculated the timing. Then at the darkening sky, with the cloud cover breaking up showing an occasional patch of blue. As he replied his voice sounded strange, confined, as the sound was, inside his head.

"They want to bring us to before we reach clear water. If Trench takes us he'll kill us all, regardless. Not much point in trying to keep the *Miranda* afloat, if we're going to die anyway."

Pender thought about that for a second or two, to ensure that his captain was talking sense. He, too, had heard the screams from the *Planet.* Then he grinned, his white teeth flashing in the fading light.

"All guns, Captain."

Harry smiled back. "And grape, Pender. He'll hate that."

Harry looked across the narrowing gap, as the *Rother* edged down on the *Miranda.* True to his salt, Trench remained beside the wheel, content to let others risk their skin. He had a sudden temptation to shout back, to tell Trench that he was wrong. They were all wrong. Him, Temple, Braine, and the rest of the smuggling fraternity. He'd never put a penny towards the purchase of the *Planet.* But he held his tongue, for it would do no good. They hadn't believed him before and Obidiah Trench wasn't going to at the point of total revenge.

His voice echoed in his head again. "Keep a sharp eye out for where they place their lashings, Pender."

"Axes ready, your honour," Pender replied, but Harry didn't hear him.

They had the guns loaded in record time and the Mirandas ran them out. The Rothers jeered, convinced it was a bluff, and leapt up on to their bulwarks in defiance, jabbing with their weapons. One of them spun round and dropped his trousers, insulting them with his bare arse. A huge gale of laughter erupted from their throats and others followed suit. It was an expensive mistake, as Harry, feeling his ship rise on a wave, gave the order to fire. Every gun went off at once, shooting back in recoil and wracking the ship's frame. Harry could feel the wood wrenching through his feet. But it was the damage his guns had done that took his attention. The side of the *Rother* was completely clear of boarders.

More than that she'd sheered off, losing speed. Even Harry could hear the screams coming across the water. That was, until the *Miranda* was too far ahead. They weathered the tip of Alderney and as he gave the order to change course he looked back at the scene behind him. It wasn't over yet, for Trench was still standing. He'd wounded the crew of the *Rother,* not the ship. And judging by the sounds from below, he done the opposite to the *Miranda.* There to the south was Trench's second schooner, *Black Hull* coming up at speed. There was no sign of *Blue Checker,* which gave him some comfort.

Night was falling. In a sound vessel he would have headed north-west, into open water, in the general direction of Plymouth, relying on darkness to evade pursuit. But he knew the *Miranda* wouldn't stand it if they encountered bad weather. That last broadside had effected too much damage. A heavy sea, pounding her hull for any length of time, and she could break up altogether. Turning towards Braye was no longer a choice, it was a necessity. He'd have to fight them again tomorrow, either at sea or on land, for he knew in his heart that Trench would never give up, as long as he had breath in someone else's body.

Harry went below, only to have his worst fears confirmed. The *Miranda* was shipping water everywhere. Even now the pumps could barely cope and it would only worsen as the sea worked on the sprung planking. Down in the depths of the ship he could hear the masts groaning, loosening themselves from their seating.

Back on deck, old Gaston, who had been pushed off the wheel by Patcham, sidled up to Harry at the same time as Pender, just beating him to the captain's ear. They rattled away in French and it was clear that what the old man was saying brought no pleasure to Harry's ears. Pender could see him swearing softly under his breath, but the only word he could make out was the oft-repeated "swinge"; since it was either French, or the local dialect, it was a mystery.

Gaston's arms were waving frantically, and he seemed as upset by Harry's replies as the captain was by his information. Harry, who'd been looking at the deck, lifted his eyes to Pender's and his one-time servant thought he saw despair. Then he looked over to Patcham at the wheel. Harry's words, softly delivered, did nothing to lift Pender's spirits.

"We're going the wrong way. We should have tried to weather Burhou, it seems, that island slightly further west."

Pender followed Harry's outstretched finger. He could just make out the grey hump in the gathering gloom. "What odds does it make?"

Harry's tone was harsh. "There's a tidal bore that sweeps up this channel. They call it the Swinge. It can go as high as fifty feet, a solid wall of water which will sink every ship in its path."

"Fifty feet," said Pender, his voice full of disbelief.

Harry conferred with Gaston and the old man made a lot of noise and many gestures, which were translated for Pender's benefit. "That's an exception, fifty feet. It's more like thirty, he says."

"Well, thank God for that," said Pender, with an artificial expression of relief.

Harry looked at him coldly for a moment. Then he suddenly laughed. Pender joined in and Gaston, caught between them, put his finger to his head, gesturing to his two sons that *les Anglais* were mad.

"We can't go back, for we'll run straight into Trench, and if we go on . . ." Harry left the rest of that sentence hanging in the air. But when he spoke again, his voice had a new note of urgency.

"We have one thing in our favour. We know about the danger, and Trench doesn't."

"You're goin' on?" asked Pender.

"No choice. All the guns over the side, since they make us top-heavy. Get everything loose off the deck. Better still sling anything that might injure someone into the sea. We'll need to lash the wheel. I want the hatches battened down and covered with tarred canvas."

He bent to talk to Gaston again, asking how long they had.

"He thinks we've got about an hour. Board up the sternlights, but leave a small gap, so that when you light the lantern it will look like a glimmer shining through the drapes. Make it appear as though we've made an error in our blacking out. I want Trench to follow us. In fact I want him to try a night attack. And I hope he's right alongside the *Miranda,* just on the turn, when that water hits."

"Pity I stove in the rum," said Pender. "A tot now would cheer the hands."

"There's brandy in my stores, hand that round. But don't let anyone get drunk too soon. We don't want them drowning."

The thin sliver of light was clear to the Rothers. They used a shaded lantern to call up the schooner and put on more speed to overhaul Harry. Trench was so excited he dribbled as he explained how he would take the *Miranda* between the two ships in dark-ness, boarding her and recovering her without a shot being fired. He looked at the sky as the cloud cover began to break up and blessed the extra light that would let him see his prey.

Aboard Harry's ship the crew were working to capacity, even as they passed round the bottle. The pumps clanked away in an endless litany. Old Gaston, appraised of Harry's intentions, crossed himself, then went into another huddle with his sons. They made much, it seemed, of the changing weather, as the temperature dropped and the sky cleared. He collared Harry and dragged him on to the poop, to look over the stern.

"What is the old sod about now," said Flowers.

"Don't tempt Providence, mate," Pender replied. "That old sod has saved our bacon once already today."

Harry called softly for some rope and a boarding pike. Pender, full of curiosity, obliged personally. When he arrived he found his captain hanging out over the stern.

"We're going to jam the rudder, Pender. Gaston doesn't think we'll be able to hold the wheel, even if it's lashed, and if our head comes round even a fraction we're done for. And he also suggests we stop pumping. The higher we float, the more we're likely to broach."

"Aye, aye, Captain."

The crew were sent below, to be strapped to the side of the lower deck by ropes. Their hands were, of course, still free to pass the brandy. Harry didn't need them sober now, they might as well be drunk. Even he didn't feel very confident about survival. Gaston was up in the bows, sniffing the air, which he assured Harry would give them ample warning of the approaching Swinge. From the stern the ghostly outlines of Trench and his consort were visible as they closed the distance. They certainly wouldn't see him go over the side and slip into the cradle he'd rigged to jam the rudder.

Gaston's two sons were by the wheel with Pender, ready to run for the hatchway as the order was given. Gaston would set their course, so that the *Miranda*'s bows were aimed straight at the oncoming wave. They saw him hurry back from the prow. He took the wheel himself and spun it slightly, sending Pender to tell Harry it was time for the boarding pike. As he leant to lash the wheel he glanced over the side. The two ethereal bowsprits, rocking gently at each side as they closed in on the *Miranda*, shocked him, for he'd had no idea that Trench had actually overtaken them.

"It's time, Captain," whispered Pender.

Harry turned, and his teeth showed in the faint light. They heard it together, a low rumbling that sounded like a distant thunderstorm. Both men froze for a moment, till Pender reminded Harry that Gaston was waiting by the wheel. His hand shot out and Pender took it, returning the firm shake.

"Good luck, friend. Now get below."

Harry swung his leg over the rail and disappeared. Pender stood there for a moment, with tears in his eyes for the second time this trip. Then he spun round and ran to warn Gaston. The rumbling was now a roar and the air was full of a sudden freezing wind. The old fisherman tugged at the wheel, which didn't budge. With a glance back towards the stern, he allowed Pender to push him through the hatch.

"Lanterns out, lads," he called, as he pulled the canvas cover tight. Gaston grabbed his arm and gesticulated wildly, to add to the stream of words. Pender just shook his head. He knew as he stood on the poop that Harry Ludlow wouldn't be coming.

Harry felt reasonably safe. If the ship was heading into the tidal wave, the stern was a good a place as any to hide. If the *Miranda* went down, he'd drown a little quicker than his crew. Either way, he'd have the satisfaction of seeing what happened to Obidiah Trench. He could hear the wind whistling past the ships, but that was as nothing to the deep thundering roar which accompanied it. The very earth itself seemed to tremble.

They'd abandoned silence on Trench's ships, instead crowding forward to the source of the sound, peering into the darkness to try and make out what caused it. Suddenly, as the noise increased, so did the light, as though the crest of the great wave was picking up the glim of the stars and magnifying it a hundredfold. Faces on the *Rother* were now white blobs as they drifted closer still. Frightened men lined the decks of the two ships that straddled the *Miranda*.

They might have screamed in panic. But there could be no other sound now, for nothing could compete with the deafening bellow of the furious cascading water. He saw Trench, in his red coat. He was by the rail, his hands up in supplication as if he was trying to hold back his fate. He saw the *Rother*'s bows lift at the same time as he felt the water take the *Miranda*. Harry could have sworn, despite the noise, that he heard Trench emit a high-pitched scream. Or was it just the wide open mouth, so obvious in the middle of his beard, sending a silent message to his brain?

Then it was pandemonium, for all three ships had their bowsprits pointing to the sky. The *Rother,* fractionally off a straight course, broached first. Then the schooner, too, spun sideways, tossed like a toy boat. The *Rother* was on her beam ends in the tumultuous waves. He heard the sound of tortured wood add itself to that of the crashing water. The masts ripped themselves out of the keel. Harry was still hanging backwards, with the ropes of his sling cutting into his spine. It felt as though the entire ship was going to go under, pushing him before it. But the waterlogged *Miranda* had not risen as high on the crest as Trench's ships. Nor had it spun away from its course, for the boarding pike, aided by the lashings that Gaston had put on the wheel, held her true. Harry went under into the freezing sea, gasping for breath, but felt himself jerked upwards as the stern was thrown violently out of the water by the huge wave running under the keel.

He spun round, ignoring the stinging sensation in his eyes, to see the two vessels tumbling away in the foaming waters. They were on their sides, with masts trailing in the foam, completely broached, with no chance of survival as the tidal wave dashed them against innumerable rocks. The air around him was still full of spume and spray. But the world was quietening down, returning to normal, and he was alive.

CHAPTER THIRTY-EIGHT

"**THEN WE** put into Braye, made some emergency repairs, pumped her dry and made for Guernsey."

"And Obidiah Trench?" asked Arthur, helping himself to another grape.

"All hands," said Harry, without the least trace of the sorrow that normally accompanied such a statement. "They searched, of course. All they found was wreckage littering the shore."

"Lord, Harry," said Anne, rubbing her huge belly. "You have almost brought on my labours with your tale."

Harry's face took on a look of concern. They'd been about to take coach to London when his messenger had arrived from Peg-well Bay, requesting pardons and exemptions if they were available. Arthur was in the happy position, thanks to Dundas, of being able to oblige. Once Harry had seen to the crew's needs, he'd come on to Cheyne Court himself, bringing Pender. The coach now stood outside, waiting patiently for its passengers.

"You should not have delayed your departure. God forbid you should give birth on the road."

"I am made of sterner stuff than you, Harry Ludlow," said Anne. "I shall most certainly deliver in the Lying-in Hospital. And I can tell you, from what I hear, that attendance at a birth would make you faint clean away, regardless of how much blood, gore, and fighting you've seen."

"I do think that such talk is unbecoming, Anne. You are not a fishwife."

"Forgive me, husband. But you must own that Harry set the level."

"I will grant you that with the same breath that allows me to forbid your lapses." He turned to Harry, his face pinched in disapproval. "It only happens when she's around her brothers. James is equally bad. I do wish you wouldn't encourage her."

"I'm sorry," said Harry, insincerely, looking away from his smirking sister. Then he changed the subject to one he knew his brother-in-law would find more amenable.

"Do you think I will like my new house?"

"It's only a four-year lease, of course. But it is grand, very grand. There is accommodation in abundance and the public rooms are most spacious. The entire ground floor opens up to create a ballroom. Indeed I wondered if you'd consent to an entertainment, once Anne has recovered from her confinement. Perhaps a celebration of the arrival of an heir?"

"Nothing would give me greater pleasure, Arthur," replied Harry, beaming. "It's time I reintroduced myself in society."

Arthur almost beamed, but he avoided it by covering his mouth with the back of his hand, turning his evident pleasure into what looked remarkably like a yawn.

"Oh, I do agree. I shall, of course, invite Dundas and Pitt. It's time you met them. Then you can thank Dundas personally for exerting so much pressure on that odious creature Braine."

Harry couldn't help it. The yawn had irritated him. He wished that just for once Arthur would be less stiff-necked.

"A capital notion. And I am sure James will want to invite Burke and Sheridan." He smiled at Anne. "We'd best hide the silver, lest it ends up in as a property in a Commons debate."

"Harry, stop teasing this instant," said Anne, in that manner, peremptory and rarely challenged, allowed to women who are about to give birth.

Harry spoke quickly, for Arthur's face had that look of fraternal disapproval he so dreaded. He seemed, in his behaviour, unaffected by his wife's impending confinement.

"I must look in on Tite."

"Yes," said Arthur without enthusiasm.

"He should have listened to you, husband."

"That old man has never listened to me all the time I've known him. I told him not to fire the cannon."

Anne cut in. "It was the news that you'd survived, Harry. We were all truly frightened for you, and so overjoyed. I cannot find it in my heart to remonstrate with him."

Anne had blossomed with her pregnancy, in more ways than one. She seemed more independent of Arthur, who didn't like it one little bit. He quickly returned to the original subject.

"I find it hard to believe he forgot the recoil."

Arthur sat up, a sure sign he was getting set to make a sally. "Possibly he parked his memory in the same place he keeps his manners."

"He was in terrible pain, Pa," said Jenny. "And the cursing was just like home."

She blushed, meaning home in the old sense. Pender was still trying to get used to having his child on his knee, something Mrs Cray had insisted was "appropriate." The other two were playing happily on the kitchen floor.

"He learned his language at sea, Jenny."

"Is that where you learned yours?" she asked.

He couldn't be sure he was being practised on, but the girl had a twinkle in her eye to add to that question. Mrs Cray missed it, if indeed it was there.

"Silly old goat. He should have broken his neck, not his leg."

Tite's windowless room, right behind the kitchen chimney, was stiflingly hot. The old man lay back on his bunk bed, his splinted leg stuck straight out. But he'd provided for his primary needs. A half-empty bottle stood on the bedside table and the familiar smell of rum filled Harry's nostrils.

"Damn it, Tite," he said. "It's as dark in here as a surgeon's cockpit."

The old man slurred his reply. "That's how I like it, Master

Harry, though I never liked to see the cockpit aboard ship."

"Nor me. It's a terrible place to be after a fight."

"My God, I was in a few of those with your papa." He fixed Harry with his watery blue eyes, his old face sad. "Break his heart to think there's a war an' you ain't in it."

Harry sat on the edge of the cot, gingerly, so as not to disturb the leg. "But I am, Tite, in my own way."

"Not the same, your honour," he said, trying to raise himself up. Harry put a gentle hand on his chest to restrain him. "You'll never raise your flag."

"I can live with that, Tite. Being at sea keeps me from brooding on it."

That was a smooth lie. Harry sometimes longed to be a king's officer again. But it was not to be. He had broken their precious rules by duelling with a superior officer, then compounded the sin by his refusal to apologize, even when they'd clearly indicated he would suffer no shame by doing so. He wouldn't ask to be reinstated and he doubted very much if the navy would offer.

Tite waved his hand drunkenly. Harry moved the bottle out of his reach for two reasons. "Well, just you mind what's afoot when you're away at sea."

"Whatever do you mean?"

"You know me, your honour. I ain't one to split if'n it'll do a good man down."

Harry nodded. But it was an insincere acknowledgement. He had ample experience to prove that Tite was the exact opposite. James might be fooled by the old man's manner, but his brother hadn't been to sea with him. Harry had, as a midshipman, and he'd suffered himself from reports carried to his father by this ever-so-loyal servant, who'd sworn blind, with his best mask of sincerity, that the information hadn't come from him. Still, he had been true to his father, which, in the end, was what counted.

"That Scotch bastard," Tite spat.

That made Harry frown. The old man might be sick and drunk, just as he might dislike his brother-in-law, but he could not call

Arthur such names in Harry's presence. His response was cold.

"I think you may have overdone the rum, Tite."

"You can't defend 'im to me, Master Harry. Not since he's been at it, behind your back."

Harry stood up slowly. "I think you've said enough."

Tite was too far gone to heed the tone of reproof. His blue eyes blazed with drunken anger. "I overheard the serving girls. They was upstairs, 'not to be disturbed on any account.' Then I spied the horse in the stable. An' I heard them myself, I did, at the top of the stairs in the Griffin, all lovey-dovey to each other. 'Will you come again,' says she. 'I will,' replies the Scotch sod. 'Make the arrangements'—"

"Be quiet!" shouted Harry.

Tite stopped in mid-flow, realizing that he gone too far.

"I am aware, Tite, and have been for some time, that there is a connection between Lord Drumdryan and Naomi Smith. You will never mention it again, d'ye hear. Not to me, and especially not within earshot of Lady Drumdryan."

He was fearful now, for the tone of Harry's voice, and the look in his eye, was frightening. "Never in life, your honour. You know me."

There was little point in saying any more and Harry had no desire to play the martinet. The message had been delivered and, he was sure, understood. But there had to be a sanction. So he said something he'd been meaning to say for years. "Get well soon, Tite. And don't fret about your duties. They will be undertaken from now on by someone else."

Harry spun on his heel and left. Tite, the effect of those words obvious on his crestfallen face, reached for the rum bottle. But Harry Ludlow had, quite by accident, put it too far away.

The postman came up the drive just as Harry was handing his sister, wrapped in several cloaks, into the well-sprung coach. The warmth was deemed necessary, though it was a seasonable spring day.

"I shall be up in London before the baby is born, I promise. But I must sort out my crew first."

"Via Blackwall Reach, I assume?" said Arthur. He looked as though he was off to St Petersburg, judging by the furs he wore. But the question was no longer accompanied by the usual sniff of disapproval. Perhaps now he had a residence in London he would accept that Harry belonged at sea.

The man had three letters for Harry, with a whole sheaf for Arthur. Harry examined his. One he recognized as being from James, another from his bankers, while the third was from an address he didn't recognize in Hythe.

"Of course. I have already written to Grisham. I dare say he'll work double tides to get her ready. I've offered him the *Miranda*'s refit if he gets her ready before I arrive."

Arthur gave him a wry smile. "What a forgiving soul you are, Harry."

He stood and waved them off, then turned to go back into the house. Harry stopped, looking at it, suddenly aware that for the first time since he'd inherited Cheyne Court he was going to be here on his own. He wasn't sure if that pleased him or not.

The letter from Cantwell didn't please him at all. It informed him that Arthur, who'd apparently been making speculative investments, was being pressed by his creditors. He'd used all of his own funds and borrowed more from Jewish moneylenders. The bank, or rather Benedict Cantwell, was advising that his power of attorney be withdrawn. Harry didn't even know that Arthur had creditors, not that it was any of his business. What he did know was that Arthur was extremely honest as far as money was concerned. He was resolved to send a sharp reply. Leaving James till last, he read the second one, which was from Franks. After the usual assurances that he and his wife were well, he went on:

I cannot apologize enough for my delay in replying. But your letter, and those of your brother-in-law, followed me to Gibraltar and back again. Let me now assure you that no one has even enquired after my person, let alone threatened it.

Nor would they ever do so. Your warning set me to thinking and I now recall the evening well, though I have drawn a veil, to spare my dear wife, over the events that followed Bertles's dinner. I'm afraid that I was concentrating so much on Mr Wentworth's attentions to Polly, which were unseemly, that I never did get round to signing Captain Bertles's manifest. Nor, as far as I recall, did Mr Wentworth. As I've already said, his mind was on other things.

That is a young man who should be taught some manners. But it ill becomes a man like me to show that I have a jealous nature. Indeed, I do not, sir. It is merely that I am on constant alert, being blessed with an ingenuous wife.

He signed it Colonel Franks, which showed that he was making good progress despite her gaffes. But the information confirmed Harry's previous speculations. All his troubles had been caused by that manifest. Only he had bothered to commit himself, and in such a manner that he'd brought trouble about his head. He balked at communicating with Wentworth, for verification, and prepared to accept Colonel Franks's word.

His tranquillity, so recently acquired, was shattered by James's letter. Yet it produced stillness rather than activity. It was left to Pender to tell the servants to watch their step. He knew that Harry was on the boil, even if he had no idea of the cause. James's letter had begun so well, with much rejoicing over his safe return. Harry had reread the second part several times just to be sure. For his theorizing about that manifest was exposed as a house of cards.

Though it is not a place where any decent man would expect to receive quarter, I visited Jalheel Temple and tried to force him to assist us before Trench's trial, on the grounds that you were innocent of any wrongdoing. He laughed in my face, of course. But it is his excuse for doing so that I find odd. For reasons neither of us can fathom, they will none of them accept, to this day, that you are not a smuggler. I did my best to nail the problem of the manifest which you wrote me about, but the scrub brushed that aside. He said a very strange thing, during that unpleasant interview, which has stuck with me.

His words were quite clear: that "they had an inkling where the money had come from to buy the *Planet* before Bertles ever set sail." Temple insisted that his source was "unimpeachable," then went on to add a peculiar observation, that "a man should be careful whom he beds."

I did ask him to clarify that, but he refused. I cannot fathom what he meant, nor, I should think, could anyone. And he is not the type to ask, since dishonesty is so engrained in his nature that he would lie rather than speak the truth. But, Harry, it was said with such assurance that for a brief moment, I must confess, I was almost fooled.

Harry sat in his library, his eyes fixed on the book-lined walls. He couldn't stop the servants from lighting candles, though he'd rather have sat in the dark. And he could scarcely do justice to Mrs Cray's dinner, served on a tray, which would earn him a frown in the morning. That sentence which Temple had used, along with the words he just heard from the lips of Tite, haunted Harry. It made him recall every detail of the last seven months. He examined every word and each gesture, looking for significance. Then he picked up the note from Cantwell, alluding to Arthur's financial problems. The words "speculative investments" sprang out at him.

"This is most inconvenient, Harry," said Arthur, removing his riding clothes. "Anne is very close to her delivery. I should be in London, not here."

"What I have to say should be said in this house," replied Harry coldly.

Arthur suddenly looked guarded. "That is a very singular tone you're using. Is something amiss?"

"I think there is a great deal amiss, Arthur." Harry started to pace the room, his hands behind his back and his head pushed down on to his chest. "I fear I shall have to speak with a clarity that you may find uncomfortable."

"I am suffering from that already."

"I require the answers to some questions."

Arthur's eyebrows shot up. "Require, Harry?"

"I left you in charge of my affairs while I was at sea. I think you have exceeded your brief. I did not, for instance, intend that to include paying court to Naomi Smith."

Arthur's thin ginger eyebrows shot up in surprise. "'Court'?"

"Will you stop giving me one-word answers!"

His brother-in-law replied with equal venom. "I will most certainly do so. I shan't answer you at all."

"I know about your debts," said Harry suddenly. "Benedict Cantwell wrote to me on the subject."

Arthur put his hand to his lips, though it was a studied move, not alarm. "It seems you have been making some of those speculative investments you couldn't engage in on my behalf."

"That is true, though I can't see it is any of your concern. Nor can I fathom why Cantwell's have seen fit to inform you of my recent difficulties."

Harry heard the sound of horses' hoofs on the gravel, and cursed under his breath. The last thing he needed now was a visitor. Arthur had heard them too, and turned towards the window. But Harry's next words made his head snap round in anger.

"You have an attorney over my funds. They think I should be concerned."

That finally made Arthur bridle. "I shan't stay here another minute, Harry. If you have something to say, some accusation to lay against me, please be so good as to do so. Then I may have the chance to ignore it or refute it. If you wish to change the financial arrangement between us, then do so in writing."

The front door slammed shut, as if it had been taken by the wind. "I wish to know the nature of your investments."

"If you don't adopt a more fitting tone, you may wish till hell

394   THE PRIVATEERSMAN MYSTERIES

freezes over. I am not accountable to you for anything other than
your estate."

Footsteps thudded along the hall floor. "Not Tobias Bertles?"

"What has he got to do with this?"

The door was flung open and James stood there. His clothes
were coated with dust and his face was suffused with anger, perfectly complementing the icy atmosphere in the room.

"What are you doing here?" asked Harry.

"I've come to see you."

"It's not convenient, James."

"Damn your convenience, brother. Damn your powder, and
damn your wig."

"What are you talking about?" said Harry.

"I'm talking about a certain gentleman, a card player in Brook's
club, who wore a wig. He also had a powdered face. This fellow,
I believe, called himself Temple, when he played Lord Farrar."

"Ah," said Harry lamely, as he felt himself blush.

"Could you please forgive us, James," said Arthur. "Harry is
in the process of making some rather odd allegations about me."

Harry blessed Arthur, for he used exactly the right tone to rile
James, which might get him temporarily out of the firing line. But
James, much to his surprise, was all emollience.

"I ran into Emerson, the barrister, at Lady Jersey's."

It was now Arthur's turn to say "Ah," and blush. "I was fortunate. He saved me from having to act by his intervention."

"Nevertheless, Arthur, I cannot thank you enough. After all,
I've done little enough to earn your affection. You took a huge
risk."

James turned and his manner changed abruptly, as he renewed
his assault on his brother. "As for you, Harry, it's only by the merest good fortune that you have not completely ruined my
reputation."

Harry pulled himself upright, trying to recover some dignity.
"What I did, I did for the best."

"What did you mean when you asked about Bertles, Harry?"

It was odd how dealing with that looked like an escape route. "I wondered, Arthur, whether he was your speculative investment."

"Bertles? Are you mad, Harry?"

"Most certainly," snapped James.

CHAPTER THIRTY-NINE

"THEN I'M at a loss," said Harry.

James had explained his letter to Arthur, who was quick to pick up the drift and go pale with indignation, at the implication that he endangered them all, including his wife and unborn child, rather than admit an error of judgement, intentionally putting Harry on the defensive.

"But you cannot deny being involved with Naomi Smith. I was there, Arthur, that Halloween night. I saw the decorations and the costumes. You are the only Scotsman for miles around. It had to be for you."

"Do you really think I'd consort with an innkeeper?"

James had to intervene then. Things looked set to get heated again. Harry took that remark very badly.

"You're placing too much credence in Temple's words, Harry."

"I'm not, James. They struck a chord. Quested said something similar, the night they tried to bury me in shingle, about there being a warm bed going. They attacked this house, but when that failed they made no attempt to find you, Major Franks, or Wentworth. But Trench went to great lengths to silence me. Why? Somehow, regardless of that manifest, they were convinced that the money to back Bertles came from here. If they were so sure there had to be a reason."

He turned to Arthur, aware that he'd jumped to a conclusion, and quite deliberately leaving out mention of Wentworth's posters.

"At the risk of causing further offence, I must add that Tite saw you at the Griffin's Head. In fact, he overheard you talking to Naomi on the upstairs landing."

"So I'm now the butt of servants' tittle-tattle. I shall not set foot in this house again until that oaf is removed."

"I have told him he is retired," said Harry. "Tite has gained nothing from his tale."

Arthur, despite what was happening, brightened a little. Harry wondered afterwards if the only reason he got an answer to his question was because he'd removed Tite from his duties. Certainly his brother-in-law's voice seemed less gruff.

"I was there that day to finalize the arrangements for my investment. I met with two projectors from Edinburgh, to give them a money draft." He paused, and looked, rather sheepishly, from one brother to the other. If they'd come that far, some five hundred miles, why had he not invited them to the house? "I had no desire to trouble Anne with such a matter."

"I must know two things, Arthur, even although it affords me no pleasure to ask. The nature of your investments and your relationship with Naomi Smith."

Arthur sat silently for a moment before answering. When he did his face was like a mask.

"I have put some money into a colony in South America. The venture, and the colonists, are entirely Scottish. If it has succeeded, then I am rich. If not, penniless."

Harry felt that this was not the moment to point out that after previous expeditions, some of which had ended in commercial and human disaster, what he'd done was extremely foolish.

"And Naomi Smith?"

"Polite, and no more. I am not so stupid as to foul my nest so close to home."

"Was she expecting you that Halloween night?" asked Harry.

"She was. The invitation was the second I'd received. I met her at the Old Playhouse in Deal, and she invited me to dine, the night the Duke of York attended a performance of *Wild Oats*."

That produced a thin smile, for the conjunction of the subject under discussion and the title of the play was singular.

"I declined the first, so she arranged to put on a special event in my honour. It seemed churlish to refuse, though I did point out I had guests, and that I would be somewhat late. But I could not go, for the same reason I cancelled that dinner. Because you'd come home. But I will say this once and stress it. I was expected as a tenant looks for her landlord."

James, typically wicked, pointed at Harry and drove home a nail. "Given this particular landlord, that's rather opaque."

Arthur relaxed then, equally willing to bait his brother-in-law. "I doubt that this will please you either. The day she spoke to me on that landing, she had a visitor."

"Who?" asked Harry eagerly.

"I don't know, Harry. All I saw was a uniform coat hanging over a chair. That and a wide buff sword belt. Oh yes, there was a fancy feathered hat on the table." Arthur had turned towards James, so he didn't see the look in Harry's eye. "I dare say her interest was financial. I rather fear she worried about the possibility that I might increase her rent while you were absent."

But the look on James's face made him turn back towards Harry, an expression of perplexity on his pale face. "Does that information have some significance?"

Arthur refused a meal, or a bed, and set out for the return journey to London. When he had gone, James, over dinner, castigated his brother for his endemic habit of jumping to conclusions. Then he related what had happened in Lewes, how Arthur had been prepared to risk everything to save his life, which only served to make his brother feel worse. But James was tactful, knowing Harry needed time to think. It was the following morning, after breakfast, before they turned back to other matters.

"I take it, Harry, that you've made the connection?"

Harry answered gloomily. "I have, James, but I cannot accept it, nor see the sense in it."

"What will you do?"

Harry looked out of the window at the bright April sunshine, at the blue sky full of billowing clouds. He felt a deep sadness.

"I must go and confirm what I suspect, James. Though God knows I'll take no pleasure in it. After that, I have no idea."

No decorations now, just the place as he remembered it. White walls, dark floorboards, and aged oak beams, with rough-hewn pine tables full of Naomi's noisy customers. With startling clarity he suddenly remembered where he'd seen Bertles. It was here, in the Griffin's Head. In his mind he saw him as he had been at that dinner on the *Planet*. Red-faced and laughing, with those two odd tufts of hair twitching on his face, pouring drinks and speaking in a loud voice. This feat of memory was welcome, but did nothing to raise his spirits.

"She's not here, sir," said the serving girl, Polly. "Mrs Smith has gone off. She said she would look in at the cemetery and go on to Deal."

"Deal?"

"Aye, sir." The girl bowed her head and blushed. She'd been there long enough to know Harry Ludlow. "It's what she's being doing regular these last few months."

Harry walked out of the door. The girl forgave his lack of manners, reasoning that no one likes to lose out in love to a rival.

It was forlorn hope, for he'd not expected to find Naomi at the cemetery. He stopped his horse and dismounted at the wicket gate, then entered to look at the great Portland headstone which stood over the grave of Tolly Smith, her late husband. The angels and carved cherubs, with their fixed smiles, seemed to mock him. He looked at the wild flowers, now withered, haphazardly laid on the sparse grass.

"She's not been here today, has she, Tolly?" Harry asked the carved stone. Then he moved round to look at the other grave he'd seen her tending that winter day, when he'd come back from visiting his tenants. The stone was small and the decorated covers, set to keep out the overnight frost, had been moved to one side. He looked at the verdant grass, the carefully tended spring plants, then at the name on the stone. After a long and thoughtful pause, he walked slowly back to his horse, setting its head in the direction of Deal.

Braine was sitting in his damp room at Sandown Castle as though he hadn't moved for months. The look he gave Harry was even less friendly than the last they'd exchanged, though it was tinged with respect, Arthur's connections having singed the exciseman's tail. Dundas had informed the holder of Braine's sinecure to scold his deputy or risk a Royal warrant depriving him of his living. Such a warning, from such a source, politely delivered by the Secretary of State for War, had, by the time it reached Braine, assumed the proportions of a thunderbolt.

"Good day to you," said Harry, looking behind Braine's head at the tattered poster on the wall.

Braine's purple, craggy face creased up in a look of distaste he found impossible to disguise. "It wasn't a good day before you walked in here, an' I can't say it's improved."

"Anything that happened to you, Mr Braine, you brought on your own head."

The older man sniffed and gazed into the middle distance, not wishing to trade hard looks with his visitor. "There's those that labour an' those that don't, sir. And the law of the land looks differently on each. I am of the former, so must take my punishment in silence."

"Am I of the latter?" asked Harry, surprised at the philosophical tone, which didn't suit the speaker.

"You are of those who are above the law, Mr Ludlow."

Harry had half a mind to engage him about the recent past, to prove that he was not what Braine thought, a man so powerful that any charge laid against him could never hope to succeed. But that would achieve nothing. And anyway, he didn't care what the man opposite thought of him. But he was not about to let Braine off entirely.

"You could have acted differently."

Braine positively spat at him. "How?"

Harry glanced at the tattered poster again. "Take young Charlie Taverner, for instance. How soon after he died did you know who'd done it?"

That made him adopt a guarded look. "Who says I knew?"

"You did," replied Harry.

"Never!"

"You did, Mr Braine. In that cellar, just after you'd dug me out. Perhaps the painful memory loosened your tongue." He saw the look of alarm in the other man's eyes, but it was mixed with disbelief. "Not in so many words, I grant you. But you left me in no doubt."

Braine thought that Harry was intent to deprive him of his living and there was fear in those eyes now. And even if he had been zealous, he knew he could not stand against him. But he plucked up the courage to bluff.

"Sayin' it's one thing, provin' it's another."

"I don't care about smuggling," said Harry. "I have my own concerns to think about. But you? Do you expect me to exact retribution for what you did? You've lost your soul, Braine, and that's punishment enough."

Harry's voice rose, echoing off the stone walls. "You lost it the day you dug out Charlie Taverner, the day you discovered that one of your younger men had been murdered, and did nothing. I stand corrected, Braine. You did more than nothing. For the sake of your own skin you embraced the man who had the boy killed."

The sound of pounding footsteps grew louder and since the chamber lacked a door, Braine's assistant, as scruffy and as unkempt as ever, burst straight in. He was breathless from his running, but he got the message out very clearly. "Come quick, your honour. Jalheel Temple has been skewered. He's naked in his bed, stone dead murdered."

Braine's eyes went wide with shock. But they were fixed on Harry, not the messenger. His mouth moved but no words came, as he tried to make the connection between Harry Ludlow being here and the news that had just arrived. Then he stood up and rushed out of the room. Harry listened to his boots as they echoed off the castle walls. They died away as he cleared the keep, leaving only silence.

Harry hadn't got what he'd come for. But then he wondered if he really needed to. He stood up slowly, his eyes glancing over the date, April 10th, 1790, barely visible on the faded poster. Then, with a grim smile, he walked over and ripped it off the wall.

CHAPTER FORTY

NAOMI was kneeling at the grave in the fading evening light. Harry left his horse on top of the ridge to graze, not wanting the sound of its hoofs to disturb her. Then he walked down the hill. The wicket gate opened soundlessly, being well used. He was within ten feet of the huge carved headstone before she glanced up. It was odd the way she looked at him. The expression was the same as that Halloween night. A mixture of happiness, surprise, and sadness, though this time all her teeth showed in the enigmatic smile.

"Hello, Harry," she said, rather flatly, without getting up. Then she went back to tending her plants.

Harry glanced at Tolly Smith's grave, which had the same wild flowers that had lain there earlier in the day.

"They said at the Griffin that I'd find you here."

"My daily chore," she said softly.

"Is it a chore, Naomi?"

There was a slight catch in her throat as she replied. "I'd rather tend a live man than see to his grave."

He walked round Tolly Smith's headstone and knelt down beside her, his hand gently touching her shoulder. "I think perhaps I'm close to understanding. But I would like to be sure I have the right of it."

She looked at him, that direct fearless gaze he so admired.

"Perhaps you won't like what you hear, Harry Ludlow."

"There's always been a distance, a detachment. I suppose I thought you were just like me. I cannot say that we shared anything other than mutual regard, yet it seems incomprehensible to me that you would knowingly endanger my life."

Harry stopped, firstly so that she could respond, but also because of his own vanity. He wanted to know what had happened and why, without getting into the kind of deep discussion that would reveal his emotions, or acknowledge that if his suppositions were correct, her actions had hurt him. But Naomi had returned to her flowers and said nothing, forcing him to continue.

"When I first met Bertles on board the *Planet,* I thought I'd seen him somewhere before. I had. It was in the Griffin's Head. He was there the last time I came home."

Still she did not respond. Harry decided to be a trifle less guarded.

"He was no saint, Naomi. But he didn't deserve to die that way. Trench skinned him alive, inch by bloody inch. We could hear his screams across a mile of open water. And that with the rigging full of hanged, innocent sailors. That, of course, was before they tried to bury me alive."

She looked at him again without flinching. Indeed, there was a fire in her eyes that was quite singular. It certainly had no hint of regret.

"The crew bothers me. But not Tobias Bertles. Whatever he suffered was well deserved."

"You deliberately set out to have him killed, didn't you?" Naomi responded with a sharp nod. "You bought the *Planet?*" Another nod. "What I don't know, Naomi, is why they were convinced it was me."

"Ask yourself why it is that men are so vain and foolish. There's not one that reckons a woman has a brain."

"I always thought you had one."

"Did you, Harry? My body seemed to be of more interest, as I recall." That remark had emerged through the anger that was plainly visible in her face. But he knew that the tone was false, more a desire to justify herself than to damn him. But whilst Naomi proceeded to withdraw her sting by the softening of her voice, it was done slowly. "Was I anything to you but comfort?"

"I cannot demand an explanation, Naomi. But I do think that I'm due one. Why did you engage in this conspiracy?" Harry tried to keep his tone level, but the image of his house, burned to ground, sprang to mind. "Why was my whole family to be sacrificed to see it concluded?"

She stood up and laid her hand on his arm, her voice gentle as she replied. That tactile gesture, and the direct gaze that accompanied her words, made him regret the implied accusation of deliberate intent.

"That shocked me, Harry, more than even the hanging of Bertles's crew. And believe me I never once mentioned your name. We're alike, you and I. What I did was stirred by instinct. First Bertles, with his madcap scheme. Then the idea that I could revenge myself. I had no idea where it would lead, or the trouble it would cause. How many times have you set a course that you've later regretted?"

Harry's mind turned to the manifest, in which he listed all the details Trench needed to both suspect and locate him. That and the posters. It was an appropriate moment to remind himself that the attack on his house had not been generated by any action of Naomi Smith. What concerned him was why everyone had refused to believe him afterwards.

"It seemed so simple. Set the fool up, then let Trench know who was stealing his contraband."

"Through Temple?" asked Harry.

"That should have been enough."

"But it wasn't, was it?"

Her hand gripped his arm tightly to emphasize her words.

"You have to understand, Harry, to begin with, the name of who was backing Bertles didn't matter. I couldn't own to it myself or they might have smoked my game. Matters took a turn I hadn't looked for. You'll know where Obidiah Trench is from. Feelings about the Kent smugglers can run pretty high in those parts and he wasn't content with Bertles. Temple's not knowing cast suspicion on him. The only way he could convince Trench that he wasn't involved himself was to provide another name. And I couldn't tell him there was no one, 'cause I'd hinted before that there was, hinted at someone powerful, and close by."

"It would have been as easy to give them my name."

Naomi frowned, as though the idea in her mind was unpleasant. "Except you weren't at home, were you. An' you'd been away for near two years."

"So you shifted their attention to my brother-in-law."

"I tried to, 'cause I could think of no one else," she admitted. "But believe me when I say, even then, that I had no inkling of what harm would come. I didn't reckon on Obidiah Trench bein' such a murderous sod. Nobody did."

They fell silent. Naomi hooked her hand through his arm while Harry mulled over what she'd said. Arthur thought she was sucking up to him. And all the time he'd been a pawn in Naomi's game. But had he not been just that himself and for a lot longer than his brother-in-law? She looked at him closely, for the first time betraying a trace of the genuine affection he always felt existed between them. She made that sigh that presaged the beginning of a long tale.

"There were four men I hated, four men who ruined my happiness. Bertles was one of them. Probably more than any of the others since the method they used was his idea. He didn't come near the Griffin for three years after Tolly died. But I knew him, right off, as soon as he walked through the door. Those daft hairs on his cheeks. He was a slippery one and no error, with his big talk and short purse."

"He told you about Trench?"

"He did. Though he never let on what an evil bugger he was, just that there was a rate of contraband across the water, waiting to be picked up *gratis*. We could pinch a few cargoes and then retire on the proceeds."

"And all he needed was a ship?"

"The money for a ship. It wasn't to be like a partnership. He was no more taken with the idea of a smart woman than most men."

Harry looked at the small neat headstone. "The exciseman Braine wasn't convinced Bertles was guilty. Are you?"

"I didn't need convincing. My husband told me before he met his maker. The whole thing was carried out at his bidding. He even boasted of it."

"Tolly?" Her eyes were on him now, searching to see if he could add it up. "I know he didn't have an unblemished past."

"Tolly was retired from the smuggling game. But he kept in touch with his old gang. They'd all come out to the Griffin's Head to get drunk an' talk over old times. That's how I knew what I had to do, for they was always talkin' about the good old days, and some bad ones, including the time the Kent smugglers had clapped a stopper on the Hawkhurst gang."

"Smuggling's one thing. Many a body's resulted from a heated encounter. But cold murder is something else. I find it hard to believe that Tolly would do that."

"He wasn't really a bad man, Harry. But he had one fault that he couldn't control, and that was jealousy."

"The difference in age," said Harry lamely, for Tolly Smith had only ever had one thing to be jealous about. She exerted enough pressure on his arm to induce him to walk away, and they made their way around the graveyard, casting an odd glance at the moss-covered headstones.

"He was a sick man, and old, that couldn't pleasure his young wife, an' hadn't done for two years. I didn't look elsewhere for pleasure, Harry, it just happened along. And when it did, even though I tried, it was too strong to pass up. Tolly knew he was dying and so did I. But that didn't put a stopper on his pride. He couldn't abide the thought of anyone else in my bed, even if he was gone to meet his maker."

"Are you sure it was just that?"

"I won't say that the Aldington gang didn't get something out of it. The Preventatives were causing trouble. It scared the livin' daylights out of the rest of them."

"Go on," he said.

"What else is there to say? When Trench's stuff went missing he started looking to see who was robbing him. It didn't take much to point him towards this part of the world and I'd primed Temple to tip him the wink. But he was a bit sharper than I thought. He didn't try to find Bertles himself, but he let Temple know that if it didn't let up he'd feel free to take it out on any Deal boat he came across. Temple demanded I tell him when the next sailing was due. He claimed he only sold Bertles to Trench to keep the peace."

"Some peace," said Harry sharply.

"That was when he came after me for another name. He kept asking about you, and I kept ducking the answer. But he knew too much. You were close, powerful, and one bought tankard of ale would be enough to glean the rest of the story about us. I tried to convince him otherwise, but he said he had written evidence. I couldn't say he was wrong without letting out the whole story."

He could see no point in remonstrating with her. Naomi knew the consequences of what she'd done as well as he did. Being in the grip of an obsession, she probably didn't care. Nor did he wish to ask how he stood with her now, for he thought he knew the answer. It wasn't a shared sense of freedom, at all. Naomi was the subject of constant attention from men at the Griffin's Head. What better way to deflect that than to be involved with Harry, a man who was powerful locally and rarely home. But his reason for not asking was that if it was the truth he didn't want to hear it said.

"You killed Temple today, didn't you?"

She looked at the sky, which was darkening slowly.

"Why are men so stupid, Harry? There's not one that doubts every woman wants him. Fat, thin, stupid, or toothless, they're all

the same. Once Bertles had finished his first trip, and proved himself, it was time for the next stage. I went into Deal. As luck would
have it, the new Fencibles were having their first drill and there
was Temple smack in the middle on his horse. Catching his eye
was easy, just as easy as it was to let him think I was soft on him.
Temple thought that in his shiny uniform, there was nothing to
match him. There he was, in all his finery, with his red coat, his
feathered hat, and that damned buff belt he was so proud of."

They'd come full circle, back to the point in front of the smaller
of the two headstones. As Naomi looked at it the wistful tone
evaporated, to be replaced by a hard-edged, callous voice which
Harry had never heard before.

"I wish you'd met him, Harry. You would have liked him, for
he was a bit like you. He was man to charge the guns and no
error. He wasn't like Braine, content to sit inside his dripping
walls and take what the gangs threw him. He went after them,
doing what he was paid for, and proved how easy it was to get
results with a bit of effort. That's the real reason they helped to
do him in."

"And me?" Harry asked, even although he promised himself
he wouldn't.

"No one came as close as you to wiping his memory." She
laughed humourlessly. "But then no one else got the chance."

"So it wasn't to save on your rent?"

She could easily have demurred, said something to mollify him.
But he could hardly complain if, instead, she demonstrated that
streak of honesty he'd always admired. "I don't love you, Harry,
if that's what you're asking. But I reckon you know that already.
Perhaps it started as convenience, but it wasn't hard. You're a
good man, and handsome, who could make me laugh. I need that
sometimes."

He tried, but failed to keep the bitterness out of his voice. "Only
sometimes. Then it's as well I was frequently absent."

"If you're hurting, I'm truly sorry. But don't ask me to be sorry for the four men that killed him. They took the only man I ever loved and buried him alive. And since they own the law and had terrified the excise, nothing happened. I swore revenge every time I tended these flowers. But I had to wait four years till Bertles showed up with the means."

She turned to look at him again, tears beginning to run from the corners of her eyes. "An' I had to hide my grief. Tolly died within the month, knowing how much I hated him. Bertles went as I would have wished, for the shingle in the cellar was his notion. Every strip of his skin that Trench removed was well earned. Temple died because he thought that I couldn't resist his handsome uniform. He thought he was going to bed me at last, after months of effort. His sabre was just laying there, waiting to be used."

For the first time Harry noticed that her hands were covered in dried blood. Temple's blood, which she hadn't bothered to wash off. Then he looked at the date on the headstone, April 10th, 1790. There was a jarring note in the end of her story that he could not dismiss. For all Naomi's strength and character, let alone her behaviour, he found it hard to see her committing murder in such a calculating fashion.

"I cannot believe you waited for the very day?"

His dissenting tone seemed to alarm her. Her reply was hurried and nervous. "I wanted one of them to expire on the right date. God knows, I've died every day."

"Why did you kill Temple, Naomi?" She sobbed and her shoulders slumped. Harry recalled the words of the exciseman who rushed in to tell Braine that Temple had been "skewered." "He was naked when they found him. And he was in his bed."

The tears flowed copiously now and her eyes pleaded to be forgiven. "I thought I'd made amends, thought that you were safe. Gratifying him seemed a small enough price after the trouble I'd caused. But he laughed at me, Harry, afterwards, and told me that he had a cellar, just for you, waiting to be filled."

Her hand went out to the headstone and her fingers ran over the lettering.

"CHARLES TAVERNER"
BORN AUGUST 24TH 1762
DIED BY FOUL MEANS
APRIL 10TH 1790

"I lost him. I couldn't stand by and lose a friend the same way."

Harry stood up abruptly. Naomi could not have come and gone at the Hope and Anchor without being observed. There could be a hue and cry after her at this very moment. He searched his mind for a place to hide her and settled on his ship. Perhaps with good legal help he could get her off a capital charge. If not, then he would need to get her away to a safer place, perhaps the Americas. Time was pressing and he needed to move swiftly. But he had just one more question requiring an answer.

"You said there were four men who buried Charlie Taverner alive. You've only mentioned three."

Her hand wiped her eyes, but the tears kept flowing as she looked at Harry in the gathering gloom.

"Yes. There were four. Tolly Smith, Tobias Bertles, and Jalheel Temple. The other one was Cephas Quested."

"Who is now a witless fool."

"That won't save him. After I stuck Temple, and dressed myself, I called for him. He came like a lamb, dribblin' and grinnin'. Then I put the sword in his hand, Harry. Quested might go to hell for the wrong killing, but go he will. He'll swing for sure, witless or not."

Motoo Eetee

Shipwrecked at the Edge of the World

Swimming for their lives from the senseless wreck of the American sealing ship *Dove*, four men escape—Thomas, a headstrong young sailor; Harrison, the affable, inventive ship's carpenter; Mr. Morgen, the *Dove*'s pedestrian first mate; and the aging Captain Tobit—bungling, short-sighted, and fanatical. Bruised and naked, they find themselves cast away on an uncharted, uninhabited island in the far South Pacific where the bounty and beauty of all that surrounds them are at odds with the old structures of shipboard life. Within the new order dictated by nature and the struggle to secure the simplest food, clothing, and shelter, the old divisions between officers and men, especially between Thomas and Tobit, nevertheless grow deeper. Which voice prevails in the end—nature or human habit—is the essence of this book's gripping climax.

"Irving Rogers knows about ships and he knows about the sea. He understands sailors, the good the bad and the mad, and what it is that makes them want to sail the oceans and how they might behave when things go against them. And he can tell a story. I thoroughly enjoyed *Motoo Eetee*."
—*David Donachie, author of The Privateersman Mysteries*

Motoo Eetee

Shipwrecked at the Edge of the World

IRV C. ROGERS

ISBN 1-59013-018-9 • 400 pp., maps
$24.95 Hardcover

"Extraordinary, and very hard to put down. It's exciting, thought-provoking, and extremely moving, an adventure of Old Testament starkness mixed seamlessly with symbolism and philosophy. The sea and sail-ship elements are impeccable, from the handling and rigging to the characters of the officers and men."

—*Jan Needle author of the Sea Officer William Bentley Novels*

Available at your favorite bookstore, or call toll-free:
1-888-BOOKS-11 (1-888-266-5711).

Or visit the McBooks Press website **www.mcbooks.com**
and read an excerpt.

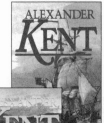

"All of the heroic elements are here.

...Good, solid stuff that still packs a wallop."
—*The New York Times*

"One of the foremost writers of naval fiction."
—*Sunday Times of London*

"Critics of his first two books dubbed Kent a worthy successor to C.S. Forester. . . . This hardly seems fair, for Kent's writing is fresh, singular, and worthy of judgment solely on its own high merit."
—*Philadelphia Bulletin*

"For adventure and action, a prize."
—*Saturday Evening Post*

Meet Richard Bolitho—

"From midshipman to admiral, this is [Richard Bolitho's] story, a story of England's navy, and of the young America, and of France through bloody revolution; a story of the ocean itself."

—ALEXANDER KENT,
from the new preface to *Midshipman Bolitho*

LOVERS of fine nautical fiction—fans of Patrick O'Brian, C.S. Forester, and Captain Marryat—will be delighted to meet a valiant new hero, Richard Bolitho, and to follow his exciting adventures.

Beloved the world wide, the Bolitho novels (numbering 25 volumes) have sold nearly 18 million copies and have been translated into over twenty languages. Now, for the first time in more than a decade, Richard Bolitho is back in print in the U.S.

THE ALEXANDER SHERIDAN ADVENTURES
by V.A. Stuart

FROM THE Crimean War to the Indian Raj, V.A. Stuart's Alexander Sheridan Adventures deftly combine history and supposition in tales of scarlet soldiering that cunningly interweave fact and fiction.

Alexander Sheridan, unjustly forced out of the army, leaves Britain and his former life behind and joins the East India Company, still in pursuit of those ideals of honor and heroism that buoyed the British Empire for three hundred years. Murder, war, and carnage await him. But with British stoicism and an unshakable iron will, he will stand tall against the atrocities of war, judging all by their merit rather than by the color of their skin or the details of their religion.

V. A. Stuart wrote several series of military fiction and numerous other novels under various pseudonyms, her settings spanning history and the globe. Born in 1914, she was in Burma with the British Fourteenth Army, became a lieutenant, and was decorated with the Burma Star and the Pacific Star.

1 **Victors and Lords**
ISBN 0-935526-98-6
272 pp., $13.95

2 **The Sepoy Mutiny**
ISBN 0-935526-99-4
256 pp., $13.95

3 **Massacre at Cawnpore**
ISBN 1-59013-019-7
240 pp., $13.95

"Stuart's saga of Captain Sheridan during the Mutiny stands in the shadow of no previous work of fiction, and for historical accuracy, writing verve and skill, and pace of narrative, stands alone."

—*El Paso Times*

DAVID DONACHIE is an avowed lover of

naval fiction with a streak of mischief. A best-selling author well-known to European audiences, Donachie— as Tom Connery—is the author of the popular *George Markham of the Marines* novels, also set during the Napoleonic Wars and telling the land and sea adventures of His Majesty's Royal Marines. Under his own name, Donachie is the author of a multi-volume biographical novel about Lord Nelson and Lady Emma Hamilton.

A Scot by birth, he lives in Deal on the Channel coast of England, where he works to keep his inspirations in motion.